ise for

BEHOLD *the* BIRD *in* FLIGHT

"Terri Lewis's enchanting *Behold the Bird in Flight* might sound like a fairy tale at first—a medieval queen in her castle, a cruel king, a lost love—but this tale of Isabelle d'Angoulême is one firmly rooted in history, shining a light on her life as well as the role of women at large. What a brave undertaking this is, and Lewis does not let us down; her gift for intriguing detail and wonderful storytelling will hold the reader captive."
—Jill McCorkle, author of *Old Crimes* and *Life After Life*

"Isabella d'Angoulême was a complicated queen, villainized by the English chroniclers. But the adolescent Isabella was a young girl with hopes and dreams and fantasies we can all relate to. A wonderful, engaging story!"
—Sharon Bennett Connolly, Fellow of the Royal Historical Society and author of *Ladies of Magna Carta*

"Immersive and filled with drama . . . transports the reader back in time to a remote yet deeply human moment when war echoes through the stone corridors of medieval castles and love still finds a way."
—Carrie Callaghan, author of *A Light of Her Own*

"Lewis masterfully blends a fictional narrative with real-life historical figures and a real-world setting. Isabelle lives in a time when women and girls are treated like property—daughters are 'sold for the richest husband or the best alliance.' This story chronicles Isabelle's fascinating life. . . . Readers will surely relish following along with and championing Isabelle, who gathers strength and wisdom as she matures."
—*Kirkus Reviews*, recommended

"With a vivid imagination and writing evocative of the era, Terri Lewis transports readers to the royal courts of medieval Europe. Amid a tapestry of political intrigue and forbidden passions, her characters defy the harsh realities of their day to find love against all odds."

—Jude Berman, author of *The Vow*

". . . an alluring portrait of a young queen caught in a web of lust, power, and royal politics . . . dazzlingly lyrical prose with a complex plot of love gone awry . . . sure to enthrall lovers of historical fiction."

—Peggy Joque Williams, author of *Courting the Sun: A Novel of Versailles*

"*Behold the Bird in Flight* paints a compelling picture of Isabelle of Angoulême, a young woman torn between her own aspirations as a human being and the desires of the men that preoccupied her life . . . The author does an outstanding job of exploring Isabelle's resilient and resourceful nature . . ."

—*Readers' Favorite*

BEHOLD THE BIRD IN FLIGHT

A Novel of an
Abducted Queen

Terri Lewis

Copyright © 2025 Terri Lewis

All rights reserved. No part of this publication may be reproduced, distributed, or transmitted in any form or by any means, including photocopying, recording, digital scanning, or other electronic or mechanical methods, without the prior written permission of the publisher, except in the case of brief quotations embodied in critical reviews and certain other noncommercial uses permitted by copyright law. For permission requests, please address She Writes Press.

Published 2025
Printed in the United States of America
Print ISBN: 978-1-64742-910-2
E-ISBN: 978-1-64742-911-9
Library of Congress Control Number: 2025900945

For information, address:
She Writes Press
1569 Solano Ave #546
Berkeley, CA 94707

Interior design by Stacey Aaronson

She Writes Press is a division of SparkPoint Studio, LLC.

Company and/or product names that are trade names, logos, trademarks, and/or registered trademarks of third parties are the property of their respective owners and are used in this book for purposes of identification and information only under the Fair Use Doctrine.

This is a work of fiction. Names, characters, places, and incidents either are the product of the author's imagination or are used fictitiously. Any resemblance to actual persons, living or dead, is entirely coincidental.

NO AI TRAINING: Without in any way limiting the author's [and publisher's] exclusive rights under copyright, any use of this publication to "train" generative artificial intelligence (AI) technologies to generate text is expressly prohibited. The author reserves all rights to license uses of this work for generative AI training and development of machine learning language models.

In memory of my mother who loved history and believed I could write.

Also in memory of the history teachers who lit the fire,
Mr. John Roberts at Wheat Ridge High School and
Dr. Alan Breck, professor at the University of Denver.

Some of these things are true and some of them lies.
But they are all good stories.

—HILARY MANTEL

There's always a temptation, I think, among some historical writers to shade things toward the modern point of view. You know, they won't show someone doing something that would have been perfectly normal for the time but that is considered reprehensible today.

—DIANA GABALDON

CONTENTS

PART ONE: Angoulême, France: 1199

1. Great and Dreadful Day . . . 1
2. Suffer the Little Children . . . 9
3. The Air Shall Carry Thy Voice . . . 14
4. Go Ye into All the World . . . 20

PART TWO: Lusignan, France: 1199–1200

5. Behold, I Stand at the Door . . . 35
6. Whom Thou Lovest . . . 56
7. Give Your Daughters unto Us . . . 69
8. Ye Shall Celebrate . . . 79
9. For Dust Thou Art . . . 86

PART THREE: Royalty: 1200

10. That Thou Shouldest Rule . . . 95
11. To Gain a King . . . 113
12. Whither Thou Goest . . . 123

PART FOUR: The Return: 1202

13. Be Ye Not Unequally Yoked . . . 145
14. Strength Unto the Battle . . . 154
15. Thy Wound Is Grievous . . . 167
16. Perfect Love Casteth Out Fear . . . 176

PART FIVE: Escape and Capture: 1205

17. The Furnace of Affliction . . . 203
18. Love Ye One Another . . . 212

PART SIX: Progeny and Losses: 1207–1213

19. Be Ye Fruitful and Multiply . . . 235
20. The Wages of Sin . . . 244

PART SEVEN: The Path of War: 1214–1216

21. A Tempest Stealeth Him Away . . . 269
22. Curse Not the King . . . 285
23. Afterword . . . 307

Author's Statement . . . 309
Acknowledgments . . . 311
Credits . . . 313
Further Reading . . . 315
Questions for Discussion . . . 317
About the Author . . . 319

The Plantagenet Empire as Inherited by King John

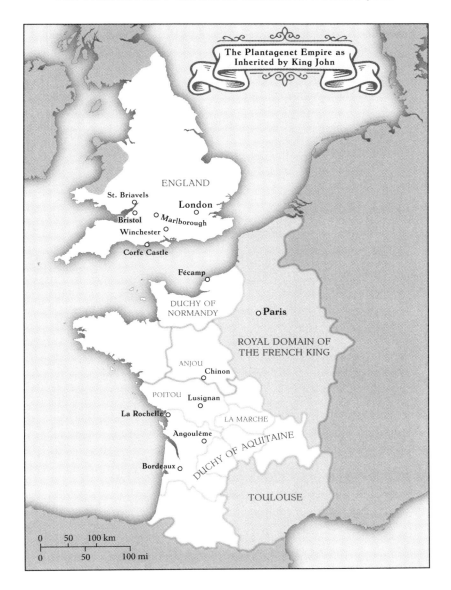

Map by Erin Greb Cartography

PART ONE

Angoulême, France

1199

1

GREAT AND DREADFUL DAY

On the last ordinary morning, Isabelle skipped up the wooden stairs to the castle walk, flung off her hated head covering, and shook her hair into the warm August air. Overhead, an arc of moon floated ash white in the blue, held by the invisible hand of God. She imagined His fingers pinching the tip of the sickle and then leaned out between the stone teeth, pretending to fly. She was like the moon. No, better to have wings. She'd be a hawk, sailing over the great woods where foxes hunted poor little rabbits. She loved rabbits. And the fluffy sheep, the spire of the Angoulême cathedral, the lavender garden, the orchard heavy with her favorite apples. All that was hers, or would be when Papa died. Oh, but what if she died first? People died all the time. Last week, their seamstress had the flux, but she was older than Papa. Nonetheless, Isabelle leaned on the cold stone and prayed for their lives to continue, then crossed herself, giggled, and flung her hair left and right, letting its gold glitter and catch in her eyelashes.

Too soon the cathedral bell struck the opening of the city

gates, and with a sigh, she replaced the constricting wimple—Maman insisted all proper girls wore them—and prepared for the daily lesson required of every daughter who'd someday run a castle. She was learning to turn vinegar barrels, weigh wool, and trim candles, important tasks but less fun than three years ago when she was eight and had lessons in folding linens, picking strawberries, and her favorite: feeding the chickens. The birds mostly ruffled and clucked around her feet, but one always flapped up, squawking, trying to break loose into the world. Isabelle named her Poulette and pretended the little chicken lived in her heart. She might wish to be a hawk, soaring in the world, but in her real life, she felt exactly like the little chicken.

Her current lessons were serious. In a year and nine days she'd be twelve and deemed a woman old enough to marry. Papa would betroth her to someone powerful, a seigneur or count with a grand demesne, and away she'd ride with her husband. The thought of running her own household—no Maman telling her what to do—set Poulette hopping in her chest. She'd name all the dogs, require honey balls and eels at every meal, and command featherbeds for everyone, even the children. Sobering, she rubbed her palms across her chest. Still flat. She needed breasts soon; men seemed to like them.

The bell stopped chiming and she went down the tower stairs to her lessons, reviewing Maman's rules on each step: *Keep clean, even in thy lower parts.* Hop down a step. *Stand tall, so as not to be seen as unworthy.* Hop. *Read the Bible.* Two hops for that one. *Learn thy lessons.* Maman meant especially Latin and its hated nouns. Just yesterday she had learned *adflatus*, masculine, fourth declension, a breath or blowing. *Adflatus e terra.* Blown from the earth. Like flying. Paulus, her tutor, said girls were not capable of learning Latin. *Zut*, she knew her conjugations and was going to prove him wrong. *Amo, amas, amat, amamus, amatis, amant.* A word for each step and there she was at the bottom.

As she crossed the wide bailey, swifts, like slices of moon, whirled overhead, men labored, women carried, horses came and went. All as weary usual. Today's lesson was measuring spices and cloth, so much better than opening stinky vinegar kegs. When Maman turned the key in the chest, the scent of pepper, cinnamon, and cloves brightened the cold larder. The spices came from faraway places like London, Venice, or even Jerusalem, where Richard Cœur de Lion had traveled. A perfect name, Lionheart. She was certain he'd been tall and brave; Papa said he had red hair. The greatest disappointment in her life was that he'd not visited Angoulême to honor Maman, whose grandpapa was a king. Sadly, he'd died last spring, but she would always cherish his memory.

Maman lifted the scale. "Weigh out a dram of nutmeg for Cook."

Isabelle chose a piece and sniffed. "Could I have this?" The little ball rolled on her palm.

"Indeed not. Put it on the scale at once."

Nutmeg weighed, wrapped in cloth, and secured in Maman's pouch, they went to a locked room with a single narrow window. Lining the walls, carved wooden coffers held stores of wool, linen, and silks. Isi was learning fabric names, production methods, and how to measure for mantles, vests, and tunics. Maman lit a rush lamp and opened the chest; out flew the scent of the lavender that had been strewn between the folds to keep moths away.

First, Isabelle identified fabrics—linsey-woolsey, scarlet tiretaine, brocade, linen, common hemp. Some of the wool was lumpy as if still on a sheep; other lengths were fine-threaded and dyed a rich red. In a special compartment, wrapped in finest linen, lay the valuable silk. Clouds of color slid on her hands. She chose a length of pale bitter green like the woods in spring. "Could I have a dress of this, *s'il vous plaît*?"

Maman snorted. "Silk is for women. You have a year to wait." She pushed Isabelle aside and pulled out a russet worsted. "Our laundress requires a tunic. Use your lesson. Measure and cut." Wool worsted. Scratchy, heavy, and stinky when wet. Poor laundress.

After her lessons, Isabelle was sent to the great hall where Papa held council with the steward, the constable, and the chamberlain. "When you're grown and your husband is away at war or on Crusade"—here Maman crossed herself—"you will oversee the castle and must know things your papa discusses." She meant crops, animals, new buildings, keeping the peace.

Ah, but Isi wanted her husband to love her and admire her beauty—her breasts. Also to give her presents like those Papa brought Maman: a tortoiseshell comb or a little wooden box with a rosary inside. She longed for a fancy pin to close her mantle, to sparkle and wink when she skipped, but Papa said jewels were expensive and she was too young. *Pismire.*

The hall had been readied for council: floor cleared of servants' mats, family bedding removed from the dais, and the privacy curtain opened. Isi often peeked under that curtain. Just last night she'd seen a chambermaid with beautiful breasts pulled into her lover's bed. Giggling at the memory, she sat on the edge of the dais where Papa lorded over the council from a heavy carved chair. The steward sat on a simple box seat; various other men had three-legged stools. Hugh, visiting from the distinguished Lusignan family, sat cross-legged on the floor, his red-gold curls flickering in the light. If he shook his head and roared, he'd be like Richard Cœur de Lion. She leaned on her elbow and imagined him galloping on a horse, waving a sword, rescuing her from . . . she wasn't sure what.

Papa glanced her way and cleared his throat—*pay attention*. She nodded and widened her eyes at the tally of cows, lambs, goats, chickens, horses. Numbers floated like dust motes. She endured the pantler's complaint about firewood required for village ovens and shuddered at the butler's report of a young cupbearer killed by a falling keg. Only when the master of the wardrobe spoke did she perk up, hoping to get a new tunic, but no, the topic was weaving supplies.

At last, her father dismissed the men. "So, daughter, what did you learn today?"

She leaned on Papa's chair, tracing the carved vines with her finger.

He caught her hand. "Come, you are almost grown. Surely you learned something."

Then she remembered. "I learned I'm not to get a new tunic."

He chuckled. "Would you like one?"

"Yes, Papa. In green." She'd not mention Maman had said no.

"I will speak to the wardrobe master. Now, on your way."

The thought of a silk tunic wakened Poulette who pecked Isabelle's stomach with excitement. She skipped from the hall, snatched a piece of lavender from a bunch Maman had placed in a niche, and waving it like a banner, went to look for her friend Alain.

In the kitchen, which always smelled of blood and fire, Alain's mother was chopping chicken. *Thwack, thwack.* Poor chicken—she hoped it wasn't Poulette. A small boy turned a lamb haunch on the spit, and Alain was scrubbing an array of pots with sand. She tickled his ear with the posy. "Yesterday at supper, you had a hole in your shoe."

"You weren't to notice!" He swatted her hand away. "Mother sent it to be mended before today's meal." He held up a bare foot. "She says I may not serve with my toe showing."

"I notice everything." She scowled and said in a deep voice, "You shall accompany me to the orchard."

"I'm supposed to finish the pots."

"I am to be a countess, so you must obey."

The butler rolled a barrel of ale into the room, causing a fuss, and they escaped, running across the bailey, out the gate, and down to the orchard where servants knocked branches with heavy sticks and women gathered the fallen apples into baskets. Here and there, ladders leaned. Isabelle snatched two apples and tossed one to Alain.

A villein in a tree yelled, "Here you, put that back."

"It's the Mademoiselle." A woman with a fruit-filled apron shrugged.

"But the boy?" A servant swung his stick in Alain's direction.

"Leave him alone." Isabelle flung wide her arms like a future countess. "This is my land, my trees, my apples." She stamped. "I can give one to my friend if I want. My father, Count Aymer, allows it." She grabbed Alain's hand and pulled him down the rows of trees to the orchard's edge where they sat in the shade, eating. Behind them, apples thumped pleasantly onto the grass. One of the men sang. The air was full of bees; black clots gathered on fallen apples fermenting in the heat. Alain stretched in the grass until, in the distance, a woman yelled.

"Helle fyr. That's Mother." He stood to run. "Ow." He snatched up his foot. "Ow, ow, ow."

"Bee sting?" Isi tossed away her core and laughed. A breeze flirted down the rows of trees. Buzzing filled the air.

Alain collapsed, whimpering. "Owwwww." He rocked back and forth.

Isi rolled over to him. "Silly. It's just a bee." She grabbed his foot and sucked out the stinger, giggling. Still, Alain cried. "Don't be a baby. I've been bitten three times. It doesn't hurt that much." He scratched at his neck, and his fingers, swollen like sausages, stopped her breath.

"I can't breathe." His eyes bulged.

"Devil got him." A man crashed down from the tree. "See that red on his neck? Mark of the wicked one." Apple pickers began to shout. Women ran toward them, strewing fruit. "The evil beast is here."

Fear scrabbled through their words and into Isabelle. Was Alain possessed? A girl in the village, taken by the devil, had been hung. Would the devil jump into her if she touched him? She crawled close to his ear. "Alain, pray the devil away. Pray, pray." He turned his head. His lips! Enormous and mottled purple. The baby fuzz on Isi's arms prickled; she shrieked and tumbled away. "Who are you?" She began to cry.

A woman crouched over them. "'Tis the devil, sure." She pointed at Isabelle. "You put a curse on him."

"'Twas only an apple." Paulus said evil entered the world through an apple. Had the village girl eaten one? Isabelle shivered violently.

The woman shouted to the others. "See, see, the devil serpent."

"I want," Alain choked out. "My mother." Men with large sticks crowded them.

"Help him," Isi begged, but they only shouted more.

"A demon spell, wickedness . . . evil!"

"Isi." Alain's tongue writhed like a pink rat. Every inch of her wanted to flee, but she couldn't leave him alone. Praying for safety, she took his hot hand.

"She killed the lad." The crowd pressed close. "Witch!"

The dreaded word flung out, skittering to Isabelle, crawling into her belly. Shudders racked the crowd. Hands, gnarled or young, made the sign of the cross. "Witch daughter."

She flailed her arms against the bodies, the heat, the noise. Suddenly, she was wrenched aloft and swung high, breath gone, unable to scream, mauled by panic. She was to be hung. *Thud*. She dropped to earth, safe behind a tall back. "Stand away." Hugh, his red curls alight, grabbed a stick and swung it sideways; a man fell to his knees, cursing. "How dare you. She is a count's daughter."

Alain's strangled cries burst from his purple mouth. The crowd panted. Hugh pointed the stick at a woman. "The lad needs help. Get his mother." When the woman started slowly away, he raised the stick. "As if it were your own child." The woman ran. He took Isabelle's trembling hand and, straddling Alain, held the pole aloft like a sword, hair awry and flaming. "Fall to your knees and pray that he doesn't die. Or if God wants him, pray his soul to heaven."

In the moment before the word "witch" reemerged, Isabelle felt safe.

2

SUFFER THE
LITTLE CHILDREN

*I*sabelle knelt in the family chapel. Hands clasped tightly, fingertips numb, she bowed her head and exposed her neck, waiting for God to strike her like He had Alain. *I tried to save him. You know it's not my fault.* Had she just blamed God? Would He be angry? She tensed for a blow, but He ignored her.

If there must be a funeral, and there must in order to send Alain to heaven, Isabelle was glad it was in their own chapel. Alain had been afraid of the massive Angoulême cathedral, its carved animals peering through tangled vines and the rows of holy men standing on little shelves. *She* was scared of the echoing arches inside. As she once confessed to Paulus, the chaplain and her tutor, "I always feel little."

"So you are meant to feel. God is great and powerful. You are nothing."

Pismire. She was going to be a countess. At the time, she'd held her tongue, but now, sitting on the cold stone bench staring at Alain's wooden box, she understood. The chapel was small, the wooden box even smaller. How could that be? Her friend always seemed big, sprinting, turning cartwheels, climbing the tallest tree. She closed her eyes, powerless before God, who could have saved him, but hadn't bothered. Maybe He wanted Alain's company. *You're a father. Please take care of him. He'd like wings. Amen.*

The candles were lit, formal beeswax for a funeral, not stinky tallow, and Maman came to sit by Isi. Alain's mother and father huddled behind them, but where were the others? When the old seamstress died, the chapel had been full. Emptiness swirled in Isi's stomach. Did no one care about Alain?

O quanta qualia sunt illa Sabbata. One of Paulus's acolytes began to sing, and Isabelle filled with words. *Quae fessis requies, quae merces fortibus.* A song about rest. And *fortibus, fortibus*, what did that mean? Oh yes, brave. What a good song. Alain dared everything. He'd climbed the creaky wooden stairs to the guard tower, leaned way out to throw acorns at those below, then ducked away. A sob mixed with a giggle popped up from her chest. Maman nudged her sharply and Isi bowed her head. Yesterday they'd been together; now he was in that box. *Requiem aeternam.*

The singer started a new verse and then Papa appeared, standing next to the coffin and opening the Bible. Papa? Where was Paulus?

As her father intoned the words, Alain's mother wept steadily. Another cook had come in and she, too, sobbed, but now Isi couldn't cry. Her eyes were drilled by candle flames, her hands and feet heavy, cold. Papa read quickly, finishing before the candles burnt down a single inch. Maman would be pleased. *Oh, don't think of candles.* Alain was gone. She stood to follow the servants carrying the little box to the graveyard for more prayers, but Maman stopped her.

BEHOLD THE BIRD IN FLIGHT

"We need to pray at his grave, Mama."

"We can't." The heavy chapel door thudded shut.

"But we always . . ."

"Enough. Your papa had to argue with Paulus for this small service. He knows how much Alain meant to you, but the devil took him and he cannot be buried in hallowed ground. We won't speak of this again, do you understand?" She took Isi by the chin. "Look at me. You must forget your friend. There is danger now."

In Maman's eyes, Isabelle saw her own face. Very small, as if her mother's look had shrunk her. She whispered around the pinching fingers. "Because I am a witch?"

"You are not a witch. You know that. But those in the village . . ." Maman pressed Isabelle close, her familiar scent of cinnamon and incense bringing safety into the chapel. "You're getting so big." She wiped her eyes and began pinching out the candles. "Come along. Time for studies."

"Please, may I stay and pray for Alain?"

Maman hesitated, then lit the rush lamp lying at the foot of Mary's statue. "You may stay until this goes out." She placed it on the stone with a loud scrape. "Remember, not a word, not even to Paulus." She was gone.

Isi bent over and sobbed, her fingertips touching the statue's base. Alain was damned to writhe in hell's fire. He'd not have wings, nor fly in heaven. She wanted to pray, but with all the candles snuffed, the space fell away from the prick of light. A darkness like death. She would die too. Not soon, she hoped. In a flare of rushlight, the statue's shadow wavered, cool air swept her ankles, and Isabelle clutched Mary's foot. Frightened, she swallowed, dried her eyes with her hem, and knelt. *Dear Mary, you love children. Jesus was your son. Don't let Alain go to hell.*

Mary's nose, carved by an unskilled workman, was crooked.

11

She stared down it at Isabelle, stone eyes flickering in the light, and Isabelle held her breath, waiting for Mary's sign, but when the rushlight guttered and the room plunged into black, she dashed out into the sun.

ISABELLE'S ELEVENTH BIRTHDAY fell two days after the funeral. Usually Maman would order a picnic in the orchard, a place which now filled Isi with terror. Kind Maman understood. They ate in the formal garden within the castle walls. Paulus said special prayers to ward off the evil eye, Papa carved a rune into the wall and made her touch it, and Maman gave her a garlic bulb in a small sack to ward off the devil. "You are to wear this at all times. And you are forbidden to leave the castle."

Now, like a lid on a pot over a great fire, the portcullis was kept closed and the household fermented. Cooks, seamstresses, laundresses ran through the bailey, up and down the stone stairs, in and out of the armor room and the stables. Servants, swollen with fear, mumbled prayers as they passed through the turmoil. Demon rumors trickled through the portcullis and spread among the servants at meals. Paulus was stern, Maman all elbows and duty. At night, bonfires were lit in the village and pots pounded to scare away the devil. Isi remembered the hanged girl and thrashed in her bed, attacked by *what-ifs*. *What if* the villagers set the portcullis on fire? *What if* they abducted her? Tortured her for witchcraft? She quivered and prayed, awaiting an attack despite the twenty-foot walls protecting the bailey.

Once, when she cried out, Papa rose from his bed and led her atop the castle tower. Below lay all that was now forbidden her—the garden with its lavender, the river and fields and forest— but he tilted her face to the sky. "Remember, *ma petite*, your star."

In the swirl overhead, one star, slightly pink, winking and ready to send her prayers to heaven. Given to her by Papa when she was seven and since forgotten. He put his warm arm around her. "Talk to Him now."

She wanted to ask for safety, but the breeze shifted, carrying from the village the pounding of pans and shouting. Her stomach knotted. "Will they come for me?"

"I would never allow that." Papa pulled her close.

"Must I stay inside the castle forever?"

"Ah, *ma petite*." He knelt to look in her face. "Perhaps we should send you away."

Poulette gave a tiny squawk, the first since Alain died. "In a little cart?"

"We shall see."

To go away meant horses. Her own cart out into the world. *Universum*. Isi's cousin Matilda, favorably married at twelve, had been sent off in a cavalcade of gallant horses and a painted cart bedecked with banners of her new husband. Isi leaned into the night and imagined traveling across the land, the Angoulême coat of arms snapping red and gold. The breeze shifted, a cow lowed into the silence, and she prayed to be sent away.

3

THE AIR SHALL CARRY THY VOICE

Hugh de Lusignan waited in the wide meadow for the falconer. He loved to fly the birds, but today he couldn't shake the grip of the Angoulême castle, hunkered on a distant hill, stained, outdated, and made even darker by his agitation. Tomorrow he was to escort Count Aymer's daughter to safety in Lusignan. He'd saved her once; wasn't that enough? A memory of bringing the howling crowd to its knees eased him slightly, but the imminent homecoming shuddered tension back to life. He'd been sent to Angoulême to ferret out if the count was preparing to attack a borderland rightfully Lusignan's; he'd heard naught but of crops and village thieves. When he got home, he'd be questioned endlessly, his father certain danger still lurked and that he, Hugh, had failed to find it. He stamped through the grass, muttering. He was fifteen. Other boys his age were already squires, training to be knights, but he'd been deemed unworthy and sent out to spy.

Above him, the sky streamed blue over the froth of the forest, and he imagined God up there with the angels and whoever else He deemed worthy. Hugh's fervent prayers to be allowed to squire had gone unanswered. If he could fly up and burst into heaven, the air thin and fragrant with incense, he'd beg for help. He wanted . . .

The falcon master nudged Hugh's shoulder. "Concentrate. A single talon could take your eye." He tossed over a leather glove. "We've many birds to exercise today." He pointed with his chin at a lowly cadger who toiled across the wide field; strapped to his shoulders was a wooden frame heavy with hooded birds. "You'll fly the merlins."

Merlins. Ladies' birds. Hugh strode away, field burrs catching at his leggings. He was a man, by God's bones, even though his father forbade him to joust, to carry a shield. If given the chance, he could ride into battle alongside a knight, proving himself capable of leading true believers to the Holy Land. Brave and stalwart as his grandfather and great-grandfather. Galloping across deserts, upholding the honor of his family. Making his father proud. His hand clenched as if to a weapon, chain mail heavy on his shoulders, he squinted against raging sun. Distant cities waited for him to conquer . . .

"Master." The cadger panted up, his carrier laden with two gyrfalcons and a peregrine in addition to the merlin. "Put on your glove."

Demeaned by a servant. Hugh lifted his chin. "Are the birds wearing proper jesses?"

"Yes, young master." The cadger flicked the leather thongs attached to the bird's ankle.

Stung by *young*, Hugh held out a gloved fist. Hood removed, the bird landed with a whack, talon points punching through the leather and increasing the angry flashes in Hugh's body. He was the son of a count, a descendant of men who went on Crusade, worthy of a peregrine, not this diminutive thing.

The falcon master shouted, "Set her loose."

Internal fist shaken at his impotence, Hugh catapulted the merlin skywards. Away it soared, bells jingling, high over the field, skimming the meadow with a swoop, then back into the blue. Hugh longed for that freedom. To be home with his . . .

"Bring her in."

Rewarded with rat flesh, the merlin relaxed, heavier on his arm. The cadger, who smelled of dung, replaced the tiny hood and took the bird.

Now the falcon master released the peregrine. Its jesses snapped Hugh's hat. "By God's bones, you . . ." He bit back further angry words; the falconer had the ear of the count. Rudeness would be reported to his father. He could just hear the lecture.

When the birds were well exercised, he left the men, their condescension and arrogance, and wandered along the wooden stockade protecting the village. Just inside the gate, two boys flailed at one another with sticks.

"Take that." A crack of stick.

Swish. "Take that yourself."

"I'll cut your heart out," yelled the littlest one.

"That's not how to hold a sword." Hugh couldn't help himself; someone was always correcting him. He would pass it on.

The boys stared, sticks dangling at their sides.

"Here, let me show you." Hugh took a stick from the littlest fellow. "Do like this." He lunged, the sword pushed straight out. "That's a thrust. That's how you pierce a heart. You try."

The boy's wobbly thrust almost toppled him into the dirt, and Hugh smiled. "Good. Now, you."

BEHOLD THE BIRD IN FLIGHT

As the lad with a skinned knee stepped forward, a passing villein noticed Hugh's fine leather boots and lifted his cap. "Good day to you, sir."

The children goggled. This was a sir?

Hugh nodded at the man, then sliced the stick through the air. "See? That's how you remove a head." The children's eyes snapped back. "One swish and your enemy dies."

Great laughter. With Hugh's encouragement, they were soon thrusting and swishing and kicking up dirt. "Keep practicing. One day you may go on Crusade."

"In hook svincy," the boys chanted in unison as Hugh walked away.

"In hook . . . ?" He puzzled it out: *In hoc signo vinces.* "By this sign I conquer," motto of the crusading Templars. Where did lads learn these things? He was grinning when a girl stepped from a hut and tossed a sparkling rope of water.

Hugh's momentary entrancement with the shining drops like the sound of bells evaporated when it hit his boots and the girl howled laughter. An "x" of thread on the neckline of her tunic proclaimed her a prostitute, and he grabbed her shoulders. Her breasts bobbled under the coarse garment. Reminded of other breasts under pale blue linen, he slid his palm over these and his body leapt up. Unwilling to break the feeling of a different, much loved girl in his arms, he avoided the laughing face and pushed the prostitute into a room that smelled of vinegar and tomatoes. A single band of sunlight lit a lump of bread on a crude shelf. He reached for the hem of her shift, but she twisted away.

"It costs. Even for fine-looking young men."

"I have . . ." He had only lust and an ache for his Lusignan love.

The girl retreated further. In the dark, he couldn't read her eyes. He found an offering stuck in his belt. "A feather. To wear in your hat."

"Hats aren't allowed."

"From the count's gyrfalcon for your wall. Proof someone from the castle visited." He held it out. *Please take it, please. I must have* . . . For a brief moment, he thought how fun lust was, how surprising, then he brushed her face lightly with the feather.

She snatched it and stepped into the doorway for a closer look. Light pressed through her shift, and her curves called to his hands. He stepped close, smelling smoke on her hair, unlike his lover's scent of incense.

"You're from the castle?" She turned the feather in the sun.

"Yes." He was rubbing against her, no longer caring about her looks or the eyes that watched him all the time. Focused on the fire building inside, he managed to choke out, "I'll be a count someday." Not in Angoulême but Lusignan. As if it mattered to the girl.

She pulled away, stuck her payment into the piece of bread, stripped off her tunic, and let him into her soft parts.

WHEN HUGH HEARD he was to return to his father's castle, the name Marielle arced like a comet, pure joy, until Count Aymer said, "You will accompany Isabelle." *Maléfice.* Alone, he could gallop straight home, but Isabelle was young and her cart would pin him down. She'd cry and beg to stop and ignore his commands, even though he'd saved her.

But wait.

Marielle would see him at the cavalcade's head, crossing the bridge, his horse brushed, banners flirting. A leader. He could . . .

The count lifted an eyebrow and cleared his throat.

Hugh stuttered, "I will endeavor to keep your daughter safe, even with my life." He would prove himself worthy.

"That particular sacrifice won't be necessary." The count laughed a short bark. "I will send my own guards, a *posse comitatus* of trusted men. You will keep her company and prepare her for Lusignan."

Companion to a mere girl? His heart objected. Yes, a lovely *jeune fille*, well brought up with that alluring yellow hair but still a girl and unworthy. Ah, but the shouting villagers, the threats. Danger, perhaps an attack, and he could . . . Hugh made an effort to smooth his face. "Certainly, sir. What would you like her to know?"

"Your father has pledged to foster her and continue her lessons, particularly Latin. Her writing in that language is lacking and . . ." Count Angoulême brushed away an unseen swarm of gnats. "However, she has been little in the world and is inexperienced. You must prepare her for your mother."

His mother? The gnats clustered around Hugh. "I know not what you mean, sir."

"Remind her to curtsy, to keep her elbows off the table. Show her where she will sleep. Perhaps you can . . . Well, do your best. She is my only heir and must be safe."

Hugh understood the threat burning on his words. A frightened peasant with an arrow or a blacksmith's tool, even a stone, could strike Isabelle dead in the name of God. She must flee and he, Hugh, would help. A thrilling adventure, so like a Crusade which held, at its heart, the saving of something precious. He'd rescue Isabelle a second time.

4

GO YE INTO ALL THE WORLD

*A*t the long plank table on the dais, Isabelle ignored the bowl of eels in wine, usually her favorite. On the morrow she was to leave for Lusignan. She'd prayed for this departure, but tonight she was unable to swallow and Maman, who usually exhorted her to eat, remained silent. Below the dais, laughter, jokes, benches squeaking with excitement. The celebration slapped her cheeks; they wanted her, the witch, gone. Tears were rising when Papa pushed aside his trencher and said, "Come with me, child."

Expecting he'd take her to the comfort of her star for a last visit, a tear fell. But no, he led her across the dark bailey where dreadful shadows flickered and a snorting horse startled her. At the gate, he said, "Wait here," and disappeared into the night porter's niche. Left alone at the edge of the portcullis, the smell of fresh fields pulled Isi upright. Small creatures rustled; overhead swept millions of stars. God's world. Her fear eased.

Papa touched her shoulder. "Come silently." He led the way, shielding a rush light. Isi hesitated. What about the bonfires? The villagers?

BEHOLD THE BIRD IN FLIGHT

"You are safe," he whispered, nodding back at the guard who'd emerged from the niche to keep watch.

Isi stumbled, then hurried to follow him, slipping dark and small into her papa's shadow. As they walked, grasses brushed her legs; the forest creaked and she gripped her mantle. Where were they going?

Inside the forest's edge, Papa stopped and lifted the lamp. "Do you see the mound?" A small pile of raw dirt marked with a stick. "'Tis where Alain lies. Go and pray." He handed her the light and stepped back. "Hurry, child." His quiet words emerged from the dark as if the voice of trees. Three leaves fell across the edge of the lit world and she wanted to run, but there, there was Alain and he needed her. She knelt and said a Paternoster, the only official prayer she could remember. Paulus would be so angry. After amen, she added, *Holy Mother, please let Alain come up to you*. Staring into the glimmer of sky, she waited for a sign as she had after the funeral. Because Alain was innocent and must be allowed into heaven. An animal shifted nearby, a mouse or a fox. Or Papa, impatient. The pressure of dark, of hopelessness, her heart closing down, then a fiery bit broke free from the rush lamp and flitted into the tangled branches. A sign. A loosening. She was fully in God's world with its foxes and stars and the smell of leaves. Alain was saved and Papa, invisible as God, held her safe. She made the sign of the cross and then, whispering *adieu*, she turned, ready for the morrow.

IN EARLY DAWN of the eighth month of the year, the family gathered in the tiny chapel where Paulus intoned a prayer for the safe journey of the *filia* of the house. As he conjugated the Latin words, dropping them in front of the Lord, Isi leaned against her papa. The Virgin stared, reminding her: Alain was dead and she must travel to a foster family for safety. No one wanted her here. She crossed herself.

When the service finished, Isabelle stepped outside and her heart lifted. In the bright bailey, horses stamped, puffing and snorting like old men after a banquet. Mules groaned under their loads: her bedding, plus hooks and nets and knives, iron pots and spoons and tankards, dried meat and fish—gifts for the Lusignan household. In addition, a brass astrolabe for Hugh's father, a length of silk for his mother, and a small box of spices, all to underline Angoulême's wealth.

Isabelle herself wore a new green tunic, secured from Maman through long argument: Had she not earned womanly silk by wearing the garlic without a complaint? Should she not arrive in Lusignan well attired? Maman would not want them to think poorly of Angoulême. Isabelle giggled at her success.

A crowd had gathered to see her off. Soon she would pass through the portcullis to the wide world. She stood tall and walked with her papa past the mounted guards, her protection on the road. Servingwomen shifted on the edges of the courtyard; male servants whispered of the road's dangers: highwaymen, river crossings, kidnapping for ransom. Surely they exaggerated, but when Hugh's horse whinnied and reared, Isabelle clutched her gown. The silk soothed her.

A small wooden cart reposed amidst the clamor, canopied on three sides against sun and rain and prying eyes. Inside, her personal trunk with its glittering nail heads and a cushioned seat to ease the ride. She was truly leaving. Poulette fluttered and a servant handed her a small basket with dried fruit and a loaf of bread. She wanted to skip and laugh, but Papa stayed her with a gesture.

Paulus stepped forward, the bailey hushed, and the assembly knelt as he made the sign of the cross over her. Then Papa lifted her into the creaking cart, the little flags snapped, and her whole body lit with the need to move. She silently urged Hugh—*start, start*—but the castle gate remained closed, the cart immobile. She peeked out. Papa was staring at the chapel waiting for Maman.

Women quickened their prayers; men lowered their reins. Low-spoken words pattered into the waiting. At last Maman appeared at the chapel door, head bowed and crossing herself. Isabelle stifled a cry, feeling for the first time the loss of her mother. Who would brush her hair now? Who would remind her to stand tall? She leaned out, waving, but her mother simply called, "God go with you." Isi filled with entreaties—*Please, Maman, I need*—but Papa gave the signal and the heavy cart lumbered like a reluctant ox toward the portcullis.

"Wait." The word burst from Maman. The horses halted and she ran to touch Isabelle's fingers. "Take care for your dress, obey Madame Lusignan, make us proud." She stroked Isi's wrist—"Be brave"—then whirled toward her husband. "Did you give her a knife?"

"You were in charge of her belongings and the chest."

Maman stepped toward him so quickly that he backed away. "She is also your responsibility."

The murmur of women praying ceased.

"She needs a knife for meals. The Lusignans will think us savages if we send her without one." The countess swept her arm toward the sheathed knife that always hung at her husband's belt. "Give her that."

Isi knew the knife with its ivory handle was special, given to Papa when he was a child; he used it to cut rope, to clean his boots, and cut meat at the table. Only once had he allowed her to hold it, and now he covered it with his hand.

"Give it her," Maman whispered, her eyes like pins.

Papa stared at her. She didn't move. Shortly he sighed, untied the sheath, leaned into the cart, and retied it to Isabelle's belt. Under the shelter of the canopy, he said, "Never take this off, child. Never." He ran a finger down the leather, then dropped his hand. "Use it only for food. Do not cut yourself. And I beg you, do not lose it."

Isabelle smiled at him. "I promise, Papa. Tell Maman I shall miss her." Her heart spiraled into her throat. "And you." His eyes brimmed with feelings, and he lifted his hand to touch her. Propriety stopped him. He stepped back, nodded to Hugh, and they started away.

As the cart thumped hollowly over the castle bridge and jolted down the hill toward the village, Isabelle peeked back at her home; Poulette, who'd pecked inside her chest with excitement for weeks, collapsed into a sad pile of feathers. Who would sit on the dais and smile at Papa? Who would tease the guards and ask Maman questions? She curled on the cushion, weeping, until a great commotion of galloping and shouts forced her to lift the canopy's edge.

"Stay inside, Mademoiselle!"

Along the road, a mob of villeins had gathered, crossing themselves, shaking scythes, roaring, "Devil, death to the witch."

Isabelle crouched and took out the knife. Papa said to use it only for eating, but she needed it now. Shrieks and bellows rose through the dust, and the cart bucked and tilted in the horses' haste. Her entire body a pounding heart. Knife held at the ready. Only when the chasing men fell back to tiny dots did the cart slow, and gradually Isabelle stopped shaking. She scratched

"Angoulême" on the floorboards, a talisman, then slipped the knife under the chest edge, handy. The cart thumped on and on, so she practiced Latin conjugations—*fugio, fugi*: I fly, you fly—but soon past days lay heavy on her eyes and she slept.

A large jolt woke her. Knife in fist, she peeked through gaps in the canopy. Horses still strode protectively on either side of the cart, offering glimpses of the riders' leggings: one poorly dyed and filled with burrs, the other wrinkled on a skinny calf like the underside of a mushroom. She laughed, laid the knife aside, and smoothed her silk dress, determined it wouldn't be crumpled or ruined by dust as Maman warned. Hugh lifted a corner of the canopy and asked if she needed to stop, but the tone of his voice made her say no. He handed in bread smeared with honey.

By the third hour, despite cushions, she was bruised and flinching at every rut. No wonder riders complained, although a saddle must be easier. She leaned out to touch the foot of the rider with the wrinkled hosen, who turned out to be a guard she had often teased. "Monsieur, I want to walk."

The guard shouted for a stop and Hugh returned. "That is not allowed, Mademoiselle. Your mother was very particular. Something about your shoes and silk."

The shoes were new. "I'll take them off."

"By no means. You must stay in the cart." Hugh signaled and the cart jounced forward.

Now the little space began to press on her, the canopy glowing as if it were the sun itself, sweat trailing spiders down her neck and along her rib cage until she bubbled like a cook pot.

She tried poking her head out the back where guards might not notice, but dust and a vision of Maman, her hands on her hips, pulled her inside. Eventually she fell asleep again, and when she woke they were in the forest, shadows moving slowly across the cart's canopy like terrible dreams. A cliff, a dragon.

On the day he died, Alain had asked if she was afraid of dreams.

"Only when Papa is away."

"Can dreams come true?" Alain plucked a leaf of grass.

Unsure, she said, "Maybe if they come from God."

He turned on his stomach. "*Écoutez*. I dreamed about the stone men that stand outside the cathedral on their shelves. They hopped down and pointed at me, yelling. The noise was *angoissant*. God with his snake hair came down to chase me. My legs shook so much, I woke up." He lifted his head. "Do you think I'm damned?"

"You go to Mass and you pray, don't you?"

"Mother makes me." Alain twisted a corner of his tunic. "I don't always mean it when I say I'm sorry."

Afterward, the bee and the devil. Isabelle closed her eyes and crossed herself. When she opened them, a leaf fell softly onto the canvas, a shadow hand. She knew it was God's signal: He'd let Alain into heaven.

BEYOND THE HORSES' legs, trees slid past: birch, oak, maple; her papa had taught her the names when she was still a child. Now, almost grown, the Bible said she must put away childish things. She rubbed her chest softly, thinking of her married cousin, tunic billowing over breasts.

The cart jerked to a stop. "Tree across the road. Bring the axes." Around the shouts of men, birds sang. Songs like those at home, a warbler, a finch. Hours away, but the world much the same. How could that be? Isabelle slipped out of the cart and drifted through the trees, craning to find the well-hidden birds. There, a warbler. She tried whistling the intricate notes like Alain had taught her. It tickled her lips and made her laugh.

"Mademoiselle." Hugh ran up behind her.

What was wrong now? Maman's rules never mentioned whistling.

"Mademoiselle, we are ready to depart."

Again the cart, lurching along roads that were dirt or occasionally stone, left by the long-ago Romani. The iron-rimmed wheels clanged, mules brayed, and when at last they stopped for the night, a sunset red as a cock's comb signaled fair weather on the morrow. She walked a short distance, ate bread and salt meat, climbed into the cart, smoothed out her tunic, and lay down. Except for the birds, this wasn't as much fun as she'd expected.

In the night, she woke, thinking she was on the dais in Angoulême, her parents' bed thumping, but it was only an animal in the forest. Suddenly, she ached for the familiar sound. She'd overheard maids joking about her parents making babies. Often she'd lain on her mat, wishing for a sister. Someone to help with the daily tasks. For Maman to scold. She'd had only Alain.

They left the forest, traveling again through fields, stubbled now from harvest; here and there she glimpsed poor women stooping to gather spilt grain. Was this the world? How did those women live? She rattled in the cart, her hips bruised, enclosed. She wanted sun. She wanted freedom. At Poulette's dare, she untied a canopy corner to wafts of air and passing clouds. Wimple firmly in place, she stood. Glory, hallelujah! Sky shimmered overhead like the moat surface on a windless day.

"Mademoiselle Isabelle, you mustn't." Hugh galloped back from the front of the cavalcade; men swiveled on their saddles.

"Halt, halt," he cried. A guard snorted as the cart stopped. Even the horses turned their heads to look.

She laughed up at him, at his curls and stern look. "Why mustn't I?" His eyes wavered and she laughed again, showing her teeth.

"It is forbidden. Your complexion." Hugh shifted, his saddle squeaked.

"Are you my mother? We are out in the world." She searched for a stronger reason. "It is tremendously hot under the canvas. Shall I be cooked? Could you explain that to your father?"

"Your complexion will be quite red."

"Your father won't notice. My papa never spoke of it." She stamped her foot and the cart rocked. "I will do as I please."

A guard laughed softly. "Wild child, rod well spared."

Hugh slouched, pulling his hat lower, losing power as his eyes disappeared in shadow. "Your father placed me in charge. You must listen to me."

"You are too young to be in charge." She pulled off the wimple, shook her hair free, and stared directly at him.

Hat ripped off, he stared back. Little ripples started in her stomach. She took them to mean he was only a boy and couldn't command her. She wouldn't flinch away. His horse, bored, shook its head, jingling the harness, and Hugh relented. He gave the signal.

As they moved, her inner ripples turned to laughter. She had knocked him off his horse with ne'er a lance. She waved her arms and leaned forward, alert, bracing herself against the ruts as the wind teased and flirted, tangling her hair. She shook her head, swung it free.

A length of time passed with no people, only blackbirds leaping from the field like ash from a fire. She craned to see them rise, squawking out warnings. Once a huge bird, its wings tucked into a wedge, crashed from the blue and took a blackbird to the ground.

"Gyrfalcon kill," Hugh shouted.

The cart rolled past the larger bird, huddled over the smaller, beak deep into the body, ripping out strings of red, feathers scattered around the feast. Isi had seen killing of animals, neatly done with a quick slice, but this was different, this was wild. She wanted to be brave, but Poulette quivered and hid.

On the second night Isabelle woke, frightened by a tapping sound. They'd stopped in a woods, but when she peered out, she could see nothing; the night was black as blood pudding. No comforting rush light. No Papa or Maman. She held her breath, listened. The sound increased, restless on the leaves, and then thunder: God's hand smacked the earth and set the rain loose to splat against the canopy, chased by roll after roll of God's anger. She'd made Him angry by taking off her wimple. She prayed an Our Father.

All around her, tree trunks were lit and quenched. The tethered horses shied, flashing white, ghostly, and when she closed her eyes, they reared behind her eyelids. In the noise and dark, she could believe in ghosts, despite Paulus who said the only ghost was the Holy One. Gathering her bravado, she said, "I am no longer afraid of the dark." To prove it, she lay down and was almost asleep when a hand probed her foot. Fright blasted through her.

"Mademoiselle, 'tis only I who am keeping watch over you whilst the others sleep."

She recognized the voice of the guard from home. She pushed at his hand. "What do you want?" Her best Maman imitation. "I was sleeping."

"I pray you are not afraid. The thunder is fearsome."

The grip eased and she snatched her leg away. "I am perfectly accommodated. I thank you."

"Let me come up and push the rain off your canopy. It is become a small pool and I'm afraid 'twill soak through." The cart rolled with his weight, like to tip over, then he was in the space with her.

She wondered at her fear; she knew this man. Papa had sent him. She pressed against the chest to give him room. He pushed the canvas, and when a small waterfall proved his concern real, relief was like a stone taken from her shoe. "I thank you."

"You are warm enough? I thought you might be chilled." He sat next to her, muscled, damp, smelling of horse and ale. "You are dry?" His soft words nipped her ribs. She sat straight, breathing against his bulk. Then he patted her hair. The impress of his hand. The stroking. "I saw your lovely hair." He took a handful. "Like a gold flag." The hand cuddled her shoulder.

Isabelle twisted away from the lingering touch, but it made no difference, the space remained crammed and stifling. "Are you wet?" His hand smoothed down the front of her tunic. Her body froze. "Nothing of interest here, hey." The guard hiccupped and pressed closer. One of Maman's most important rules: no man shall defile your body before marriage. He wouldn't dare. Would he?

She tried to breathe. Was he just being kind? No, no. She forced herself to push at the hand, to stammer out, "I am quite dry, thank you."

The guard leaned forward, expanding, pressing her hard against the cart wall to stroke her bare ankle. "You are perhaps a bit damp here." The hand slid to her knee. "Or here. Let me warm you." Her voice locked in her throat; her skin shrank as the hand dragged her deeper and deeper into slimy water; she had seen such on the moat, green, shiny, swaying slightly. The thunder had ceased, but rain roared through the trees and inhaling the roar, she began to kick. The hand paused; an arm encircled her waist. She flailed against him, butting with her head, pushing at the heavy body. She needed the knife. She bit him, freed an arm, fumbled for the weapon, and stabbed, once, twice. The suffocating weight fell away. He crashed into the rain, swearing, bellowing. The camp awoke.

Swirls of shouting. Stamping through mud. Calls for light. Horses strained against their tethers, whinnying, as the guard was dragged away. Left alone, Isabelle reached out into the rain, splashing handfuls of water on her skin. She must wash him away. Maman must never know. His fingerprints smoldered on her calf, her thigh.

In time Hugh came with a rush light and tapped softly on the cart's body. "Mademoiselle, are you all right?"

She covered her eyes. "Where is he?"

"We have tied him to a distant tree. You are safe."

"I do not feel so." Hugh's eyes, misshapen by the flickering light, were black holes.

He reached in and took her hand. "I pledged your father I would keep you from harm with my life. May I come into the cart?"

Isabelle wanted Maman. She needed Papa. She would accept Hugh.

He took her silence for assent and climbed slowly in. "I will stay awake so you may sleep."

He smelled of horse and pine; his body barely brushed her, and she felt the kindness he meant. Her fingertips warmed slightly; her shoulder blades unclenched a fraction. "I fear I have . . ." Had she ruined her tunic with blood? Was it right to think about that when she had stabbed a man? "Is he dead?"

"By no means. You must sleep." He turned his back to her. "We arrive tomorrow."

She touched his arm. "What should I do with the knife?" Her voice quavered. "It was Papa's." She sobbed once, twice. "He will be angry that I used it so."

"He will be proud that you protected your honor. Now sleep."

She tried but the woods were loud with sudden noise: squirrels twitching with dreams, a rider's snore, the spring of a branch released when an owl took flight. She lay on the cushion, shuddering, not from cold but from what she now knew. When toward morning Hugh's head slipped onto his arms, she watched him sleep and gripped the knife to keep them both safe.

PART
TWO

Lusignan, France

1199–1200

5

BEHOLD, I STAND AT THE DOOR

he morning sun seemed reluctant to rise. Eventually, darkness cracked, revealing solid trees. Minutes passed, more light, leaves fluttering to the forest floor. When Isabelle could discern the men sleeping around the cart, her grip on the knife loosened and she wakened to her body and memories. The insistent bulk of the guard. The stains left by his groping fingers. Swarmed with horror, she nudged Hugh awake. "I need to descend."

After the night's rain, the road resembled ancient porridge. Hugh swung her down onto a wet mat of leaves beside the road. "Where is he?" Hugh pointed, and she walked in another direction, trembling. Behind a bush, she lifted her overdress to look at her thigh. Unmarked, but burning with a hand-shaped blot. She scrubbed at it with a fist of wet leaves, then pounded, slapped, kicked. Her body revolted her; nevertheless, it was hers. She would never be rid of it. *Throw off this mortal coil.* Her papa said that at Alain's funeral; at the time it made it her terribly sad, but today she understood the need.

When she calmed and returned, Hugh said, "I have sent him ahead with a warder." Isi was so grateful her knees unlocked; Hugh caught her stagger. "He was pale with the loss of blood." He carefully placed her upright. "He will be taken to await judgment, either of my father or of his heavenly Father, should he fail to live." She noticed how his arms warmed her ribs. He said, "Are you able to continue?"

The cart loomed and Isi retched. "Is it far to the castle? Could I walk?"

"Many leagues." He peered into her face. "You shall have my horse. Have you ridden?"

"Only a small pony." His horse was gigantic.

"Alaric is gentle." Hugh's eyes also. "I think you will find yourself well accommodated." He helped her onto the saddle, placed her feet in the stirrups, and showed her how to grip with her knees—she controlled a shudder when he touched them— then walked, leading the horse on the last lap of their journey. The horse's scent rose, warm, safe; Hugh's hand gripped the bridle, brown, smooth. She'd remember that hand, not the other. In the sun, fine golden hairs glinted on his wrist; the knuckles seemed solid. Held in his kindness, she allowed Poulette to lie down.

The Lusignan castle, new stone with a multitude of towers, blazoned with pride. Perched on a cliff above the river, it had no need of a moat. The stone walls had teeth, its parapets dented the sky, and many arrow-loops overlooked the countryside, insuring the safety of the villeins and others in the village. It made Isabelle quiver. How dare she ride into this glory? Would Hugh's family want her? Surely Papa had made certain. A ghost of doubt brushed her neck: Papa had also sent the guard. She rubbed the ghost away. He had given her the knife. Meant to cut meat at the table, not to stab a man. Her thoughts ran every which way, a field of wheat in the wind. The knife! Where was it? Had she lost it? No, it was tied at her belt, clean, no blood. Hugh must have . . . his hand, his back. But never again would she travel by cart, not even if they put her into chains. And if the guard died? Would she be accused? She covered her eyes.

"Are you afraid?" asked Hugh.

His voice stopped the swirl of thoughts and suddenly the Lusignan castle bloomed in the sun, a small flag at its very peak, its white walls stretched between the little round towers like a sheet between chubby laundresses. Isi leaned forward on the horse, comforted by the soft neck and the steady gait. "Why is it so pale?"

"Father ordered new ashlars. The outer walls had darkened with time, so he had them refreshed over the summer."

"It's beautiful." Isabelle twirled a piece of mane and thought of her home, the stains running from the arrow-loops, the small guard house, the rickety wooden steps she and Alain climbed to throw acorns.

"'Twas not done for beauty. Father says we must project strength and prosperity. And villeins unable to pay their yearly fees were well put to work."

Isabelle imagined Hugh's parents inside, arrayed in clothes as new as their castle. She brushed at her skirt. "I can't go like this." Her gown was thick with dust, crumpled and blood spotted.

"I know a fine seamstress, the mother of . . ." He cleared his throat. "A friend."

The seamstress, Alina, worked in a daub and wattle house, lit only by the sun. Now, cooler autumn days having arrived, a fire burned in the center of the room. The smoke was meant to escape through a hole in the roof, but Hugh stood at the door, coughing. "Mistress, I require your assistance."

Alina, slightly stooped, eyes red-rimmed, emerged to assess Isabelle's gown. "'Tis ruined." She shook her head. "The girl's right thin, but perhaps my daughter's outgrown overdress would serve. Come down, child."

When Hugh helped Isi from the horse, Alina turned her head aside and laughed.

Standing as tall as she was able, Isabelle said, "My ruined dress is no cause for mirth." She brushed at the blood.

"I beg pardon, Mademoiselle." The seamstress eyed the dirt road. "'Tis only that your face is the same ruddy hue as the stains on your dress."

Her complexion. Isi touched her cheeks. Her skin was hot and tight as inflated pig bladders. Maman would be furious. She should never have taken off the wimple.

Alina put a hand on her arm. "Come. We shall repair what we can." She pulled her into the smoky cottage where the cast-off gown proved too wide and quite short. "You have a goodly growth, Mademoiselle, for one so young. We must repair your own tunic." It was brushed with a straw broom to remove dust, a powder was applied over dirt spots, then Isabelle was made to stand over incense. "To refresh the scent, Mademoiselle." Finally, because the blood markings on the front couldn't be disguised—"I'd need to pound it on the fountain's stones and lay it in the sun for several days"—Isabelle was given a length of pale green linen to fasten over the stains with her belt. "Girt yourself tight so the fabric cannot loosen."

Cheeks burning, waist cramped, bruised from battle with the guard, sleepy from the eventful night, and exhausted from riding, Isabelle remounted the horse and entered her new home, determined not to embarrass Papa or Maman.

INSIDE THE LUSIGNAN bailey, the courtyard bustled like a village street. Maidenly propriety meant she should keep her head down, but with so many things to see, Isabelle stared at the leg of a dead goat waggling over a cook's shoulder, an ale wife sloshing her bucket, a pair of priests arguing. In the center of the recently swept stones, a large poplar flourished, already touched by autumn and glowing like a copper pot.

"Welcome home, young count." A swift bow from a man in a stained shirt. Hugh tethered the horse to the tree and helped Isi down. "*Le jeune maître*, welcome." "*Grâce a Dieu* you are safe." Everyone who passed acknowledged Hugh; Isabelle was invisible. She had a moment's pang. This was his house; he had friends and duties. If Alain were here, they'd laugh at the goat leg and her papa would have complimented her riding. She longed for a greeting, a curtsy.

Scuffing her feet, she made herself small and followed Hugh inside where wooden stairs confused her. "The great hall is above?"

"Mother had it moved up when the keep was rebuilt. The old hall is now a kitchen." Hugh tugged her elbow. "Can you move faster? Father will be waiting."

She was going to meet his father. She rehearsed proper greetings as she followed Hugh, already estranged by the straw on the floor strewn with lavender, pale and medicinal, unlike the friendly marigolds her own mother used. They passed through several large rooms—a buttery, a pantry—then in a room filled with armor and weapons, Hugh paused.

"That is my grandfather's sword, and that helmet is from an infidel he killed on Crusade. My family goes on Crusade. Father has gone, and I will too." He seemed in no hurry to move on; Isabelle studied the banners with the Lusignan coat of arms, the blue and gray stripes not nearly as nice as her father's red and yellow checks. She clenched away a pang of missing, vowing to represent Angoulême properly.

Suddenly, Hugh inhaled and pulled her into a room where several women were spinning. He dropped Isi's elbow and faced the women. "Greetings."

"*Le jeune seigneur*." A woman dropped her distaff, which clattered to the floor. "*Vous êtes revenu*." Greetings flew around the room.

Was that his mother? Surely the woman who'd dropped the distaff was too young. Uncertain if she should bow, Isabelle glanced at Hugh and startled at his odd expression, smooth but with wolf eyes. For some reason she was sure the guard who'd entered her cart looked the same.

The woman bent to pick up her wool. "Greetings to you . . . I, I." She stuttered to a stop. "Sir."

Not his mother, but certainly discomposed. Her flush reminded Isabelle of her own face, and she bent her head. Hugh spoke softly—"Thank you for your kind greeting"—grabbed Isabelle's hand, and pulled her into the great hall.

Against all propriety, Isi gaped. A fire burned, not familiarly in the middle of the space but in a masonry opening like a small room on the outer wall. Fabric with embroidered soldiers hung high against the stone, and on the dais, a long *table dormant* hunkered, never to be moved. Maman had asked for one, but Papa

BEHOLD THE BIRD IN FLIGHT

said it was a foolish waste of space. Where did Hugh's family sleep?

Hugh dropped her hand as a woman came across the hall, speaking Latin. "*Salutem. Tu es tuti domun.*"

Isabelle recognized *Salutem* but, surprised by the Latin, missed the rest. She surreptitiously pulled at the slipping green fabric. *Keep thyself clean.* Maman would be so angry.

"*Salve, Mater.*" Hugh kissed the woman on both cheeks.

With a jolt, Latin awoke. This woman in silk was Hugh's mother. Latin phrases twirled through her mind like cloud wisps. What should she say after *Salve? Sum felix? Gaudeo? Me felicem?* She couldn't remember the proper form to express pleasure. And exhaustion. Was it *Taedet* or *Taedeo?*

"*Ubi Patris?*"

Isabelle understood Hugh expected to see his father. *Where's Father?* Slightly relieved that her Latin was returning, she placed her hand over a bloodstain and struggled to follow his mother's words.

" . . . *absens . . . regis postulatio.*"

Hugh's father was away; "*regis*" meant king. Understanding had almost arrived when she noticed the edge of Madame Lusignan's overdress glittered with silver thread, and her concentration broke. Maman never wore silver thread. The crisscrossed pattern formed boxes, and in each box nestled a tiny knot. Instantly she wanted it. Words streamed past her, unheard.

Hugh tapped Isabelle's shoulder. "*Alors ici*, Count Angoulême's daughter, Isabelle. She is accustomed to *parler français*, Mater."

"She needs to improve her Latin, or so her father said, but for now . . ." Madame Lusignan stepped closer to Isabelle, fanning her hands wide. "Mademoiselle, welcome."

Isi's comfort at the return to her native language disappeared when Madame reached out to touch the green fabric cinched at her waist. The hand, although soft with well-trimmed nails—not black with hair—sent a fiery rod through her and she clamped down a shrieking. She must represent home. She was safe here.

"I understand there has been some trouble with your dress. We shall fix that shortly. No need to hide, *ma petite*." The hand lifted Isi's face. "Ah, I see. You are quite red. Surely your maman spoke about preserving your complexion. *Tant pis*, we shall get some salve and then we shall see what to do with you." The silk flared as she turned.

"Mother, I think Isabelle is more in need of rest than salve."

"Ah, *mon fils*, ever kind. Take her to the solar, and then see to the horses. The steward is traveling with your father, and the constable has been consorting with town whores. I don't trust him to provide proper care." Again the whirl of silk. She strode across the hall.

Solar? What kind of castle was this? The embroidered eyes in the hangings stared, Madame Lusignan called to a group of men as if she were a man herself, the fire seemed lonely and distant in its little house, and Isabelle of Angoulême was dissolving like tallow in lye. She longed for home. *Are you tired, petite chou? Take some barley water before your prayers*. Every night Maman sent her to bed with those words. Every night, that is, until her last one in Angoulême. *Go to bed and remember, you will represent our family out in the world. Be proud and strong. Pray every day*. Maman had talked softly while combing Isi's hair as they sat behind the curtain of the dais. For once, she'd not pulled at the tangles nor shaken Isi's shoulder with a command to sit still. *You are almost a woman. Remember that and your manners. Chew with your mouth closed*. Now in this new castle, this new home, Isabelle nudged Poulette. She had ridden a horse, stopped an attack. She would succeed. When Poulette raised her head, Isi draped the green fabric over her arm, called out, "*Merci*, Madame," to the back of the silk dress, and followed Hugh across the hall.

The solar was a large room up a second set of stairs that ran along the inner wall. Isi's trunk had already been placed in the corner with other trunks. There were several pallets scattered about and in the middle of the room was a bed, much like that of her parents. Two little windows, oddly wavy, let in light. Isi wanted to walk over and look out, but her eyelids had other ideas.

"This is yours." Hugh led her to a pallet with layers of straw-filled sacks, a single feather bed, and on top, Isi's pillow and blanket from the cart. He pointed to a niche. "The *necessarium* is through there. Try not to step on any of us if you need to use it in the night." He took the green fabric from her. "I will return this."

Isabelle sat down. Late afternoon sun oozed into the room like plum jelly, rich, almost purple. Sounds from the great hall drifted in. No shouts or clattering armor, only a gentle speaking like distant thunder rolling away in the clouds. As she stretched out, images lifted from her mind like a flight of birds: Hugh arriving in Angoulême, Hugh pulling her away from the angry men in the apple orchard, reaching into the cart to comfort her, leading her into this new place. Remembering Maman's injunction, she whispered, "Lord, watch over him and me. Amen." She curled under the cover and, as if hit by an anvil, slept, safe for now.

Clutching the fabric, Hugh used the peephole his father had ordered in the wall of the solar to look down into the great hall. His mother was talking to the priest, and several villagers awaited her attention. He looped the green fabric over his arm, went quietly down the stairs and along the length of the long hall. If caught, he'd have to explain the borrowed cloth. Passing unnoticed into the weaving room, he breathed easier. The short woman was no longer spinning, and although the remaining women giggled, they kept working as he walked through.

The horses were stabled. He received greetings as politely as he could, then hurried out the gate, fabric still over his arm. In the village he resisted the urge to run, to fly, to gallop. Despite his stately pace, when he arrived at the seamstress's house, he was panting. The sun was slipping off to sleep, wrapping itself in the evening mists, but no matter; in the dark room a glimmer quickened his breath. "Is your mother gone?"

"To stay with the dyer's wife."

"Come here where I may see you." Every part of him was reaching out—his hands, his heart, his cock.

When the seamstress's daughter took a small step toward him, he flung the fabric over her back and pulled her close. At last he held his Marielle, her soft roundness, the tip of her breast in his mouth, the bristle between her legs parting for his hand. He planned to go slow as she preferred, but he'd been away too long and, falling onto the single chair, he lifted his tunic and wrenched her onto his lap. In a trice, it was over.

Marielle pulled the tangle of green fabric from their heads, laughing. "Next time will be different, will it not?"

"I swear it."

"Come lie down and show me."

Afterward, they lay in the dark. From time to time a straggler passed outside, rush lamp trailing light like a bit of comet; otherwise the night was black as the heart of an infidel, but no matter. Hugh's hands had eyes. They saw the fuzz on Marielle's arms and around her hairline, the curve of her breasts where they flattened into the rise and fall of her ribs. This, the softness in his life where all else was hard: the castle, Alaric's flank, Father, even the falcons whose fluff belied taut bone and beak. His hand slid down Marielle's stomach—clouds, strawberries, velvet. When his little finger popped into her belly button, she rolled onto him, breathing laughter like bubbles in his hair. Her weight was the only pressure he longed for. "Marielle, I shall marry you."

The giggles stopped and she pulled away. "No." Her hand, soft from working with the wool, covered his mouth. "Do not hope for that. Your father will have other plans."

"Whither thou goest, I shall go." She couldn't argue with the Bible.

"Honor thy father and thy mother." Years of attending Mass.

He took hold of her long hair, knotted now from their love-making, and twisted it through his fingers. If he had a comb, he would tease it smooth, tickle her ear, kiss her eyebrow. "Father will want what I want."

"Your father will want what is best for your land, for your kingdom. I have nothing to give. Mother has nothing to give. Do you think your father will be satisfied with this tiny holding? You must want more."

"Your mother has you to give. You are everything." Her body was hardening. To keep the softness, he said, "I shall delve into his thoughts without saying of whom I am speaking."

"Do not ask, Hugh. Swear it to me."

He made the vow, but as he pulled up his hose, he wavered. This was his woman, the only one he would ever want. He must confront his father. He pushed away an unmanly quiver and vowed to find a way.

IF ISABELLE HAD allowed it, the huge castle with its many servants and extended family could have swallowed her, but determined to represent Angoulême proudly, she lengthened her spine, sharpened her gaze, extended her steps, and kept her new gown, a gift from Madame Lusignan, clean. She didn't widen her eyes when she learned the windows in the solar were set with expensive white glass. She used Papa's knife with care at meals, and on the day she glimpsed her attacker being carried across the bailey, she kept her composure. She made herself new inside the newness.

Day began with chapel, a familiar ritual in an unfamiliar location, discovered the first night when she wakened, groped along the wall toward the *necessarium*, stepped through a door, and, reaching out, touched nothing until a railing hit her knee and she almost fell into black space. Madame heard her cry. "Stay still, *petite*. I'll come get you." In the morning light, Isabelle saw that the chapel encompassed two floors. A small balcony off the solar meant the ruling family could easily attend Matins, even if not fully awake.

After chapel came studies—Latin, math, religion, history— another constant with new twists. In Angoulême, history had been of the English Norman kings such as Richard the Lionheart, once her father's liege lord. The Lusignan liege lord was King Philip, so history was of France and Isi learned about her own great-grandfather, Louis VI, called Le Gros. Why had Maman never mentioned he was fat? Louis's son married Eleanor of Aquitaine, who became Maman's aunt until the marriage was annulled and Eleanor married a duke of Normandy who became King of England. It was all confusing, but imagine marrying two kings. And Eleanor's son was Richard Cœur de Lion. Somehow they were related. Isabelle Cœur de Lion sounded *très* grand.

Of all the newness, morning council surprised her most. At home, Isi's mother had convened the daily council when Papa was away, but Maman merely nodded yes to the steward and the reeve. Madame, on the other hand, asked questions, looked at the numbers, and directed the men. Isabelle vowed when she was a countess she'd be like Madame; in council she sat straighter and leaned forward so everyone would know she was listening. One day, Madame announced with crossed arms and tight mouth that King John was coming to visit. As the steward and the marshal roared—the cost, the cost, how long would he stay, how many horses and men must be housed and fed—Isabelle squirmed with Poulette's mad pecking. John was brother to Richard Cœur de Lion. She could hardly wait to meet him. She began practicing her curtsies.

Poulette awakened again on the day the bailiff said, "The Angoulême man died last night of canker from the stab wound." Heads turned toward Isabelle and her face flamed. She had killed a man. Would she go to hell? What would Papa say? Would she have to give up her knife? She was so good at cutting her meat. No, no, what kind of thought was that? She must pray for his soul.

"What does Madame wish? Shall the matter be brought to the manorial court?"

The men's eyes fluttered on Isabelle's face, but Madame's eyes bored like awls into Isi, who was trying not to cry.

"I think we must have a formal judgment. Her family will have no desire to pay a boon to the dead man's kin." Here Madame cast a small smile at Isi. "Mademoiselle is almost grown and quite strong."

The praise stopped her tears. Of course she was strong. She would save her family. Hugh's eyebrow lifted slightly, recognizing her strength, and she smiled, not at him but at the embroidered soldiers who witnessed her courage from the wall.

After council, she went to the room where the women spun, accustomed to sitting there after Nones, learning to use the distaff. Much of her day was spent with men, so it was a relief to walk in on women pulling wool into thread and talking. Isabelle felt smoother there, her legs and arms loosened as if rivulets of water flowed through them. Agatha and Marielle, only slightly older, had become her friends. How different from being with Alain. No running or digging, no chases, no hiding; only talking and spinning. Agatha, from a tiny village unattached to any castle, had been sent because her father hoped she would marry a Lusignan villein and live in safety. Marielle's presence had been required by Madame because she was quick with the spindle and her thread was fine and serviceable. The women talked of cousins and storms, of favorite animals—ducks for Agatha, sheep for Marielle, rabbits for Isi—of the new shoemaker's apprentice, the quantity of soap still to be made, and of dancing, because at Castle Lusignan the company often danced in the great hall.

Today the room was silent. Not a woman raised her head when Isabelle entered. The younger women stood to spin, but the older ones sat on stools that scraped on the stone as they shifted. The twirling spindles whispered softly and occasionally tapped the floor. Isabelle piled combed wool on a distaff and began to spin.

Finally, Marielle spoke. "We heard the news."

"About the manor court." Agatha stopped spinning. "Did you really kill him?"

"Not on purpose." A lump formed in the thread somewhat smaller than the one in Isi's throat. "He was on me."

The older women shaped their lips like little money pouches but didn't speak. Marielle took Isi's distaff and smoothed the mistake. "Then you had good cause."

Because her hands were trembling, Isabelle stood straighter and gripped the distaff as if it could pull her to safety. "What will they do to me?"

"Nothing," said Marielle and Agatha together. "They will ask questions."

"Might be that they will require an ordeal," said an old woman leaning in the corner. "To prove before God that you are innocent."

"Like the fletcher's apprentice. Hiding iron tips in his apron for his father."

"*Judicium Dei.* God's judgment."

"God won't punish Isabelle," said Marielle. "And the apprentice's hand healed."

"The water warn't boiling properly. He's a thief all right."

Isabelle bit her tongue so as not to moan. Why had Papa sent her here?

"He never filched nothing," said Agatha. "I saw him marched into the church, and how he reached into the boiling water to grab the stone. His hand was right scalded. Red as sunset. He a'howling. The priest saw and attested."

Marielle swung her spindle with force. "Three days, that hand unwrapped, skin pink and no putrescence. God found him innocent."

"I'm of the mind his family used some witch's potion. The very devil is in that boy."

"You only say that because he teased you." Marielle touched Isabelle's shoulder. "You need not worry."

How could she not? Maybe God was punishing her. When

she'd read about His wrath, the fire and brimstone, she wondered if it hurt to be turned into salt. Had her blasphemous thought made God angry? And she'd neglected her prayers, despite Maman's exhortation. She'd really tried to pray, but Lusignan's newness got in the way. At night, she couldn't find her star; the other stars caught her prayers and sent them back. In chapel, the incense didn't waft her pleas up to heaven; it only made her cough. And the Virgin's statue, carved in wood and gilded, impressive and stiff, made Isi long for the stone Mary of the crooked nose.

In desperation, she focused on the men who would sit in judgment, smiling politely in council and keeping her mouth closed. She was heedful of Hugh, who had witnessed the attack. Oddly, he seemed to be avoiding her, running off to town every chance he got; maybe he thought she was guilty. Only when she was riding—Madame insisted a countess must ride well—did worry ease. As her horse stamped along the path, the trees, now leafless, stitched the sky to the clouds, the air shimmered with smoke and the smell of apple butter, birds lined stone walls like tiny black runes. Why would a God who created all this pay attention to her? If He did, He knew she loved His world and would protect her, but if He was too busy to notice a thin girl, she would have to protect herself. She gathered flint into her mind, preparing. She never thought to send for Papa.

FOR THE TRIAL, hangings of blue cloth embroidered with fleur-de-lys, symbol of King Philip, were placed in the great hall upon the *table dormant*. Crackling torches lined the walls, and a tremendous fire had been built against the early November chill. As Isabelle entered, the crowd of servants, visitors, and family members was standing aside for the man from the previous session who was being led away, white and trembling. What had he done? Had he not proved his innocence? *Lord, be kind to him.* If she was generous and good, the Lord would be kind to her. *Do unto others.* That was what He demanded, what she was trying.

Three men wearing the king's insignia sat at the table, menacing faces in flickering shadows. Her wild heart battered her ribs, her breath. *Be merciful to me, Lord.* She panted slightly. The fire crackled. *You know I am innocent.*

She was led next to Hugh who touched her shoulder and, when she turned her head, nodded gravely. She'd not seen him so serious and it shook her from prayer. Suddenly, Alain's ghost charged past, waving a stick as a challenge; she must master this. To rouse her bravery, she stamped her feet on the wooden floor. *Thump, thump.* Her heart beat louder.

To her left, a woman, not old but bent and squinting, wiped her rheumy eyes with a bit of rag. From time to time a man in a black doctor's cap patted her back; at her side fidgeted two young girls, unkempt, ill-dressed, staring around the hall.

Noise from the crowd echoed on the stone walls, and when a man on the dais began speaking, Isabelle missed his first words, but he stood, scraping back the heavy chair, and the crowd quieted. "Madame Guillot, in the name of King Philip, we are here to hear your grievance and to decide upon recompense."

The doctor nudged forward the woman who stood, pulling at her apron. "Me, myself, has been nursing my husband. The doctor will say such." She looked at him. He gestured for her to continue. "Just lately himself has died. 'Twas no need. He warn't old. That young hussy"—she pointed at Isabelle—"tempted him with her yellow hair, luring him into her carriage. He war only doing a kindness, and she stabbed him. And I now alone with two daughters. How will they marry? How will I keep my household? We are without sustenance."

The official smoothed his beard. "Monsieur le Docteur, did Guillot die from this grievous wound or another cause?"

"Suppuration of the wound, Monsieur. He was in the main healthy."

"Thank you." The official spoke briefly with his colleagues and then pointed at Hugh. "You are a witness?"

"Yes, your lord." A large log crackled and crashed in the fireplace.

"Proceed."

Hugh spoke slowly. "The man called Guillot was stabbed at night while my company, which was escorting the *jeune fille*, slept. He had been designated to guard her, to be wakeful and ensure her safekeeping. We roused suddenly when he fell howling from Mademoiselle's conveyance."

"Was there rain?"

"Yes. And tremendous thunder." The crowd shifted; thunder meant dark spirits coiled in the air.

"You slept while the Mademoiselle was in this storm?"

"There was a canopy over the cart, sir. She was well protected."

"Would said canopy have gathered rain?"

"Undoubtedly. But . . ."

"Thank you." Again he whispered with his colleagues, one of whom gestured repeatedly at Isabelle.

Hugh leaned toward Isabelle with his comforting smell of horse, else she might have fallen.

The head official pointed again at Hugh. "We now take up the matter of the yellow hair. Was it on display?" Here the crowd began to murmur. A young girl without her wimple. Ungodly.

"Not at night."

"At any time?" The coming answer shattered Isabelle's breath.

Hugh straightened his tunic and twisted his shoulders, glancing sideways at Isabelle. His sorry look shot cramps up the back of her legs. "*Oui*, Monsieur. Mademoiselle Angoulême had ridden a fair part of the day standing up in the cart without her wimple. 'Twas a hot day, and I believe she wished to be in the air."

"Feelings are of no consequence here."

Isabelle's body jerked. She had only feelings.

"We wish only to ascertain if the hair was loose and full of temptation?"

"She's a witch." The wife threw up her arms, waving the rag. "She killt a young boy with her wiles in Angoulême. Now she killt my husband."

The crowd in the hall broke into talking, shifting, crossing themselves until the bearded official slapped the table. "Silence in the name of the king."

Isabelle could scarcely breathe. Tremors overtook her ribs. Torches flamed in her gut.

"Monsieur Lusignan?"

"The hair is yellow, but none of my party remarked on it. I don't feel it tempting."

The frightful torches guttered slightly and hope brushed her. Later, in bed, she would cry because Hugh didn't delight in her hair, but now she took a breath.

"Turning to the accusation that Mademoiselle is a witch. You were in Angoulême, which pays allegiance to the Norman king, not to our liege lord Philip Augustus. Their ways may be strange, welcoming to witches. What say you?"

"This cannot be. She is among the faithful. Attentive in chapel. I was there with her many a time." Hugh raised his hand as if taking an oath. "When the young boy died, she was stricken with sorrow over his death, praying every day. A true witch would not enter the sanctified ground."

"You swear this."

"Solemnly."

Isabelle stepped closer to his strength.

"We shall therefore discount this accusation and judge only if she is a temptress who lured a man to his death. Thank you. That will be all." The officials talked softly among themselves, and gradually the hall filled with sharp-bladed whispers.

Hugh smoothed his tunic and murmured something Isabelle didn't hear. She was waiting for her turn to speak. She had been there. She was the only true witness. The terrible thunder. The ghostly horses and the smell of ale. A sharp beak—not little Poulette—struck her stomach and chest until she thought to fall to the floor. She longed to huddle against Hugh and hide her face. The ghost of Alain returned. *Find your courage. Be lionhearted. The Lord said the truth will set you free.*

She lifted her face to the talking men and stepped forward. She did not shout, but spoke clearly. "I, I wish to speak." The murmurs dimmed. "You must hear me. As the accused, I will defend myself. I will one day be a countess. Attend to my words." The officials turned, their hands raised in protest, but before they could say anything, she stamped another step closer and cried, "I am no temptress." She ran her hands down the front of her overdress. "See me." She turned sideways. "I am flat, still a child." It was bitter to say those words, but she understood she must. "What temptation is here?" She ripped off her wimple and shook out her hair, causing a thrill around the hall. "Yes, God made my hair yellow like the sun. The sun draws me, like to like. The men traveled free in the air, but I was immured, a prisoner. Which of you would choose to ride enclosed in a cart? With the sky and sun, the trees and birds of God's creation hidden from your vision." Excited, she pointed at one of the officials. "You?" Before he could reply, she continued. "No, you go like a man goes on his horse. Soon I will be a woman, but now I am a child and I only stabbed Monsieur Guillot when he tried to make me a woman before my time."

In the silence that followed, the points of what she had thrown into the air glittered. Hugh took Isabelle's hand and pulled her back, whispering, "You must apologize."

"My lords, forgive my outburst. I have only told the truth as a countess must. God forgive me if I have sinned." She thought better of adding: *but I have not*. She gripped Hugh's hand, anger and fright draining into its warmth while she waited for the men to decide. If she was to endure the boiling water, her hand might never feel this again.

At length, the officials stood, and the hall was instantly quiet. The bearded man spoke. "We adjudge Monsieur Guillot culpable. Mademoiselle is free to go. There will be no boon levied."

Her body lit with pride and she cast away Hugh's hand. She alone had saved her maman from shame and her papa from the fine. She would be a proper countess, with power.

6

WHOM THOU LOVEST

Hugh, buoyed from a visit to Marielle, galloped across the drawbridge to find the inner bailey massed with horses, grooms, and shouting squires. His father had returned from fulfilling his duty to King Philip Augustus. Hugh's inner sky clouded. Soon he'd be called to account for his Angoulême visit, so he dallied in the crowd, brushing his horse, cleaning his shoes, wishing to be invisible, but presently a knight appeared. Père required him. He mounted the dark stairs to the great hall and edged into the room.

"*Fili mi.*" Père opened his arms. In his father's embrace, so powerful, so knowing, Hugh could scarcely breathe. "Come, tell me of your findings."

The arm around Hugh's shoulder grew heavier as he proved unable to recall the number of knights or horses, or if the smithy forged crossbows, or the fletcher worked day and night. He stammered out a vague certainty that no plans were being laid for an attack, adding, "I believe all is well."

"Do you not understand?" His father's arm dropped. "Count

Angoulême is a threat. He claims our marches, panting for the rents and amercements to fill his treasury." He leaned into Hugh's face, breath a hot bellow. "If he succeeds, he will attack our lands. Only the threat of Philip Augustus keeps him away. And now King John, the Norman usurper, is coming to us. He is a wolf and shall stay God knows how long, draining our supplies, demanding to see the accounts, and should he join with Angoulême, who knows what will befall us."

Belatedly Hugh understood the watching eyes, but his memory held only normal castle rounds. Unable to appease his father—he could direct his mother, a woman, but Père turned him into a child—Hugh tried diversion, telling of how Isabelle had been blamed for a child's death and called a witch.

His father laughed. "Villeins, ever prone to fright. The girl is but a child. Soon to be of marriageable age, though, and brings a fine dower."

Hugh, wallowing in his humiliations, didn't notice his father's keen look.

With Père's return, the rhythms of the castle changed. Madame Lusignan moved to more usual womanly territory, harassing cooks and laundresses, meting out spices, checking household supplies, and riding in the afternoon. Council became loud, manly. Knights tromped through the bailey, teased the spinning women, stamped into the great hall for meals where they jostled on benches and shouted at their squires, who yelled in turn at the pages.

Hugh longed to be among them, polishing a shield, seeing to the hooves of a horse, or simply sitting with a knight, *his* knight, at the table. When he'd turned fourteen, properly a man, he'd asked to begin what he envisioned as his future life, but his father forbade it. "You are an only son. You must live to take a wife who will bear children." Now, although cowed by his past failures, he secretly worked daily at driving a lance against the quintain and running for stamina. When he mounted Alaric to visit Marielle, he'd gallop and leap small stone fences, even though forbidden to do so when riding alone. Someday Père would recognize him.

AFTER THE TRIAL, Isabelle found her place in the castle. Before she had moved through it like a badger in a burrow; now it moved around her. She was among the first offered salt at the table, Madame deemed her skilled enough to be a riding companion, and the tutor praised her Latin. Isi puzzled over the difference and could find no outer change: the servants, meals, evenings spent dancing or listening to the troubadour remained the same. Perhaps it was because her chest had puckered slightly around her nipples, a sign, she fervently hoped, of bigger things to come.

She enjoyed her new ascendancy until two knights declared devotion to her, asking for her favor. One knelt in the spinning room—Isi thought he had dropped a coin—making Marielle and Agatha giggle and the older women harrumph. Another youth galloped up as she rode and grabbed her hand, almost unseating her. "The Lai of Guigemar" recited by the troubadour said expressions of love should be treasured, but she felt only confusion.

"What can they mean?" Isi was walking with Marielle around the bailey. Chill December but no warmer inside because many rooms lacked a fireplace. Even in the great hall, despite a raging fire, drafts blew behind the hangings, rippling the embroidered men into life. "I don't yet have a full woman's years."

"They wish to plead for your favors before the others." Marielle flexed her hands, stiff from the cold.

"Others? There will be more?" Isi stopped walking and stared at her friend.

"Many, I assure you. Come, walk on, 'tis cold." Marielle wrapped her mantle tighter. "You are tall, your hair is golden, your complexion fine, your teeth small, strong, and white. You will be a countess. Such is the dream of all men." She made a mock bow to Isi.

"*Pismire.* They require only my person? What about my thoughts and feelings? I desire conversation and love of my whole self. If they care for ladies only as for horses, I shan't be a lady."

"You've naught to worry." Marielle covered her mouth as she laughed, her breath white. "Where silence is expected, you speak. Where eyes should be downcast, yours rove like foxes. Did you not hear the troubadour? 'The lady was of tender age, passing fresh and fair, and sweet of speech to all.' Such you should be."

"That *lai* is trifling." Isi scuffed through a skim of ice. Maman told Isi she would be a lady, but that meant directing servants, ruling a castle, wearing fine clothes. Like Hugh's mother. "Madame doesn't speak sweetly."

Marielle glanced around and then whispered. "She is no longer of tender age. Sweetness is required of maidens. Look at me."

Although a maiden, Marielle would never be a lady, that much Isabelle understood, but she recoiled from the idea. "You speak wondrously well. I had not thought on sweetness, but it is so."

They continued in silence, Marielle's eyes on the ground, Isabelle puzzling things out even as she enjoyed the world: a leafless tree tangled like embroidery or a chaplain carrying fresh linen from the laundry. The fletcher hauling fresh-cut branches for his arrows passed and a branch caught on Isi's mantle; she started to scold the varlet, then remembered sweetness and grabbed the angry words by the tail. She was honey, apple butter, a sugared almond.

At the main gate, a guard berated a villein. "Ye dankish gudgeon, the maître will not see you until tomorrow." Dankish! The word dropped into the sea of Isi's thoughts with a splash and she laughed. She'd not be sweet. She'd shout like a man, like a dankish gudgeon.

"Mayhap you are right." Marielle's words drifted like smoke on her breath. "Sweetness has won me nothing. Which of the knights do you favor?"

Isi conjured them, middling tall, one face arrayed with a large mustache, the other with a mole. Neither appealed. "Why must I choose? What does it mean?"

"It means little. You will give the chosen knight a small token, mayhap a scarf or bit of sleeve, which they will carry into tournaments or battle." Marielle wrapped her cape around her head and pulled the end across her face. "Who shall it be?"

"Geoffrey has blue eyes; Aydmar's name is almost the same as Papa's." Isi hopped a few steps to warm herself, the new cape with a raccoon collar, Madame's gift, failing to keep out the damp.

"Do you regard one above the other?"

"Both are boring. They swear undying allegiance, talk of lances and battles, read me poetry. Neither speaks as well as the troubadour. Wasn't it funny last night about the knots?" In the *lai*, the knight Guigemar tied a girdle around his lady's waist as a covenant of love.

"Knots?" Marielle peeked out from the cape.

"Do you not remember? Only the true lover could undo it. I've tried to tie such, but they always come undone. Hugh undid the last one in a trice." Isabelle didn't notice Marielle's blush.

BEHOLD THE BIRD IN FLIGHT

"Poor Guigemar. Do you think one has to suffer to find true love?"

Marielle drooped. "Yes, love means suffering."

"Have you been in love?"

"Never. Well, almost. Once." Fidgeting. "He didn't read poetry."

"So you didn't love him?"

"Something like that." Marielle walked away, calling back, "Just choose one. It's only a game."

Isabelle didn't think love should be a game. Choosing a knight must be serious, like lessons and riding, something to practice for her future. She could speak passable Latin when required; now she must learn to be a proper object of love. She resolved to be a new kind of love object, one who counted for other than her face or hair.

On a Tuesday after council, Hugh stood below the dais, waiting while his father and the cordwainer discussed shoe leather. Through the hall's high windows, sky bloomed blue as stained glass and as transparent, and he longed to be out in God's house. Marielle and Alaric waited; he would ride both this afternoon, but first he'd ask Père about marriage. Hugh rubbed the faint mustache on his upper lip and cleared his throat, glad for his deep voice. He noticed his père was getting stout, skin like a burnt Yule log. When he died, not soon, *grâce à Dieu*, but soon enough, Hugh would order a shield emblazoned with the cross of the Crusades and seek to join the Templars. Marielle would cry when he left for Jerusalem, but she'd be proud. She'd tend to the castle with the reeve's help. He wanted her to remain soft, not tense like Mother, and upon his return . . .

"So, what do you want?" Père jumped down easily from the

dais. "Time is short. I need to check the horses. The damned constable has been riding them excessively. Then I must see the carpenter about a chair for your mother, the chandler is dipping into the beeswax, or so the reeve says, and vines growing on the south wall must be removed. Endless work."

"I will walk with you." Hugh strode, manly. He could do this.

They passed down the long hall and into the spinning room where his father made a jest—"Ah, my little spiders"—and the chatter stopped. He plucked Marielle's thread, setting her spindle swinging, and she blushed. Hugh choked back the urge to slap his father's hand and kept his eyes on the floor, the greasy straw, the faint purple flowers.

Isabelle smiled and spoke up. "We only spin, never plot."

"Ah, well said. This is the little witch, *n'est-ce pas?*" Père stepped closer. "Perhaps 'tis only she is bewitching. What say you, Hugh?"

"Yes, Father." His lopsided smile was intended to tell Marielle she alone held place in his heart. He waited, dread growing as his father's eyes roamed the bodies until, internal threads totally frayed, he jerked his head sideways and managed to move into the armory. His father followed, strolling, surveying the weapons as he had surveyed the young women, a bit more hands on here, touching a helmet, testing the tip of a lance, lifting a sword. "By the stars, Mademoiselle Angoulême is a real beauty. Wide hips. She'd not leave a man without an heir. When she gets her full growth, she'll make a fine wife." He dangled the sword. "Young breasts. Perhaps she'll be mistress to a powerful man."

"Father!" Shrill. Hugh lowered his tone. "She defended her honor."

"'Tis true. And her dower is much coveted. So a wife then." Père grinned and stabbed the air. "But that other one with the silken lashes. Her ample curves and her eyes make me think she would be a delight. A peasant surely, and perhaps not so fastidious." He swung the weapon. "Do you know her name?"

The sword slashed at his heart and Hugh strangled out, "No."

"We shall ask." Replacing the weapon, his father walked on.

Hugh lagged behind, imagining Père in Marielle's bed, his heavy body, his hairy back . . . No, no; he would grind down her beauty, harden her, take her away. But she could not refuse the *maître*. His steps stuttered, his fists locked. Seeking control, he floated her in his mind, a softness of clouds, fleece, clotted cream. The points of his nerves dulled slightly. They passed down the stairs and he rehearsed what must be said. *Her name is Marielle, and it is she I shall marry.* No, a preemptive tone wouldn't do. When he'd demanded to be a squire, his father immediately set against him. *She is a suitable wife, you noted yourself. Fit to bear my son.*

He stumbled, missed a stair, almost fell. His arguments would be for naught; sons, yes, but many a woman bore them, and neither Marielle's beauty nor his feelings counted. Marriage was only to increase holdings or power. His own *cousines* traded away for connection, for largesse, or a promise of peace. And Marielle's family had nothing, were nothing. Hugh slid his hand on the wooden rail, driving a splinter into his palm, glad for the pain. He was a child; she had understood better than he. He cringed down the last stair, exhorting himself. *Don't give up; you must have her. Only think carefully before you speak.*

His father stopped in the bailey—a shambles of jousting and wrestling, capers to hone fighting skills—to join his knights, laughing, shouting, clapping here a man on the back, there on the arm. To Hugh they were dogs, wrestling in fun until hurt was caused, then teeth emerged. Were he allowed to squire, he'd have honor. Strength. But these *knights*—he spit the word inside his head like a seed—these contemptuous curs were only at play. Second or third sons they, who would never have a wife or legitimate child, they sought ladies freely for chivalry or physical pleasure. But he was a first son and must have a wife. Therefore if he was not to be a squire, he would have Marielle. The logic was impeccable. His back straightened and he gripped his fist against the splinter.

After endless minutes, Père broke away, found the carpenter and ordered a fine chair emblazoned with the family crest. Next, in a small room that smelled of beeswax and tallow, the chandler's accounts proved to be in order. The gardener was duly instructed to remove the growth on the outer walls lest it provide egress for enemies.

On every step, through every room, on every path, Hugh stalked behind his father, thoughts rumbling like boulders. Be strong. Say *omnia vincit amor*; love conquers all. No, no, Père would laugh, call *amor* a scant sword. A phrase from "The Lai of Guigemar" gave him some relief: "In such a love as yours there is nothing to be ashamed." He folded the words around his desire. When the last duty seemed fulfilled—his chance to speak—Père said, "Let's have a bit of fun."

He led the way to the mews where two gyrfalcons, four peregrines, and several merlins were tethered to perches. At the scent of men, the birds flapped, rising, settling, *kak-kak-kak*. Dust motes floated, the floor was littered with feathers and droppings, and in the corner, mice cowered in cages, waiting to be dinner. Determined not to be like them, Hugh smoothed his tunic. "Father, I will speak to you as a man speaks."

Père raised an eyebrow. "Certainly. But first . . ." His father tossed him a glove and pointed out a peregrine. "Is she not beautiful? Newly captured and in need of training. Try her on your arm." The bird stepped up to the offered fist. Père said, "There, a man with his falcon. What did you wish to say?"

His father's recognition of him as a man impeded Hugh's speech. Should he ask to squire and from a position of strength, obtain Marielle? No, no. He blurted, "I wish to marry."

His father guffawed. The startled bird flapped against its tether. "Perfect, my son, perfect. I, too, wish you to marry, to beget many sons." He leaned on the falconer's bench. "Have you a young woman in mind?"

Marielle almost rattled free like a pebble down a cliff, but he'd promised. "She is within our castle."

His father rocked back on his heels, grinning. "I believe I know whom you mean. As yet too young, but 'twill make a fine match." He stood upright and clapped his hands. "Her father will be amenable, of that I am sure."

Father? Marielle had no father. Horror crept up Hugh's ribs. Too young? What young girl, not a servant, lived in the castle? The talons gripped his wrist and suddenly, with a flash of yellow hair, he went blind with knowing. He slashed his arm against the name. The bird screamed warning, which set off the other birds; the mews became a flame of shrieking.

His father still laughed. "I am delighted beyond words. Your choice matches perfectly with the need for peace with our neighbor. Say nothing of this until terms can be established. I will send a messenger to Angoulême. How King John will rage when he learns of our liaison. I delight in the thought." He pulled on a glove, untethered a gyr, and took it onto his fist. "As proof of my pleasure, my young scion, I give you the bird you hold. Train her well. Then perhaps, I will allow . . ." He ruffled the bird's back. "We shall see." He stepped toward the door, heavy-footed, experienced.

"Temper your new acquisitions with gifts. These for the bird." He gestured toward the mice. "For your intended we shall find something suitable. A gold circlet or perhaps a length of silk. You decide. I'm to the hunt." And chuckling, his father left the mews.

Hugh stared into the eyes of the peregrine, now his, and realized that of the two things he had long desired, he would gladly give this one for the other.

NIGHTS LENGTHENED, TORCHES were lit in the great hall, and the company danced against the dark, swirling through smoke and flickering light as the lutenist plucked out the rhythms. Isabelle had settled on Geoffrey of the blue eyes, the second son of a noble family and destined for the military. She hoped to behold the sea in his eyes; he had composed her a poem with just those words. He'd also given her gifts. A little pouch with a piece of cinnamon from Jerusalem and a rabbit. Agatha said he should have given her gold, but Isi loved the bunny. She named it Twitch, and fed it bits of dried apple while stroking its long ears.

On the night she planned to bestow Geoffrey with her favor, a bit of scarf to be tucked into his helmet, she wore a new tunic with a tiny embroidered trim of silver thread, very like the dress she had coveted on her first day in Lusignan. The kitten-soft silk—Madame not being so strict as her own mother—whispered, silver glittering at her ankles. Inside the gown, her body filled with delicious quivering as she stood at the solar window; outside a star flared, golden, sprinkling light on her face. She laid her cheek against the cold glass and smiled. This was the beginning; she would have everything.

The first dance was an estampie, much beloved, and although Geoffrey held her hand in the circle, its sliding hops made it difficult to speak. She'd anoint him during the rondelet, calm and perfect for talking: two circles, men inside, women out; three steps right, look into the eyes of the man standing opposite with a small curtsy, take his hands and circle round. With another three steps, change partners, thus moving around the circle. As the company gathered into formation, Isabelle practiced the words she'd say when she touched Geoffrey's hands. "I accept you as my knight." Agatha said the phrase was proper.

The lute was plucked, the recorder joined in, her skirt swished, and the dance began. Isi started opposite Hugh's father. She honored him with her best curtsy, circled, took three steps to the right, and counted ahead. Four changes and she would stand before Geoffrey. She smiled, glittering her teeth at her second partner, practicing. Circle round, three steps to a young squire, new to the dance and blushing. His eyes were blue—like Geoffrey's—so she tried to deepen her look, to send little arrows to him. Was she doing this right? The flute joined the music, her partner glowed red, and she almost giggled with pleasure. Something inside her was pouring out; she would be a proper love object. Three steps to Hugh's eyes. Brown, rich and dark like the mystery in holy wine. A little internal tremor; yes, this was right. She reached out to him. She'd held his hands before—the night of the attack, at the trial—but now his touch warmed her elbows, her shoulders, her neck; her cheeks trembled with smiling. They circled, her eyes joined his. She felt a slight regret when the dance compelled her three steps to Geoffrey, his eyes blue surfaces on which floated the wet stones of his irises. She curtsied. His hands trembled in hers, the flute trilled like the silver twinkling at her hem, and her feet stepped around him, little cat paws. Now, now was the time to speak. Behind her Hugh danced with Marielle. She let go of Geoffrey and took three steps to the right.

After the rondelet ended, she climbed alone to the solar, shaken and confused. Outside the window, the heavens glittered. She sighed a ghost on the glass, rubbed it away, and crossed to the peephole to watch the dancers. Geoffrey blundered past with one of Madame's chamber ladies. How clumsy he was, his feet too big; he wrote a commendable poem, but no, his hair was awry, his ears stuck out. Now the company lined up for the carol. When the psaltery's gentle notes floated like snowflakes into the great hall, Hugh led, stepping in the curving patterns, so tall, jerkin falling straight from his wide shoulders, hair curly and burnished. Had he looked so in Angoulême? How long ago that was, sitting in council, Alain still alive. Suddenly, she missed Papa as she'd not missed him for months. And Maman. Homesickness trickled on her cheeks. When the music ended, she stripped off her dress, crawled under the pallet furs, bursting with . . . what? She scooted all the way down so if anyone entered, they would never know she was there. Below, company began to sing.

She wakened to silence, a mysterious moon sliding past the window. The soft light reminded her of a blown dandelion and she lay still. The chaplain often said, "Be devoted to one another in love." Tonight the words coated her with longing; light sifted on her face; a dog bayed.

Hugh entered the solar, shirtless. She'd often seen him so, but in the fresh light, he was new: skin draped like a swath of brown silk, muscles flexing, sleek as a cat. Her heart surged and she hugged herself. Her belly prickled, then her thighs, and she brushed her body for fleas but found nothing. Even after Hugh sank onto his pallet, the prickles remained. Something had launched within her, grinding and slipping like the stone at the mill. But not heavy. Moonlit and urgent.

7

GIVE YOUR DAUGHTERS UNTO US

nside Alina's house, the fire had burnt to cinders; outside, sun nicked the icy stillness. Hugh sat behind Marielle, combing her hair, gently teasing out the tangles caused by their lovemaking. When it was smooth, he wrapped his arms around her and leaned his face into its warmth. She filled every inch of him, her hair, her breasts, her smile. His hands glided over her softness, pulling the old blanket tighter against the chill, and spreading his palms across her belly for warmth.

Marielle shifted slightly. "There is your son."

His son. Yes, someday they'd have a son.

Marielle pressed his hands tight against herself. "There."

For the first time he registered the swelling. With surprise and joy, he flung up his arms and toppled off the pallet. Quickly, on hands and knees, he crawled back to her and nestled his head against his son, separated from him only by her beloved skin. She laughed and twirled one of his curls around her finger.

His hope burst out. "Now Père will have no choice. We shall marry."

She jerked away. "No, Hugh. No." Grabbing the blanket, she covered herself. "You know this isn't reason enough."

"It is. He shall allow it." When she covered his mouth with her hand, he kissed it.

Marielle pulled further away. "You cannot force him; he will marry you to whom he pleases." She ran her thumb across his cheek. "I know that and am resolved to bear it, having only two requests." She hesitated, then said softly, "Our boy shall be made a page."

"*Mais, oui*. And a girl shall have dower enough to marry." He could do this, make it happen. He crawled under the cover. "What is your second wish?"

"No one shall know the child is yours." She turned her head away, picking at the daub that held the walls together.

This he could not accept. His son, his pride. "No." Memory of Père in the mews tightened his voice. "Even if we can't marry—but we will—he is my son. We shall name him Alfred Bartram after my grandfather." She shook her head violently. He turned her face and looked in her eyes, trying to measure her feeling. Even in the vague light, he could see she had withdrawn, her eyelids quivering, her mouth turned down. If he fought his father, he would also fight her. If they ran away, Father would find them, and how would they live? His father supplied everything. Would it be different if he were a squire? Why was love so complicated? Hugh wished for the simplicity of war, yes or no, live or die. His lover began to weep. "Marielle, I must tell Father if I am to meet your first request. You can see that. Why are you afraid? He will keep a vow of silence, I am sure." Had he already accepted they couldn't marry? He gripped her arm.

She shook him off. "From your mother? If Madame learns of a child before your betrothal to Isabelle, she will send me away." Marielle hiccupped and pressed the heels of her hands to her eyes.

Reality squeezed his gut. The betrothal. "In Christ's name, Mari. Don't speak of it."

"Hugh!" Her hands flew to cover her belly, eyes wide around tears. "If you make God angry, harm will come to me or the child." She crossed herself and quickly said a Hail Mary. "Charters have been sent to Angoulême and returned. We can do nothing."

Hugh moaned. He was bound to Isabelle against his will. What use to be a first son? "Do you hate me?"

"My feelings are as they ever were. But Hugh, think long. Would your father hold our secret?"

"He must." Marielle's arms were covered with goose bumps. She needed a fur to keep her and his child warm. That he could give her. He clenched his hands, then rose to clumsily rebuild the fire.

"Leave it. Mother returns soon, and I am wanted in the spinning room." She reached out her hand. "Only promise me."

He knelt next to her. "I vow on all that's sacred."

The heaviness of that vow melted into elation as he strode from the village to the castle. A son. Proof of his manhood. Father, in pride, would agree. How could he refuse?

Père was in the smithy, talking to the blacksmith while an apprentice drove the forge fire with bellows. The small room was full of flame and steam, but Père leaned on a wall, relaxed, his face sagging slightly, nose red from a night's drinking. He smiled at Hugh. "Greetings." He motioned the smithy away and leaned back, hands crossed on his girth. "I have great news."

"I, too, have great news." Hugh threw his arms out wide. "I'm going to be a father." Heat bloomed on his face.

71

His father lurched vertical, eyes sharp, body tense, a hunting dog pointed at its prey. "Of course you are. That Angoulême girl will get us many heirs." He grabbed Hugh's arm. "The engagement with her considerable dower was confirmed this morning." The fire roared and he maneuvered Hugh against a wall. "I don't believe that is the fatherhood you were celebrating," he hissed. "Who is the girl?"

"I can't speak here." Hugh pointed his chin at the servants.

"Never mind them. Who is she?"

Like peregrine talons, Père's hands demanded an answer. "She, she . . ." At the last moment, Hugh blotted out Marielle's face. "I don't know her name." He regretted his inner falter; he had meant to say something else. "In Angoulême. A dalliance."

The grip loosened slightly. "Lusty boy." His father jerked him close. "How came you to hear this from Angoulême?"

His hot breath sunk Hugh's hopes. Père would whisper to Mother at night in their bed as Marielle foretold; she'd be sent from the castle. He must fight, but how? Père held all power. "Her father, a cadger, sent notice." The lie, a simple puff of air, would send him to Satan's fire. God forgive him, he had no choice.

"A cadger's daughter. I hope she was a beauty." Père released Hugh and turned to the smithy, shouting, "I need new lance tips, and the constable says a horse has thrown a shoe." The smithy nodded, pulled a piece of iron from the fire and struck it with his hammer, sending a shower of sparks onto the carefully swept floor.

Hugh turned away, crossing himself. A glance at the scorching forge reminded him of his fate should God find his lie unforgivable.

"We must send some coins to the man for her proper care." Père pulled a handful from his money pouch. "Make sure he receives these. Come, 'tis time for council. I want you there when I announce the betrothal."

Hugh stared at the coins' bent edges; they would buy at most a woolen blanket for Marielle and swaddling for the child. So meager an offering. He prayed for his son. For himself, his weakness. Leaving the heat of the forge for the icy bailey, he forced a smile, hoping the wind would freeze it on his face for the betrothal's announcement.

In the great hall, men and women gathered, talking, wondering that they should be called midday. Musicians stood ready. From the dais, Père raised his hand for silence. "Let us celebrate. News has come that Aymer, Count of Angoulême, will betroth his daughter to my son, Hugh de Lusignan. The ceremony will take place shortly, and they will marry when the girl is of age. The marches remain ours."

When trumpets and drums sounded, Hugh's heart tore. Once betrothed, he'd be bound to Isabelle forever. He glanced across the room and was stunned to see Isabelle, arms held slightly away from her body, face lifted and joyous as if she had been named queen. For a moment, she was the young girl he'd rescued. She had no idea she was ruining his life. Before he could reach her to say so, the crowd thronged him with congratulations. Then Père, amidst the laughing scrum, raised his hands and shouted, "As befitting an engagement of such import, there shall be games." The yelling increased. "Nay, nay, not for you churls. For the squires."

Hugh's gut clenched. *For the squires.* He had lost everything.

"In April, after Easter celebrations, Count Angoulême will arrive, bringing a multitude of knights and squires. Our own squires shall be led in the games by my son." He put his hands on Hugh's shoulders. "I have seen you striving to gain prowess and reward you with this boon." He gestured at the young men. "Prepare well. Become the knights you are meant to be."

Père deemed him able to lead! How proud Marielle will be. The last dreary year of longing dropped away. He was a man, would have a child, would marry. His father would esteem him, send him on Crusade. He vowed to make it happen.

When the shouting died down, Hugh knelt before Isabelle and kissed her hand. It was dry, shaking slightly, skin smooth over long, thin bones. So delicate. Her beauty tugged at him, but he could not love her, his heart already given away. He stood and avoided her eyes. She need never know he had no choice or that he longed for someone else.

ON THE FÊTE *de l'Annonciation*, the much-anticipated day in March when Lenten fast could be briefly broken, the main meal included a white soup, venison, and wine custards with dates and honey. A true feast. When Isabelle was sated, she and Marielle went outside, calm and ladylike, two friends walking in the orchard. The bright day whirled around them, the apple blossoms just coming into bloom, a gambol of clouds in the blue.

Isabelle was glad to have her friend back; when the spinners heard about the betrothal, there had been laughter and congratulations, but afterward Marielle disappeared from the castle. Isabelle puzzled at her absence until Agatha gossiped that Marielle was with child, father unknown. The spinning ladies drew tight the strings of their mouths. Now the puzzle changed: Why hadn't she told her best friend? Bereft, Isabelle spun and waited. After a few weeks, Marielle returned as if nothing had happened, but she refused to reveal her lover's name.

Today as they walked, the unanswered question pecked like

BEHOLD THE BIRD IN FLIGHT

Poulette of old. A brief gambol might assuage her curiosity, so Isi suggested a small run.

"The midwife says I must move like a flatboat on the river."

"You don't look particularly flat." The secret made Isabelle sharp, not like a knife but like the points of crocus leaves just showing. "Marielle, *la belle ballon*." She patted her friend's bulge and took off, weaving in and out between the tree trunks, glad for the sun, the smell of dirt, the flashing birds, and the edge of wind. When the pecking ceased, she returned to her friend, panting.

"You are so swift." Marielle raised her eyes and smiled. "Poulette?" Isi had long ago told her about the internal clucking.

"Gone, thank goodness." She picked a blossom out of Marielle's hair, considering a plan to nudge the secret free. "You put me in mind of fair Melusine."

"Do not speak of faeries. 'Tis unlucky."

"But she built this castle." Isi gestured behind them. "And afterward was turned into a dragon, for no reason."

"You know the reason. Her lover betrayed her secret." Marielle stopped abruptly.

"But how awful to be a dragon."

"True." Marielle sighed. "But Melusine had the right to be angry." Head tilted away, she glided on.

Isi felt snubbed by the secret, unnecessary between friends such as they were. She pulled a tree limb and let it bounce free. "I, for one, understand the lover's desire to know." Her neck and cheeks prickled with frustration. "But unlike him, a secret is as safe with me as with a dead fish at the bottom of the river."

"Don't talk of death!" Marielle crossed herself and her belly.

Isabelle also crossed herself, and then paused as if thinking. "I'm sure it wasn't only the lover. She must have told someone, else it would have eaten her insides."

"They say not."

Isi remembered how Maman had unearthed the truth about a goblet dropped into the moat: persistence. "She protects all things Lusignan. When a child born of the Lusignan line dies, Melusine howls in sorrow."

"Isabelle, stop." Marielle hurried ahead, waddling slightly. "I really am leaving."

"Don't go." *Pismire.* She wasn't going to tell. "It was just part of the story." Isi grabbed Marielle's hand. "I shall talk of something else." They walked in silence. The tree branches filigreed the sunlight and Isabelle lifted her face. This would be her orchard when she married, when she conceived. Her step stuttered. If she wouldn't speak of her lover, perhaps she would speak of . . . Isabelle took a breath. "Shall we sit?"

"On the ground? How would I ever rise?" Marielle patted her belly.

Isi pulled her friend's gown tight over the waiting child and was surprised at how large she had become. "How long?"

"Two more months, or so the midwife says."

"Are you afraid?"

"No. God will protect me."

Isabelle breathed a quick prayer. Many women died. A cook in Angoulême, blood rushing out of her as she stood by the fire, not even time to lie down. Perhaps it was a sin to hide the father and Marielle was in real danger. Before she managed words of warning, Marielle cut her off.

"Do not speak again of danger, Isabelle. I am eager for my child to come into the world." Marielle smiled her irritating secret smile. "I am to seclude myself in the lying-in room right after the bohort."

The bohort to celebrate her betrothal, then in a few short

months, her twelfth birthday and the wedding. Wind lifted Isi's skirt. Time, so swift. Her breasts puckering, sparse hair between her legs. Womanly marks she had longed for, but what of the wedding night? The marriage bed. Her parents' bed had thumped often enough in the dark, and she'd seen animals. But it couldn't be like that, all the snorting and squealing. Would Hugh snort? Her stomach flopped, fish in a net.

Marielle touched Isi's arm. "I've changed my mind. Could you help me back up if I sit on the grass awhile?" A patch of green velvet spread away from the orchard toward the garden. "My feet pain me."

"Of course. Take my hand."

Marielle lowered herself carefully and settled back, swollen feet sticking out from the edge of her overdress.

"Let me rub them. Maman used to rub mine when I couldn't sleep." Marielle's gesture said no, but Isabelle persisted. "No one can see us." She unlaced Marielle's shoes and began rubbing her ankles, keeping her face down as she looked for courage. "Marielle"—she shut her eyes—"I need to know what it's like."

"Swollen feet?"

"No, I mean . . . when you are with a man."

Marielle lay back on the grass and wafted her arms in the air. "I love spring. Everything so alive, so as God made it."

Isabelle kept silent, squeezing her friend's toes.

Marielle sighed and covered her eyes. "It starts with kissing. At first you think kissing will be enough. Like clouds, like when you're in chapel and feel desirous of God, totally giving yourself over to Him. It isn't enough, but maybe when his face, his mouth moves to your breasts and his hands stroke, maybe that will be enough. But no. He undoes your hair, lifts your dress, and every moment you are yearning, and at first you don't quite understand, but it's like eating honey, you can't stop. Then his hand goes between your legs and he slowly touches you open." Marielle's arms floated in the air. "Your body knows it's time. It's like the moment in chapel when incense floats and the tiny bells sound *ting* and your prayers are sent to heaven. He finds your soft spot, you want to be joined to him, and you let him in." Her arms dropped to the grass.

Isabelle's body was responding to Marielle's words. She imagined Hugh's large brown hands on her own body; when she was married, she would let him in. But . . . she remembered the tiny hole. "Doesn't it hurt?"

"The first time, yes. Afterward I walked as if I had a squash between my legs. But it didn't stop me. Once he had broken me open, I wanted his hands, his shaft, his mouth. It's a lovely thing."

Marielle's words evoked in Isi memories of girls drifting into the great hall to be pulled down and absorbed into their special knight, of whispers in fields and moans in dark corners. The flush on the face of a servant in the morning as she shook out the sheets or made the fire. For the first time Isabelle understood it was everywhere. Her body was running toward her own moment of cracking open, and the thought thrilled her. It must be wonderful. She could hardly wait.

8

Ye Shall Celebrate

he fields fuzzed with green and the cheer of bird-song. Daily, Isabelle sought Hugh. She'd find him mounted, but before she could offer proper greeting, he'd slip away to business in the village or to join Père in the fields. Once King John's messenger required his attendance. She understood. Like her papa and all men with power, he must see to Lusignan and the villeins. No matter. She could wait because Easter was coming and they would walk side by side to church. She imagined speaking softly, telling him about . . . what? She decided she'd ask questions. What was the name of his horse? Did he like eels? Was he partial to the name Grégoire? She wanted to know him and for him to know her. That was love.

The celebrations began on Good Friday in the Lusignan cathedral. When all the candles save one were blown out, Hugh and his father lifted down the heavy wooden cross with its burden of Christ, laid it on the altar, and covered Him with newly embroidered linen, ready for the grave. Isabelle prayed with the rest of the congregation, but in the middle of a *Salve Me*, she was struck by a fierce attachment, not to Jesus but to Hugh: his strength as he lifted the statue, his care as he laid it down, his piety as he knelt to pray. Was the feeling blasphemy? She pressed her palms tightly together. Why should she not love him? In a few months, she'd be twelve and they'd marry. Her elbows were weak and her heart expanded like a moon rising to float over the fields. *My heart leapt up before my beloved.* Dizzy, she gripped the edge of the bench so as not to fall, closed her eyes, and prayed for Hugh's love, sneaking peeks at his long eyelashes and his shoulders, until, at the very end of the service, afraid to be damned, she covered her eyes and prayed for forgiveness.

On Easter Sunday, she walked beside him in the procession to the cathedral. Her feelings threatened to collapse her knees. The gold swirl at the tip of the priest's new crosier sent glints of light over the crowd, and Isabelle pretended they were the reason she kept glancing at Hugh, but when he returned her glance—*my heart leaps up*—she forced herself to look skyward, to the distraction of God's blue. Overhead, clouds piled like river foam and she imagined angels and Mary, nodding approval.

When the choir began to chant, she touched Hugh's hand as if by accident, but he didn't seem to notice; he must be praying. She longed to walk alone with him in the fields or maybe in the garden where mint grew, but was afraid to ask. Perhaps he would write her a secret poem like Geoffrey. He was to be her husband. *My beloved.*

Three weeks after the Easter feast of lamb, jellies, the first fresh herbs, broth with bacon, and river bass baked in a sauce of almonds, pounded crayfish tails, and spices, Isabelle waited in the great hall with Hugh and his family for the arrival of her papa to seal her betrothal. She hoped he wouldn't swing her around as if she were still a child.

He noticed her reticence and merely clasped her tightly. "*Ma petite fille.*"

"Not so *petite*, Papa. *Voilà.*" She twirled. "See my new dress."

"Very beautiful," Papa laughed. "But not as beautiful as the wearer."

Suddenly, she remembered their nights on the Angoulême ramparts and longed for home. The great well, the moat, the strips of land reaching out to the forest. Her ribs pinched when she thought of leaving Hugh, but no, she would return. Maman would be glad. Surely Alain's death had been forgotten.

In the evening she took Papa to see her rabbit, and as he stroked its long ears, he explained how the Lusignans claimed the land of La Marche, which rightly belonged to Angoulême. In marriage, the two families would be joined in peace. No war, no killing, and she would be countess over a much larger demesne. Pride rose in her and she reached for her father's hands in the soft fur. She would stay.

The day of her formal engagement, the hall filled with knights and squires, the reeve and chamberlain, Madame and Père. Isabelle was sorry her own maman wasn't there, but as Papa said, someone had to see to their castle. In recompense, Maman had sent a tunic for the ceremony: magenta with an overgown of pale green silk, very like the dress she had ruined, but with tight-fitting sleeves ending in a long swath of fabric, a new fashion. With her braids wrapped in white silk and wearing a mantle of deep blue with a tiny fur collar, Isabelle imagined herself a queen.

The musicians played a simple march, the crowd quieted, and Papa offered Père a silver bowl filled with cherries for fortune and fertility. He then announced he betrothed his daughter on the advice given by Richard Coeur de Lion before he died. The name shot through Isabelle. He would be looking down; she vowed to be a good wife.

In return, Papa received three pears in a silver chalice, symbolizing his daughter's womanhood. Isi laughed secretly at those words; her breasts were still nascent. A stroke of worry—would Hugh be disappointed?—then the chamberlain laid forth vellum and quills and asked Isabelle if she freely entered into this marriage. Smoothing her cape, heart in full flight, her words sang in the hall: "I shall marry you, Hugh, Seigneur de Lusignan." Seals were affixed, and the chamberlain lifted a cushion on which was laid a circle of tiny golden leaves interwoven with silver tracery. Hugh stepped forward and fastened it around Isabelle's neck. His hands were cool, but the gold burned; from this day she would be marked as his. She tried to look into his eyes, but abashed, he knelt before her. Her ribs opened and an angel entered in, just like Mary at the Annunciation. Panting slightly, she touched his hair, the springy ringlets like ferns, lions, bedclothes; she thought to lay her face in his hair—now he would love her—but when he didn't glance up, she slipped back inside her formal self and nodded at her father.

Hugh rose, bowed slightly, and said, "I must prepare for the games."

She called after him, "I wish you success." He didn't turn.

HUGH SAT ON the horse chosen by his father for the tourney, breath whooshing inside a heavy helmet. The top of his head ached with the weight; the nose guard smelled of metal and fire. *Whoosh, whoosh*; he breathed and concentrated. This battle might be mock, but injury was possible. Even death. Across the lists, his Angoulême opponent wore a flat helmet. Was it safer than his own round one? Through partially blocked peripheral vision, he caught flashes of other squires, waving swords, bumping shoulders, bellowing war chants. *Whoosh, whoosh.* His stomach gurgled. He shifted uneasily, but the horse was steady, calm, more accustomed to battle.

Now his father announced the rules from the pavilion. Knights leaned into their squires, giving last advice, confirming swords and lances were blunted. Those squires who couldn't afford a weapon or hadn't been given one by their knight carried heavy cudgels. The knights left the fighting area, leaving the squires alone in the lists, and Hugh's father pointed at him. Oh, yes, the gesture. He took off his helmet. Assailed by bright colors, snapping flags, and the noisy crowd outside the fences, he nudged his horse toward the pavilion where Isabelle sat, with Marielle slightly behind. Hugh rippled with tenderness for her heavy body under the lavender mantle, his son inside. He bowed, certain Marielle knew she, not Isabelle, was in his heart. For a moment, Isabelle fidgeted with her sleeves, the long swath of fabric floating slightly as both fathers looked at her, Père frowning, Papa with a smile. She then turned to Marielle who took a bit of fabric from her belt—bright blue—and kissed it. Hugh felt the kiss up and down his spine, but Marielle only meant this is how to do it. Isabelle kissed the cloth in turn, and reached it out to him. He forced himself to smile as he tucked it in his belt, and replaced his helmet. He was ready.

The teams drew back. Hugh gripped the horse with his thighs, with his maleness, his strength; he meant to win and glorify himself before his love. The musician blew a trail of notes, and the combatants were released into a melee.

Surrounded by running men, shouts, and glinting weapons, Hugh galloped forward, his lance ready, concentrating on the point that trembled toward his opponent. The edge of his sight was buffeted by the sea of men, a glimpse of a hand on a sword hilt, a cudgel's arc. This was how one drowned. Through the waves, the blue and gold of his opponent's shield came at him. His horse stumbled slightly and the tip of his lance bounced sideways. He pulled it back with all his strength, aiming for the bright shield. He braced. *Slam*. A judder in his bones, a slash of pain, and he was unhorsed, flat on the ground, struggling to breathe. Fighting continued around him, he tasted dirt, feet scrambled near his face. He must rise. Up, up. His horse snorted and pawed nearby; he heard the metallic whisper of chain mail as his opponent dismounted. He could still win. Use the sword. He staggered up, ribs biting into his torso, and threw off his helmet, the better to see. He fumbled for his weapon. Lifted it and turned. The blue shield was upon him and he swung wildly, metal clanking on metal, the crowd incandesced in a shout, and he fell into darkness.

ISABELLE WAS FIRST on the field, sliding under a rail, ignoring Papa's shouts. She wove through fighting men, wailing loudly. Swords halted midair, her dress was torn, some men took up her cry—*Hugh, Hugh*. Fighting ebbed in the center, gradually guttering out.

Her love lay on his back, eyelids fluttering like tiny moths. She touched his cheek, felt the slight rubble of his new beard, called his name. She meant to take his head in her arms, but Père pushed her aside, shouting for men to help. Madame thrust Isabelle further away, took her son's hand and pulled him to a sitting position. His eyes opened with a gasp. Blood was running into his eye, but he smiled up at his mother. "Did I win?"

BEHOLD THE BIRD IN FLIGHT

"Yes, my son. He went under your sword." She probed the wound. "'Tis but a scratch."

Relief like spring, like May, bloomed in Isabelle. She longed to follow Hugh as he was helped from the field, but surrounded by sweating burly men, she was unable to move. Across the field, her papa helped the Angoulême contender. The curve of her father's back, the care with which he lifted the young man to stand, how he placed his hand on the boy's head brought fire ants to her arms, her neck. Papa had always stood with her and with those she loved, but now he gave not a glance to Hugh limping off the lists. *Papa*. She willed him to look at her, but the air remained empty. "Papa." Whispered. Then suddenly, as if a portcullis crashed into place, Isabelle separated from him. She was bound, had given her promise, and like a martyr at the stake, in pain but also in ecstasy, she burned with the knowledge that she now belonged, not to Papa and Maman, but to Hugh and Lusignan.

9

FOR DUST THOU ART

sabelle wandered the great hall, half listening to men grumbling about heat, a missing goat, the storm that had ruined some crops. Despite the certainty she belonged in Lusignan, she missed Papa. She wandered to the spinning room to find Marielle, but it was empty. A hot day—under her wimple, little spiders of sweat; maybe the women had gone down to the river to cool off. She'd find them. Madame wouldn't expect her to ride until Nones. As she stepped into the bailey, her friend Agatha crossed, leading the pages, seven-year-olds sent to the castle for training. When first put in charge, Agatha had moaned, "I'd rather be spinning," but today she was laughing and skipping, trailing little boys like comet tails. She swerved over to Isabelle and, as she passed, yelled, "Marielle's baby is coming."

The women would be in the birthing chamber.

Isi ran, crossing herself and praying. *Let Marielle be well, let her child be well*. The chamber, set in the outer bailey, admitted only women; its door and windows were closed, meaning Marielle labored safely. Still, Isabelle had to pray for her friend.

She bypassed the castle chapel and headed to the cathedral where God would hear her better, pausing at the castle gate. The gardens and fields spread freely before her, and great clouds like the voice of heaven boomed across the sky; over in the town, the cathedral's double towers reached upward, sending replies. She felt all of God's glory. He would protect her friend.

She raced through the crooked village lanes to push open the iron-studded door and squint in the semidarkness, her gasps echoing against the great stone arches. On the altar a beeswax taper burned, and in the alcoves a few tallow candles flickered, lit by other petitioners. Yes, God lived here. She ignored the statue of Saint Margaret, the patron of pregnant women, and went straight to Mary whom she trusted. Kneeling, she asked her to keep Marielle and the baby safe. Then, remembering "In sorrow thou shalt bring forth children," she added a petition to lessen Marielle's pain.

A carving of Melusine hung above the door. Isabelle quailed to see the spread wings and staring eyes, the open mouth spewing dire prophesy. Marielle had been frighted when teased about the legend, so though it was a sin to pray to an idol, Isabelle begged Melusine to leave her friend and the baby alone.

Fear rattling in her stomach, she raced back to the birthing chamber, where her terror multiplied. The door and wooden window coverings had been flung open; the baby needed help emerging into life. Praying steadily, Isabelle slipped inside and huddled against the wall to peer through the gathered women who had undone their girdle knots to help the birth. She saw only an empty bed against a wall, and in the middle of the room, the birthing chair, also empty. Where was Marielle? Frantic, she turned left and right. Preparations waited on the sill, a honey jar and a pot of almond oil to rub on the newborn. The scent of almond mingled with another, metallic and cruel: blood. The dirt floor was red with it. Isabelle's knees failed and she slid down the wall. She'd seen animals slaughtered, but this blood was human.

Then, there, Marielle! Pacing along the opposite wall, hunched over. Her cries! Deep frightening moans as if she would move the world. Clawed by fear, Isabelle crossed herself against the image of Melusine howling when a Lusignan child died. No, no, the child wasn't born yet. Marielle's lover hadn't betrayed her. *Let the baby emerge, let it live.* The piercing moans ceased, replaced by panting as of a terrified dog. Isabelle closed her eyes and prayed to Mary. *This is my friend. Please save her.*

Marielle stumbled on a pile of swaddling. The midwife caught her and took her to the birthing chair where she collapsed, white-faced, cheeks dragged down with pain, mouth pinched and disappearing. Two women held her upright; two others took her hands as the midwife reached under her tunic, rubbing ointment on her belly and between her legs. A woman whispered into her ear and she shook her head violently. The woman crossed herself. Fear solidified in Isi's stomach; the midwife turned. "She's your friend. Go! Bring someone to shoot an arrow. And a priest."

Ever praying, Isabelle ran. An arrow to open the gates of heaven, to allow the soul through, to release the body of the infant for the priest to baptize. She could save them both if she ran fast enough. Just inside the gate, she collided with Agatha. "Marielle needs a priest."

Agatha understood immediately. She yelled at the little boys to stay by the tree and sprinted away.

Who to shoot the arrow? A guard? A squire? Isabelle whirled. Whom did she trust? Hugh, only Hugh. And there he was, coming through the gate. She seized his tunic. He hardly knew Marielle, but he would help if she asked. "Please, please, we need an arrow. Marielle's baby must be released."

"She's in labor?" Hugh dropped the wooden box he carried and stared at Isabelle, slack.

She pinched his arm. Unseemly, but this was urgent. "Run as if it were me." He flew away.

HUGH PANTED ACROSS the bailey. How had he not been told? Marielle's baby, *his* child, was coming. He should have sensed it, felt her pain, but he had not, and now the very one who stood in the way of his happiness brought him the news. Breathing harshly, he bounded up the stairs to the armory. A pox on Isabelle. His steps stuttered. *Don't think of her.* Think only of Marielle. He grabbed a bow and arrow. Two lances crashed to the floor; he kicked them away. Pushing past the steward on the stairs, he rushed into the bailey, stumbling through small pages gathered around the tree. Shouldn't someone be watching them? If they were his . . . He ran faster, buoyed by the thought that his own son was coming and he, Hugh, would bring him safely into the world. For a terrible moment he couldn't remember where the birthing chamber was, but then he saw Isabelle standing at the door, waving her arms wildly.

Gasping, he forced himself to slow; haste would give him away. His shaking hands dropped the bow and it took three tries to seat the arrow. Finally, with all his strength and love, he pulled. *Snap.* It was gone, up and over the field where sheep stood like small clouds against the new green. Was it high enough to alert God? In his haste, he had brought a single arrow. *Please, Lord.*

AT THE DOOR, Isabelle prayed the arrow to heaven, and then turned to the claustrophobic room, the priest already inside, saving a soul in peril. His stout body blocked her view, but a trickle of fresh blood broke free from the clot of women and Isabelle began to quake. She could just see Marielle's tormented face, mouth stretched wide around her teeth, dark bruises haunting her eyes. Isabelle felt her pain and reached back to Hugh for comfort. His bow clattered to the ground, then his hand gripped hers. They stood joined for minutes until the low murmur of the women inside broke with a cry and the midwife, her dress bright with blood, lifted the baby for the priest to bless.

Isabelle released Hugh and pushed through to Marielle and held her hand, cradling her head. Around them, women began to keen, and Isabelle prayed to Mary for mercy, but it was no use, the priest took up the holy oil and began last rites. When Marielle's head lolled back and her hand went slack, Isabelle joined the keening.

Close by her side, a woman knelt, swaddling the baby and weeping. Why was the child still in this dreadful space? Isabelle reached out. "Please."

The woman gave her the small package. "'Twas a boy."

'Twas.

Isabelle staggered into the doorway, pressing the diminutive body to her heart, willing him to life, but pink was already draining from the tiny face, a terrible sunset to his only day on earth. As she sobbed, a violent wind rose, snapping at the swaddling.

BEHOLD THE BIRD IN FLIGHT

Hugh understood her tears were not of joy. "Is it a boy?" He could scarcely say the words for fear he'd break down. Startled by his voice, Isabelle stepped back, then after an anguished moment, laid the child into his outstretched arms. He leaned against the wall for support and peered down at his son. He hadn't known it was possible to ache so, God crumpling him into nothing. The wind howled—Melusine mourning the loss of a Lusignan. The swaddling, hastily done, threatened to unwind. Nestling the tiny body in the crook of his arm, he tried to straighten the fabric. Isabelle reached out to help, both of them leaning over the little face, now completely gray. She smoothed the wrinkled brow, he touched the tiny mouth, and she palmed Hugh's cheek. For a moment he saw her as she really was—her kindness, her fortitude and beauty—then pain sliced the vision away.

Inside the room, the women wept and prayed.

PART THREE

Royalty

1200

10

THAT THOU
SHOULDEST RULE

King John rocked in his saddle, bearing down on Lusignan, intent on rents still owed. He paid little attention to the forest's summer canopy or the July-golden fields, although he noted the vigorous stalks of wheat and rye. It looked to be an abundant year in Poitou, as in England, thank God. One less worry. He glanced back at his retinue, a trail of grumbling squires, household knights, and a handful of whispering barons, the latter a major worry. Also wives, money, wars, heirs. He had no heir because his wife was barren—ex-wife thanks to the pope, that old *busard*; plus his kingdom was embroiled in wars, leaving him to bear the staggering cost of arms, soldiers, travel, horses, arrows, lances, trebuchets, all because the damn treasonous French lords kept changing sides. Weaselly nobles clamoring for permission to marry widows. Actually, a boon, that. New husbands paid for the privilege of titled wives. But there was never enough. Empty coffers haunted his dreams. Damn his brother and his Crusade. Honor to God and all, but fie on Richard, incurring that immense ransom, building the foolish chateau in Gaillard. What value a castle stronghold when it further drained the treasury? Had his brother stayed in the kingdom where he belonged, the wealth would have remained in England. *It would have been mine.*

As John rode, he considered how to regain his French holdings. Anjou and Maine had been overtaken by his nephew, furious to have lost the kingship he thought rightfully his. John grunted satisfaction. Arthur be damned, too young to lead, impetuous, addlepated, and worse: he bowed to the French king, which meant another war. God's bones, curse the man. Aquitaine was still English—surely Mother would keep it secure—and Normandy held with King Philip's covenant, safe for now, but he must remain alert. Philip would use any pretext to grab it back. And the counts of Poitou, Lusignan, and Angoulême, quarrelsome churls who chose their liege lord based on gain, required vigilance and his best spies.

Would that he could dismount and walk away to a little village. Amusing to dress as a villein, find a comely woman to bed, hear common gossip about his royal person. Ah, but he'd miss the jewels, the furs and down bedding and bountiful ladies, the handing out of privilege, the obsequies of the loyal few. Men essential to stand against his nephew. Again he reviled Arthur, panting to be king, gathering jealous traitors to steal his very throne. That war, if it came, would cost dearly. He was traveling to Portugal to snatch a rich wife, a princess whose dowry would refill his coffers . . .

"Sire." The man riding beside him leaned over. "Are you in pain?"

Grunting again. He must control that. John smiled, more wolf than dog. "No, William. Thank you for your concern." He needed only silence and time to sort out what would be required. "They expect us?"

BEHOLD THE BIRD IN FLIGHT

"A messenger sent two days afore. Count Lusignan claimed honor at your visit. We are welcome."

"We shall stay a fortnight. The men will be glad for the rest." He, too, was in need of rest. Portugal was far, and the father of the intended bride must see him in good health. Ruddy, strong, powerful. Make the father fearful; obtain the daughter at small cost. John overlaid the size of his gain from Portugal with the loss of Anjou and Maine; the balance was in his favor.

Sun dappled his hands on the reins, glinted on the hilt of his sword; birds flashed through the trees. All were nothing to him; only the trail of power riding behind held meaning. He was rightfully king, despite Arthur's claim. He would be king until he died, God willing and his wits remain keen.

In the late afternoon, the cortege emerged from the woods. In the distance, a village, sloping fields, grain whisked by wind; beyond lay gardens, a vast orchard, trees bent with fruit; and towering over all: the castle, lively with flags and guards. Boats were moored on the river that ran in a horseshoe around the whole demesne, and men traveled up and down the road to the gate. Instantly John coveted it.

He called a halt. "William, send for my best cloak and tunic. And a messenger to announce our arrival. I desire a proper welcome."

William dismounted to attend the king. Shouts traveled up and down the line, and soon a squire walked forward with the required clothing. John dismounted, unbuckled his sword and handed it to William. Off came his light mail, his travel-stained tunic, and stretching out his leg, he allowed the man to brush the dust from his hose. He flexed his arms and arched his back. Still strong and lithe. Like a young man, only thirty-three, the age of our Lord when He was crucified. John snorted as the tunic was placed over his head. Jesu, being a Man of Peace, couldn't have been half as strong as he himself, a man of the sword.

As the last sunlight fell over the edge of the castle in God's eventide blessing, John led the troop forward. Ahead of him on the road, three horses broke clear from the village and cantered up the hill. He squinted. One of the riders was a woman, without wimple or cap, hair streaming as if a river, pouring, frothing, gold as sunlight. Only a peasant would ride like that. He expected the trio would be barred entrance, but they galloped freely into the outer bailey and did not reappear.

That hair. Oh, to have a wife with golden hair. Symbol of his power and richesse. The Portuguese princess was bound to be brown—eyes, hair, skin—resembling her Spanish brothers-in-faith. John called for his garnet-and-pearl pin. He'd fasten it on his tunic, and when he found the wench, servant or not, use it to persuade her to his bed. Across the river and up the hill he galloped, flags flying. To his gratification, trumpets sounded and the Lord of Lusignan, Count of La Marche, appeared with his wife to greet him with proper obeisance. He would rest, obtain his rents, and then travel on to Portugal.

DURING THE DAY, Hugh treated Isabelle, his fiancée, as expected, riding and dancing with her, but he slept with nightmares of a stone effigy in his bed on the sham wedding night, cold radiating from Isabelle's flat torso, relations forbidden by God until she was fully a woman. He ached for Marielle, riding alone in the forest, galloping madly, fighting tears no one must see because Marielle had been a servant, a nobody to all but him. Sometimes he rose before dawn to pick daisies in the field and bring them, covered with dew, to the grave where she lay with the

BEHOLD THE BIRD IN FLIGHT

baby. He remembered his arms around his dying son and longing raked his heart for the boy. Once Père asked about the coins for his bastard child in Angoulême, and he said they'd been sent. He'd given them to distant nuns for prayers. His love mustn't languish in purgatory; an angel on earth, she now belonged in heaven.

His feelings toward Isabelle veered here and there. Some days he shuddered: she was a witch; how else had she managed the betrothal? Other days he remembered her innocence, how she shook when he saved her from the crowd, from the guard. How she'd wept with him over his son. Could she really be both? When they walked, she battered him with questions. "Where did you get your horse? Do you favor eels or honey balls?" He'd mumble and walk away. Why should she care? She was to bear his children, be his helpmate, not his friend.

Once after a dream of trying to breathe life into his son, he woke, gasping, to find her leaning over him. "You were crying out. Are you ill?"

He closed his eyes against the oval of her face. "No." He wanted to push her away; he wanted to cry in her arms. "Please, leave me." Only when he heard her rustle onto her pallet did he dare move, gripping the crucifix he wore and praying for peace.

IN A FORTNIGHT Isabelle would be a woman. And a wife. What once had seemed pleasure now held dread. What did it mean to be a wife? Sleeping with Hugh on his pallet, yes, she looked forward to that, to his warm hands opening her body as Marielle had described. But once she had lain with Hugh, children would come, and she didn't want to die like her friend. Also, a troubadour's song haunted her: *Lovers give each other everything freely, under no compulsion of necessity, but married people are in duty bound to give in to each other's desires.* The Countess of Champagne had written those words. A countess who knew the world. If Hugh didn't love her by the time they married, it would be too late, and clearly he didn't, barely speaking as they walked, galloping ahead when they rode. His eyes downcast in the dance. In Angoulême he had smiled at her. Lifted her to safety. What had changed? She wanted love, not duty; passion and companionship. She imagined his praise at her embroidery, or sailing in a little boat, grooming a horse together, speaking about Paris before bed.

Desperate, time running out, she paced under the tree in the bailey, cogitating. Riding or dancing, people and movement surrounded them, but if they could sit quietly in the gardens, the roses, marigolds, lavender, and foxglove would pull forth his feelings. He'd touch her hand and write a poem for her like Geoffrey had. A better poem, of course.

But as the day of the wedding neared, Hugh's heart still fled from her. Despair dragged her footsteps and pressed her in her bed. With Marielle gone, Madame frightening, and Maman far away, who could she consult? Her only friend was Agatha, who cared for the pages. She would have to do.

Isabelle found her in a shed surrounded by the seven-year-olds cleaning rust off helmets, bucklers, and shields. Pails of sand stood about, as well as pots of oil. The little boys wiped the metal with oily rags, sprinkled sand on the dirty spots, and scrubbed with small stones. The shed was hot with energy and sun bouncing on the canvas roof; it smelled like cooking. Agatha walked among the children, patting some on the head, nudging others to greater effort.

"Why are you here?" Isi asked. "You were only to see that they ate properly and slept."

"Seems I'm clever with them," said Agatha. "They like me."

She tickled the neck of the nearest child with the tip of her braid; he giggled and swatted at her with his rag, leaving drips of oil on her apron. "Perchance you need a small boy. This one I'd gladly give away."

"Not today," Isabelle laughed. "On second thought, I'll take that one." She pointed to a little boy scrubbing with all his might. "His diligence is exemplary." She turned her back partially to the children. "Can we talk here? I need your advice."

"Speak away. They don't listen to anything an adult says unless it's pointed directly at them."

"You're sure?"

"Mademoiselle Angoulême," Agatha intoned, "I regret to inform you that the castle is on fire."

Isabelle startled, but not a head raised, so she blurted out, "I need to make Hugh love me. He esteems me, he's said so, but that's not enough."

Agatha put her hands on her hips. "Esteem is enough when you're married. Do you think Count Lusignan loves Madame? They're the biggest trees in the forest, standing side by side, knee-deep in esteem, but love? I troth not."

Isabelle nodded. She had never seen them touch.

Agatha added, "Doth your father love your mother?"

Isabelle remembered their distance, Maman with the women, Papa resting in the garden alone. "He is Mother's second husband." Isabelle shrugged. "Her first was the Count of Joigny. Perhaps she loved him. She told me they traveled together often to Paris."

"Paris!" Agatha twitched her apron. "I have such a yen to see it. I hear they wear velvet cloth, fuzzy like a pelt. And have proper tournaments and honey at every meal." She smoothed her wimple. "Most like I'll never go further than Poitou. Lucky you, leaving Angoulême, seeing the world." Agatha sighed. "What say you of the king?" The lower-ranked servants had been sent from the great hall into the kitchen for meals; John and his retinue required space. "Is he tall and fair?"

"Scarce tall as I. But not unpleasant of face. Brown hair, oddly worn."

"English style, Cook said. She who has never left Lusignan. She bubbles like one o' her pots. Brushed down on the forehead, was it?"

"Yes." Isi giggled.

"And his finery?"

"Silken tunic fastened with a button. Royal blue. Purple hose. A pair of cordovan boots, shined and cuffed."

"A button? I ain't never seen one, but methinks I'd like it. Pins take so long."

"He wore a pin too, but not to fasten his cloak; only for *richesse*. A pearl encircled by glittering red stones. That pearl! I wanted to touch it with my tongue. Surely 'twould have a delicate taste."

"I long to see him. I think . . ." Agatha was interrupted by a shout of laughter from the little boys. One miscreant had put the helm he was polishing on his head where it sat crookedly, covering his eyes and dripping oil from the nose guard onto his tunic. His companions began banging their stones on the metal shields and throwing sand at each other. Agatha strode into the melee, shouting, slapping here a head, kicking there a leg, until it subsided. She lifted the naughty boy by his arm. "Go at once to your squire. He shall punish you."

To escape the shed's heat, Isabelle stepped outside, loosening her wimple and shaking out her hair. The little chap had just slunk off when King John and his companions rode through the gate. Quickly repositioning her wimple, Isi called to Agatha. "The king." They curtsied as the horses passed.

"Not so kingly," said Agatha. "A hole in his hose at the knee. I expected leastwise a peacock feather in his hat. Count Lusignan be grander."

"No need for grandeur when riding. Today's banquet is in his honor. I wager he'll wear *vêtements plus grandes*."

"Mark every detail." Agatha ducked back to her charges. "Very good, lads. Enough for today. Return thy work to the armory." As the children were gathering up the heavy armor, Agatha poked Isi's arm. "Come, I have a thought that may be of service." She grinned. "Jealousy. In *The Art of Courtly Love*, Monsieur Capellanus says jealousy increases the feelings of love."

Isabelle stared. Agatha was a servant. "How do you know this?"

"These lot"—she indicated the boys—"must learn much nonsense as part of their training." She nudged the nearest child with her toe. "You. What's the fifteenth rule of love?"

"When made public, love rarely en, en, endures."

"That's number thirteen, you witless flap-dragon." One of the larger boys recited, "'Every lover regularly turns pale in the presence of his beloved.' Number fifteen."

"See?" Agatha lifted her chin. "I know some things. You have only to make Hugh jealous. 'Jealousy, and therefore love, are increased when one suspects his beloved.' Knight Geoffrey begged for your favor. Make Hugh love you by dallying with him."

"*Pismire.* Not Geoffrey. He is the most boring man." Isabelle helped Agatha gather up the last piece of armor, then burst out laughing. "I know how to forge Hugh's jealousy." She held a shield up as if an umbrella and took a few steps, swinging her shoulders. "I shall make the king fall in love with me."

JOHN HAD RIDDEN out early with William Marshal to discuss plans for Count Lusignan's morning council. As they cantered through the forest, he noticed neither the shafts of green light nor chipmunks running for cover, tails pointed straight toward heaven. He was calculating how much of his plan to entrust to William. His sworn baron, yes, but William had once espoused Arthur's claim to the throne. A mewling, bawling child. Unfit to rule. Speaks only French. The English people would hate him. John's mustache lifted in a small smile. How they cheered when he, himself, was crowned and rode through the streets. Even his dying brother Richard had come to understand that John, not Arthur, should reign.

John wafted a meager thank-you to Richard, undoubtedly still in purgatory, despite the fortune donated to the monks for intercessory prayers. He added a scornful chuckle to his other brother, dead and gnashing his teeth because his son Arthur would never rule. Fortunate that old William Marshal, beloved of the barons, heard Richard on his deathbed name John as successor. Yes, perhaps William was trustworthy.

"Sire, begging your pardon, but you are grunting again." They had stopped in a clearing. Light pricked out the waving grasses and pinpoints of daisies; profound silence prevailed but for the horses' snorts and the faint creak of the saddles. "Perhaps we should return." William bowed slightly. "The sun is halfway up the sky." A wind fluttered the top of the trees; a thrush flung out its song.

John nodded and turned his horse. Naming William as Earl of Pembroke had nailed his fealty; he was now honor bound to serve and if anyone believed in honor, it was that old man. Today he would help spear Lusignan. John looked forward to the council, testing his wits against the count and winning the sum he was owed. As they rode, he outlined his plan to William.

When they cantered across the bridge and entered the bailey, John again glimpsed the golden hair as it was tucked into a wimple. The entrancing girl pulled another wench from a shed and they both curtsied. Surely a servant. He would offer a gift, a small jewel, perhaps the little garnet set aside earlier. "Did you see that girl?"

William turned to look. "There were two, Sire."

Amusing, William's earnestness, so ever courteous, acknowledging all women, beautiful or not. "The one with the hair. Tall."

"Ah. Isabelle Angoulême." At the stable, William dismounted. "Did you not mark her yesterday?"

Hellfire and damnation, was he to notice everything? He had marked the paltry supper, the nervous hands of the servers, the stain on the cloth covering the table, but not this girl. John pushed down his growl and said mildly, "The Poitou fashion hides much beauty." In his personal travel bag was a larger jewel, blue, glittering, or perhaps . . . He fingered his pearl pin. "Angoulême's daughter?" Even countesses could be persuaded, as he well knew. Future countesses, wives of barons, lords, earls. He smiled, remembering.

William took the reins of John's horse. "Betrothed to the young Lusignan."

"The devil!" John dismounted and walked away, calling over his shoulder to the groom, "A measure of oats as well as straw." For the honor of a king-in-residence, Lusignan would pay to feed his horses. His mind turned again to Isabelle. Betrothed to that boy. *Him* John had remarked earlier. Smooth of skin, tall, but somehow cowed. That would work in his favor. But how to snatch her? One glorious night. Was that too much to ask? A reward for being king, surrounded by the disloyal and the treacherous, hounded by wives and lack of money, always on guard against the knife to the throat, the forced bending of the knee, the stink of failure. "Is she of age?"

"I believe she has not yet had her monthlies, although her twelfth birthday falls in eight days' time. On that day she is to be married."

John sorted through possibilities as they climbed the stairs and passed through the armory and the spinning room, where now Lusignan's family bedded—the solar given up to him—and into the great hall. Silence dropped over the assembled men, his own knights standing in clots among Lusignan's. Everyone bowed. John focused.

"Greetings." Count Lusignan stood on the dais, dressed in a silk tunic and a cloak of cloth of gold; he wore a glittering belt from which hung a heavy sword. "I hope your ride was enjoyable. The weather is fine, is it not?"

There was a single chair on the dais. Lusignan sat. Lolled. His men snickered softly. A wild boar pounded John's viscera, but he pushed it aside and strolled toward the dais. Calm, in control. His men would see and remember.

"Where is place for the king?" William crossed his arms, not so calm. The floorboards creaked as the assembled knights shifted and braced.

"He is not my king," said Lusignan. "Philip is my liege lord, he to whom I bend knee." He gestured toward John. "But you are welcome."

John kept his hand from his sword, but barely. "I am not your liege lord, true." He spoke softly, his eyes spiking Lusignan upright. "But like the greater Lord . . ."—here he crossed him- self—"I can give and take away." He mounted the dais. There was

BEHOLD THE BIRD IN FLIGHT

a slight metallic whisper in the hall as hands heavy with rings were placed on swords. "Unlike the count, my host, I have no need to sit," he announced to those in attendance. "I shall stand." He leaned over Lusignan and whispered, "Don't play with me. La Marche is yours by my grace." He smiled, the pink of his tongue showing between glittering teeth, and when the count started to rise, he stepped in front of the chair, forcing him to sit, and said loudly to the assembled knights, "I thank you for the welcome and look forward to eating and drinking with you in peace." His voice was rough with the effort not to knock Lusignan from his chair.

A squire appeared with a large carved chair and another with a crown. John briefly acknowledged William's service, donned the crown, and sat. "Now we are in council. I find myself required to ask about the La Marche rents due me." He pulled himself taller and leaned toward the count. "It has been six months in your possession, yet my exchequer reports no remittance."

"I have no knowledge of those rents." In his turn, Lusignan leaned forward, cheek twitching. John held his eyes sharp and settled his crown more securely; the count blinked and beckoned to a man on the side of the hall. "Bring the accounts." The combatants turned away from one another. John crossed his legs.

The attending men, alert and braced during the exchange between their leaders, slackened. Hands unclenched, a murmur sifted through the hall. As they waited, John eyed those in attendance. His own knights were tired; many now leaned against the walls, and several coughed. Good to tarry here some days. Even better that Lusignan would have to provide.

Then he noticed the girl and she blotted out all other thoughts. Earlier, in the bright sun, her face had been bleached, but in the dim hall, it was a pale luminous oval. His palm itched for her cheek, the long neck. Damnation. He could not see her body, but . . . Another thought forced him to his feet. Shortly he must shout and curse at the idiot Lusignan. She would be frightened.

He turned softly and took a step toward the count, hands clasped behind his back. "Lusignan, let us clear the hall. We have no need of armed men. We require only space and a snatch of time to review the accounts. Why keep them standing?" John spread his arms to underline his reasonableness. "If they leave, your servants can prepare the tables for the banquet."

Lusignan hesitated, then nodded. He started to stand, but John put a heavy hand on his shoulder. "I shall send them away."

John beckoned to William and, leaning down, said softly, "The Angoulême girl is over there. Take her out with you and prepare her to sit with me at the banquet. And ready my embroidered green tunic, the cloth of gold mantle, and the girdle with the jewels." He straightened and gestured for the hall to be cleared.

With the men gone, the hall relaxed into stone and shafts of sun. John waited, thinking of the coming banquet, what he would say to Isabelle, how he would captivate her with his courtly conversation. He might even compose a poem. He had just started—*ah, mes désirs brûlent*—when a small table was placed on the dais. On it, accounting records, a jumble of vellum pages, so unlike his own neat pipe rolls. Here, as in all things, he bested Lusignan.

He focused. This stiff-necked, scurrilous wretch would not cheat him of monies owed. John scanned the pages carefully, reading aloud sections concerning larger amounts. "'Robert de Courtine, three *livres* for rent of the *forêt* paid. A further ten *livres* for pannage.'"

John paused, surprised at the amount paid in pannage.

BEHOLD THE BIRD IN FLIGHT

Perhaps he should levy more in England. He had countless forests where countless men kept their pigs. John pointed to the line. "De Courtine must have many pigs." Remembering the slim fare at last night's table, he added, "Perhaps we will feast on one today." Lusignan shifted in his chair. John continued, tracing his index finger along the accounts. The information was not as detailed as his English pipe rolls and was recorded with slovenly writing. Barely legible. Lines marked out, sums recalculated.

"Roger, thirty-three *sous* for the farm, two *livres* for profits of the mill. Paid in two tallies, quit."

When he read aloud, John used an insulting silken tone. "Gervase of Creuse paid sixty-three *sous* and owes twelve." Once he crashed his fist on the page, stood, then sat again. "By amercement of Count Lusignan, Ernald owes one *livre* for false pleading." His growl shrunk Lusignan in his chair. Let him tremble, the roguish, reeky lout. A full share of this wealth belonged to England, and he would have it. He was a king.

In his concentration, John ignored the tables being placed in the hall and covered with cloth. Bread was set out, large slices to be used as trenchers, smaller pieces to be piled with salt. An ornate silver salt cellar awaited the high table. There were chalices and spoons and pitchers of ale; at the end of the hall an ewer of water stood for the washing of hands. A tray clattering to the stone caused John to look up.

Ah, 'twas late. He must dress for the banquet and for the young Isabelle. *Fie, regrettable name.* Ten years wed to the other Isabel, Countess of Gloucester, and only bastards to show for it. He required a son to reign after his death. To whom he could bequeath England, Normandy, and Aquitaine, intact. He must start again, and soon. Mayhap the Portuguese princess—nay, he'd think not on her, only on the beautiful Isabelle.

He rolled up the parchments and rose. "I believe there are fees due me. My man shall determine the sum owing. We remain in Lusignan until such time as it is paid." John would occupy the solar as long as he stayed, leaving the count and his family to the spinning room; his host must also feed John's men and horses in addition to his own household. Lusignan would soon acquiesce.

John was pleased to find William waiting in the shadows at the back of hall. Ever vigilant. "You have her reply?"

"She slipped out with the men. Sire, you are sure about this Mademoiselle?" William held one shoulder tensed in a slight shrug, a sign of his worry. "The Portuguese princess awaits you."

"We have not ceased to consider the princess. But tonight we shall sit with that damsel. Speak to her."

When William bowed, John turned away satisfied and, as he mounted the stairs to the solar, returned to the accounts. He would advise his man to make the amount owing enough to cover his progress to Portugal. Many *livres* in hand would ease a portion of his worry.

LIKE THE OTHERS, Isabelle left the hall when dismissed but remained in the spinning room as the knights and squires clumped through the armory and out into the bailey; she could hear them jostling on the stair, shouting under the tree. She didn't look for Hugh; she would ignore him until she enchanted the king and he, Hugh, jealously declared his love.

Once the men had gone, the room's cool air settled around the pallets and Madame's bed; echoes from other spaces floated from stone to stone and the day subsided into stillness. Isabelle waited. Perhaps the king would pass through the room. She smoothed her wimple and dress. A bouquet of distant laughter bloomed and faded. She sat on the edge of the bed and wiggled her toes against the tickling moss stuffed into the tiny point of her new shoes, admiring the small band of embroidery across the arch. A gift from Madame, for the wedding. *Wedding*. Eight days.

Minutes fluttered by; the room remained empty. She tapped her toes together, singing softly, "*Un, deux, trois* . . ." When a pair of men's shoes moved into her sight, she was afraid to raise her eyes lest it was the king and he had been watching her foolishness.

"Mademoiselle Angoulême?"

She jumped to her feet. "*Oui*." Not the king. Older, mustache only, body thick and straight as an ancient tree. Thin hair worn in the odd English style.

"I am William Marshal, knight to King John." He bowed slightly; she could see streaks of scalp between the strands. "Please sit. May I join you? Standing on cold stone makes my feet ache."

She was relieved he spoke of his feet; potential lovers spoke only of their hearts. As they sat, he groaned a little. She felt he would take off his shoes if he dared. Should she offer him that comfort?

"The king requests you to sit with him at the banquet." Monsieur Marshal was rubbing his shoulder.

At the high table? With the king, Père, and Madame? What a beginning for her plan. She would smile, showing her perfect white teeth, nod down at Hugh sitting below, and take as much salt as she wished. She wanted to jump up, but instead wrapped her arms around herself and gazed toward the ceiling. A small bird had flown into the room. "I would be pleased to join him. I thank you, Sir William."

"*Seulement* William." He rubbed his leggings. "I must change; these are full of burrs. You, too, must wear your best gown."

No need to tell her that. She sat straight in what she took for a womanly manner and transformed her inner laughter into a mild smile. She had already thought through her silks; green, blue, red the color of raspberries. Yes, that one, with the circlet from Hugh, her new shoes—she tapped them together softly—and girdle of cloth of gold, which was not to be worn until her wedding day, but surely sitting with the king . . .

William turned to her and drew back her wimple. "If you want to please John"—he didn't say *the king*—"leave your hair free. 'Tis a fashion much admired in England." He slid off the bed. "Oh, and talk. John likes women who can speak well." He left, limping slightly.

11

TO GAIN A KING

he assembled company, hands washed, grace said, settled into the banquet. John sprawled in his seat at the high table, aware of Isabelle on his left, a stray hair crossing her cheek. He could brush it away, but he checked himself. She was but a colt and might startle. A satisfactory first course arrived: leek-and-rabbit pie, chicken sauced with pounded almond, quinces in honey and ginger, multicolored jellies. He put small portions of each on the trencher he shared with Isabelle. She murmured, "*Merci.*" Nothing more. He turned to William on his right, but he conversed with Lusignan. A strange man, William, always courteous, but a demon in the tournament lists. John would be more like him, driving at the quintain with a lance, practicing with the sword, but time, time. He had none. Reports and rebellions, papers and messengers and the meddling pope. In recompense, he was king and had wisdom, and acuity. And power. He'd put the barons into place. His mustache lifted in a smile.

The girl coughed and he turned, expectant, but she merely

blushed and reached into the trencher to cut a bit of chicken. Bah, she was a child. What had he been thinking? Better to have requested Madame Lusignan, though that lumpish maumet would not draw so many glances. He adjusted his crown and moved his shoulders, causing his pin to send glints of light into the hall, reminding all who was king. He gestured for more ale. Would the damn girl never speak? William had been right. The Mademoiselle was straight as a stick; only two tiny bubbles declared a girl inside the tunic. She'd not yet had her menses and therefore would not, could not be in his bed. He'd keep the little garnet, though it would complement her dress. She at least chewed with her mouth closed and refrained from wiping her hands on the tablecloth. Mannerly, *grâce à Dieu*.

The course was almost finished when she said, "You are the brother of Richard, Coeur de Lion, are you not?"

Devil take her! Always Richard, his fame, his glory, not a thought for those left behind when he sashayed off on God's work. Damn him. John nodded and chewed on.

"When I was little, I called him Coeur de Dragon."

John raised his eyebrows. There a thought—his brother as a fire-breathing dragon, burning everything in his path. He turned to her.

"I wished to be called Isabelle de Sangliers. It sounded bold. A name to keep me safe, but Maman said I was ridiculous."

Isabelle of the wild boars? Where did she get these ideas? Surely she had not been taught such, but interesting. He'd not mention his father called him "Lackland"—a fourth son, no holdings—in the days before he gained power. Nor that his own ex-wife was secretly La Inutile, the useless. "You are to be married. De Lusignan will be enough. Or perhaps Mademoiselle Signet. A ring to be worn and cherished." He filled with chuckles. "Perhaps

Isabelle, La Cygnet." How apt, for truly she was a swan. Long neck. Fair skin. He was enormously diverted.

Isabelle laughed. "You speak so well. I wish that Hugh . . . Monsieur Lusignan Le Jeune would speak to me so nicely." The girl glanced down to where her fiancé sat with his mother and sighed. "Is it not important for husbands to speak to wives?" She leaned her face on her hand, then quickly removed her elbow from the table.

What to answer? She would be a wife, like any wife, bearing children or not, dying or not. What did a man say to his wife? He'd said little enough to his. "Things will change when you are wed, in a man's bed, bearing him sons. When are you to marry?"

"On my birthday, August twenty-fourth." She frowned slightly at the date, mood shifting. She was like a summer afternoon, sun, sudden cloud, a bit of rain. "On that day I shall be a woman. When were you born?"

"December, long ago." He joined her in the rain . . . Dear Lord. He'd be thirty-four at Yuletide and had naught but barons at his back, wanting more, giving little. He must wed, crush Arthur, regain the Angevin lands from Philip, that French *horreur*.

"Had it been August, you could be John the Imperatorius." She took a pinch of red jelly, then a piece of quince.

He tugged his beard in surprise and laughed.

Isabelle dropped her chin. "Is my Latin incorrect? *Imperatorius* means 'August,' does it not?"

"Your Latin is perfect." So enchanting. He offered her a piece of chicken.

DURING THE SECOND course, of Wensleydale cheese, venison, and honey balls, Isabelle, delighted she had spoken well, admonished herself to stay calm. The hall, lit with heavy candles, echoed like a great bell, like the cathedral at Easter, when the risen Christ was the center of the story, but tonight she, as in a *lai*, damsel fair of face and gracious in manner, was the center. The men below stroked her with their eyes. In her excitement, she wanted to run along the tables, laughing, touching their necks. She sat, shoulders loose, hands floating above the food with little flourishes of glee.

John offered her more honey balls. She smiled at him, her best smile, the one she used when dancing the rondelet, then pulled a handful of hair over her shoulder. The king had called her a swan. She stretched her neck, felt the possibility of powerful wings, pinched some salt, not because she needed it but because she could. Smiling like Marielle with a secret, she leaned down toward Hugh, willing his entrancement, but he only stared into his chalice. Were her arms longer, she'd reach out and turn his chin toward her, just like Maman had. He would see himself reflected in her eyes and be happy. They would . . .

"You will be a countess, will you not?"

She startled into the world of the high table. "When Papa dies." There she was, in John's eyes. Was his beard soft and comforting like her poor rabbit? "I pray it will not be soon." She crossed herself, both for her papa and for the stew with carrots.

"When you are countess, will you accept me as your liege lord?"

She was French; Lusignan bent knee to Philip, and her marriage would be here. But she was sitting with John. In confusion, she shook her head no, then yes.

"Your father accepted me as liege when he came to Gaillard."

Relieved Papa had answered for Angoulême, she said, "Gaillard has special windows with little places carved in the stone where one can sit to look out over the countryside."

"'Tis beautiful. The river runs free and is full of fish."

"Eels?" His face was old, but his eyes pulled her.

"You are fond of eel?" He placed his hand on hers.

The hand confused her at first, a king's hand, then a sense of safety rose up over the noise and movement of the servants passing food and the knights' loud laughter. Behind the tables, their swords stood in the shadows, leaning against the wall, waiting. She laid down her knife.

THE THIRD COURSE was the most magnificent, including loin of veal with gilt sugarplums, a sturgeon covered with powdered ginger, and a reconstructed peacock, feathers and claws embedded in the cooked flesh. The meat stuck in Hugh's throat; the tansy cake revolted him. When at last the eating was done and the hall was cheerful and ale-sodden, the king rose. Throughout the meal, Hugh had been unable to countenance John sitting in the center, his father's place, his hand grazing Isabelle's hair as if by accident, enticing her to laughter as she salted her fish and her veal slices and her apples. The cur, king or not, had usurped his family. They slept in a room where servants worked; his mother had been pushed from the high table to make place for Isabelle. Ruttish lout.

The king stood, quieting the merrymakers, and took Isabelle's hand, announcing, "I wish to recite a part of 'The Lai of the Dolorous Knight.'"

Dolorous? When Hugh snorted, his mother elbowed him hard. Was King John lachrymose, repentant, in pain? No. Hugh stared down at the table, the stained cloth, the spilled sauces, the trenchers of bread sodden and brown. He was dolorous. He hated the smell of ale, of men, of meat; the whole hall made his stomach spasm.

In a resonant voice, John began to speak, shading his words, stroking his beard. "In Nantes. Nay, in Lusignan." He smiled at Isabelle. "There dwelt a dame who was dearly held of all. She was passing fair of body, apt in book as any clerk, and meetly schooled in every grace that becometh a maiden."

The cur knew naught of Isabelle. She was his. How dare he make claim, king or not. *See how she blushes.* Hugh wanted to yank her from the high table.

As he spoke, John's pin flashed and glinted. Flaunting power. Oh, to strike him down.

John kissed Isabelle's hand. "So gracious of person was this damsel, that there was no knight could refrain from setting his heart on her, though he saw her but one time." He finished and removed the pin, fastening it to Isabelle's flat chest. Hugh's fists clenched. Were the Lusignans so poor that he, the only son, had naught save a small silver crucifix? He grabbed it and pulled, the chain rasping his neck, while John kissed Isabelle, once, twice, on each cheek. The churl took and touched and used what he wanted. He, Hugh, could do nothing. Inside him howled a wind, Melusine betrayed. The falcon he flew, the woman he would marry, the prayer he must say, all chosen by others. A slash of rage cracked his long compliance and shot toward John. *Finis.* He would do and choose for himself henceforth. He turned to his mother. A hard glitter forged her eyes and he knew his hatred was right.

WITH THE MEAL over, Isabelle was unsure of what to do. Servants began clearing the hall for music and dancing; John spoke with William. Should she leave? She couldn't go up to the solar where John was quartered, and truthfully, she loved the high table. A glitter of attention remained on her arms, her neck, her hair; if she stepped down, it would dissipate. She must talk to Hugh before it was gone. He would see—he must see—that she was more than a demesne. He would love her.

Distracted by the movement of servants carrying away the ewers and setting aside the trenchers for the poor, she hesitated and suddenly the glitter fled, leaving scraps, dogs, and the flight of days before her wedding. A realization quivered her ribs: When she was Hugh's wife, who would she be?

"Would a walk in the garden please a young maiden?" John offered his hand. "We can enjoy the setting sun and return for the entertainment. The roses are in full bloom."

Again the feeling of safety, of certainty in the warm hand. She touched the jewel on her dress. His eyes were even with hers; he was smiling. She said, "The campanula are also blooming. Royal purple in the clustered bells, as if meant for you." Her heart calmed. "A stone bench was added to the garden this summer. It has legs carved like griffins. I love to sit there."

"So we shall sit. Come." Her papa had always swung her down but now, with great courtesy, John helped her step from the dais. She didn't notice Hugh standing in the shadow.

Across the great hall with the King of England, strolling down the path where clouds of lavender bloomed. Scents washed by, seeming to match the color of the flowers: a light fragrance shaken from the campanula's bells, from the pale lavender came a perfume like Madame's powder, and there, the pink rosebud she'd noticed yesterday, open, sweetness in its folds waiting to be inhaled. Isabelle felt herself as one of the flowers.

The king walked with her, his boots crushing the stones.

She lifted the glittering pin to her mouth, touched the pearl with her tongue. No taste, but little waves and hollows on its surface emerged. Hers. Like a bell, her heart rang with the glory of it.

At the bench set between pierced stone screens, she sat and puzzled at her happiness. She had craved the eyes at the banquet, but now she delighted to be hidden. With John. She turned and stroked the rose lightly with her fingertip, then smiled up at him. Now they would talk and he would know her.

"You are very like that rose." He stood at his ease, leaning lightly toward her. "I believe it would become you more than the pin."

Unconsciously, her hand covered the jewel and he laughed. "I see you like my little trinket. A beautiful woman deserves many gifts."

"Not yet a woman." When he drew back, she added, "But betimes."

His mustache lifted. "Soon you will be lovely beyond mortal measure." He reached out and caressed a strand of her hair. "You are a treasure of gold." He spun the strand between his fingers, the evening sun reflected on his face, silent. She must start conversation, as she had at the high table. Ideas splashed through her mind: horses, embroidery, Crusades, hunting dogs. Then she found, "Is it different in England?"

He looked sharply at her. "Different?"

She was unsure why she'd asked. She didn't want to hear of gardens or farms, places she knew well in Lusignan and Angoulême. She tried for clarity. "Do you do things other than we do here?"

"Ah." He touched his beard.

Perhaps he understood. She waited for the world to open.

John clasped his hands behind his back. "Differences." Bees buzzed in and out of the roses. "There is a grand fair every year

BEHOLD THE BIRD IN FLIGHT

where cloth is sold. Merchants come from all over England, from Turkei, the fabled East, even France. My grandfather gave the charter for this fair to his jester"—here Isabelle giggled—"and for three days the unruly crowds buy and sell. At night there is such entertainment as Lusignan has never seen: acrobats, musicians, puppets. Sometimes there are punishments for those who break the law, but mostly there is dancing and displays of rare animals."

Ignoring the punishments, she said, "Animals?" She hoped he would mention a lion, or maybe a griffin, but he said, "Bears. Dancing bears. Clumsy and poorly treated, wretched creatures, but the crowd loves them." He stretched his arms and flexed his fingers. "I have renewed the charter and my treasury is much enriched by this fair. Soon I will have . . ." He stopped and looked at her. She wished he would continue his thought, but he said, "The fair is on St. Bartholomew's Day, August twenty-fourth."

"My birthday!" A faraway celebration on the day she was born. Out in the wide world, her day was important. It made her own small observance seem more festive.

"Would you like to see the fair?"

It rose before her, the crowds, the music, the bears, the piles of cloth. "Do they sell velvet?"

He laughed. "Perhaps. There are rainbows of color, blue plunket, red escarlate, the gold and silk of baldachin, fine tissues in green and brown and puce. With your golden hair, you should wear the finest plunket. I shall send a piece for your cloak." He stretched out his hand to her. "Come, the dancing will begin shortly. We shall enjoy the Basse Dance together."

As they stepped from between the screens, Hugh stood in the path. "Sire, she dances only with me." Isabelle gasped slightly. How fresh he was, hands on his hips, hose pulled smooth, his tunic dropping straight and unstained from his shoulders. As the slight shock ebbed, she realized what he had said and thrilled like a harp. The fair, the dinner, the eyes fell away and she moved toward him. He was going to love her.

"'Tis only a dance and gracious of the host to allow me my pleasure." In opposition, John grew taller; not as tall as Hugh, but radiating power. Isabelle felt it. He was a king. Hugh didn't flinch.

Rocks on the path pressed against her soles as she silently urged Hugh to claim her. She'd be a loyal and loving wife. He must want her now, before they married. Afterward would be too late.

"I see you take your pleasure as you will." Hugh crossed his arms. "She is to be my wife and shan't be touched but by me."

John flicked his eyes toward Isabelle, then back to Hugh. "Strong words of love."

She had prayed for this moment.

"'Tis not love. She belongs to me, given by her father. When her demesne and mine are combined, we shall be strong and do as we please."

Isabelle's heart disappeared, her fingertips went numb, all the garden's scent fled.

"I am aware of the first statement; it remains to be seen if the second is accurate." John gestured and one of his knights stepped from the orchard and walked toward them. "Now, you will allow me to escort this fair maiden to the dance. The choice of partner shall be hers."

The knight arrived and placed his hand on Hugh's shoulder. John held out his arm for Isabelle and as they walked down the long row of lavender toward the great hall, she looked for but failed to find her pride, and so she leaned on him, shaking as if from ague. In her pain, she understood for the first time the wounding of Cupid's arrow.

12

WHITHER THOU GOEST

hat night, Isabelle danced the Basse with John, held upright only by her tight dress and the thought she would be a countess. Afterward she left the keep, stumbled across the bailey, and climbed the inner stairs to the wall walk. It was cloudy. Beyond the castle, black reigned, the distant hulk of forest more felt than seen, the fields a vague glimmer, a single flicker of a rush lamp in the village. That little light, perhaps a lover returning home, stabbed her heart, and she crumpled against the wall, muffling her cries lest a guard come. *'Tis not love*. Hugh wanted only her inheritance; he didn't care that she loved him, that she spoke well in French and Latin, knew how to make ale. He cared not for her or her thoughts, only for Angoulême, for the fields and village, for the cattle and horses.

Sorrow scraped her body into mist. She'd be a ghost bride. No one would notice or care because her hair, hands, dress would remain; only the core of herself would be gone. She tried to still her crying, to let her heart go numb. The silk dress puckered with tears. She was learning what women knew, what

Marielle, Maman, even Madame knew: women themselves counted for nothing. Only sons and dowers. She ached with the hurt of it. *'Tis not love.*

Although August warm, the sides of her ribs, her fingertips, her feet in the new shoes were icy, the circlet from Hugh frozen on her collarbone. For warmth, she pulled her hair around her neck and her hand brushed the pin. The pearl and the garnets seemed to give off heat. Enclosing it softly, she relived the Basse, the warmth of John's hand, the skin malleable, a gathering of little bones across the back under her thumb. As they circled the floor, he had turned to her often, smiling, and when the music stopped, although Hugh tried to take her away, John ignored him and brought her ale in his own chalice, standing for a moment, asking if she would like again to walk and talk in the garden. She would have gone, but Hugh pinched her elbow and pulled her to Madame.

She arched back to the smear of stars. John had conversed and answered her questions; her small joke in Latin made him laugh. Flushing slightly, she cradled the pin, gathering all her questions and with each—Are there castles in London? Do fine ladies ride in the fields? Do you eat rabbit?—Hugh's painful pinch eased and she returned to her solid self, her body remerging.

Across the bailey, she could see the candles being snuffed in the keep and the torches quenched. One by one the arches of the windows went dark; she must return. She leaned far out from the parapet where wind lifted her hair, bringing the smell of harvested wheat and under it, the scent of something wild. Wolves in the forest, raccoons in the orchards, voles in the fields. Eating what they pleased, moving freely, choosing, but still God's creatures, still loved by Him. She would find a way to make her life like theirs. Suddenly exhilarated, she swung her hair in an arc; a sense of flight rippled from her arms, down her torso. Tonight her new life would begin. Although she was bound by her word to marry Hugh, she would no longer love him.

JOHN SPOKE WITH Isabelle as often as he could—as she embroidered or walked in the stables among the horses, at the high table. It eased his worries to hear her talk, to answer her questions about castles and journeys and tournaments; her delight lifted him. She asked repeatedly about his dogs; he told her their names, how Brutus, the biggest, was as gentle as a cat, while Gyrus chased his tail and needed to be restrained lest he rush into the hunt and force up the pheasants too soon. When she laughed, a breeze crossed his heart.

Unused to asking questions about other people's lives—lives that seemed distant, grasping, tricky—he was fascinated how freely she told him about hers: that she once had a rabbit, loved horses—he must remember to mention his first pony—and that her maman had strict rules, which he appreciated. And she seemed utterly unafraid of him. Women he met stuttered and blushed, their sideways glances expectant of a gift, which could be useful, even with baronesses, depending on what one desired. But Isabelle asked for nothing; the less she asked, the more he wanted to give: a hank of lace, a bit of foxglove to tuck into her bodice, an old coin.

Day by day the Portuguese princess faded; here, in front of him, was a vivid girl-child. When he and William rode for exercise, he spoke endlessly of her. "She dances with grace, does she not? Her Latin is well-formed. When she laughs, one must join in." He avoided mentioning her hair because after the first night Isabelle had kept it under her wimple, her glory hidden although her arms glistened with a fine flaxen down that promised a golden fleece between her legs. When he imagined himself wed, for the first time he felt desire, not duty. Isabelle in his bed, her hair spread, her knees wide. Enjoying the rising in his cock and the rhythm of his horse, he said, "How did she come to such beauty?"

"From her mother, Alix Courtney." William reined in to a walk, causing John to slow. "I saw her once at a tournament. Many a knight vied for her favor. At the time she was married to Count Joigny." William stretched.

"Joigny?" John slapped his horse into a trot, shouting back. "That was years ago. You are an old man." He urged his horse into a canter, making a wide circle though the fallow field, the high grasses swinging past his feet. When he returned, he said, "What is her lineage?"

"Alix's grandfather was King Louis VI of France." William raised his eyebrows. "That makes Isabelle a suitable choice for a noble, one might say queenly, wife. But Sire . . ."

"Always one step ahead." John chuckled and galloped away again like a young squire; William's eyebrows went higher, the sun beamed, the scattered clouds remained white and innocuous, and flights of birds rose from the grass.

BECAUSE SHE WAS betrothed, Isabelle must spend time with Hugh; Madame and Count Lusignan expected it, as did Hugh himself. She had made her decision, but when she danced an estampie with him, walked her horse alongside his, or simply looked down at his curly hair as she sat with John at the high table, she found it inconceivable she no longer loved him. Little hands reached out of her chest to pull him toward her. When he smiled at his père, face open, eyes crinkling under his dark lashes, her heart flew like a merlin. Once, flushed from dancing, he spoke to her: "The music was very fine, was it not?" She heard the passion in his voice and ached to lean against him. But his face would close, his voice harden, and she knew she must turn away. Slowly, she created a little witch inside herself that cackled over and over, *You shall love John*.

AUGUST WANED. JOHN attended chapel upstairs in the family's space. Ignoring the chaplain droning the familiar Latin, he knelt, genuflected, and stood as required, all the while reviewing his worldly options.

The cost of continuing to Portugal would consume the rents from Lusignan; the princess's dower kingdom would be separated from his by many days' ride. Difficult to govern. Easy to be cheated. Plus, if Hugh married Isabelle, when her father, who knelt to England, died, Hugh would kneel to Philip, taking Angoulême from him. More land lost. But with stealth and cleverness, he might marry Isabelle himself and reinforce Angoulême's allegiance.

He imagined the barons, those grim and tricky louts, pleased at a productive alliance. Another source of income to ease their requirements. Less leaning on them for remittances. Astonishing, their reluctance to see his need, *England's* need. A king must appear strong and with resources lest another—he felt Arthur's raised sword—forced a way in and took everything.

William nudged him. The Agnus Dei complete. John knelt.

Count Angoulême would demand a high price for her. Such beauty and a countess. La Marche? He chuckled at the thought of taking the valuable holding away from Lusignan. What would be the price? War? Lusignan would appeal to Philip, a not inconsiderable enemy. Philip supported Arthur and would use any excuse to gain England for himself. The logic curled about John; thorns stuck his ribs and he clenched his hands until the nails turned white, then Isabelle rode across his thoughts, hair aglow, full of questions and beauty. Damn the cost. His heart wanted what it wanted.

Amen. Go with God. He crossed himself and leaned over the balcony to see her still kneeling below and his mustache lifted. What cared he about a small war? The treasure would be his.

When the chapel cleared, John said to William, "I have decided to marry Mademoiselle Angoulême." He leaned on the stone railing.

William pinched his mouth slightly. "Sire, she is engaged."

"True, but not yet a woman. Canonical law states no child can consent to marriage. She must renew her vow when she is of age."

"I see you have considered carefully. And Lusignan?"

John kicked the bench in front of him. "I would gladly humiliate him."

"It may mean war. Philip will be angry."

"I care not. He has injured me beyond bearing, taking my lands, supporting my nephew against my true kingship. With Angoulême safely on our side, we regain strength, and I, a young wife to bear sons. For England. For the Angevin strongholds."

William hesitated, shifting his weight, one shoulder tensed. "How shall it be done? Lusignan has paid what is due. The men are restless and we depart on the morrow."

"Depart we shall. I shall speak to her today. Come to the solar after the meal."

HUGH LEFT THE chapel, eager for morning exercise. Today he joined the squires in the outer bailey jousting against the quintain. When he rode into their midst, a path cleared and he ran at the straw target with extra force, scoring a solid hit, jarred but still astride. Flags on the castle snapped in the wind; young men galloped, shouted, laughed; pages on the field's edge played their own games. Exulting in his strength, Hugh stood in his stirrups and threw his lance. It arced, landing point down and quivering. There. His mark. This afternoon he'd fly the pere-grine; in the evening he'd dance. A new troubadour had arrived. Tomorrow the king and his retinue would be gone and Isabelle would belong to him alone.

He would ask her to put away the pin. Demand if necessary. Why be endlessly reminded of John? Once she had complied, he would do as his mother advised and speak kindly to his companion in life. Momentarily he flushed, remembering Isabelle's pleasure at the king's gift, but he willed his heart to quiet. Kindness was required; she was but a woman, incapable of understanding a man's necessary striving against kings. She still wore the golden circlet he had given her; she could easily give back the king's bauble. He'd say what his mother said: "Queens are an unhappy lot." He'd speak to her with kindness and save her again.

"THREE DAYS 'TIL you marry." John and Isabelle sat on the garden bench with the griffin. "I leave on the morrow."

The questions Isabelle had prepared flew away. He'd spoken with such ease. Would he miss her? She found no regret in his profile. His beard and the slope of his nose didn't alter under her attention. On the morrow, she'd have no one to talk to, no one to offer her jewels or poems. She'd no longer sit at the high table. Suddenly John sighed and her hopes lifted. She moved so the pin sent tiny red glints onto his tunic. When he didn't turn, she said,

"I shall be sorry when you leave." Her little witch spoke: *He has a fine nose; he is a king.* With a little shudder of love, she touched his hand.

He breathed and turned so sharply she started. "Will you come away with me?" His hand smoothed her back. "Nothing to fear." He touched the pin, then ran his finger along the side of her neck. "If you consent, we shall go to your father's house. He has horses waiting for you, part of your dower."

She didn't hear the words; she was waiting for his finger to wake her body as Marielle had described, but there was only the cool nail scraping and a small prickle. She willed more; she wanted more, shudders and openings, caverns and explosions of love.

"Isabelle?"

He looked at her with such intensity. She must rise up to him. She made herself into a roaring springtime river and poured her weeks of longing for Hugh into a word: "Yes."

"She has agreed. You shall accompany her." John was dressing for the evening's entertainment. "I must not leave early."

"What do I tell her?" William shifted away from his bad hip.

"Say that I have asked you to take her to her father. That she will be safer with you, that stealth is required because kings are attacked on the road, and so on." John held out his arms to the knight who was dressing him. "You are to leave after the first dance. I shall dance to the end and then join you as fast as I am able. Our knights depart before dawn and I have arranged for her trunk."

"Let us pray no one sets up a cry." William stepped to the door. "The devil will stir if Lusignan uncovers your plan."

BEHOLD THE BIRD IN FLIGHT

"The lout." John laughed with anticipation as he chose a pin from the many offered by the knight. A star sapphire, said to attract love. "Go with God."

IN CONFUSION, ISABELLE followed William away from the dancing, out into the bailey where horses waited. Did her simple yes mean this leaving? She'd not thought of quitting Lusignan so soon. She wanted John's love to bring Hugh to her arms. No, no, she wouldn't love him. But did she love John? Her heart scrambled for understanding as she stood, wind whisking her dress, music falling from the great hall's window. She needed John's quiet voice and warm hands. The moon, almost full, had a little slice missing. She felt cut by it.

William brought her horse, its shadow mingling with those of other horses shifting on the stones. She mounted. The noise of the hooves, the clatter of bridles and the opening gate clutched her heart; now Hugh would come, but they rode freely into the night, through the rising river mists, past the village. Why was she destined to always leave?

On the journey, she found safety with William. No yearning, no anger, just riding under the moon that powdered light on the fields, on the mane of her horse. Her pale hands glimmered; her silk cloak floated behind. Frogs in a mad chorus. She let her mind go blank as on and on they traveled, through the ghostly trees, past lakes and fields until her eyes fluttered down, her body melting into sleep, almost falling but for William's shout. He took her onto his own horse where she leaned against him as they rode endlessly on.

HUGH HAD DREAMED of soaring like a peregrine, swooping over the river that cradled the castle and out across the fields, sun's glint on his feathers, the world spinning below. He wakened lighthearted, smiling; today the king would be gone. He found the solar empty, not a trace of John or his servants; he leaned at ease against the window. Morning was well begun and down the hill miniature villagers like those in his dream hurried about their business under a pale-washed sky. First Matins, then a perfect day for riding; he'd invite Isabelle and as they rode, explain to her how to be his wife. He should have spoken weeks ago, but every time he thought to begin, memories of Marielle flooded him and he'd turn away; today he would be strong and kind. He would offer Isabelle . . . what? Everything belonged to his father. But he must give her something so she would know her life with him would be pleasant. The king had read the *lai*; Hugh would offer more than words. He would swear eternal fealty. Even love. When the troubadour sang of love, Hugh noticed women listened with shining eyes and flushed cheeks. He wanted Isabelle to look at him as she had when he saved her, with gratitude and appreciation. She'd not been the one he wanted—Marielle slid past like a ghost—but her flinty moments intrigued him. Standing in the cart, her hair like a flag. Speaking at the trial. He would reason with *that* Isabelle, a girl so different from his lost love that pain would ease.

His parents came into the solar and he stepped with them onto the chapel balcony for Mass. Isabelle didn't join them. Strange. Perhaps she'd forgotten the king was gone and was below. He daren't lean out until the last benediction, but even then he didn't see her. Perhaps she'd gone to the cathedral's morning service on this, the last day before she wed; he knew naught of the rituals required of women. A special candle lit. Obeisance to

Mary, Mother of God. Then cast all away and climb into bed. He felt a little stirring, but no, she must remain a virgin until she had her bleeding lest God punish him with childlessness.

He walked casually through the keep, searched the stables and forge, passing the well and into the outer bailey, but she eluded him. When he recognized a young woman who used to spin, he put his hand on her arm. "Have you seen Isabelle?"

"Her trunk was loaded this morning."

"Her trunk?" Hugh arched back, gripping the sleeve. How could that be? The girl must be lying.

"Sir." She tried to pull away, but Hugh held her fast, almost tearing the fabric.

"Loaded, you say?"

"Yes, sir. Onto a cart."

"You told no one?" His face was close to hers; he could smell garlic. "What is your name?"

"Agatha. A page was sick." Her lips quivered. "Isabelle said she was to fetch dower horses from her father's house. It was a secret."

Hugh dragged the shaking Agatha to the count who heard the tale with disbelief. "Her wedding is tomorrow. How think you she will return in time?" He yelled at a servant, "Where is Mademoiselle's trunk?"

"I, sir, I am a cook and I . . ."

The count collared the hapless man. "Find it."

Because the family's belongings were being moved from the spinning room back to the solar, there was much running up and down stairs, shouting and swearing. Shortly the servant returned, head bowed, hands clenched. "Sir, 'tis not here, Sire." He flinched away from the count's swift blow.

Agatha's tears turned to howls. The count shouted for someone to check the stables, but Hugh stood dazed. She had run away? From him? He could give her everything; everything he had wanted to give to Marielle would have gone to her. He was good. A Godly man. His pulse galloped; his thoughts scrambled until he focused on the moment when John fastened the pin to Isabelle's dress. Hugh remembered her, slim as a blade of grass, strong, eager, full of pride as the king's touch transferred power to her. The power to decide for herself. He had not paid attention, had let her go. He grabbed his father's arm. "She has gone with the king."

Père's shouting stuttered. "The, the . . . Why say you so? She would not dare. Nor he."

"She sat at the table with him, wore his jewel." Like a dry haystack, Hugh flared up, swinging his arms, pacing wildly. "I must ride after them. Stolen. My love taken from me." Did he mean Isabelle or Marielle? It mattered not.

Hugh's father yanked his arm hard, almost bringing him to his knees.

"You will not catch them, even should this be true. But if 'tis, we shall have her back." Père's face was purple, his lips strangely pale. He bruised Hugh's arm with his grip. "John is vassal to Philip. The French king will force her return."

"Father, let me go now." Hugh jerked against the grip. "Paris, endless messengers, planning. Useless." He heaved against Père's hand. "By the time we are prepared, the nefarious churl will have . . ." Hugh paused, panting. Whatever John's plans, he must stop them. With a violent twist, he shook himself away and dashed to the stable. He galloped through the gate, chased by shouts and wailing.

BEHOLD THE BIRD IN FLIGHT

SITTING ON A bench at the edge of Angoulême's great hall, Isabelle could scarcely keep her eyes open. The hall reeked of onion, ashes, and roasted goat; her thighs ached from riding, her hands from gripping the reins and then William's cloak. She wanted to ask for Maman, but she was so tired. She leaned against the stone, struggling to understand why no one spoke to her. Was she to be punished?

At a table, Isabelle's father and King John laughed over drinks; Papa had ordered wine instead of ale and Isabelle could smell it, slim, fruity. It made her sick.

She longed to slip away and hide in the buttery like she'd done when she was little. But no, she was no longer a child; today she was a woman. She brushed her torso, her thighs; nothing had changed. *Were the men disappointed? Did they laugh at her sameness?* She waited for their eyes, but none came to her. Yesterday in Lusignan, today Angoulême; yesterday a child, today a woman. No difference except in the words or where she sat. Slowly, under her exhaustion, a new understanding glittered like a shard of glass: she was always herself. She went with herself everywhere and did not change. God saw her soul and judged. Overhead a small bird flew in and out of the rafters, trapped in the great hall. Its cries wounded her, as if it, too, knew a terrible thing. Her ribs ached. She pulled her legs under her cloak for warmth.

William stepped into the room. "Sire."

No one but Isabelle heard. Kind William. She could still feel the bulk of his body supporting her, keeping her safe. His courtliness as he lifted her off the horse in Angoulême, his arm around her shoulder to help her inside.

"Sire, a report."

The king glanced up. "Shortly."

Isabelle thought to greet him, to bring him to her bench so

he could rest his feet, but she was molded to the wall. William stood quietly. A servant came to the table and dripped wax onto a paper into which the king pressed his signet ring.

She let her eyes close.

"Any pursuers?"

"Only the young count."

Her eyes sprang open. William leaned against the table.

John stood, nose close to William's. "Lusignan captured? Brought here?"

Hugh here? Isabelle gasped. Would he be angry at her?

"No, Sire. I thought it best to send him back under escort. Your plans shan't be disturbed."

"You should have let him come. He'll raise the sleeping dragon."

Hugh with a dragon. She almost giggled, then realized he wasn't coming. She'd not see him. Tears leaked on her cheeks.

"It will take time. Meanwhile you can marry and return to England."

John sat. "Ah, well planned as usual. We shall prepare for their response." He offered William wine and was refused.

Was she to go to England? She wiped her face with her hem. Too late to see the fair, but there would be other new things. Eyes closed, Isabelle conjured white castles, dancing bears, piles of silk and jewels. At last, Maman came. She loosened Isabelle's wimple, then touched the pin. "Very fine. From the king?" Overhead, the bird flew and sang.

Isabelle nodded. The heavy pin pulled at her dress. Her body sagged under its weight.

"How well you have done. Your father is proud. Today he received a charter from the king. La Marche is ours." Maman stroked Isi's hair. "You are exhausted. The bishop will be here soon, and you need only affirm that you are today a woman and renounce your promise to Hugh. Say 'twas given when you were not of age. Then you shall accept John. Afterward you can go to bed."

Renounce Hugh? The bird's cries slid into her stomach, sharp, distressing. How did this happen? Her mind tumbled back to the beginning, Alain, Marielle, Agatha, Hugh. Sitting here with Maman, the path to this moment trailed behind her like a snake, hissing and slithering. The old yearning started up, but she summoned her little witch. *You shall love John.* The words covered her ache. She had done this. She was a woman and would be . . . a queen? A consort?

Maman tapped a reminder to sit straight. "Tomorrow you are to go to Bordeaux to be married in the cathedral where John's mother wed. 'Tis a strange choice, but with it I believe John mocks King Philip. After Eleanor's marriage to King Philip's father dissolved, she wed John's father. Mind, Eleanor will be your mother-in-law. She has a will like armor. Take care you don't trouble her."

Isabelle tried to keep the story straight, but the names spun round and round. Only the words *love John* remained like a spike in the ground. She held on to them.

"Remember, you will be a queen. I raised you for such but never thought . . ." Maman kissed her as the bishop entered the great hall.

FOR EVER AFTER Isabelle would associate marriage with the smell of the sea. As she stood with John on the Bordeaux cathedral porch, gulls called overhead and a salty breeze lifted her pale blue overdress. People gathered, whispering *the king*, staring at her splendor, at the silver braid on her sleeve and hem, the pin, the cloth of gold cloak, all gifts from John. She stood straight as a stalk of wheat, trying to look solemn; the birds whirled among the wispy clouds, and she exulted in the glittering eyes of people wishing to be in her place. John said, "I receive you as mine, so that you become my wife and I your husband." With a quiver, she said the same back to him, the bishop blessed them, and she was married. So few words to become a wife. Did that make it less impressive? John took her arm and they passed under the tall columns into the cathedral for Mass, and when they sat, he drew her close with his arm, his hand caressing her side. She knew it was not yet time, but she waited for her body's response. Nothing.

WILLIAM LED ISABELLE into a large room in the bishop's residence. Three windows arched along one wall, under them several carved benches, and grandly, in the center of the wooden floor, the king's bed, assembled and piled with embroidered cushions, fur pelts, and a large striped coverlet. Isabelle's confusion at the lack of sleeping pallets fled when she realized the bed was for her. And the king. Crossing herself, she prayed. Her body would never open in this chilly room.

Shortly John entered, smiling, toasting her with his chalice. "To my wife, and soon-to-be queen."

Queen. Said for the first time. Her little witch came to attention.

John took her hand. "I have sent messengers to prepare for your coronation. My subjects shall love you as I do." He pulled her close and whispered against her cheek. "There is no sun here, so your complexion is safe. Take off your wimple."

William cleared his throat.

Isabelle was glad to remove it, because John's hand seemed

demanding of her own, his thumb rubbing her palm, his nail rough. Once she had removed the covering, she didn't know where to put it.

John set down his chalice, took the wimple, tossed it into a corner. "We shall find you a serving maid, but tonight William will unloose your braids. He has a wife and is more accustomed to pleasing a woman than I, having long avoided my first queen." The king stepped away.

Isabelle startled to remember there had been another queen, but William's touch gentled her breath. William didn't love her; his hands were anonymous. Shortly her hair fell free down her back. She shook it loose. "I have no comb."

"Ah, but I do." John stepped behind her and began to tug it through her hair.

"Ouch." The king knew nothing about combing hair. "Start at the bottom." Then, thinking she had been too demanding, she added, "Sire."

He laughed. "I'm John, only John, your beloved husband."

The word *husband* bounced on Isabelle's ribs and she gasped slightly. Her husband was combing her hair. Not what she expected. She forced herself taller, prepared for what might come.

William said, "A quarter hour, as agreed," which Isabelle scarcely heard, but when he left the room, closing the door with a slight thud, she felt she should have said farewell. Followed him to the door with full courtesy. The king—John—tossed the comb to the floor and began stroking her hair. She could hear him breathing; his face was pressed into her neck and she wanted to step away but he had an arm around her waist. The other hand roamed down her back and she panicked.

"I am not a horse that you should so feel my withers."

John laughed. "So you are not." He released her and sat on the bed. "Take off your shoes. You cannot sleep so."

Shoes made no difference. She wouldn't sleep. His hungry eyes would tear her apart. Slowly she took off the new leather shoes. Now she expected he would approach and kiss her, but he took up his chalice of wine from the floor and sipped, simply staring. She swallowed again and again, anxiety pinching her throat. Did she displease him? The troubadour sang, "*A maiden fresh and fair to his desire.*" Perhaps she wasn't that maiden. She could simply say so and leave the room. But where would she go? She shifted her bare feet on the rough stone. She was a wife. A chill crept across her body. Was that all? Was this love? The witch wouldn't waken. Isabelle was alone, pressed into herself by John's heavy gaze. In his disappointment, he would put her aside like his first wife. She'd be sent back to Angoulême in shame.

John set down the chalice with a clank and she jumped.

"No need to be afraid, *petite*."

"Not afraid. Just cold." Goose bumps on her arms. Toes going numb.

"So you are, but stay a moment longer."

Isabelle did as her husband commanded. He lounged, smiling a little. Everywhere his eyes touched her, she twitched; a pheasant awaiting the hunter.

"My poor bride." He picked up a small fur from the bed. "You are quite chilled." Stepping close, he wrapped it around her shoulders. She laid her cheek into the softness, glad for the separation it made between her head and her body, because now the king embraced her and her body revolted. His scratchy beard, not soft as she had imagined. He pressed closer, his little sword alert, and moaned in her ear. Frightened and ashamed of her fright, she cried out, "Are you hurt?"

BEHOLD THE BIRD IN FLIGHT

A short laugh broke on her neck. "William!"

William stepped into the room. She wanted to offer him a place to sit, but could not, not with the king so near, one hand on her shoulder.

William stared only at John. "Sire, we require God with us lest Lusignan . . ."

"Bah!" the king roared, and Isabelle cringed. William bowed his head.

John released her. "Don't be frightened." He turned to William. "Bring in the woman."

William nodded to the open door and a nun stepped into the room, her long habit rustling against the stones, a rosary glinting at her waist, her collar whiter, more brilliant than any Isabelle had ever seen. Isabelle's fear ran toward her for safety.

John pointed to a bench in the corner and the woman sat. "Before you, my wife, retire for the night, there must be music. Sweets, fruit, more wine."

William beckoned, and a small table and two chairs were carried into the room. Isabelle slid the chair further away from her husband's before she sat.

John raised his eyebrows slightly, but merely said, "My delightful queen. We shall go to Chinon and I shall give you such wealth. Niort is a great demesne. I shall give it to you because of the pear trees. Do you like pears? There is a fine herb garden and fig trees. The villeins's rents are munificent and we profit greatly from the sea . . ." He paused.

"Shall I have a crown?" When John took her hand, she struggled not to shrink away.

"You shall have the world. And when those"—his hands hovered toward her chest—"are grown and you are ripe, you shall give me a child in return."

The musicians entered; Isabelle drank wine and asked the king about Niort, Chinon, and his dogs. Finally, William sent the musicians away and she followed the nun to a quiet cell. Relieved to be alone, she undressed. The pin winked at her—*you are going to be a queen*—but her former delight was ruined by the thought of spending night after night with John. The dreamed-of life collapsed around her. She would have to summon the witch if she wanted to survive.

PART FOUR

The Return

1202

13

BE YE NOT
UNEQUALLY YOKED

Wind thumped the sail as Isabelle's ship left the coastal mist behind, and she blessed the cloudless summer sky. She'd endured two years in England—icy chilblained wet dripping dark London, where water tasted of moss, and apples were never eaten raw. She was a queen, crowned in full glory before the fat barons at Westminster Abbey, but *England* pulled her face into a knot. Only now had her husband allowed her to visit France, summoning her to the military camp where he waited for King Philip's attack. John often ranted that the damned French had used their marriage as an excuse to seize English land. Now men would hack each other into blood, arrows would pierce innocent horses, and many would die. Because of her simple *yes*. Her inner sky darkened, sorrow quivering across her ribs.

She shook herself back to the sky. Light like thinnest parchment, birds skimming the sea. In front, unseen as yet, sunlit France with its orchards, vineyards, rivers, and small hills, joy and breath. But John had forbidden her to travel further south than Arques. She wasn't allowed home to Maman and Papa in Angoulême. Longing drenched her. Waves beat on the boat.

John had kept his promise and taken her to the St. Bartholomew's Fair. She laughed at a sudden memory of the stunned man who sold her a length of the coveted velvet. *The king, the queen.* Long trails of whispers, and when she turned, holding her cloth, pale pink like blush on a pear, people bowing low between the horses. The velvet tunic was in her trunk.

A sailor approached. "Madame, your maid says . . ." Pulling up her inner queen, she gestured him away. *Mal de mer* kept her English maid below, freeing her to lean on the rail and conjure France in blessed solitude. Maurelle, the maid, had been chosen by John to spy; she spoke incoherent French garbled with Anglo-Norman and Latin phrases from the Mass. Isabelle pinched her lips. She'd pleaded for Agatha to be brought from Lusignan, but John refused. Pigheaded and suspicious, her husband thought everyone plotted against him, especially the Lusignan brutes. She lived long days, constantly watched, constantly blamed, because Hugh—*his curls, his smooth skin*—didn't want her. Overhead, John's flag, *her* flag, snapped; the sail billowed.

Shading her eyes, she strained for France's edge. Nothing yet. Wimple removed, hair shaken free—no care for her complexion—she practiced smiling like a queen, nay, like a wife. John loved her smile, said it gave him hope. She turned to all sides, hair glinting, arms unfurled like wings. *Be hopeful and of good cheer.* A gull swooped to the rail; wind frisked past her ears. Slowly, a plan formed. She was a queen. She would ask, no, demand Maurelle to stay behind on the boat when they landed. For a moment, she would breathe the air of *la belle France* alone. Draw castles in the sand, skip stones. A real smile arose. And faded. In the end,

Maurelle must come ashore and William must deliver Isabelle to John, who would want . . . A tide of darkness. She willed the wind to blow the thought away, but 'twas no use. His hairy body, clenched fingers, clinging attention. She crossed her arms tight, protecting her ribs. During his months of absence, little knots of nipples had loosened and bulged into small breasts. Several gowns had to be given away. She could no longer sleep on her stomach for fear of crushing them, and when she ran, they bounced. Today she wished they'd fall off.

The night before they sailed, Maurelle folded a tunic into the chest and commented that soon the flux would appear, bringing sons; Isabelle clearly understood Maurelle's word, *filii*, taken straight from the Mass, the double *ii* like a shudder. John had kept his vow, but with her flux, their unconsummated marriage would end. No more nights alone while John satisfied himself with a baron's wife or the sister of a man of power. How the court women hated her for not keeping him in her bed, for allowing him to cajole, buy, or force favors. She'd hoped when he went off to fight for the Angevin lands, those same women, relieved of his attentions, would forgive, but the tight clusters knit with gossip or jokes never opened for her. Only men favored her with greetings, questions. Trained in Angoulême and Lusignan councils, she could answer with intelligence, but her words meant nothing; they were speaking to her blond hair and burgeoning body. Eyes found her, brave hands casually brushed in passing. A few tried to woo her with courtesies and small gifts, but she turned them away, her core hard. Her body had never opened.

She liked John well enough when they rode or talked or danced, but when he embraced her, she could say to herself *husband*, but his touch was ever strangling, even when he rubbed her hands with scented cream or stroked her hair. Marielle had either dreamed or lied. In a few days she'd be fourteen, but she held no hope the new year would make a difference.

The ship forged through the open water; sailors shouted among the cargo or clambered up the sail like monkeys. Isabelle leaned and worried. Then a thought cut her breath like a knife. *I shan't go back.* She pressed her hands against her chest, gasping, then flung out her arms. Yes! She would ask John to put her away as he had his first wife. He should be loved by a woman experienced in bed, a true consort. She was unsuited. Young. She wavered, thought of the velvet, the crown, but no. She would go home, speak French, walk with her father, find a friend. No longer a queen. No longer Madame. Just Isi.

WHEN THE DINGHY left her on the French sand, she took off her shoes, lifted her gown, and splashed along the glitter of waves. William had yet to appear. Perhaps her ship had been blown off course and he was waiting on another beach. Behind her, Maurelle, knee-deep in water, unloaded small chests; other boats rowed toward shore. Now was time, fly away!

She crossed her arms, gripping her elbows, held back as if by reins. Once she'd fled. This time she'd do it properly. She quailed at the thought of speaking to John, but no, she must. Anxiety sent her dashing past the cargo littering the beach: trunks, barrels of flour, linens, arrows, new-made helmets and armor. Crates of pigs, squealing louder than the surf. Panting, she laughed aloud. Her first moments in France.

Soon William rode over the hill, leading her horse. Behind him thumped carts to haul away the supplies. She waited, holding her shoes as he dismounted. "Madame." He bowed.

She wished he would swing her up in an embrace as her

father would have done, but he was only a courteous baron and she was the queen, as he often reminded her when she raced through a castle or rode without her wimple. She expected him to scold her now, a cross between Papa and Maman, but he refrained. Dear William. She would regret leaving him.

She tucked her hair away; he helped her into her shoes. She expected more news, greetings from John, but he stood shifting on the sand, shoulders hunched, eyes downcast.

"What is it, William?"

"Madame, your father has succumbed to fever. I greet you in full honor as Queen of England and Countess of Angoulême."

Papa. A wave broke behind her; there was sand under her nails and in her shoes. Papa dead. Gone to God. The pigs clamored. She turned away and closed her eyes, and when William placed his hand on her shoulder, she leaned against him as she had against her father.

"I must . . ." What must she do? "I must go to Maman."

"Madame, that is too dangerous. The king has forbidden travel but to his encampment."

She stiffened and pulled away. "Maman will be alone." William was shaking his head. What use was it to be queen? She had the urge to scream, to batter William, but no, she *was* queen. A ruler, but always ruled. Papa was dead; she must . . . She found a plan. "John would not forbid me to pray." Cunning she'd learned during two years in England lifted her chin slightly. "He needs the Lord's help. I will pray for him and for my father." She was a queen; she could command. "Is there a church near?"

"Yes, Madame, the abbey of the Benedictines in Fécamp is within riding distance."

"We shall go there at once. Send word to John that I come on the morrow. He will allow this."

Isabelle mounted and waited while William gave orders, then followed him away from the sand along the cliffs. *Papa has died.* The words crashed like the sea below, over and over, never tiring, constant. Against the noise and rhythm of riding, she wept into the wind, remembering a letter. She'd been embroidering when John leaned over her shoulder, touching the threads. "That is quite fine. We shall hang it in our room." He ran a finger down her neck, then nestled his chilled hand under her dress; he smelled of horse and leaves. "A message came today from your father, reports on the rents from La Marche. At the end he sent you his blessings and mentioned a new stone chair or platform from which you can look out on the garden. I hope you understand. I do not. His Latin is not as good as yours, *ma chérie*."

Long-ago nights on the castle walk with Papa, they'd looked at her star and he'd asked about her *leçons*, but once, as they leaned out over the parapet, he described benches he'd seen in Coeur de Lion's castle, Château Gaillard. She'd begged him to make one for her, so she could sit and dream at the sky. Papa put his hand on her shoulder. "A bench shall be yours, *ma petite*." But there had been no time; Alain died and her life whirled into new shapes commanded by God. Why hadn't He allowed her to sit on the new bench with Papa? Why did He take away those she loved? She leaned forward against the warmth of her horse. Papa had never seen her wearing the crown. Like petals falling from a pear tree, grief opened her heart and a tear dropped onto the horse's mane, sliding along the coarse hair to fall underfoot.

"Madame?" William slowed his horse.

Isabelle straightened. "Is it far?"

"No, Madame. I have sent a messenger ahead. They will have food and lodging prepared for you."

"First I will pray. Then I will speak to the abbot."

Because of repair work on the abbey church, the stone exterior was covered with ladders and the ground rutted from the hauling carts, but inside the ceiling soared away as in Angoulême, and Isabelle felt God peering through the high windows. A comfort, a steadiness against change. She went as close to the altar as she dared and knelt to pray. *Requiem aeternam.* Latin fell between her thoughts. Maman needed her—*Dona eis.* John commanded otherwise—*Domine.* Always he commanded. The past two years battered her like a winter wind. *Et lux perpetua luceat eis.* Slowly other words, words she had heard in the English court, filtered into her recitation. A woman, Isambour, and King Philip of France. His shame. She sat back on her heels and allowed her prayer to be overtaken by remembered gossip: hurrying past a tangle of tittering women, stray words biting the tops of her ears. King Philip had had a wife he didn't want and had gotten rid of her.

Requiem aeternam dona eis. Requiescant in pace.

Isabelle looked up into the arches. *Forgive me, Papa. You were proud I married a king, but I have a husband I do not want.* She didn't mention King Philip, who'd asked the pope for annulment on the grounds of non-consumption. Papa needn't know that. Head dropped, she tried to pray again, but her mind wouldn't stop. If an unconsummated marriage could be annulled, perhaps John would allow her to leave. He could remarry. Habit held her on her knees, but inside she rose toward the pale arches, bidding farewell to England. And John . . .

She bowed her head—*Absolve, Domine, animas omnium fidelium defunctorum*—offering up the first of many prayers required to release Papa from purgatory. She wished she had coins to pay the monks to pray for him, but John maintained she had no need. She would ask him to send silver, but first she must speak to the priest to confirm what she'd understood from court rumors.

His name was Benoit, the blessed, a little round man who squinted at Isabelle before he bowed. He smelled of stale incense, and his robe was dirty at the knees from kneeling. When he asked how he could help, she gestured William away, then stammered, "I need to know what constitutes marriage in the eyes of God."

"My child, what question is that? Do you need to make a confession?" His squint deepened.

She wanted to slap him for thinking she'd given away her favors. "No, Father." Using the word brought tears; her lips quivered.

"Come, we shall sit and you shall tell me your troubles."

As they walked toward the priory, Isabelle realized she mustn't tell Benoit she no longer wanted to be married. By the time they were seated, she had invented a woman at court, a cousin named Maurelle who'd asked for help. "She wants to be properly married, Father, and has asked me what the holy church says. I am merely a layperson and cannot tell her."

Benoit leaned forward and put his hand on her knee. "You may tell your cousin that marriage consists of three parts." He pulled back with a jerk and folded his hands. "The partners must be of equal rank. A cousin of yours would find no impediment there." He smiled slightly. "The woman must be given by her father and dowered." He sighed. "Finally, the marriage is completed by sexual consummation. If your cousin is troubled, possibly the last has already occurred?"

Isabelle bowed her head to hide her face. "No, Father. The family is poor and there is no dower. If that is required, I shall ask my husband to provide such."

"A kind and Christian thought, my child. 'Twould keep your

cousin from sin." He reached out to take her hand. "Are you certain you have no desire to offer up a confession?"

Isabelle slid her hand away. She would confess the lie on the morrow to another priest. She ate a meager meal and slept in the cold monk's cell where her own bedding had been placed. For that warmth, she gave thanks. She also pleaded with God to hold her menses back a while longer because she couldn't hide them from John while they were in encampment. Even if she could, Maurelle would tell him; he would consummate their marriage. She'd be bound to him forever.

14

STRENGTH UNTO THE BATTLE

In the spring of 1202, Hugh longed for the quiet of Lusignan. Paris was overrun with construction on the new cathedral to be called Notre-Dame, and the Île de la Cité swarmed with masons, carpenters, and blacksmiths; carts hauled stone, tile, loads of wood, great bells. As he'd foreseen, the plan to rescue Isabelle had required years of waiting. Of standing around with Arthur, John's nephew, an arrogant boy-man who often announced he'd do this or that when he was king. Their discussions about supplies and horses for the coming attack were constantly derailed by passing nobles who wanted Arthur's favor, merchants who wanted Arthur's business, or preening women swinging their sleeves who simply wanted Arthur.

The rollicking Parisians with their loose manners reinforced Hugh's ambition to repossess Isabelle. Her grace and polite address would make him a proper wife. He would try to love her—not like Marielle of course, but that couldn't be helped. Some nights, overwhelmed with the difficulties of planning the rescue, he'd lie abed and conjure moments they'd shared—her tenderness with his son. Galloping in the sun. Once he'd entered a room where she embroidered and she'd sprung to her feet, scattering colored thread, begging him to take her for a walk in the garden where the strawberries were ripe. At the time he thought her childish, but now he envisioned going out during the day to care for his fiefdoms and riding home in the evening to her chatter and her bed. Yes, she would make him a good wife, and after they had a fistful of sons, he might go on a small Crusade, but that would be later. First to bring her back.

Finally, after two years, Philip called Arthur and Hugh to court and, straightening from a table full of maps, announced they would attack on two fronts: Philip would harry John's encampment in Arques, a valuable seaport in the north of France, and while John was embattled there, Arthur and Hugh would lay siege to John's mother, Eleanor of Aquitaine, in Mirebeau. As Philip said, John couldn't be in both places at the same time, and the old queen, once captured, could be exchanged for Isabelle.

The opening attack at Mirebeau confirmed Hugh's expectations of war: a scramble of screaming and mayhem and arrows; men, horses, squires shot dead, women fleeing, skirts flapping, fruit and bread dropped, a baron wounded and enemies captured, but this first excitement was followed by days of sitting in the field, eyes on the old pile of stones. Rain or sun, day and night, Arthur, Hugh, and the knights must keep vigil there lest one of Mirebeau's inhabitants escape to bring help.

The building of a trebuchet war-machine brought a burst of activity. Ambitious Arthur strode around the workers, shouting as if he had knowledge of construction. While he pushed and threatened men working in the hot sun, Hugh gladly sat under a canopy, anticipating the machine's clank, the swish and crash of rocks flung against the castle walls. He pictured the old queen as a black spider deep in a center of stone, hollow-cheeked, hands dark with age, plotting for her son John. A pox on her. Pound the castle to dust; exchange her for Isabelle. Old for the young.

Tasked with providing supplies, Hugh organized forays into the countryside to locate and commandeer bread, eggs, chicken, hay, all required to feed the soldiers and their mounts. Once he returned with a pig and the men shouted and clapped him on the back. Once a useless volley of arrows flew from the castle. Otherwise they simply waited for the old queen to run out of food and give up. If he had known war's boredom, he'd have saved himself years of yearning to be a squire.

He entertained himself by working with the pages; most were ten years old and eager to be fourteen and squires, so he organized play to strengthen them. Today they were at stickball with pine cones and a bit of wood. Hugh would hit a cone, calling, "Crispin, catch this if you can." Crispin and Neville ran and fell, shouted and laughed with the other boys. Hugh stood gladly in the sun, teasing—"Faster! You've naught but spindles for legs," or "Ha, a triumph." In those games, he came to understand being a father. Had his son lived, he'd be two. Would he be walking, talking? Hugh didn't know and had no one to ask, but he imagined curly red-brown hair like his own, flopping and swaying as his little son ran to greet him.

Alone, at night, he approached his memories with care so as not to break down: grabbing the arrow, waiting outside the birthing room, Isabelle, bent with weeping. How she reached out to help with the loose swaddling. That gesture and her tears had somehow folded her into his heart, eased his pain. Someone had cared as much as he.

BEHOLD THE BIRD IN FLIGHT

Now, as Hugh stood musing, stick dangling from his hand, a pile of pine cones at his feet, he was struck from behind. A sharp intake of breath, but it was only Crispin, his favorite. "You're our prisoner." Surrounded by cheering little chaps who'd organized the attack, he spun, laughing, as he tried to loosen the little monkey clinging to his back. "Surrender your silver and your horse." He fell to the ground, laughing, and the scrum of children tumbled on him. They rolled and shouted and kicked; he felt only joy.

JULY LAY HOT on John and his companion as they sat outside the tent, squinting at the chessboard. While des Roches contemplated his pieces, a great heron swooped up from the field: sword-like beak, powerful wings, legs trailing like pennants. Its glory pressed John's sternum. His breath rose; his thoughts gathered and sang. *I am a mighty king. I defy Philip.* Never would he bend knee to France. Let Philip mass his knights in the distant Arques woods; let him plan and plot. He, John, would prevail and soar like that heron.

Across from him, des Roches bent over the board, sweating, determined to win. John envisioned a millstone in the man's head, slowly grinding as he puzzled out his next move. He was an admirable administrator, but French. Was he to be trusted? A fair price—the promise of a bishopric—had been paid for his support, but if he won this game, he might think there was more to be had. The greed of men, never satisfied with their lands, their wives, their holdings. Des Roches moved his pawn. Fool. John moved his rook, blocking the next move. A sea breeze eased the heat from time to time.

Across the mown field, hidden in the shade of the forest,

King Philip massed with his knights, straining to invent a plan of attack. John's encampment was surrounded by clear land, impossible to surprise, easy to defend. Hah! Was he not as good a tactician as his brother Richard? He could wait forever. *Relent Philip, go home.* John grinned and moved the knight, strengthening his position.

Behind the tents, his mercenaries shouted, staging mock battles, keeping their mettle. Good men, trustworthy, paid for by the barons' silver, scutage from dim and stubborn men with ambition beyond their simple manors or occasional fortress, men who complained bitterly about paying. Bah. Their silver would return the glory of the Angevin lands, a glory that accrued to them as well. He was a king, responsible for dozens of castles, and bound to manage and defend England, Aquitaine, Poitou, and eventually Angoulême. Only a ruler understood the workings and urgent needs of a vast empire.

John moved his queen, blocking any chance des Roches had of escape, though the lout had yet to recognize it. As he waited for him to see the trap, he mused on Isabelle. His treasure, coming today. How he'd greet her depended on many things, most of all her growth. Four months absent. He would get a son on her, but only if she was ripe. Currently God smiled on his projects; no need to force Him to anger. John would wait for her readiness and for Philip to give up. His mustache lifted as he moved his queen again. Checkmate.

With a jingle of bridles, William appeared, his back slightly slumped with age but riding easily; behind him rode Isabelle, alert, reins held high, hair bound in plaits beneath her wimple, for which John was glad. Better the others not see her beauty and be set to dreaming. Bah, they were hired fighters with nothing; he was king and deserved her.

BEHOLD THE BIRD IN FLIGHT

He wanted to rush to her, to smell the delicious place on her neck, to answer her endless questions, but in front of des Roches he held back, offering formal greetings, taking her hand, helping her dismount. Before he could ask about her journey, she began bubbling words. Her father had died. There was need for Masses. He, John, must pay. "Send silver to the monks at once." Her battering voice unbalanced him. Women always cared about these Godly details. They didn't understand that kings always went to heaven, as did counts. It might take a while, but they got there. Because, of course, they could pay. Richard was probably there now, cavorting with the angels, gloating at the country he had bankrupted.

John pushed the thought away and concentrated on his wife. "Of course, my treasure, I shall give what you ask." He eyed her body, hidden under a cloak. *Soon, soon.* "You had a comfortable journey?" Observing the courtesies owed a woman, he took her arm, pulling her slightly against him. Her outer delicacy hid a pillar of iron. "Come inside." He slid his hand under her cloak as they walked, assessing, cock springing to life.

William came to his side and whispered, "Sire . . ."

Would the man never leave him alone? "Go." John directed Isabelle into the tent. "You are tired. I shall send refreshment." Then a fierce whisper to William. "How know you she has not had her flux?"

William didn't flinch. "Maurelle."

"She is certain? She might lie. No, no, I pay her well." John slapped his chest. "Why am I surrounded by the untrustworthy?"

"Maurelle is loyal and she says no." William touched his king on the shoulder. "Be kind. Remember, your wife's father has died. She wept long in the night."

Growling, unready to face her sorrow and wishing for relief

159

from his desire, John called for ale and entered the tent. Isabelle had removed her cloak. Her fullness cheered him. He laid his hand on her wrist, trying not to think of other places he wanted to touch. "I regret the loss of your father. He was a fine man. A loyal man." He stroked her hand lightly and, hoping to avoid tears by replacing the death with a happier thought, said, "But now you are a countess in your own right."

She pulled her hand away. "You will keep your promise about the money?" Her voice wobbled. "I can't bear for him to be in purgatory."

He checked a flare of anger. He had acquiesced to her every demand; why did she not respond to him? "Yes, my treasure." Her red eyes and the blotches on her complexion shamed his lust. "I shall send enough for prayers in perpetuity." He wondered briefly how much that would cost.

Isabelle sobbed once, then gripped John's arm. He could feel her hand quivering. "Maman is now alone. May I not go to her?"

"Only when the danger from Philip is past." Travel meant a risk of kidnapping or worse. The thought of losing her killed his desire. "Until then, I fear for you." She leaned against him, crumpling into sobs; he held her close, like a father, soothing, giving her a bit of cloth to dry her eyes, offering more ale. He needed her laughter, her mad runs, her delight when he took her to the fair or gave her a bauble. She was his treasure.

Slowly Isabelle calmed and John was contemplating his next move when, with shouts and a crash of armor, an unkempt fellow burst into the tent and fell to his knees. William entered, sword drawn. The man raised his hand to stay the blade. "Please, I must speak to the king. I come from Mirebeau. From the king's mother."

John gestured William's hand down. The man staggered to his feet, brushing dirt from his knees, trying to cover the tear in

BEHOLD THE BIRD IN FLIGHT

his sleeve. Dried blood flecked his cheek; his beard was knotted. "Sire. Your mother suffers under a siege."

John stood. "Eleanor? By whom? I thought her in Fontevraud Abbey."

"It being vulnerable to attack, she left for Mirebeau where your nephew Arthur has pinned her for several weeks. Provisions are low and she is ill." The man was thin enough to prove the lack of food.

"How came you here?" William, suspicious, sword still drawn.

"Lowered at night to the river from a secret window. Chosen because I know how to swim. I have traveled for five days." He unfastened a pouch from his belt and offered it to John. "From your mother, the queen."

"Former queen. Your queen is here." John gestured toward Isabelle, then opened the pouch. It contained a small piece of vellum with his mother's seal. "No other word?"

"'Twas done in haste. She asks only that you come at once."

"Impossible." Damn mother. Ever against him until she had troubles. "I cannot leave. Philip will overrun Arques." Pacing, John flung his arm out, striking the side of the tent, which rippled and boomed.

"Sire, I can hold him." William sheathed his sword. "The lady requires you."

"I will not abandon the field." Time and again accused of leaving a battle. For once he'd not be a soft-sword. 'Twas Mother called him so. Also Lackland. Pushing him away for Richard. Laughing at his failures. He'd not rescue her; he had excuse enough.

"Sire." Isabelle crossed to him. "John," she whispered, "you must."

"I have said no." He turned away. She was not to meddle. He would decide this.

"Your mother gave you life. She needs you now." Isabelle flung back her hair. The blotches on her cheeks deepened.

"This is not for you." John sent the two men from the tent with a look. "Isabelle, I will not hear this."

"I have a mother." Her breath began to wheeze. "Like yours, who is in great need." Hands fluttering across her eyes, she burst into weeping. "John, you must. Go to your mother." She pushed him toward the opening in the tent, but he made himself into a rock. "Do not leave her alone." She began hitting his arms, his shoulders. "If not for her, do it for me." She flailed against him until he picked her up and forced her to sit on a chest. She cried loudly, swinging her head back and forth, slapping at the air. "Your mother. Alone. Save her."

John hated women who cried, who demanded. Isabelle's mother would be ashamed of her, so wild and angry, so unlike herself. He had been hasty in his marriage. He drank some ale, swallowing against the sound of her sobs. *Do it for me.* He had already done everything for her, without success. She was full of joy in her life, but not because of him. He wished her to turn to him, to pour herself out freely, not enticed by a bauble or a fair or a plum, but only by his very self. He paced the edge of the tent, shaking his head against the heat, against her cries. Bah.

He strode into the air and stood before the field from which the heron had risen, a decision surging in his gut. "Ale for the messenger." He shaded his eyes, squinting into the power of the sun, then whirled. "William, you shall hold ground here. Des Roches comes with me." A test of loyalty. He'd drive south with speed. With power. He thrilled at his prowess; the camp came to life with shouting and neighing horses.

He reentered the tent and knelt before his queen, taking her hand. "I acquiesce."

Isabelle was hiccupping. "You will do this?" She rubbed her eyes with the back of her hand. "You will stop Arthur?"

"Yes. I shall cut Arthur down and save Mother. When I return, you will be glad." *And wholly mine.* He ran his hand down the length of her back. "Stop crying, my treasure. I leave you safe with William." He stood, taking up his helmet, his sword. For her he would risk his men, his very self, and save Eleanor, who didn't deserve to be saved. But surely with this stroke, he'd win Isabelle's true love. He left the tent, shouting for his horse.

H E   W A S   G O N E . Despite the pressure of sorrow—a vision of her own maman, alone in the great hall—Isabelle's skin eased. The effort to resist John drained her; at every moment she must create armor around herself. When he returned from saving his maman, she would beg him to release her.

Slowly a realization seeped upon her: someone in France wanted her back, was fighting for her. Not Hugh, she had no hope of that, but if she could be in Angoulême, then maybe . . . Her hiccups lessened; a slight buoyancy rose in her chest.

Although it was hot, she donned her wimple. Pressure came not only from John; strange men, young boys, those who could only look, never touch, impinged on her, their desire for her body or inheritance pressed against her life. They cared not for her thoughts or feelings. John listened; he had taken her to the fair, to the new cathedral in Chartres, boating on the Thames. She wished she could swear eternal love to him, but no. Cold lived inside him, a winter of dark skies and frozen lakes. Perhaps his work as king demanded it—counting fiefs, raising armies, reviewing legal warrants and grants of land, settling disputes, levying fines, appointing bishops. He was always with the minister of the exchequer, surrounded by papers. She sighed for him and went outside.

The messenger sat on the ground, holding his ale, skinny, bedraggled, stricken. He must be hungry. Isabelle gathered up the chess pieces still on the table, took them into the tent, and came back with the plate John had ordered for her—chicken and a pile of cherries. "Come." She took the man's arm. "Sit and eat." She stood quietly by as he devoured the chicken and began on the cherries, spitting the seeds to the ground. When he finished, she sat in the second chair. "Tell me about Eleanor. I have not met her."

The man, realizing he was sitting beside the queen, stood abruptly, almost knocking over the trestle on which the table balanced. "She is an honorable lady."

"How does she look?"

The man fidgeted, scuffing his feet. He had holes in his shoes. "She is old, Madam. But her eyes be still fair. They can pierce a man . . ." He ducked his head.

Isabelle laughed. "I have heard so. Is she kind?"

"Ah, Madam Queen, I cannot say. I be working in the stable. 'Twas only I could crawl through the little window and swim that sent me here. 'Tis a burden to save the queen." He ducked again. "Former queen."

"Did you see knights around the castle?" Isabelle hoped there were few so John would return safely. If he were killed, what would happen to her? Papa was dead. How would she find a new husband? Could she and her mother alone hold the ancient land?

"I heard tell of more'n hundred. Arthur and the young Lusignan be the lead."

As if she had passed down a long corridor, snow blowing through the windows, July's heat turned bitter cold. "Lusignan is there?" When she said his name, her heart claimed him, her little witch forgotten.

"Yes, Madam, I did hear. Hugh the younger, much gossiped about. Him seen playing with the pages. A foolish labor. Siege is a grievous task."

Gripping her composure tightly, Isabelle thanked the messenger and walked into the field where recently the mercenaries had played. Dizzy, she thought to fall, but breathed deep, crossed herself, prayed. She had sent John to kill Hugh.

HUGH ROLLED FROM his pallet into the grass at the edge of the forest. The smell of pine drifted into the early cool; a gray sky awaited sun. By his side, a lump of resin he'd readied for a new game. He imagined cavorting and gleeful cries, Crispin's tousled hair. Satisfied, stretching, he fell back to sleep and dreamt he was inside a barrel rolling down a hill. Stones thrummed against the wood. *Thumpty thumpty.* He wanted to escape, but the barrel pinned him. *Thumpty thumpty.* Loud, frightening. He tried to cover his ears and woke, but the thumping followed him into wakefulness. Not a dream. From deep in the earth, the sound of galloping horses. He jumped to his feet and, grabbing his sword, screamed, "Attack, attack!" just as the first knights burst onto the field.

His men rose, staggering with sleep and fear, fumbling for weapons, tripping on their armor. As the attackers rushed the field, a lance caught Hugh squarely on his hip and he fell, arms shielding his head from pelting hooves. The field flailed with flashing swords, bodies, shouts, horses shrieking. From the castle, flights of arrows. The portcullis opened and fully armed knights streamed into the melee.

Hugh saw the pages, huddled, stumbling, crying, Crispin rubbing sleep from his eyes. Neville, wakened to nightmare. "Go to the river, run, run!" Shouting, he scrambled to his feet, blood streaming down his leg. Waving his arms, he limped toward the expendable boys, mouths to feed, unskilled. "NO!" He was too late. Two armored men cut the lads down. Pain came to life, rolling from his hip, up his ribs. He vomited, then fell, howling, in the grass.

Half an hour and it was over. Bodies and clothing scattered on the field, the trebuchet burning, such rebels as still lived gathered and securely tied, attackers arguing over the bounty of armor and horses. Hugh was dragged to his feet and shoved against Arthur; they staggered and fell.

High on a lathered horse, King John removed his helmet, a wide grin splitting his beard. "We came with fearsome speed, did we not? Two days. My brother had not done better." He poked Arthur with the tip of his sword and laughed. "Think you to be a king? You unprepared squidling." He loomed over Hugh lying in the bloody grass. "You wanted my wife. Like a true queen, she sent me here. You are not fit for a laundry maid." He commanded a soldier, "Bind his wound and secure them. In Chinon I shall decide their fate. The ghost of my father rejoices." He sheathed his sword. "And send word to William Marshal that the siege is lifted. Isabelle shall join me in Chinon."

Isabelle . . . Pain stopped Hugh's thought. He gasped into the bloody dirt and began to pray for the young lads. Just before he passed out, he heard the king shout, "You shall all die on this field if my mother has been harmed."

15

THY WOUND IS GRIEVOUS

When des Roches rode into the camp, calling for William, Maurelle was combing Isabelle's hair. Isi flung away, out of the tent. If John had been killed, her life could start over. For the sinful thought, God punished her with John's win. She gathered the loose hair in her fist and forced herself to nod as des Roches bragged of the thrilling success, of many rebels still living to be ransomed. How the field had bled red, horses and armor taken. How the old queen staggered out from the castle, thin and diminished, and John knelt to kiss her hand.

At last William asked what she dared not. "Arthur? Hugh?"

"Both alive. Grievously injured. Taken to Chinon where they will bring fine ransom."

Isabelle's heart! Hugh lived. When next she saw John, she'd ask for annulment. *Soon, let it be soon.* The month had turned to August; shortly she'd be fourteen. The wretched Maurelle predicted daily her first flux.

William, always solicitous, said, "Shall Isabelle return to England?"

Isabelle's fright turned to joy when des Roches said, "Nay, the king will have her in Chinon."

THE FIRST DAY on the road, Isabelle galloped until it seemed her bones would shatter. When William shouted for her to have pity on the horse, she slowed to a walk, but her spirits cantered on. She would see Hugh. She would be free. They could . . . She stopped her thoughts. She had broken her vow; Hugh would no longer want her.

On the second day, a rest at Château Gaillard. She hastened to find the stone bench set into an arrow slot. The sun was setting, purple shadows long and melancholy. She sat, rubbing her cheek against the rough stone. Her papa had seen this bench. Had kept his promise to build her one. She yearned to be in Angoulême, leaning against him, looking at this sunset. Perhaps Maman sat there now, weeping under this same sky. Isabelle wept herself.

William laid a gentle hand on her shoulder. "You must rest, Madame. We have yet two days' ride." He led her to her assembled bed; he didn't mention her tears.

On the fourth day, the arrival in Chinon slightly eased her pain. More beautiful than she remembered, its white walls stretched above a wide mirror of river, blunt ends of the towers blooming with flags. Here she had come with John after her marriage, and here he had given her immense lands. She had no need of them now, as he often reminded her. He would give her everything she wanted. Hadn't he once sent a keg of strong wine and a gold cup while he was away? Gifts of his love. With a pang of impending loss, Isabelle realized he might take back the pearl pin and the cup when he set her free.

The path leading to the castle jostled with villeins: women

carried baskets of eggs and pears, a young boy strained to move a dead cow in a cart, men swung handfuls of squawking chickens. Inside the gates, horses and men packed into every corner, right up to the edge of the ditch that separated the two parts of the bailey. She had forgotten the narrow bridge that crossed to the grounds in front of the Saint George Chapel. There were guards stationed on the bridge and on the walls, all focused toward the main keep where the rebels had been incarcerated. Like stacked barrels threatening to fall, the Chinon bailey was overcrowded and dangerous.

William escorted her to a bench inside the great hall. "Stay for a moment, Madame. I wish to speak to the king without the distraction your presence brings." He limped quickly to where John huddled with three men. Isabelle wondered why a man so old continued to serve. He had a wife, a home, and yet he was here. Men were like griffins, displaying their courage, trying to fly, often crashing. She strained to hear, hoping for word of Hugh.

William bowed. "Sire."

John roared with glee. "Two hundred captured! The entire rebellion quashed." He smacked his hand on the table. "But now I've to feed and house them." He gestured toward the bailey. "Ransom comes slowly. Messengers, bargaining."

"Perhaps all are not worth the trouble."

"I'll have land or silver from each, no matter how paltry. Daring to rise against me?" John tugged at his beard and grinned. "But wasn't I splendid? Isabelle knew I could do it. Where is she?" He rose.

"Stay a moment, Sire. What of the leaders?"

"There she is, my treasure."

He strode toward Isabelle, who braced.

"The leaders, Sire?" William limped beside him.

"Arthur is locked away. Young Lusignan sorely injured. I will gain a large sum for his ransom if he lives." Here he embraced Isabelle, holding her fast, which was fortunate. "If he lives" had turned her knees to water.

He spoke over her shoulder. "I trust no one to care for him. I am surrounded by spies, resolute enemies. How glad I am to have you here, William. And you." He nuzzled his stiff beard into Isabelle's neck. "If he dies, I will lose piles of sorely needed gold." He began kissing her hands.

"John." Isabelle, disciplined, didn't pull away. "Hugh is feverish?" She felt him harden. To loosen him, she rubbed her cheek against his.

"Ah, my treasure, ask not about him. You are here, *grâce à Dieu*."

"He needs care?" William, ever on the lookout. "If he dies, you will lose the ransom and deepen Lusignan's enmity. Perhaps Maurelle could serve . . ."

"She serves only my queen. I pay well for her loyalty." He pushed Isabelle away, holding her shoulders. "Look at my beauty. A woman in figure. Surely she's ready."

As John's eyes scraped up and down, Isabelle's mind filled, eddies and rapids. No flux yet. Would he believe her? Might Maurelle lie? Where was Hugh kept? Injured, without care. Close to death. Suddenly she understood what was required and her mind stilled. She smiled at her husband. "Allow me to oversee Lusignan's caretaker. I have learning in the care of wounds, and my presence would hinder messages and plotting."

"He was your betrothed." John's grip on her arms didn't ease.

She stilled herself more, relaxing her shoulders, her hips. "Long past. Did I not send you to capture them? Now the rebels are in your strong hands." She reached up to kiss his neck. "They must pay." Isabelle, voice firm, nodded toward her ring. "I am yours, my lord. Let me be of use to you." John's eyes narrowed, shifting across her face. No need to feign. She was loyal to him as king; she just didn't want to be married to him. She tilted her head and glittered her teeth in a perfect smile. "When he is well and you receive a fine ransom, I will ask only for a ruby and a length of amber silk."

John chuckled. "My little merchant, trading, dealing." He released her. "So it shall be."

William stared at Isabelle over John's shoulder. She prayed he would say nothing. When, after a breath, he raised his eyebrows, mouth firmly set, she knew she was safe.

THE VILLAGE SURGEON, Lacombe, waited for Isabelle at the ancient Saint George Chapel across the ravine in the older section of the fortress. William accompanied her at John's behest, his fears not completely assuaged. The guard bowed slightly and opened the door into a room lit by a narrow arched window. It smelled of vinegar, burnt flesh, old incense. Crude pictures painted on the walls showed Christ's passion, blood dripping from his feet and side as he looked down at a group of misshapen disciples mourning under the cross with Mary, her halo like a plate. The wooden altar was empty but for a cloth and a bronze candlestick left from long-ago Masses. Isabelle shuddered, remembering John's father had died here. Let it not be an omen.

Lacombe hurried ahead to where Hugh lay unconscious and uncovered on a bench concave from years of wear. His hip bore a desperate wound, the torn flesh surrounded by yellow pus and a dark burnt rim. "I cauterized him to stop the seepage of blood."

Lacombe touched the ashy skin. "We can only hope his humors are in balance and that he will heal."

Crumpled bloodstained cloths lay under the bench. Isabelle called the guard. "Please take these away." William stood aside, watching. She longed to embrace Hugh, but she lengthened her spine and held the aching under her ribs away from her words. "Lacombe, when were you last here?"

"'Tis two days now."

"No one has seen him since?"

"The guard brings food and ale."

Isabelle faced the altar and crossed herself. In her peripheral vision, Hugh's feet, white, narrow, toes slightly bent; she wanted to clasp them. She glanced at his hip, then away. "Why is his wound uncovered? 'Tis unsightly. If he awakes and sees it, he may think himself dying." She locked her face into a look she had learned in two long English years, older, more capable, never shown to John, but put on today for William. "The king has commanded he live." She took a moment to be certain her face was stable. "Has he a fever?" She glanced again at Hugh's feet.

Lacombe laid a hand on Hugh's belly; nicks on his fingers attested to his service as the village barber. "Yes, Madame."

Isabelle pinched her own wrist to keep from weeping. "Why has no one taken care?" Her voice quavered only slightly.

William walked to her side. "Madame, this is too much for you."

She held up her hand, palm out. "I can manage."

Lacombe clasped his hands. "I recommended a daily cleansing with vinegar to fight suppuration, and poultices of yarrow." The man started to take Isabelle's hand, but remembered who she was and knelt. "The king would allow neither me nor my woman to attend the prisoner."

BEHOLD THE BIRD IN FLIGHT

Lacombe's gesture reminded Isabelle of her power. "Your woman must come now. She shall ask for me and I'll bring her here." She turned again to the altar, wishing to pray, but the only words chiseled behind her eyes were *He must live.* She crossed herself again. "Have you coriander for his fever?"

"I can supply such." Lacombe hesitated, glancing at William. "Perhaps Our Lord is punishing him for rising up against the king."

Isabelle's witch reared up, but she held herself in check because this short spindly man had necessary potions and salves. "Bring me what is needed immediately. And cool water to bathe down his fever." When the door closed, she turned to William. "John will be wanting you in council. I will see that proper care is taken."

"Keep Lusignan alive." William leaned forward slightly. "Only that."

"I shall do my best." She needed him to leave; her face was slipping into perilous softness. "Do you think I would betray my husband?"

"Take care, Isabelle." William touched her arm. "We both know this is dangerous. The king trusts you as he trusts no one. If that is broken . . ."

"He need not fear." Frozen words to push him away. "I will do what is necessary, nothing more. By God's grace, I am Queen of England, *with the consent of the archbishops, counts, barons, clergy, and people of the whole realm.*" Such had been said at her coronation; usually it amused her, but today the words braced her queenliness. William understood, bowed, and slowly left the room.

Only after he was gone did she look into Hugh's face, his lips thin and clenched, his curls matted. Her chest crackled with sorrow. The fever's pallor lay beneath sunbrowned skin; goose-

173

flesh covered his arms, but his forehead burnt to the touch. Where were the coverlets? She wanted soft cotton, the warmth of fur, but there was only an embroidered linen cloth on the altar. Without hesitation, but asking God's understanding, she genuflected, slid the candlestick aside, and took the cloth to Hugh.

Before she covered him, she took in the whole of his body. But for the wound, his torso was the same smooth swath of skin, tight over muscle. The king's skin, like well-worn hosen, came to mind, but she pushed away all thoughts of John; here was only Hugh. His sharp ribs rose and fell; when had he last eaten? Fever should be fed, but along the wall wooden bowls with crusted gruel and a full mug of ale, untouched. She must bring him to consciousness. She whispered in his ear, "Hugh. Hugh. 'Tis Isi."

He remained unmoving. One of his arms had fallen, dangling almost to the floor. Carefully she took his clammy hand, wishing it alive and warm as when they'd danced. She stroked it into warmth, squeezing, pulling the fingers, willing him to waken. Failing, she placed it on his chest and covered him. Still the poultice hadn't come. She sat at the head of the bench and took a comb from her little bag to comb lice from his hair. He murmured slightly. His eyelids twitched. What did he see in his sleep?

Lacombe returned and set a small, evil-smelling wooden mug under the bench. She was swabbing the wound with vinegar when he said, "If he regains consciousness, give him the potion. You should . . ."

She didn't pause, dipping a fresh rag into water and placing it on Hugh's face. "I know to cool the fever."

Lacombe couldn't help himself. "When it warms, refresh it."

"Thank you for your advice." Isabelle pinned him with her eyes. "Send your woman tomorrow. What is her name?"

"Genevieve."

BEHOLD THE BIRD IN FLIGHT

Once he had gone, she knelt by the bench, checked the still-cool rag, and leaned her face onto Hugh's chest to pray. She pressed so hard that the embroidery left a trail of flowers on her cheek.

16

PERFECT LOVE
CASTETH OUT FEAR

he door closed and Hugh dragged the cloth off his face with shaky hands. *Isabelle. (Isabelle!!)* Perhaps a hallucination. When Lacombe had cauterized the wound, Hugh passed out; since then the very real comings and goings of the guard folded into strange dreams: a peregrine gnawing at his hip, swinging on a meat hook over a fire in Satan's kitchen. Fearing to be executed, he feigned unconsciousness; surely he'd not be tried for treason if he was senseless. But Isabelle said the king commanded him to live. Doubtless John wanted the pleasure of seeing him hung and kicking, more entertaining than a dead body in a cart.

He wrapped the linen cloth around his thin shoulders and dozed, Isabelle trailing through his dreams like the milk galaxy, full of light and far away, saying, "Here is your son."

He woke at her voice to an empty room and staggered to the wall to drink a little, swallowing repeatedly to keep it down. He dared not sit, unsure he could rise again. *He must live.* John's trick, his delight in games. On the road to Chinon after the attack,

John dismounted to walk alongside Hugh, who bounced on a sledge; he admired the summer day in a loud voice, then leaned in to whisper, "We can free you. Only say where Arthur is." Every jolt of the sledge sparkled pain through Hugh's body, but he thrilled to think Arthur had escaped. John then laughed at the cruel jest. Arthur, boastful and hapless, was also prisoner. Had he died?

Shuddering, Hugh lurched back to the bench to wait for Isabelle's return. His chest ached where her cheek had lain, but he must be careful; she had married his enemy. Had she not vanished to England, he would not care as he did now. New, this foolish longing. Isabelle walking under the trees, swishing her silken sleeves. He could hear the swishing. No, that was his own breath. He fell against the bench, head hot and whirling, a boar on a spit.

He'd say to the king, "You took my betrothed. I didn't love her then, but I do now." No, he'd not say the last. John would only taunt him. He teetered on the edge of the bench. Isabelle held out his son, alive, kicking tiny feet . . . To marry and have sons, denied by God and the king. A life filled with hunting, banquets, dancing . . . Isabelle whispering, "The music is fine." He toppled off the bench and, unable to rise, drank Lacombe's potion, struggling not to retch. Afterward he prayed—*Salve Me*—then reached into the dark, through horse hooves, sun winking through trees, the weight of Isabelle on his chest, until he found again the most important thought: he must live.

He woke, dreadfully thirsty, but he'd not call the guard for help; accidents happened at night; bodies hauled out in wheelbarrows at dawn. He dozed until daylight streaked the rough-edged stone and gilded Mary's halo. To her he prayed: *Please send Isabelle.*

ISABELLE FOUND HUGH on the floor. Genevieve placed a pallet of fine linen on the bench and Isabelle called the guard to lift him. "Take care. He's not a beast." She'd forgotten a coverlet and hesitated to ask the straggly-bearded guard for help—he seemed aged, unsteady—but she must. Ignoring her inner queen, she spoke as Isi. "Please, send to the laundress for a cover." The man bowed and left.

While Genevieve bathed Hugh's wound with vinegar, Isabelle stood before the altar, focused on the rim of Mary's halo and praying, strangely relieved. She poked at the feeling. Was it because God's grace kept Hugh alive? Because the guard had obeyed and Genevieve seemed so capable? Sudden understanding straightened her back: she'd not see John today. He had men to question, letters of ransom to write, messengers to send. She hardened at the thought of his touch, his smell as of old tapestry, his prying fingers. She must ask for release; she'd never be a good wife to him, God forgive her. An internal warning slithered across her skin. Perhaps she should speak to William first. The king trusted him and he would know the right words. And John did love her. His face softened when she brought him stories; to the barons he showed only his crisp edge. She had eloped for his courtesy and listening, the pin, the admiring eyes. In a chapel, she must tell the truth, even to herself. She peered at Mary's painting. *Help me know what to do.*

Outside the narrow window, gray clouds spread like mouse fur over the sun; the river shifted and flowed. She wished her life to be like the river, calm with currents unseen, joined to a man who knew and understood her. Courtly love lived. The heavy door scraped open, and the guard placed a coverlet on the end of the bench. "I thank you."

When Genevieve finished, Isabelle indicated the empty mug

and wooden bowls. "Take those away and ask the guard to bring fresh ale. Also chicken and a pottage."

Genevieve left, only to return. "He says the king has ordered only gruel." The guard stood in the doorway, nodding.

Isi wondered about the life of this bent guard. Completely unkempt, he certainly lived alone. She laid her hand on his arm, felt his slight palsy. Her mind circled the problem. If she sent Genevieve, she'd have time with Hugh. She needed to ensure the guard remained outside. This time her queen arose. "You need only to stand guard. Not to fear. The king has put me in charge." She inclined her chin toward Genevieve. "This woman will bring what I ask. If John wants Lusignan to live, he must have nourishment. Madame, go to the kitchens and say it is at the queen's request."

After they left, Isabelle waited several minutes before leaning over Hugh. Genevieve had half covered him, but his skin, wan from confinement and pain, still drew her. She knelt and placed her hands on his chest. In John's pelt she was lost, but touching Hugh's silky skin, she was mirrored. Clear. Unfettered. She was about to lay her head down when Hugh grasped her wrist and whispered, "Isabelle." She tumbled away from his weak grip, pried open the heavy door, and fled the room.

HE WAS TO die after all. She knew it and had ordered food. A last meal before hanging. Hugh pulled the coverlet over his face and, trembling, began his final prayers.

ISABELLE STOPPED OUTSIDE the door. The guard turned to her, astonished. "Is Madame in danger?"

179

"No." *Wits, fail me not.* She sneezed loudly.

"God keep your lady."

"I was afraid the noise would waken the prisoner. He needs sleep." Now what? She must wait for Genevieve but loitering here would seem odd. She turned to the guard. "Do you live in the village?"

"'Til the woman that was my wife died. Now I keep myself here. Guarding as you see."

He was very thin. "You should eat more. Do they not give you food?" Isabelle's heart, open to Hugh, also took in the guard. "You need strong ale. You look unwell."

"I thank you, Madame, but 'tis age. I feel well as old bones can. And I like my work."

"I'm sure you do good service." She had nothing more to say, so she bent and pretended to take a stone from her shoe. When she rose, Genevieve was crossing the bailey with a basket and a mug.

After the food had been placed on the bench, Isabelle said in a low voice, "You must leave. He still sleeps. I'll wait to see if he revives. If he does, I shall feed him."

"Yes, Madame." Genevieve hesitated. "Perhaps it would be better if you called me. I am accustomed to helping injured men."

Isabelle settled next to the basket. "I am sure your help is wanted for others. Leave this to me." She lifted a small platter of chicken from the basket. "Tomorrow you will be required to do the vinegar bath." Isabelle could feed Hugh, but she didn't trust herself to look at his wound.

Genevieve curtsied. The heavy door scraped open, Isabelle glimpsed the guard, then it swung slowly shut and she was alone with Hugh. "Are you awake?"

He turned on his side, head still under the cover. "I am to die, am I not?"

BEHOLD THE BIRD IN FLIGHT

"What? Of course not." She picked up the chicken. "Come. Eat. You need your strength." She tasted it: chicken pounded with almonds. Nourishing. "You shall be set free. We must only wait."

"For what?"

"For your father to pay the ransom, as he is sure to do." She gently pulled the cover away from his face. "Hugh . . ." She had no idea what to say, so she broke off a piece of chicken and fed him, then held his head for ale. When he could eat no more, she combed his hair—how pleasing his curls. She left, saying, "I shall return *demain*."

She gave the guard the remaining bits of chicken and an apple after he made fast the door.

HUGH'S NIGHT WAS long again, and the next day he pleaded with her to stay after he had eaten. "I feel better with you here."

She touched his cheek. "The fever is leaving."

When she took her hand away, he imagined its imprint, small and somehow golden. Dreading another day of silence, he said, "How find you the court in England?"

She crossed to the window. He looked for words that would entice her back and remembered her love of the rondelet. "Do they dance? Are there musicians?"

She turned, leaning on the wall in silhouette. For one awful moment he thought she was going to leave, then she said, "There is dancing every night. 'Tis a big court, filled with many fine ladies and barons. John . . ." When she hesitated, Hugh feared the name had stopped the words, but she continued. "Many musicians. Harp and recorder and lute. Have you heard a bladder pipe?"

He shook his head.

181

"'Tis much like a bagpipe but strange in shape." Isabelle shook her head slightly, as if awakened. "The sound is like this." She held her nose and began to sing, tentative at first, then stronger, swaying her hips and shoulders until she broke into giggles. "I could never dance when it was playing."

Hugh propped himself up on his elbow. "How strange."

"Once a villein played a rebec. The barons laughed at its uncouth sound and the ladies covered their ears. I felt sorry for the man and nudged John to give him some coins."

"You have a kind heart."

Isabelle swatted his words away. "Kindness is not prized at court. Men with their affairs care only for power. Women to dress well and gain gossip." She turned her back to him. "I only try to be happy."

Hugh saw how much she had learned, how bitter the learning was. "There are many ways of happiness." He, too, had learned and now understood his own way was to be with this woman. To have sons with her. To have more conversations like this one, perhaps while walking in a forest or sitting in front of a great fire.

Isabelle said, "They say prayer brings happiness. I find mine in talk and listening." She told him about Alain and his grave in the forest, about her rabbit.

He so wanted to tell her about the slain pages, about the turning of leaves against the sun, about his foolishness, but he was wounded, weak, and dared not. "Tell me more."

Isabelle came to take Hugh's hand, curling her thumb between his first and second finger. "This is how hands are clasped in the English dance. Strange, is it not?"

His skin sprang to life and he closed his eyes; blossoms swirled against the red.

Suddenly, Isabelle pulled away and walked around the room,

singing. Soon walking turned to dance. Wilder and wilder she twirled until she bumped into the altar and the candlestick crashed to the floor. As she bent to pick it up, the guard hobbled in, holding his sword. "Is Madame safe?"

Hugh pulled the coverlet over his head.

Isabelle hid the candlestick behind her skirt. "Completely. I thank you for your concern." She stared at the guard until he pulled the door closed.

Isabelle's dancing glee had infected him. "The way your braids swung. Like a willow tree in the wind." He let his thoughts pour out. "Graceful. Teasing. But you are strong inside. The trial. Speaking to those men. I thought you would burst into flame." He laughed out loud. "Isabelle of Angoulême, you are an entrancing bundle of . . . of . . . contradictions." He lay back on the pallet, exhausted from his outburst. And with weakness, reemerged fear. "Please say you can save me."

She knelt again. "You are going to live."

Hugh touched her neck. "The golden circlet." He traced the edges of her betrothal necklace, then wrapped an errant wisp of hair around his finger.

"I never take it off." She leaned closer and he pulled her down into a kiss. She tasted of almonds, her cheek like silk. He smoothed her neck, cradled her shoulder blade. He wanted her to stay forever, but she curled away and slowly stood, hands covering her face. "You shan't die," she whispered. "I promise." Then she was gone.

WHEN SHE LEFT the room, Isabelle was trembling. Hugh's kiss had opened a crack in the wall of her body. If she allowed it to widen, what would pour out? Words, surely. Feelings like butterflies or falcons. Stars. All she contained and had never known. Marielle was mistaken. The body didn't open. It broke into parts and flew away.

"Come, Madame. Sit." The guard indicated a stool. "You look right shaken. Need I punish the prisoner?"

Isabelle crammed down her newfound self. "I thank you, but no. I am well. The sun struck my eye of a sudden." She smiled at him, sorry that she had left the remnants of food behind. "I bid you good day." With a long breath, she sashayed across the grass, crossing the bridge and swinging her sleeves, but at the main bailey, she sobered. She must pose two questions to William: one about Hugh, the other about her marriage. It was urgent.

John had long barred her from daily council—men's work—so she waited outside the great hall until William appeared. "Sir, will you accompany me into the garden?" From his reluctance—he always made time for her—she understood his feet ached. "We shall only sit and enjoy the flowers. I have no need of exercise."

On a bench shaded by a pear tree, terror in her heart blocked the questions. She spoke of flowers, the fine amaryllis and clumps of bluebells. William crossed and uncrossed his legs, thoughts elsewhere; soon he would make excuses and leave. She must start. "When John receives ransom, the men will be set free, will they not?"

"That is usual." He looked at her for the first time. "Without their armor or horses. Those are forfeit to the king."

Hugh was safe. His father would send ransom. But every certainty had an exception. She probed. "And if ransom is not received?"

"John will decide man by man. He may marry a rebel's daughter to a loyal baron. He may force the man to serve at war or take away his fee farm. However, the leaders . . ."

BEHOLD THE BIRD IN FLIGHT

In William's pause lay danger. Her heart pressed blood against her throat. "You mean Arthur."

"Also Hugh. Philip must send a fine ransom for them, but even if he does, I have counseled John not to release them."

The scented flowers pressed against her voice. "Even though ransom is paid?"

"They are traitors who threaten John's holdings in France."

"But to be locked away from their fledgling lives." She couldn't speak Hugh's name lest she confirm his fate. "Arthur is so young."

"And has many years to gather discontented lords with which to harry John." William took her wrist. "While he lives, war will never stop."

She shook off his hand and stood. "Killing is a sin."

William sighed. "Perhaps there are special rules for kings." He shifted on the stone, then clasped his hands. "Isabelle, understand this. While Arthur lives, John will not have peace. England will not have peace. Many shall die in war. Think. A single man offered against dozens. And fistfuls of silver lost to fighting that would better serve elsewhere. No, Arthur should be tried as a traitor and executed. Hugh also."

Isabelle turned her face up to the tree. She tried and failed to hold back a tear. "This cannot be."

"Madame, men of power must fight to keep their power, whatever the cost. My own father offered me as hostage to an enemy when I was but six years old. My life was forfeit if the truce was broken. Father did not intend to honor the truce; he merely needed time to rearm his men."

"You are alive."

"The enemy was weak and I laughed when they put me in the trebuchet to be flung at the wall. I charmed them as only a child could. My father's enemy could not give the order. I lived and he paid for weakness with defeat."

A small path had opened. She could be engaging, distract John from this course. She nodded at William and stood.

"One moment, Madame."

She hesitated, her back to him.

"I know well your feelings for young Lusignan. They are natural. He was your betrothed. But you, yourself, chose John and are now queen because of that decision. Be glad and leave this alone."

If kings had special rules, so must queens. She locked her intent deep before speaking. "Thank you for your advice." Isabelle looked over her shoulder at him, her face absolutely calm. "I take it to heart." Gathering up her sleeves, she walked away.

JOHN SENT THE groveling Chambort away in disgust, a man without land, no wife, no daughters. Useless. Joining the rebels with nothing to lose, but much to gain, had the rebels prevailed. John growled, then remembered the ransoms Philip would be forced to pay, 40,000 *livres* for Hugh alone. Silver to buy loyalty from knights who no longer fought for honor, for England. Bah. He frowned at Chambort cringing out the door at the end of the hall. He would go and . . . speak against the king, stir discontent. John's mind stopped as if his horse had fallen from under him. Where was William? He needed advice. Men shifted and murmured in the hall; outside a tambour announced a messenger. His mind restarted with an idea, his own, excellent and cunning: release Chambort, offer him a bit of land, earn his gratitude. *He will then speak well of me to others in Poitou.* John shouted for the sheriff and arranged it, only keeping Chambort's horse and such armor as he had. One less mouth to feed. The great hall smelled of men, food, piss, and blood. Now that John had thought and acted like a king, he was inclined to ride, to hunt, but no, there were others to see. Silver to gain. A small respite, then. He called a servant. "I wish to see my queen."

Gnat-flecked sunshine slid through the high windows, but he moved to the shadows at the back of the hall so as to see her clearly when she entered. To the point, she would not see him. When Isabelle knew his eyes were on her, she smiled tirelessly. Tilted her head, asked endless questions, but when he wasn't there? Once he had come to their bed after a night with a forgotten countess or daughter to find Isabelle sleeping, her face scattered with moonlight. Long he stood, trying to divine her dreams, her thoughts, but the face remained cool and closed. Even her eyelids still.

He shifted deeper into shadow, pondering women. Their value, bearing children. But afterward? Always a difficulty. His brother Richard's wife still living, still demanding silver, servants, support. His first wife crouched in the castle to which he had sent her—he'd forgotten which one—sending messengers to trouble him. Heaven forfend the current Isabelle heard of queen's gold, a custom he had dropped. One mark for every hundred of silver that came into his treasury. Bah. What need had she of gold? He provided. Generously. He brushed a few crumbs from his tunic and smoothed his beard. She married by choice. She should be thankful he took so much trouble to get her.

Shortly Isabelle came into the hall, her long braids wrapped in silk, the hem of her skirt in motion but the curves of her body still. She hadn't seen him, of that John was sure, and yet she held herself like a chastened dog. Stiff, guarded. He stepped into the light, smiling, holding out his hand. "Come, I'll order us some honey balls."

"Nay, my lord. 'Tis too hot."

Her hand was cool. He pulled her close and felt her tension depart, as if willed away. Her calm face, meaningless; in her eyes, nothing. "How have you been keeping yourself?"

A slight tremor, a tender ripple on water. "I have done as you asked. Watched those who care for Lusignan."

Perhaps the injury disturbed her. Perhaps something else. With words like little knives, he carved away at her reserve. "How fares he?"

"Better, my lord."

"He'll live?"

"The girl says so."

"He was once your betrothed."

"'Twas long ago. I married you."

"No conspiracies? No hasty whispered messages?"

"None."

"You touch him? Feel his cheek for fever?"

"No, Sire."

He thought to see her bleeding, but she remained intact. Test her further. Best be sure. "If he is well as you say, I shall order you away." A movement in her waist under his hand, a slight clench, nothing more. Her eyes came to his and she glittered a smile; her loveliness made him hesitate, waiting for the clench to loosen. It did not.

"He is a dangerous traitor. His father will pay a large ransom for him."

Perhaps she hoped Hugh would be freed. Unthinkable. Finish this. "You are forbidden to go to him."

He placed his nose against hers, staring into her eyes. "And now, my treasure. What was it you requested?"

She twisted slightly and leaned back in his arm.

"A length of silk and a ruby ring." Her cheeks rounded with a smile.

"You shall have them." He felt no pleasure, but he pressed her breasts and forced himself to laugh. "And the other upon which I wait?"

"Not yet, my lord."

He stroked her silky waist. "Such a fine woman." Lust prompted him to take her to his bed, devil be damned, but as always came the crackling of fire at his back, the roar of hell promised to sinners. His hand dropped away. "You have vowed to tell me." Her body was completely still, alien.

"With pleasure, John."

The sound of his name relieved his anxiety. She was his wife, he treated her well, and soon he would lay her down and in his pleasure, make sons. "Go. I have more men to see." He pushed her away. As she walked through the sun, he saw a glimmer of curve and dance return to her body, and as if handed a messenger's parchment, he knew: He must look in on Lusignan.

IN THE COMFORT of Isabelle's presence, Hugh couldn't stop talking. She listened carefully, smiling, tilting her head. He told her what made him laugh and what made him sad, the sons he hoped for, the joy of riding in the forest, the color of the feathers on his peregrine, his hatred of peas.

"Peas?"

"When I was a lad, I escaped my mother and snuck away to sit with the apprentice cooks." His throat clotted at the inane story.

She slid her soft shoe under the pallet and wiggled her toes. "Don't stop."

"'Twas summer. I hid crouched among boys shelling baskets

of peas. Soon I was shelling and eating. How pleasing the pop when I bit into one. I ate until Mother found me and paid doubly for my gluttony with a sound beating and a massive gut-ache. I've never eaten another."

"My poor Hugh." She laughed and combed his curls with her fingers. "Are you thirsty?"

He nodded and Isabelle held the mug. He had strength to hold it himself but reveled in her arm around his shoulder. She was married, but the last Courtly Rule stated, *Nothing forbids one woman being loved by two men*. He bent up his knee so she wouldn't see his desire.

She set down the mug. "Tell me of something that scared you."

He'd not admit to fear, but she pulled him close, turning him inside out, and a truth rose. "The moon. I thought it the eye of God. When round, He was awake, then night by night it slowly closed, He slept, then slowly woke. That was God's time, long and forever, while my time ran on so fast." Her closeness made it difficult to talk. He swallowed. "I could do anything during the day when He wasn't looking."

She pulled away. "But the moon is sometimes visible during the day."

He stroked her wrist. "My teacher pointed that out. Such terrible things I'd done when I thought God wasn't looking. I was sure He would strike me dead." His hands slid into the softness inside her elbow.

"You were only a boy."

Her kindness. He put his forehead against hers, smelling pine and vinegar.

She blinked against him and said, "I love your tales. No one has ever told me so much about themselves."

"I feel we could talk together forever." A notch inside, a mark of knowing: she was not his old love but he loved her. He sighed and joyfully took her face in his hands.

IN THE KISS, Isabelle lost herself: the soft edge of his beard, his warm mouth, his taste of ale and cheese. He wreathed around her like a vine. Her body understood; her knees dropped open. His hand slid on her thigh, rippling her stomach. Behind her eyelids streaks of light. Doused in pleasure from his hands, his mouth, she thought not of what Marielle said, nor of what she expected. There were bells, shouting, a celebration, someone calling her name, "Isabelle, Isabelle . . ."

The heavy door heaved open. Isabelle shoved Hugh away and was on her feet by the bench when John strode in, the room a spinning top, twirling on its point. The ringing between Isabelle's legs continued, unseen. Thinking to stop it, she stooped to the jug of ale. The spinning top wobbled and fell.

"You were not to come here." John's voice iron, hand on his dagger.

"The girl was ill. I brought food." She poured ale into a mug.

John yanked away Hugh's blanket; he rolled to the floor, but John saw his manhood. His dagger glinted and stuck in the pallet. Then John was kicking Hugh and screaming, "She is mine!" *Thud. Thud.* The wound opened and bled red on the coverlet. John scrabbled for his knife. "I shall see that you never . . ."

"John." Isabelle's tone was sharp, cutting.

He broke off, panting. Hugh leaned on the bench, blood sluicing his thigh.

Isabelle walked toward John, her curves soft and moving. When she handed him the mug, her fingers lingered on his. "You are king. Don't demean yourself. He's naught but a silly boy with dreams of glory." Her calm came from two years' practice in England. She picked up the knife and the platter of uneaten pasties and left the room. Behind her, John's frenzy of kicking reverberated in her torso, but she forced herself to walk toward the guard's safety.

John strode after her, roaring back at Hugh. "You'll never be free. Not for all Philip's gold."

Isabelle was handing the platter to the guard when John knocked it away. "I feed you, dolt. Not the queen." She knelt to pick up the pieces. John jerked her to her feet, tearing her silk dress. "Never kneel in front of a guard. You are a queen. MY queen." He pushed the guard to his knees. "Pick that up."

Isabelle gathered up her skirt. "I require a new dress." She hesitated to cross the bridge, fearing John would push her into the chasm, but the guard cried out and she turned. John held him by his straggly beard, kicking and shouting. "The queen is no longer allowed into this room." She wanted to help the old man, but she had to save herself. She rushed across the bridge. John followed, tracking her as she wove among the horses and servants in the bailey, trying to escape. She was breathless and shaking, when he cried out for his horse, and she slowed, safe. For now.

Knowing he would ride for several hours did little to soothe Isabelle's witch, back many times over, cackling and flapping as if at a wolf. Slowly she walked, avoiding the eyes. She passed the room where John's bed lowered, all dark damask and ebony. She had yet to sleep in that bed, but soon. *Don't think about that.* First she must save Hugh. Her mind roamed. Came back to the bed. In its covers lay a path, one so terrible she cried out in denial. *No no no.* In her own room, she paced, searched for other means, and finally wept herself into acceptance. It would work. It must. She bathed her red eyes and called for Maurelle.

BEHOLD THE BIRD IN FLIGHT

"Oh, Madame, your dress."

"I fell while running."

"You oughtn't to run. Sir William says so."

"Be that as it may, I must change. A light linen shift, it is so hot. And take down my hair. I'm going to rest."

"Madame doesn't feel well?"

"I ache."

"Here?" Maurelle touched Isabelle's belly. "Perhaps it is the flux. I often ache before it arrives."

"Yes, yes. Is there a potion?"

"A woman in the village can provide such."

"When I am changed, you must go at once. On your return, set it before the door. I wish to sleep undisturbed. You may have your leisure until supper." Isabelle watched closely for a squint, a slight jerk. Maurelle said only, "Thank you, Madame."

Isabelle spun with inner panic until she spied her maid hurrying through the gate. Now, now, she would fix this; Hugh must not die. Clenched to calm, she put a light shawl over her hair and keeping her head down, went to the kitchen where the cooks stopped in astonishment. *The queen, the queen.* The usual smell of blood and fire.

As queen she spoke. "I have been stricken with hunger. I require honey balls and some of whatever meat is prepared. Put it in a basket." She would hold back death.

Food in hand, she blended with the crush in the main bailey, then hesitated at the chasm until a cart fell, sending dead goats across the stones. In the uproar, she swiftly crossed.

The old guard, head hanging, sat rubbing his leg.

Regretting she hadn't brought a potion for his pains, she knelt beside his stool. "I am come to ask pardon for the king. He's a kindly man, but when angry, he forgets himself."

The guard abruptly stood. "You aren't allowed here."

She prayed silently, fervently. "I've brought you food to replace that which was kicked away." Isabelle uncovered the basket. "You mustn't be left hungry."

He leaned toward the basket. "Them honey balls?"

Well chosen. "Yes." She moved the basket away from his trembling hand. "They are yours for a small boon."

The guard pulled back. "The king said . . ."

She spoke quickly. "He is riding. You yourself saw him leave. He shan't return soon." She took a breath. "I am asking."

The guard stood straighter, looking away. "You want time with the traitor." A sideways glance. "What for?"

"I shall ask him to swear allegiance to King John. To keep us all safe." Isabelle held the basket out. "Just a few moments." She let him take a honey ball, then dropped the basket on the ground. "Come, open the door." When he complied, she said, "Lock it after me and leave it so until I knock. I swear no one will come." Praying she was right, she slipped inside.

Hugh stood in front of the bench, naked and tense. When he saw her, his shoulders dropped. "Isabelle." Her name, whispered with wings.

"Why are you not in bed? Your wound." It oozed blood.

"You think me a coward?" He wobbled slightly, then straightened.

"No." Her eyes slid to his soft penis, nestled in brown curls. A coil between her hip bones began to loosen. "I know you to be a man."

"I thought they were come to kill me." He sat carefully on the bench. "I was to die standing up."

"You shall not die." Despite the bruises from John's kicks, the skin on his chest shone. His ribs, like a harp, called her hands.

"How not?" He moaned slightly. "You should not be here. He will kill you too."

"I am his queen." As he struggled to stand again, she saw his rage and fear and it ignited her own. Her hands began to shake. The plan must succeed, or they both would die.

"The king saw plain my desire. He will hang me."

"No." She stepped closer. She needed a moment without John looming over the room like the figure of Christ on the wall. "I'm going to show myself to you as in 'The Romance of the Rose.' Afterward, I will ask you to swear." Before he could speak, she slipped off her shoes, outer tunic, inner shift and stood plain before him. He sighed once, desire rising; his eyes pricked her skin and her body bloomed into radiance. She became the moon, an entire night sky. When she stepped closer, his hands took over from his eyes, his touch not wooden but shaped into every part of her: hair, shoulders, breasts, causing her coils to further loosen. When he pulled her onto the bench and licked her belly button, she giggled, but when he stroked between her legs, she mastered rising ardor and said, "No."

Shaken, she pushed him aside. "We cannot. I must remain virgin for the king." He pulled her back and kissed her, groaning softly, then walked to the window, leaving her sprawled on the pallet inside her own surprising skin. She closed her eyes, cherishing the feeling.

"What shall I swear?"

That we shall do this and more. She opened her eyes to a smear of blood on the white sheet.

She was going to perish. Hugh also.

No, no.

Only blood from Hugh's wound. Her breath returned.

"Will he come now? Was this just a kindness?"

Isabelle donned her shift, her wimple. "Did you not feel my love?"

Hugh turned from the window and nodded. Isabelle waited for him to come and kneel at her feet—the troubadours sang it so—but when he didn't, she touched the circlet on her neck. "I always wear this. We were betrothed." She put on her outer tunic. "But you didn't love me."

"It was only . . ." He pressed his forehead against the stone. "There were reasons I could not."

The slice of sun on the floor went dark and she wanted to ask what the impediment, but there was so little time and she feared his answer almost as much as the entrance of the guard. Perhaps he needed time for love to grow. Yes, this she could hold and believe. Still, she braced. "And now?"

He didn't kneel, but nodded firmly. She longed for a return to passion, but saw they had moved past that to another part of their lives. The nod would have to be enough. "You told me of your desire to have sons and live at Lusignan. I can give you sons." Her breath knotted and the words dissolved even as she tried to speak them. Finally she whispered, "Swear you will wait." She bowed her head. "Will marry only me." Her throbbing fingertips echoed her heart.

He swung his arm in dismay. "You are married."

She did not tell him of her desire to be released from John. That was now only a dream. Today, this hour, would have to be the softness in her life for what was to come. After tonight she'd be bound forever to John. Pulling on her shoes, she mumbled, "John is old and much at war. He won't live long."

"If he has his way, neither will I." Hugh leaned against the wall, the sun on his hair as the first time she saw him crossing the bailey in Angoulême.

BEHOLD THE BIRD IN FLIGHT

"I promise I can save you, but only if you swear." She shuddered, waiting for his answer.

He knelt. Her knight, her beloved. Her hands in his hair.

"Isabelle of Angoulême, I swear on God's honor that you shall be my wife if you help me to live." He laughed harshly. "If I don't live, my vow's of no use."

She pulled him to his feet. "Take care of your wound. Eat well. I shall send messages when I can." She kissed him and her body flared into life, but time ticked on, relentless. She knocked for the guard. John would be waiting.

THE HARP PLUNKED a tune while disorderly men fidgeted at tables, knives drawn in readiness for meat. The noise suited John. His own loyal men. Well paid, good fighters. And those captives, their ransom, with which to buy more loyalty. He took a draft of ale. Below the dais, a man stood, looking to the great door, waiting for Isabelle. As was he. *Disloyal errant wench.* The hair on the backs of his fingers rose. If he gave her the damned queen's gold, would she be his? Another long gulp. No, by God's Wounds, he'd have her freely or not at all.

"Sire, you are growling." William, seated on his right. "Shall I ask the servants to begin?"

"We wait for my queen." He clenched his teeth against the stone in his throat and reviewed the earlier scene in the chapel. She was fully dressed. The man cowered. She could not love such a one. She belonged to him alone. A successful warrior, a good hunter (three pheasants brought down and a stag this afternoon), and now England's finances eased by ransoms he had won. He drank again, then conjured the golden hair, which he had fully possessed, if not yet her body. He was her husband and her king.

She must love him. Why was she with that traitor? Bah, he'd sent her there, as William had reminded him. John settled his crown; ale smoothed his turmoil. As William also said, a satisfactory day in many parts. Philip withdrawn from Arques and sending fifty thousand *livres* ransom for Arthur. Thirty for Lusignan, but more to be had from his brute father. John drained his cup; the servant poured more.

Where was Isabelle? Should he beat her? Banish her? As always, many decisions to be made, hundreds of paths, and he alone, as king, to decide. What if he chose wrongly? No, impossible. God had anointed him. Given him power. Suddenly, the power of the young man in the chapel raged behind his eyes. He'd kill him for what he had seen, but Isabelle, his love? His queen. He'd send her away to some clammy heap of stones. Gilbert de Clare in Hertford, espoused to William's daughter, loyalty certain and he a cold, stingy churl. Let her appreciate what he gave her. He was about to command service of food when Isabelle entered.

Gradually, the great hall silenced. Only the harpist played on.

She walked slowly through the music, wearing an overdress of palest blue tucked into a golden girdle. Her underdress was pink, embroidered with golden thread, her hair loosely bound with silk ribbons, her sleeves like streamers of sky. But her clothes didn't command the silence. That walk! Curves moving like waves, sliding down her waist to her hips and up to her breasts. John stood and the men joined him with a great scraping of benches. When she reached the dais, she held out her hands. "My Lord. Please excuse my lateness." She spoke sweet and high, a lover's voice. "I heard of Philip's withdrawal. There is to be a celebration, is there not?"

He took her hands—the long fingers, white and scented with lavender—and lifted her up to the dais. So light. So beautiful. She

BEHOLD THE BIRD IN FLIGHT

sat and turned to him, the curve of her breast beckoning. Perhaps he'd not send her to Hertford. 'Twas too far. He'd secure her in London.

As they ate, Isabelle often leaned across John to speak to William. At first he reared back, avoiding contact, angry, but she seemed not to notice, chattering about horses and boatmen and gardens. He stopped flinching away. Sat like a stubborn bull—in control—until her scent of roses and something musky loosened him. Her hair brushed his hand, once drifted against his cheek. When the last course, fresh pears and cheese, appeared, she cut a pear and offered it to him. Holding her wrist, he tongued the pear from her fingers. Released, her hand floated down onto his thigh. "John."

He scarcely heard, concentrating on her touch, her fingers on his skin.

"You are truly a king tonight."

Tonight? Every day, every hour he carried his kingship. And she, who of all his subjects should be loyal, dared go against him. "Don't speak to me. You were . . ." His words were cut off by her fingers, by the roar of his lust.

"I have a gift for you." Her eyes glinted; she reached deep into him.

Why be angry? This was what he had wanted: she was coming to him. He had made no promises of jewels. He sunk down into pleasure. "What shall I receive?"

"I have gotten the thing you have long desired."

When he understood, a thrill shook him. Thank God. He finished the ale and crashed the mug down. Now. He wanted to throw her on the table, but no. She was a queen, not a laundress or even the daughter of an earl. "Let us go then. I will take my gift in private."

"First, my husband."

Joy to hear her call him that. Tonight he would be a true husband.

"First, a boon." When he nodded, she took his hand, placed it on her breast, and leaned across to William. "My husband is going to take me away."

William came to attention, eyebrows raised.

"But he wants you to know that when the ransom is come, Lusignan is to be freed."

The breast seemed new. Her body ready for him to possess. Her nipple, more exciting for being behind the silk. He would rip the dress from her when . . .

"Sire, is this so?"

John fumbled for her knees under the table. She was kissing his ear.

"Sire?"

What was it? No matter, he must get her away. "Yes, yes."

"Swear it, my husband." Her thigh pressed against his.

"I swear. Lusignan shall live." He picked her up and carried her out of the hall. She wept with excitement in his arms. *My treasure.* Tonight she was his to enjoy, and after she would be truly his wife.

PART FIVE

Escape and Capture

1205

17

THE FURNACE
OF AFFLICTION

As the court traveled through the English summer and into fall, Isabelle saw birds everywhere, omnipresent, like God. Flushed from fields with urgent cries or wheeling overhead. Flocks of starlings darkening the sky, buzzards raking their feather-tips into the day. Men with hawks, peregrines, and other falcons on their arms as they rode, as they walked into the great halls; birds and men alike preening, showing themselves strong, well-feathered, murderous, and capable of flight, seen and seeing.

Isabelle, too, had an omnipresent bird, carried secretly in the hollow under her rib cage, soft but with a beak that scored her heart when it turned its head toward France, toward Lusignan. The bird of longing.

JOHN WAITED IN the great hall of Marlborough Castle for the village petitioners, Isabelle beside him, her beauty marred by pinched shoulders, blue lips, and red nose. She was much diminished since he first took her to bed three years ago, and as yet no sons; he prayed she wasn't barren. "A fur for the queen." John's command voiced irritation as much as a desire to help.

Servants scurried away, slipping on the muddy stone floor; water oozed down the walls and dripped from the hole in the ceiling, sizzling into the central fire. Everywhere sneezing, coughing, smoke.

When the fur came, his wife disappeared into it like a child, thin and angular. *This bloody uninhabitable castle.* No wonder Richard gave it to him. A fine hunting forest to be sure, but in February? A pit of slime, mist, cold. Where were those damn petitioners? Bound to be underfed, groveling for a market charter. Bah. Let them come. A quick no. He must take Isabelle to a warmer room.

Next year he'd winter in London. Or Windsor. He sighed for those apartments, the great fireplaces. None of this damned draft, table hangings aflutter, mouths frozen tight, not a smile to be seen, although God knew John had nothing to smile about himself, what with that damnable lout King Philip with an eye on his crown, overrunning his Norman lands. Had Philip stayed in Paris where he belonged, he, John, would have dry hosen and clean shoes instead of this progress through the country, showing himself in his royalty, beneficent, but also living off the barons— that at least a boon—reminding his people he protected them so they'd pay their rents and scutage. By God's grace, 'twas not war's season. Come summer, with all that was due collected and in his coffers, he'd batter Philip back to Paris.

Isabelle broke out coughing. "Wine for the queen. Not some dregs." She had eaten little the past months and was too frail for winter travel, but he needed to show his treasure. She should

BEHOLD THE BIRD IN FLIGHT

understand the travails of which he spoke every night after doing his duty. Duty? 'Twas more pleasure, but he wouldn't think that word lest the damn abbots complain to the pope, another hot coal in his shoe, the not-so-innocent Innocent, claiming only he, the pope, was empowered to approve bishops. His stomach cramped. As long as he was king, he'd choose for bishop his own man. Take the gold he needed from those fat rich abbeys. Bah. But first a son. Then crush Philip, rebuild Château Gaillard, lately captured by Philip's men. John's mustache lifted as he thought of the French digging through the latrines for the final attack. Their stinking shit-covered torment was almost worth the loss of his brother's castle.

The petitioners arrived, a veritable rabble as expected. He listened to their petition for a market and although he had planned to say no, Isabelle laid her hand on his arm, so he promised to think on it and sent them away.

JOHN BRIDLED WHEN Isabelle did not appear at supper. Instead, Maurelle came, claiming, "My lady is unwell and has gone to bed."

"Is my son growing inside her?"

"No, my lord." Maurelle bobbed her head. "She has not bled for three months, but neither is she with child."

"God's bones. I have spilled enough seed in her to plant an entire field of sons." John drank long, a better wine than yesterday. "A new cask?" he asked William and signaled for more, drank again. His men drank also, the heat of their bodies adding a scant comfort to the damp hall. A musician crouched near the fire, warming his fingers as he played.

Maurelle remained in front of the dais. He glared. "Well?"

"The queen pleads for the petitioners. A twice-weekly market. Also a summer fair, eight days, such as is held in Winchester."

John had already decided to allow a market—let them sell and earn him money, for he would have a share of the proceeds. But a fair? "How came she to this request?"

"She walked into the village."

"Damnation! You allowed this? She must conserve her strength. Why did you not stop her?"

"You know yourself she cannot be stopped."

Verily. Among other transgressions, nay, say shows of spirit, she had hidden a litter's runt and fed the mewling pup until he, John, must command it be allowed to live. She refused to remove the golden circlet her mother had given her, even after he gave her a fine emerald on a heavy chain. Worst of all, her terrible insistence on watching the traitor Lusignan sent free two years ago. He had not yet forgotten the flare of joy in her face. With that thought, the wine turned sour. He gestured for ale and finished a long draft. "Tell me, what engendered this demand?"

"The cottars have no cloaks and the crofts are right poor."

"'Tis winter everywhere."

"But the people are half-starved. No pigs run the lanes. Each house a pile of wood, mud, and unhappiness. Mere babes beg for bread."

"And because of this walk, she is too worn to come to supper." John drank again. "Return and tell her if she but joins me in a dance wearing the rose-colored wool gown and her crown, I shall grant what she asks."

"Sire, perhaps," William said quietly.

"She is my wife and will do my bidding." John drained and slammed down his cup. The night's dancing would be joyless, mere exercise to move the blood before bed. Isabelle would lighten the mood.

BEHOLD THE BIRD IN FLIGHT

When the servant reached to refill the ale, William tried to stay him, but John grabbed the flask for himself. "'Tis comfort I need."

"Then go to your queen."

"My treasure." John filled and drained the cup. "Why have I no son?"

"She is too thin. Exhausted from our travels."

"She is their queen as I am king, and she, with all of England, will suffer if God in His glory goes against me and makes her impotent."

William winced at the impiety. "The child will come when God wills it."

"'Tis either a failure of the queen or of the Lord, not mine. I have engendered Fitzroys aplenty." John growled at William's horror. "He made me king and He has abandoned me."

"Perhaps, Sire, more fervent prayer . . ."

"Bah!" John tore a piece of the meat-stained trencher and threw it toward the fire. "Where was He when Philip overran Normandy? Did we not pay thirty nuns to beseech His help?" He pounded his fist on the table; bits of food flew. "Angoulême and Aquitaine cut off." His chalice tipped; dregs sluiced onto the cloth. "I shall punish Philip." He leaned slightly, then straightened. "Where is the mewling calf?"

"Your nephew Arthur?" William set down his cup. "Held at Rouen."

"Had I only listened months ago. Trial, hang the traitor, you said. Rid myself of that hair shirt, you said, then crow to Philip." John threw back his head, roaring. "With Arthur's death, Philip's path to my crown, crushed. Less dear than war." He leaned on William, breathing hotly into his face. "See it done." He signaled for more ale.

Now Isabelle came into the great hall, her cheeks white smoke against the rose of her dress, the long sleeves bunched on her arms, her hair tangled and dingy. But she held herself upright, her crown glinting. "I am come, Sire." She leaned slightly against the dais. "One dance, and then, in front of William, you shall keep your promise. You shall do good tonight."

WHEN THEY LEFT Marlborough, Isabelle rode with John at the head of the train: servants, men-at-arms, cooks, horses, carts, and such knights as were loyal. She had long hated carts but now wished for the comfort, the hiding, but John insisted she must be seen. They stopped at the ramshackle Ludgershall and at supper John claimed he would rebuild it. Isabelle, in a moment of despair, lost control. "This shall never be. Your wars eat up all the coin." He threw down his cup and stalked from the room.

After a cold, sodden night, they traveled on to Andover under a sky iced with clouds. At every meal, whether in a tent, abbey, or castle, John fumed about her failure to conceive and urged her to eat, ordering her favorites—eels, doves, honey balls—but the knot under her ribs impeded swallowing and even honey tasted bitter. Her mind lived in France, conjuring a frenzy of possibilities: Hugh had kept his vow. Had been forced by his father to marry. Had taken a mistress. Had fallen from his horse and died. With no letter or whispered message, Isabelle took comfort in her thinning body, as if sending bits of herself to Lusignan.

She bore another stone of worry: the lack of a son. At night when John tried to bring her enjoyment—'twas known a woman must take pleasure in coitus to conceive—Isabelle made an effort to convince her husband and God that it was so, sighing as in a troubadour's song, willing her legs to open wide to John's hairy body and clenched hands. When her flux, never monthly from the first, ceased altogether, she thought the thing accomplished, but Maurelle probed her belly and said no. Isabelle prayed special pleas to Mary. *Let me have a son.* But God was punishing her. He knew she longed to be released.

A messenger arrived: the pope had rejected John's man as archbishop of Canterbury. In the furor that followed, John decided to dash to Winchester and there plot a response with des Roches, Winchester's bishop. Isabelle he'd send to the Portchester castle. "Winchester is cold and you are ill. On the south coast, my treasure, the weather will be milder. You will eat fresh fish and regain your health."

William was to accompany her, which cheered Isabelle immensely; such a quiet, listening man who sometimes offered advice she could accept. Plus he'd kept secret her illicit afternoons in Chinon from the king and she trusted his friendship.

Their smaller company set across the land. Occasionally mists lifted and distant cathedral towers or local castles appeared. She dreaded entering unkempt villages where her miserable subjects shivered and starved. What use was the sight of their queen if her hands were empty? She asked William to send them her meat and fish. She wanted only the warmth of broth. Clear broth—bits of chicken or carrot made her gag.

At times, she rode leaning against her horse's neck for warmth. William noticed and provided a fur mantle. Eventually, they reached Portchester on England's little-inhabited edge and settled into a castle on which John had actually spent coin. The hall was warm and the arched window in Isabelle's chambers overlooked the sea. She could almost see France. Days were lengthening and she often rode, William beside her, talking of jousting and his children. His thin hair fluttered at the edge of his helmet and with iron eyes, he squinted against the sun and watched for danger. Once he mentioned the ache in his feet had moved up to his hip. Isabelle marveled at his steadfast courtesy and kindness.

One afternoon as they rode along the sea, she said, "Sir, I see you are tired. You are no longer young and have been heaped with honors. What need have you to continue?"

"Loyalty, Madame. 'Tis the ground of a knight's life. I shall love the king and be his servant until he no longer wants me. Even if sent away, I shall remain his man. So I have pledged."

"Ah." She nodded, then turned her head to the relief of the sea. Her own loyalties were questionable, but she had only pledged marriage, not lifelong service.

"Isabelle, I believe . . ." His hesitation alarmed her. "May I speak?"

Isabelle gripped the horse with her knees, slid deeper into the fur lest he say something frightening, and nodded.

"I see you fading away. The king has not yet noticed but he will. What then?" He shifted in his saddle, sword clicking. "You must stop this pining."

Only that? She lifted her head and stared at him. "Do you not pine yourself? Your wife and children in comfort at the great Pembroke Castle while you ride day after day with an aching hip?"

A slight shrug. "The king's need is first, Madame."

Isabelle hunched under the damp fur. Her body was evaporating, flecks of skin and eyelash, bits of bone and nail flowing away. She felt lighter, her head floating, elbows loose. When she turned her horse toward the water, droplets of mist pinged against her cheek, sharp as longing and as unending. She halted on the narrow swipe of sand. "Do you not smell France? 'Tis over there, just across that water."

"I smell only fish and sea."

"You have no imagination, William Marshal. Blossoms. Rivers."

"'Tis winter in France as well as England."

"Soon will come the bloom of March. Our French rivers, unlike the Thames, wear no ice at their edges." She was an English river, iced, moving sluggishly, soon to freeze over entirely. Hands quivering on the reins, she leaned as far as she dared toward France, reaching her face into the mist, blotting out William and England, straining to see. She could almost . . . She slipped from the saddle.

She opened her eyes to Maurelle shrieking somewhere among the guards. William knelt beside her, holding her hand. "I will persuade John you must go to your mother."

The sand shifted, shaping to her back. At William's words, her heart opened and words flew out. "And the other?"

William removed his hand and leaned close, his breath scraping her cheek. "He shall know you are in Angoulême. More I cannot do."

Curled into her hood, she prayed, then marked the sand with her fingertip in a pledge: she would remain loyal to John but love Hugh. God must understand.

18

LOVE YE ONE ANOTHER

he Angoulême castle was in disrepair, stones cracked and streaked from rain, but as William helped Isabelle from her horse, her heart hammered *home, home*. In the great hall, shafts of bleary March sun revealed a matted darkness under the fresh layer of rushes, stones around the central fire were broken, weapons on the walls unpolished. The privacy curtain that was pulled across the dais at night hung askew. Papa would never have allowed such dilapidation, but he was gone. Isabelle huddled into her mantle, her bones aching, while Maman removed her wimple and smoothed her hair, lifting her spirits slightly. A pitcher of ale and pasties stood on a little table. Maurelle began to serve, but Isi summoned her strength. "That won't be necessary. Go unpack."

William drank and ate; Isabelle merely crumbled a pasty as Maman chronicled Papa's unrelenting fever, how he sweated and shivered in their bed until Paulus, once Isi's tutor, ministered last rites and sent his soul to heaven. Isabelle crossed herself, arm heavy with the telling. "Why is the hall so quiet?"

"With your papa gone, many knights moved on. Paulus moved to the abbey. A castle misses its master." Maman hesitated. "As do I."

Isabelle took her mother's hand. She understood the grief but could do nothing. Women suffered alone. When she had rested, she'd see that the curtain was fixed and the weapons polished. She was not only queen but countess of this castle and would take it, and Maman, into her care.

William drained his ale and said farewell; his going pulled at Isabelle's heart. "Ah, stay and rest." His tired face and limp hurt her.

"I cannot. The king wishes my advice on replacing the archbishop." He donned his helmet. "Dangerous disputes loom."

"I shall miss you." Her body was hollow, held together by bony twigs.

"And I you, Madame." He lowered his voice against Maurelle's approach. "Remember, you must take care."

With William gone, Maman touched Isabelle's arm. "Welcome home, my little queen. You need sleep." She waved Maurelle away and helped Isi into the old bed, now piled with queenly fur. Isabelle huddled under the coverlets and relived all she had done: crossing the sea, seeing St. Bartholomew's Fair, dancing in court while men wondered at her beauty and ladies frowned, sending John to rescue his mother, rescuing Hugh. Slowly, Poulette emerged, fluffing happily, and she slept.

Hugh wafted through her dream.

Within a week, she'd recovered enough to walk. She cried on the new stone bench under an arrow loop, imagining Papa outside in the garden sitting just out of view. Alain's ghost haunted her: in the kitchen where he'd plucked chickens and thrown bloody feathers, at the well where they'd dropped marigolds, and above the moat where he dared her to throw a chalice. They'd both run away when it sank with a plunk. How he made her laugh. She never laughed like that anymore. She visited the apple orchard to lean against a tree. A weak sun skidded through bare tangled branches.

"You are thinking of your friend?" Maman touched her cheek.

The kind words almost brought tears. "I should like to visit his grave."

"Grave?" The ever-present Maurelle.

"An old friend," Isabelle said.

"Has my daughter not told you of her playmate?"

Every word would go to John. "Maurelle is my maid, Maman. We share no confidences."

"Then we shall wait to speak of this." Her mother turned to Maurelle. "You may leave us now."

"But the king . . ."

"Is not here. This is my daughter. I will attend her."

Maurelle reluctantly disappeared into the keep. Isabelle grinned at Maman, her conspirator. Free from England, from John, from the sniffing court ladies. How heavy life as a queen. She sauntered between the tree trunks, icy ground under her feet, blue sky and little clouds with frisky tails overhead. In freedom, her mind flew to Hugh. Surely he'd come, but if he didn't . . . She stumbled slightly and cold slipped into her shoes. She wrapped her arms around herself. *He will come.* He'd made a vow. He must.

At supper, Maurelle approached the dais, but Isi waved her away. Let her sit below with the scattered servants, even if she told stories. Ensconced in Papa's seat and warmed by her power, Isabelle drank ale, and although food repelled her, she ate small spoonfuls from dishes offered by servants. When honey balls came—Maman remembering her taste for them—she forced herself to eat two.

As the meal petered out, the few men bowed and left, leaving a small knot of ladies gossiping at the back. Cold rose from the stone and the hall was dim. No musicians, no dancing. A servant removed the table. Wind blew freely through the empty windows and roiled a threadbare wall hanging into life. The great cathedrals had colored-glass windows. Was only God to be warm? She flinched at her impiety, but Maman was shivering. "Can I change things here?"

"What would you change?"

"Order white glass for the windows to stop the draft and employ women to embroider heavy hangings for the hall. Can I do this?"

"You are Angoulême's countess, although it is not official until your husband has come and been recognized."

A flare of worry. If John came, her hopes to see Hugh were naught. "He is pressed by Pope Innocent and must remain in England for now. I need not ask his permission." Maman raised her eyebrows—obedience to your husband in all things, her rule—and Isabelle added, "I'd rather it be a surprise for his coming."

"This I can accept. You will pay with your money?"

"Maman." Isabelle slid her cup back and forth on the cloth. "The king gives me only what he sees fit." She sipped. "'Tis little."

Her mother stared, shoulders tense, lines on her face deepening. Then she turned away, saying softly, "I have some silver hidden in a chest."

"*Merci.*" Isabelle took her mother's hand. "I want to stay until the trees have tiny knobs. 'Till they bloom."

"Write to John and ask permission to stay until Easter."

"Until May Day, until summer, until the harvest. I am glad to be here." Behind her thoughts ran words: the longer her stay, the more time for Hugh to find her.

Maurelle, leaning below the dais, ostensibly to serve, said, "Until May Day?"

Maman froze her with a look. "We were speaking of the apple trees. None of your concern."

That night, when Maurelle placed her pallet at the end of Isabelle's bed where she had been sleeping, Isabelle said, "You may take that out into the great hall. My mother will serve me."

"But I . . ."

"Ah, 'tis too heavy. Ask a servant to help you move it." Maurelle hesitated until Isabelle's stare drove her away and Maman sat on the bed, saying, "Madame, shall I comb your hair?"

Isabelle tossed a little fur pillow at her. "Don't call me Madame. I'm your Isi."

"A queen."

"Not here. Behind this curtain I shall be your daughter. Only that."

Maman loosened Isabelle's plaits, combed her hair, and helped her undress. "You are not yet well." She nodded at the shadow of Isabelle's belly. "You ate little at supper."

"I have no appetite. It matters little."

"My daughter, if you don't eat you will never be with child. During starving years, when crops failed and bread was lacking, no new children were born in the village." She touched the edge of Isi's hip bone. "You must give the king a son. That is your duty."

Isi turned sharply away. "Duty? Why is there only duty? What about pleasure?"

"The Lord says no." Maman crossed her arms and rubbed her hands on her shoulders. "But sometimes . . ."

Sometimes. Isabelle never thought of Maman as a woman with a man, despite the years-ago thumping in this very bed. Could her mother, so full of rules and admonitions, have had real love? She ducked her head and fingered the coverlet. "Was it a pleasure for you with Papa?"

In the long silence, a horse neighed out in the bailey, a servant sneezed. Finally, Maman said, "We won't talk about it. You were conceived; that's enough."

A queen could ask what she pleased, but Maman had no need to answer. She wasn't an English woman joking about bedding barons or Marielle rhapsodizing about *his* touch taking her to heaven. And although Isabelle longed to tell Maman about John and Hugh, a queen's secrets were shared only with a priest. Tomorrow she would go into the cathedral and confess her sinful thoughts. "Come to bed. You are quivering like a jelly."

"Gladly." As Maman blew out the candle, she added, "If you have cold feet like your papa, keep them to yourself."

HUGH DIDN'T KNOW who sent the messenger, nor how Père had been avoided, but the message slid little knives into his gut. Isabelle was in Angoulême. Now he must go and confess the vow forsworn.

Two years earlier, he'd arrived home from Chinon to great recrimination—*asleep on the field, the enemy gathering you up like fallen noisettes, the cost, the cost.* Père harangued him for days, ranting about the wench who'd caused the whole disaster. Hugh dared not say Isabelle, not ransom, had bought his freedom. She was his secret.

Crumpling the message, Hugh walked in the bare woods, stamping on icy piles dense with leaves. If he found a way to Angoulême, what could he say to Isabelle? He turned the past year over like a coin, trying to make his words, if not soft, at least harmless. Perhaps her desire had waned. No, she'd be constant. Dreading her hurt, he settled on "The Lai of the Nightingale": "Two friends loved right tenderly, yet were they so private and careful in their loves that none perceived what was in their hearts." He would say them before he told Isabelle the truth.

Decision made, he asked Père for permission to search for Arthur, rumored to be imprisoned in Rouen. Père scoffed—another chance to be captured, Arthur probably dead—and turned his back. "I shall go then and join the Crusaders." His father couldn't forbid God's work.

Père walked away, then turned. "Perhaps Arthur yet lives. 'Twoud be a boon with Philip to save him." He admonished Hugh to go in disguise and return at the beginning of spring planting, two fortnights distant. He also gave him a purse of scant silver.

Hugh arrived in Angoulême on market day. With Lent approaching, fish sellers predominated alongside sellers of roots and herbs and a squealing pig so underfed it would serve only for soup. The town had grown. Wood palings replaced with stone, a few houses along the dirt paths enlarged; local merchants appeared prosperous, raising wooden stalls. The cathedral still lorded over all, more grand and better cared for than the old castle.

At the edge of town, he searched for the prostitute's hut; no one would look for him there. He found the house by a peregrine feather stuck in the doorframe. Inside, a woman on a stool fed a baby. A moment's sick joy, but no, the child was too young to be his. The woman turned, and yes, it was the girl, grown and no longer wearing the sign of a whore.

She covered her breast. "Go away. You will find what you are looking for elsewhere. This is a Godly house."

"Good day, Madame. I am searching for shelter and a pallet. I can pay." He regretted spending the coin but had no desire to sleep in the woods. After leaving Chinon, he had slept gladly on feathers, but now, for Isabelle, he would accept straw.

"'Twill cost more for the horse."

The deal was made. He wanted to rush to the castle but feared he'd be recognized by the servants and news would travel back to his father. He must watch for her in town. He had twenty-six days before he must return.

ISABELLE WAITED THROUGH warmer, longer days, the forest a pale green haze, the breeze fresh, Lent looming. Convinced God was punishing her by keeping Hugh away, she went daily to the cathedral to confess, wearing an old dress, hair tightly covered so as not to be discovered. After confession, she'd watch near the city gates, wander the sparse market or down narrow alleyways, followed by Maurelle who bemoaned the mud, her feet, the crowd. Despite her attempts at anonymity, often a whisper—*the queen*—would set off flurries of curtsies and bows until she was forced to return home. After a week, Hugh hadn't appeared.

HUGH FOUND ALAIN'S grave, searched the back lanes, crouched by a bush near the castle, but his desire failed to deliver Isabelle. Hoping his landlady would take a message to the castle, Hugh wrote on parchment—*I am at Alain's grave*—but the woman demanded more coins and his silver was much diminished. He folded the parchment, tucked it in his pouch, and continued to look and wait. Nineteen days remained.

Shortly before Lent's fasting ended, he went to the cathedral to pray. 'Twas a blustery day, wind batting clumps of cloud across the blue and his hat across the plaza. A man in dirty green hosen whom Hugh had seen almost daily returned the hat with a bow. "You are a stranger?"

"Yes." Exposed but unwilling to arouse suspicion with abruptness or mystery, he managed, "From Poitou. I thank you for rescuing my hat." He jammed it back on his head, turned, and came face-to-face with Isabelle.

As if God had appeared, all things stopped. Only the wind moved. Then life ground back: townspeople entered the cathedral, a dog ran, a nun flapped past with a group of children. Hugh said, "Good morning, Madame." He bowed deeply to hide his joy.

"S-s-sir."

Her stutter reflected his heart, but her face was calm. Did she not recognize him? "I am pleased to see you again."

"It has been too long." She inclined her head.

Hugh didn't dare offer his hand.

"You know this man?" Maurelle stepped between them.

"From Poitou, he said." The man in green hosen bowed again.

"No fear, Maurelle. A son of my father's friend."

Hugh nodded to the woman, evidently a servant. She was sharply made, her face dragged down by frowns. Evidently not from the castle of old; she didn't recognize him.

Isabelle said, "Maurelle, you may leave us. I have not seen Monsieur Le Brun since I left France. I will speak with him."

"I am not to leave you alone," Maurelle insisted, hands on hips. "The king has said so."

"The king isn't here. Go over there and wait."

Isabelle's regal voice struck at Hugh. How could he admit his broken vow? He fumbled in his pouch for the parchment. "'Tis not necessary for your woman to leave. I only wanted to offer greet-

BEHOLD THE BIRD IN FLIGHT

ings. Please give this message to your mother from my family."
Hugh bowed and walked away.

"You cannot go to the grave alone," said Maman.

"Of course not," said Maurelle.

"Your opinion is of no import," said Maman, not even turning
her head.

"But the king said."

"You may leave us." They were standing in the bailey by the
stables where Isabelle had found Maman and told her she was
going to visit Alain's grave.

"But Madame didn't give you the message."

"Go," said Isabelle. She waved Maurelle away with the parchment.

"Message?"

"We met someone in town." Glancing sideways, Isabelle saw
Maurelle inside the stable but lingering by the door. She lowered
her voice. "An old friend sent his greetings." Quaking slightly
inside but counting on her mother's usual focus, she offered the
parchment piece. "I don't remember his name, but he came often
when I was little; a boring puffed-up man with curly white hair.
He used to tease me by pulling my tunic."

"Don't try to distract me." Maman glanced at the paper and
frowned. "You shall behave as you have been taught. You are forbidden to go alone into the forest."

The rules clanged into place: stand straight, wash your hands
before meals, pray for salvation, keep good company. Isabelle
had had enough. She was seventeen. "Maman, I am the queen and
I command it." She stamped her foot on the stone, eyes averted.
"I am going alone. You will keep my maid with you." She said this

loudly so as to be heard. "She needs to learn to write. Paulus is gone, so find her a tutor." Her words fell like stones; she blinked. "Maurelle, tell the groom to bring my horse."

Having stunned her mother into silence, Isabelle turned away, hunching slightly against the look Maman surely aimed at her back. So be it. For once, she would do as she pleased. She suppressed a giggle at the thought, mounted, and cantered toward the woods. A large white bird sailed overhead and she leaned back, dizzying herself on its circles, its ease on the wind. She'd be like that. Open and powerful and stretched wide. God had lifted her to be queen and she thanked him. Behind her, the old castle; in front, her love.

Hugh knelt at the grave. Her heart poured joy over him; he had scarcely known Alain, but here he was, trying to save a soul from purgatory.

He didn't rise, deep in his prayer, and she knelt beside him, sinking into the spongy ground. All around, coins of sunshine dropped through half-open leaves, birdsong cartwheeled through the branches. She moved her arm to touch his tunic, felt the rise and fall of his breath. At any instant he would say "amen" and turn to her. She readied herself, trying to still the bright turmoil, fighting against her need to fall against him.

Suddenly Hugh stood, moved behind her, and placed a hand on her shoulder. She tried to rise, but he said quietly, "Stay."

Her power melted into the damp leaves. He, a man, would rule her. Her body bolted, denying him this power. "Hugh. I shall rise." She struggled to rise, but he pressed harder.

"I must speak and it will be easier if I don't see your face."

She quailed. Reached for her queen against the blow to come, the blow she had imagined through the many days of his absence. "I shall stand, but shan't face you." She ducked her shoulder away, lifted her long dress—now stained at the knees—and stepped toward the small cross marking the grave. She prayed the sacred place would protect her.

"I wanted to keep my vow. If it had been my choice alone . . ." His words dimmed to a whisper. "My father."

Royalty mustn't cry. Her horse nickered, and she longed to be astride, riding away, pretending she didn't love him.

"I never told Père. And he . . ." Hugh groaned, the sound killing the day's softness. "I am betrothed."

She willed her skin to armor, but she was already pierced. Bleeding. Last breaths.

"The girl brings a large demesne, cattle, forest land, rents, and scutage. My father chose her."

Desperate to see his eyes, she closed her own. Her body wavered as if to fall. She opened them to the barren woods. A thin sun.

"Clémence. She is called Clémence." He dropped again to his knees, a soft thud on the earth. "Forgive me. This was not my choice. You must understand. The land, the enlarging of Lusignan, my father's power. You remember."

In the long silence, Isabelle searched herself for her witch. Only a hollow. "And the marriage?" Strangling, her voice harsh.

"Once she is a woman. Father has signed the contract. But . . ."

Isabelle stopped breathing. There was more. Perhaps Clémence was from the Orient where Hugh's uncle was king. He would be sent away and she'd never see him again.

"Clémence is but three."

Sheets of relief. Nine years until womanhood. *Perhaps the girl will* . . . Isabelle inhaled, waiting for God to strike her dead. Children died daily—scrapes, ponds, hearth fire, sickness—but no one wished a soul to heaven. She covered her eyes, Marielle's baby on her heart. "May I turn?" She ached to see him.

He knelt still, his springy curls sprinkled with light. She put her cheek on his hair, absorbing him, his essence. He circled her ankles with his fingers, and she stretched her arms down his back as his hands slid up her legs. *Nine years, nine years*. They lay on her cloak and finished what had begun three years before in an abandoned chapel, but now they were in fresh air, blessed by clouds and wind and the calling of birds. How could this be sin?

MAURELLE LIFTED A rose wool dress from the trunk, saying, "Soon, Madame, it will be warm enough for silk." A bit of parchment slid to the stone floor. A message from Hugh? Something she had missed? Isabelle stepped on it before Maurelle turned.

"I do not think these shoes fitting for that dress. I shall wear the brown." Isabelle bent to remove the offending shoes and slid the parchment into her hand. She finished dressing and sent Maurelle for ale. "I have a headache this morning."

"Your flesh is increasing, Madame. Perhaps you will have your flux."

"I devoutly hope so." That was the truth. She had no way of knowing if she was with child or if her flux was still hindered for some other reason. And if with child, whose? She was so worried she almost forgot to read the note, which was in Latin: *video, scio, scribo, ibo*. I see, I know, I write, I go. Handwriting unknown. Paulus had made Isabelle write similar lessons when she was first learning. If Maurelle had written it, what was she up to? Isabelle dropped the parchment back into the trunk. She would keep watch.

Maurelle returned with ale; Isabelle drank and declared her

headache better. "I must go into town to check on the embroidery for the curtain." Maman's silver wasn't enough for glass windows, but Isabelle had ordered a new hanging, embroidered with the red-and-gold Angoulême coat of arms. Today she would ride to town, then to the grave, although she must hurry. She had sent for a troubadour. Tonight there would be dancing. If only Hugh could see her dance, hair plaited with silk, the low-cut dress displaying the circlet, her grace and litheness. But no, he could not. Only neighboring knights and Maman were to be charmed. She would dance to display her joyful spirits: moving through the music, remembering her afternoons, and when she laughed, no one would question her.

TEN DAYS WITH her love. Soon John would send for her and she must leave. Some nights she imagined the farewell, their last embrace, her tears, his pledges. But that was for later. Now, filled with Hugh's presence, she lay on his cloak and he pretended to pluck dappled light from her skin. When an egret flew overhead, they laughed at the blur of wings and trail of legs. She told Hugh about the star Papa had given her; he confessed anger at his father's demands. She fed him honey; he fed her kisses. Only once did they disagree: she mentioned Maman's strict rules, and he said they were for her own good. Isabelle pushed him away and began to dress; he understood her need to decide for herself and apologized. She relented. They limned the wonders of their lands, the forests, the mighty rivers, cathedrals, fields of grapes, places of peace and of celebration. And they swore that those lands should someday be joined. Four more days passed.

At night, in bed next to her mother, the *what-ifs* arose. Not those of a young girl, but those of a young woman who has made choices. *What if* she had not flirted with John? *What if* Hugh had loved her then as he did now or John had not given her the pin? She believed life occurred as God willed and she must accept it, but she began to distrust His decisions. Why would He make John love her? A punishment surely, but she'd been a virgin, sinless. Perhaps because He saw all, He punished her for the myriad sins she now committed.

When Hugh departed, she'd humble herself before God and obey the priest; love on earth was irresistible, but she mustn't risk her immortal soul, yet now, in the afternoons, she forgot her soul. Evenings, she counted sins to be confessed on her fingers. On her right hand, starting with the thumb: lies about her visits to the grave. Index finger: baskets of food requested from the kitchen to include dried apples, pork pasties, a salad of the first greens, and honey balls. The rest of the fingers on her right hand for a single sin because it was so heavy: coins stolen from the castle chapel to replenish Hugh's dwindling store. On her left hand were the embraces she had accepted. Encouraged. Enjoyed. The pile of sins accumulated onto her toes and still she couldn't stop. She went everywhere alone, turned her back on Maman, and shouted at Maurelle, sending her off to her studies with the tutor Maman had found.

The fields showed faint green, soft as baby hair, making her forget God's growing anger and the punishment He would enact. Pink orchard buds knotted along branches, horses neighed, men sang, baby goats frolicked. How alive the world. She shared her joy with Hugh and he replied with his own joy at small boys run-

BEHOLD THE BIRD IN FLIGHT

ning in the lanes or playing with sticks, how they brightened the evenings after she had gone.

Daily, together, they thanked God for what He had made—the little lads, the clouds, the dark earth and blue sky. Each other. Hugh was unable to say his father expected him in two days.

ISABELLE RODE FROM the grave through the orchard; bits of pale blossom drifted into her hair and tickled against her cheek. A halcyon day, Hugh had lain upon her, his curly hair on her neck, his hip bones against hers. Her body smiled like the sun. Laughing, she galloped through the castle gate into a chaos of knights on milling horses, shouting, servants running across the bailey.

Amidst the turmoil, Maman glared up at a large man. "State your demands." The knight urged his horse close; Maman didn't flinch. "Either dismount and greet me properly or begone."

"What is it, Maman?" Isabelle could scarcely hear for hooves and shouting. She leaned over.

Her mother said, "Sent from the king."

Oh yes, John's banner. A sharp pang clenched her legs and the horse responded, almost tossing her from the saddle.

The man dismounted, bulky in his hauberk, stiff from riding. He bowed slightly. "Martin Algais, the king's loyal servant." He crossed to Isabelle's horse. "Madame." Another thin bow.

Certainly a mercenary, loyalty gained through coins, unworthy. Isabelle forced herself smooth, gave a royal nod, and turned to leave. He grabbed her foot. "You, hussy, are wanted."

Her demeanor shattered and she kicked him away. "How dare you?"

"You are the one who must answer. The king knows you are unfaithful."

227

"He accuses me of this?" Her horse stamped under her shifting weight. "Let him look first to himself. He also spoke vows." Rage and fright loosened her tongue into danger.

"Isabelle, come here."

Maman's voice smacked Isabelle. Steadied by the blow, she dismounted, stared the knight aside, and stood by her mother.

"I won't have my child, your queen, defamed."

"She has been seen leaving the castle. Alone."

"She goes to the grave of her childhood friend and prays. He was but a kitchen boy; his family cannot pay for prayers."

Isabelle marveled at Maman's blank face; she bit her lip, rising words barely contained.

"'Tis an act of kindness she does, praying him from purgatory." Her mother crossed herself.

"This is not what we have read." The man widened his stance, solid, accusing.

"From whom have you received these words?"

"The queen's own lady."

The trunk, the flick of parchment. *I see, I know, I write.* Isabelle's jaw clenched. The slithering wench. How dare she? Contempt drove her words. "You come all this way because of a miserable servant who writes but little. I don't believe you." Isabelle stepped toward him, ignoring Maman's warning hand. He was lying. "You are here to kidnap me and gain a fine ransom. Had the king truly wanted me, he would have sent William Marshal."

Algais's eyebrow lifted. "The mareschal is no longer at court. He, too, proved treacherous."

The cords in Isabelle's neck tightened. Had William exposed her? No, Algais said the queen's own lady. Maurelle. Rage ran down her neck, twisting her throat.

"You have not heard." Algais smiled slightly, almost a sneer. "Angoulême is far. After the earl delivered you here, he traveled to Paris where he swore liege-homage to Philip."

A tiny breath. This Isabelle understood. "He holds lands in Normandy. Philip is lord there."

"The mareschal should have let them go." Algais adjusted the girdle upon which hung his sword.

Isabelle stared, slaying him with her eyes. Neither he nor Maman moved, held in anger's fist. Around them, men had dismounted, horses stamped and shifted, clouds flew overhead, a dog barked.

Algais broke first, reaching into his tunic, offering a parchment to Isabelle. Much creased and reeking of sweat, the king's seal intact. She handed it to her mother, not trusting her hands to be steady. Maman opened it, glanced quickly at Isabelle, then nodded. Isabelle must return.

"Our horses and my men require sustenance. We shall rest tonight. Prepare yourself, Madame. Before dawn tomorrow, we ride for England."

How to tell Hugh? He mustn't think she had abandoned him, but whom to send? A queen had no friends. A queen was only a woman, powerless. Isabelle lay in bed, suffocating in night's silent ink, the *hows* pressed on her chest. *How* to rid herself of Maurelle; *how* to abide the horror that was England; *how* to lie with John and not flinch away? But the *how* that expanded her heart until it hurt was how to leave Hugh.

Whispers from the great hall pattered on the new curtain that separated her from Maurelle and the others. They were talking about her. Her failures. Her pride brought low. Laughing, nudging, like the women in court. *They do not know me.* She squeezed her eyes against tears, clasped the only hand that could help—her own. She would go back to London and die. Her body was dissolving . . .

"Who is he?"

Maman's words tumbled into the darkness and Isabelle's breath stopped.

"Not a stable boy. You are too old for that."

Isi's body materialized: neck, shoulders, breasts. Maman lied for her today. Another *how*, urgent, flapping like a bat. How much to reveal?

"You have been reckless. Coming back from 'prayer' with glory on your face, a sway in your body, dancing at night for someone unseen. But I saw." Maman groped for Isabelle's shoulder, gripping it tight. "Now we are in great danger. If the king divorces you, we will lose Angoulême. As your husband, he is legally count. The land belongs to him." Maman pounded on the coverlet, speaking in fierce whispers. "I am a fool. I should never have allowed you into the forest. This land is ours. Your father's, grandfather's, back for generations. We shan't lose it because you fancy a stable boy."

Maman's anger forced out Isabelle's: "Hugh de Lusignan."

A long snort. "Once yours, thrown away for a pearl pin. With rubies, if I remember."

"Garnets." For fairs, jewels, a new dress. Many a night Isabelle had replayed scene after scene, wondering at the child she had been. "I was wrong."

Maman lay back down and sighed. "When will he be at the grave?"

Isabelle felt a child again, saved from a foolishness: dress mended, thorn plucked out, burn soothed. "After Nones." She

BEHOLD THE BIRD IN FLIGHT

half smiled into the dark. Her heart eased. He would know that she hadn't left him, that she loved him still. "Maman, tell him . . ."

"I shall tell him to forget you. That you are a queen." She found Isabelle's face and turned it toward herself, though nothing could be seen in the dark. "You must become that queen. I shan't allow you to bring about our downfall."

Isabelle wanted to bite her mother's restraining hand, to shake herself free, to leave the bed and run. Her whole life, clamped. She could do nothing.

Maman pinched her cheek sharply. "Swear it."

Isabelle swore, then began to sob.

"Hush, they will hear you in the hall." Maman stroked Isi's hair. "I gave you all those rules. Why did you not understand they were for the best?" The stroking paused. "Once I."

Two words, blazing like comets, then silence. Isabelle waited, but Maman didn't move. Blinking, Isi whispered, "Once you?"

Again silence. The great hall slept. Then, "I understand better than you'll ever believe. I once . . ."

Isabelle held her breath. This was Maman speaking to her as a woman. Not mother to daughter. She willed her to continue.

Maman took her hand away from Isabelle's hair. "My second husband, the Count of Joigny." Maman's voice like the breath of wings. "With him it was pleasure."

Through the window, damp, springy air. Isabelle ached along her neck and down into her ribs.

"He was forced to divorce me because . . . well, you need not hear that." Maman turned on her side, away from Isabelle. "I advise you to stay with the rules." The real Maman returned, commanding, strong. "If you have a daughter, teach them to her. Pleasure is not worth it. You don't want her to suffer as you will. As you do."

PART
SIX

Progeny and Losses

1207–1213

19

BE YE FRUITFUL
AND MULTIPLY

As she had sworn to Maman, Isabelle played wife on her return, working to captivate John anew, forcing herself to turn smiling to him when he came to her bed. She rode with him and joined him at ceremonies, but gossip, jewels, dancing, talk of courtly love were empty. Like a fish, she swam in queenship, glistening, drowning, only the thought of Hugh bringing her to the surface to break into sun for a moment and breathe, but then, realizing he would never be hers, she'd drown again. Her single care was to eat, forcing down meat, pasties, fish, game, acquiescing to the imperative of conceiving a child.

It took some months for safety to resume, for her to walk without a shadow in the garden; as the clamp of John's suspicion loosened, she felt the need for an ally. William, though banished, the only possibility. When she dared ask after him, John roared anger at his betrayal. She whispered shock. "So loyal a man. Surely much missed by the king." She poured John wine from her own cup. "Did not William's fame make John look the stronger, overlord to such a renowned knight?"

"He pledged to Philip." John drank the wine, nevertheless.

She poured again. The earl had not stayed in Paris but returned to England. He could be in John's court, fighting for him, watching the other barons who were less loyal. "I miss hearing you speak to him. Your strength. His loyalty." *My only friend.*

William was allowed to return, and shortly thereafter she conceived. Such joy, such feasting, John forbade her to ride, to run, offered the best pieces of meat, and gave her an enameled box containing a hair of Saint Peter to keep her from harm.

Of Hugh she heard only that he was to marry. She feigned gladness, took John's hand when he told her, said, "Ah, that is well for him and Lusignan. But it makes no difference to us." As she spoke, ice shards formed on her heart that even the kicking child couldn't dislodge.

When she was six months pregnant, John sent her from court to Winchester Castle. She suspected he was repulsed by her widening body, ungainly walk, the blotches on her complexion. She also suspected he wished to dally with other women, although he excused his absence saying, "I must stay in London. These damnable barons give me no peace. But I will come to you when you give me a son."

Avoiding Bishop des Roches who'd been given guardianship over her, she paced the rooms, stopping at windows to track autumn as the trees flamed and guttered, remembering afternoons under other, French, trees. She prayed not to die, an outcome she fully expected in payment for her sins.

Maurelle had also come to Winchester, laying out Isabelle's clothes, handing her the prayer book, lighting candles and the fire. The unrepentant wretch practiced writing on a wax tablet, even daring to ask Isabelle how to spell a word. When Isabelle paced past her maid's wide back, she imagined driving the stylus into her throat, laughing as the skulking hussy bled. A spray of leaves clattered warning on the window; she held her elbows and strode away, turning her thoughts across the river to the trees so as not to mark her child, a red stain on its brow or a twisted foot. Another sin to pray against.

Evidently God saw and approved Isabelle's requests. As she waited out the final weeks of her confinement, seven people from the castle died: a drunken knight tumbled into the pond at night, a villein's head was axed open, a child fell into the fire while its mother slept, a cut turned morbid, and three women perished from autumn fever, including Maurelle, for her perfidy.

In October, days after Maurelle's funeral, Isabelle sat on the birthing chair, squeezed the midwife's hands to white, and pushed out her son. "An easy birth," said the midwife. Isabelle, body rent and aching, wasn't so sure, but afterward, lying with little Henry, named for his grandfather, she marveled that this red-faced wrinkly creature would one day be king. She carefully adjusted the bands holding tight the swaddling and vowed to teach him trust, loyalty, and love, not only of England but also France.

John arrived the day after the birth—roads mired in mud, a horse gone lame, some business demanding his seal. Mud-splattered and reeking of garlic, he took up his son. Little Henry promptly howled, his head bobbing back until the wet nurse caught it. Isabelle's breath flung away, her child endangered. John was unable to nestle Henry against his chest because of an emerald on a long chain. Did he think to impress a baby? For years she'd cherished the memory of Hugh reaching for Marielle's dying baby, pressing it close, thinking her own child would have the same, but John made a sour face and handed the squalling baby to the nurse. "Lusty lungs." Isabelle reached for Henry, but John pushed the woman aside and sat on the bed. "My treasure. A son. I shall give him the world. A pony. He must learn to ride. When he is five, he will be sent here to the bishop for his education." John nuzzled her neck. "A prince. Someday a king." Isabelle's joy contracted; she would not be allowed to shape the soul God had sent into her care.

Soon John disappeared into the work of a king, and since the wet nurse cared for Henry, Isabelle was often alone. She had no personal lady. Servants, yes, many of them, but no woman seeing to her needs day and night. Surrounded by men, roughed by their loud voices, their swagger and swords, she longed for someone with whom she could share a secret. A French woman. She told her troubles to her confessor, but his only response was to say Hail Mary's, light a candle, and give to the poor. And William had returned from banishment circumspect. When she confronted him about her need for a woman, he said, "The king knows a man will be loyal. And if not, he knows how to punish him."

She barely held back her anger. Her husband paid the men for their loyalty and had access to their families in case of rebellion. His sins were daily bruited about in whatever castle the court inhabited. Isabelle avoided gossip, but what she heard assured her John would go to hell. She said her prayers daily, confessed often, hoping to go to heaven where she wouldn't have to see him again.

Two weeks after the birth and Henry with the wet nurse, Isabelle combed her hair, pulled on her rose-colored overdress, and appeared in council to ask John for a new lady. Hoping for news of Hugh, she requested Agatha. "A friend from my childhood."

"I cannot think about that now." John's eyes drifted from her face to the rafters. "The pope . . ." John took a long gulp of ale; those in council stood with bowed heads. "Pope Innocent has consecrated Stephen Langton as archbishop of Canterbury." His eyes snapped into focus and he slammed down his cup. "I shall not accede my earthly power to the pope. I have chosen a loyal Englishman, not a whore of Rome."

The castle chaplain and William began speaking at once.

"Silence!" His shout clattered against the walls. "I shall hear no more."

The men stood like rocks fallen around the cliff that was John's anger.

"Langton is banished. Write the paper and I shall seal it. Imprison the pious. Seize their silver, their plate, their lands. Every penny."

Isabelle wanted to ask for things she needed, but as she stepped forward, her husband knocked his cup to the floor; dregs of wine sluiced to her feet.

"Enemies press us on all sides."

In the dangerous silence—did John accuse only the pope?— Isabelle's body drifted, freed from carrying the baby, but her mind kept vigil on her husband.

John slashed his arm in the air and the sheriff brought forward the book of accounts. "Here." His finger stabbed a page. "Here we are short. And here." More stabbing. "Make them pay. If they do not, send them to prison. I shall rebuild Ludgershall into a proper hunting lodge and have the new hangings for the royal apartments. Langton, indeed. I don't trust the man."

You trust no one. Isabelle curtsied, unseen, and left the hall.

FIFTEEN MONTHS LATER, John rode again toward Winchester. The bishop had sent word that Isabelle would soon deliver. Snow fell in clumps from the trees. He pulled his fur tighter, urged on his mount, and beseeched God for a second son, sign of His favor. The bishop could baptize him; at least that remained. Seven months of the damned interdict. No sacraments, no place to bury the dead, no services, not that he missed the Latin droning. He did miss the bells, but 'twas a small price to pay. Let the pope rage; he'd not bow to him. His mustache lifted slightly remembering the land and silver plate confiscated from the fat abbots, but against that pleasure stood the Scottish warlords plotting with the barons. His mustache dropped. He must ride north as soon as the child was baptized.

He called to William. "The army for Scotland?"

"Gathering now. Some fine knights have joined."

"I have enough silver to pay them?"

"If you do not buy more jewels."

"Bah, I need the jewels. I have ordered a pearl diadem for my queen. We are rulers; we must appear so. Press the abbots of Winchester while we are there. They can scarce deny an extra portion in honor of my new heir."

There was shouting at the back of the cavalcade. "The pope's messenger."

What more could that old man of God inflict on him? On England? John accepted the message and broke the seal.

William urged his horse closer. "Sire? What news?"

Excommunicati. John held up his hand against William, against Innocent, against the whole damnable struggle. *Et iam non sis Rex.* He was no longer king. Deposed. As the sun glittered through the bare branches, the snort of horses, the clank and talk of knights seemed to fall into silence, and John shook his head to clear his ears but heard only the distant crash of trees giving up their snowy burden. Hunkered down in his saddle, he folded the parchment smaller and smaller. The barons' oaths of support absolved. Another load of snow fell, blanketing his shoulders. He envisioned French glee. The pope had given Philip permission to invade England and remove him from power.

William, solicitous, asked, "The news is bad?"

He'd always have William, but he'd not tell him now. They were going to celebrate a birth. If God allowed him a son, John would know He wished him to remain king, despite what his representative on earth said. "It is nothing. Another demand to accept Langton." He stuffed the parchment behind his girdle. His sword was in place, his mind working. He would not bow. "On to the queen. To my second son."

He named the child Richard, hoping to set the ghost of his brother to rest, then rode to Scotland.

HENRY WAS TWO and Richard a year old when Isabelle regained her place at court, dancing for John when he was in attendance and keeping away from the ladies who, she knew, still called her the French whore. With passing time and discipline, her longing for Hugh had thinned to a silken thread woven through the days of overseeing her two sons and the servants and keeping track of John, galloping around the kingdom in a fury, striving to subdue Scotland and Wales, and to bully the religious orders into denouncing Langton. She still had no personal lady.

ONE OF WILLIAM'S men handed her a letter. The parchment was fine; the unfamiliar seal, broken. No privacy; the queen must be protected. "I thank you," she said to the bearer. "From whom did you receive this?"

"The sender is unknown, Madame, although the messenger said you would be glad of the message."

She didn't bother to turn away, expecting the usual pledge of honor and respect. *My own heartily beloved Isabelle, I recommend myself to you with all the inwardness of my heart.*

Intimate address, as if to a commoner. *Beloved*, not queen. Who would dare write so? Understanding slid from her mind to her hands, and she turned slightly lest they shake. At the bottom was written: *By your sworn and faithful Hugh this day at Lusignan.*

She kept her face down but mastered her voice. "To whom am I to give answer?"

"I shall be pleased to help you, Madame."

The letter was filled with nothings; Hugh had a new dog, he had caught a fledgling peregrine and was training it, his father and mother asked to be remembered to her *right worshipful husband, the king*, and *I trust you will pray for me as I shall pray for you.* These were not the words Isabelle had longed for: *Clémence has died* or *I shall defy my father.* Something stronger, but the broken seal told of circumspection's need. Only the opening and the signature gave her hope.

Surely John would not live much longer—he had already more than forty years of God's grace. And then . . . She released the thought. Proclaimed it normal for any wife, married nine years. She had been good to John. Surely God allowed an occasional grievance. Although the interdiction prohibited confession, she'd learned to clear her own conscience, to forgive herself. It hadn't been as difficult as she expected.

"Come back on the morrow for my answer." She looked in on her daughter, Johanna, two months old and nestled with the wet nurse, unlocked the spice box for the cook, relocked it when the cinnamon and cloves had been measured out, and walked to the well for some air. Finally in her own apartment, an advantage of Windsor Castle, she took up her quill. Certain her letter would be read, she began with a plain greeting: *I recommend myself to you*. She wrote about castle festivities and hopes for John's quick return from Ireland, about little Henry and Richard; Hugh should know she could bring sons into the world. She closed as he had done—*by your faithful Isabelle, the queen*—"faithful" being unusual but not dangerous. She pressed her seal into the green wax, hoping that its image of her with loose hair would remind Hugh of who she was under the mantle of queenship. Of what he had possessed and what she prayed he would want to hold again.

20

THE WAGES OF SIN

*I*sabelle felt God's anger, waking at night with a gasp to peer through a narrow window to rain, incessant rain. Because of the pope's decree, bodies were buried in unconsecrated ground, mourners doubly stricken, their dead denied admittance to heaven. John had stripped churches of silver and gold; inside locked doors, statues peered into incense-tinged darkness while clergy fled like fleas from a drowning animal. England was unmoored, festering in its unconfessed sins. John, in his intransigence, frightened her, danger snapping like fishing lines, snagging men highborn or low bred. She avoided him where possible, ducking as they passed in some drafty passageway, cringing against the stones. At night when he came to her bed, he sweated tales of courts, taxes, writs and charters, cajoling, threatening, punishing. Swearing, no matter the cost, he would retake Normandy.

Isabelle tried to protect her sons from his anger. On the few sunny days, they played stick and ball or rode or cheered knights in their jousting games. When the English fog rolled in or the skies wept, they spun tops and learned chess. Her care was to keep them safe; they must live to rule, but she would also give them some young joy.

One morning, William Marshal found them playing in a great echoing room. Isabelle stopped suddenly and Richard collided with her, yelling, "Tag!" in his little voice.

"I must speak with you, Madame." He bowed. "Best send the boys away."

She captured Henry galloping past. "Enough. We shall ride. Go to the stables." Released, he ran, shouting the name of his pony.

"Come back and take your brother's hand."

"Maman!" He stomped reluctantly back. "Why must I always drag him with me?"

"You are to be king and must learn to lead. Go now."

When the boys were gone, William bowed again, a bad sign. He would address her not as a friend but as queen.

"Madame, in a week's time, Henry is to be sent to Winchester, to Bishop des Roches's care."

"No." She dropped to the floor, gown billowing around her. He wanted the queen; she would give him Isi.

William's face closed.

"My son will not be safe. The bishop is John's man entirely, yes, but weak, without imagination, easily brought down."

"Perhaps true." William, careful, correct. "But Henry is six and should have begun his training last year. At the time, the king feared for him because of the state of the country, but now we can wait no longer. Henry will be ruler and must be educated properly."

Her little boy, gone. No more running. No more summersaults in the grass. She stood, the better to fight. "Who will teach him kindness and respect? He'll learn only power, secrecy, domination." All traits his father had mastered.

"To do numbers. Read Latin."

"Surrounded by doltish barons with their lances and falcons, who know only war and hatred." She envisioned the long jaw and thin mouth of des Roches. "Better he learn French and be civilized." She turned her back, but not before William's face twisted slightly. He thought the French uncivilized, often speaking of wars Philip had caused, the many deaths, but then he'd say, "At least the French kept to the church." Not today. "I will request such lessons of the bishop if you please."

Isabelle did not please. She had long blocked knowledge that Henry, who rode without fear and played fiercely, reminding her of Alain, wasn't hers. Born to be snatched away into kinghood. She paced, flinging her arms. "How long before Richard is gone?" She should calm, but she continued to flail in protest.

"Another year, Madame. Take comfort in your daughter."

"Comfort?" She thought to throw something, but finding nothing, threw herself on a bench. "Johanna will be sold for the richest husband or the best alliance."

"True." William sighed and murmured. "The king needs alliances now."

His tone brought her to her feet. His knotted hands, a stance favoring his aching hip. "Come, sit." She drew him to the seat.

"Thank you, Madame. The ride from Ireland set my hip aflame."

He would never quit; loyalty forbade it. Lucky for John to have such a knight, but why had he no others? "I don't understand why the barons hate him so."

William lowered himself heavily. "'Tis because he never leaves."

BEHOLD THE BIRD IN FLIGHT

"Never leaves?" Isabelle's laugh was a bark. "He is always away, in Scotland, Ireland, at one abbey or another, begging, fighting, struggling to keep England intact. I never see him. The boys hardly know him." Her children would never gaze at a star with John. Kings required children but were not meant to be fathers.

"The barons see him overmuch; he looks into their affairs, their payment of taxes, of proper scutage. When Richard was king, he cared only for his Crusade, not the barons. Henry, before him, stayed mainly in Normandy or Aquitaine. But John, having lost those lands to Philip, must needs remain on our island."

"Or go to war." Isabelle began to pace again. "He tries to set the country right, does he not?"

"Perhaps. But in his vigor, he has crushed long held traditions. His need I understand, but not his methods. Imprisoning men without trial. Impounding property. The dungeons are full. You have heard of the noblewoman and her son, forgotten, left to starve."

Isabelle had heard and shuddered with the rest of the court. "You told me yourself kings must govern by special laws."

William was rubbing his knee. "Only if all, high and low, agree. Or acquiesce."

Even in her anger, Isabelle believed the barons could not doubt John's kingship. He'd been born to it, made so by God; no man could take that away.

William added, "I fear he will lose the throne if he cannot bring the barons to his side." He stretched the leg away from his aching hip. "England needs an upright king."

The queenship fell heavily onto her shoulders. *Lose the throne?* If so, what of her children? The boys were leaving, but

247

her love still tangled around them. Maybe not love—she couldn't afford love—but they had been put into her care and she must protect them. She crossed her arms. "Can you not help him?"

"I have already spoken too much." William rubbed again at the pain in his knee. "You, Madame, might make a difference."

She paced away. "More children?" Weak sunlight falling through the high windows made pale stripes on the floor. She stepped deliberately over them, a childish game.

"Not my meaning. He must accept Langton. When he does, the pope will support him and things will be easier." William struggled off the stool. "You surely have influence."

"Less, now he has two sons." No need to mention Johanna, only two; girls meant little. Still, William's words lay as anvils at her feet, heavy, demanding attention. She bowed to them. "I will try." Tonight she would pray long, but now the boys awaited her at the stables. As she walked, she wondered if Maman had felt this crumbling sorrow when Isi herself was sent away.

CLANDESTINE LETTERS TO and from Lusignan went back and forth, sometimes quickly, sometimes not. An official message from the king could travel from Winchester to Lusignan in a week. Isabelle's might take a month. Hugh's, more. At first, Isabelle sent hers off with yearning and hidden passion, but then the fire began to fade. Hugh would marry; Isabelle bear more children. God had allowed them a few brief weeks; that must suffice.

JOHN CAME TO Isabelle's bed. As usual, he lay beside her reciting his woes, the offending barons, the powerful pope, the Scottish threat, complaints she had heard many times. She braced herself for his arm across her breasts, his beard against her neck, the smell of garlic, his rough hands everywhere, but he fell silent, staring up at the heavy bracing rafters. Summer, no need for the bed hangings, the room eerily open. Isabelle closed her eyes. What was John doing? Thinking? He should have turned to her minutes ago. Was he missing the wild child in his bed spinning tales as at the beginning of their marriage? Only traces—hair, teeth, sometimes smile—remained of that girl. She was a wife, a mother.

John said in a low voice, "Why do you never come to me?"

Come to me? She was his whenever he chose. She kept silent, the better to force him to speak.

"You are ever compliant, like a wife." His back stiffened and he turned violently in the bed. She could feel, not see, his hooded eyes. "But not wholly mine." He leaned over her, hands pinning her to the bed. "Who is he?"

She swallowed against her speeding heart. "There is no one, John." In the dim light, the lines in his face were deep. She knew his beard held gray.

His grip tightened. "How can I believe you?"

He would not believe her, no matter what she said, because it was true: she never desired him, but then, as his fingers bruised her skin, she saw a way forward. Carefully, slowly, she said, "It is because." She took a breath. "Your hands hurt me."

His grip loosened. "You have never said that before." He lay down and lifted his arm into the air, turning his hand this way and that. His hairy fingers glistened.

Released, she spoke more easily. "How does one say such a thing to a king?"

"To a husband."

Another truth. She thought of him as the king, commanding

her, using her, but perhaps he thought of her merely as his wife. He had often whispered: "Behold, the king hath delight in thee." Perhaps he loved her.

She touched his cheek, his wiry beard. "Shall I show you?" When he nodded briefly, she took his hand and began stroking the palm. "Make it soft like a summer night." His fingers were tense and curled. She smoothed and gently flexed them. Once they loosened, she placed them on her breast. "Now, softly." She leaned in to kiss him as she held his hand against herself. She seldom noticed the heat of his skin. As he touched her, the accustomed hardness, a scraping mill rock, returned. She pulled away and again stroked his palm. "Like a trickle of river over grass." Her finger slid between each of his, then she again placed his hand on her breast, slid it down her belly, murmuring, "Soft, soft," and when his hand remained pliant, she left him to explore, tracing her neck, breasts, ribs, hip bones, until her knees fell open and she whispered, "Now," and pulled him on top of her. Her cries told him of her first pleasure in the marriage bed.

Afterward he was gleeful, shaking his hand overhead and speaking of how he would retake Normandy and give her Niort.

She nestled against him. "First, another boon."

"Ask."

He was sincere but still she hesitated, finally deciding to make it personal. "I long to go to confession."

"Only that? I will ask the bishop."

"He has not been my confessor these ten years."

"Your chaplain has been sent away, siding with Langton."

"Can you call him back?"

John rose naked and stalked across the room. "Even tonight cannot make me do what is necessary for that to happen."

A beginning. She would try again.

When John accepted Langton, the pope's choice, William Marshal received praise from the relieved barons for his influence. "But," he said privately to Isabelle, "'twas you who made the difference. The country will never thank you. I, however, give you full honor." He bowed over her hand.

She smiled. William need never know of the nights of persuasion. "Your thanks are enough." Privately she stored away the moment: by helping him, she could claim his help when her need came.

HUGH LEANED AGAINST the fence as the reeve accounted for Lusignan's livestock using his tally sticks. Strips of newly planted land stretched toward the woods, the sun was high, and the world smelled of earth, oxen dung, and rain. Upon parting from Isabelle, he had forsworn all thought of becoming a knight or a Crusader, content to manage the demesne and wait for her. Sometimes even pleased. Like today: the weather, the reeve's honesty, the increase in pigs and horses. Seventeen colts!

He next spoke with the bailiff of coming needs: carts, iron tires, axles, horseshoes. Père himself was preparing to go on Pope Innocent's Albigensian Crusade. Hugh smiled. Soon he'd have charge of everything and Madame, his mother, must defer to his decisions. He intended to add a shed for the dairy maids— the reeve said milking should be held away from the barn because straw quickly soured the milk. And he'd order fresh slate for the chapel to stop the chaplain's complaints of leaking rainwater, which despoiled the holy cloths.

He'd almost finished with the bailiff when his father strode into the room and flapped a parchment at the bailiff. "Go."

The man flinched and quickly fled. Hugh, who'd never spoken so abruptly to the man, clenched his jaw, braced for a tirade.

"Your betrothed, Clémence, is dead." Père crossed himself. "Taken by spring pestilence. We shall pay the chaplain for prayers."

Dead rang in Hugh like a tolling bell. *Dead, dead, dead.* He righted a fallen stool and sat. He'd never met her but had been told she was a pious girl with brown hair and gray eyes, a girl who attended Mass without fail and carried her breviary everywhere. Perhaps she had wanted to go to heaven rather than marry. He understood some women did.

"We must find you another bride before I leave for the south. God willing, I shall return, but you must be properly betrothed before I depart."

Isabelle began to trickle into Hugh's mind. Her élan, his vow. Her joy when she heard the news. Not for the death, she was finer than that, but for his freedom, the constraints of betrothal fallen. He would find a way to write immediately.

Père paused at the door. "I shall send to Thibaut, Comte de Blois." He stepped out, only to return. "Perhaps I shall go to King Philip. He recommends a match, I pay him a large sum, you have a wife, beget an heir, and our link to the Capetians is strengthened."

Hugh's long practice in managing his father wakened. "You wish to be beholden to a king so close at hand? He has swallowed up much already and his ambition stretches wide."

Père tossed away the message of Clémence's death. "Well spoken. Thibaut, then."

His father gone, Hugh sat on a chair, prayed briefly for Clémence, then devised a plan. He must see Isabelle. Reaffirm his vow. John was old, Père was leaving. Marriage could be postponed.

BEHOLD THE BIRD IN FLIGHT

He found Père in the stable, stroking the nose of a colt. "Sir, 'twere perhaps better to inquire of King John." Hugh trembled slightly at his daring.

His father pushed the animal away. "Are you of right mind? He is deposed."

"Even better." Hugh stepped close to the little horse. "A distant lord, weak and in no position to demand much silver." He pulled straw from the mane and waited.

"*Mon fils.*" Père's eyes glittered over the soft brown nose. "Well spoken."

ANOTHER SUMMER, THE distant fields full and waving with wheat, the lambs and ewes in the pasturage stark against the green, the river's scent flowing across sun-warmed banks. Isabelle stood with John at a window looking down at Johanna, now three, squealing and chasing a bird through the bailey.

"She is well-formed, our daughter." John took Isi's hand. "Full of spirit, almost wild. 'Tis her French blood."

Isabelle had not yet begun to teach Johanna the rules; she loved her daughter's natural state, as she had been sent from God: bubbly, pliant, smiling at everyone, patting a knight's armor to hear the clang, insisting on climbing the stairs herself, one small leg at a time. And now it was too late, because she was going to give her up. She sighed and leaned slightly toward John. Tucked behind her bejeweled belt was a letter from Hugh, carefully composed, betraying no special feeling but for the usual *heartily beloved*. The letter's contents had been echoed by the message, arrived this morning under the banner of Lusignan, requesting that John choose a wife for Hugh.

Isabelle no longer expected to have Hugh for herself—their

253

love had been long ago and forbidden. But she wished him married to someone who'd care for him as he deserved; if she recommended a court maiden, John would see her loyalty and approve. Late into the night, she'd sorted through baron's daughters, nieces, wards, even young widows and found none deserving. But this morning Johanna came running, "Maman, Maman," and as the child slammed into her knees, only discipline kept Isabelle from buckling. She lifted her daughter, stroked her hair—the child she loved most, the child she'd been allowed to keep only because she'd never rule—then sent her out to play in the bailey.

Grown, Johanna would be a pawn for her father's needs, that was her role, bargaining chip or path to alliance, but if she was to be a pawn, Isabelle would have a say. She considered her words as she stood with John looking down at Johanna playing, her cap fallen, her hair awry.

"Unruly daughters are all very well." John kissed Isabelle's hand. "But the Lord has blessed me with sons. Your failed suitor in France must be envious." He smiled down at her, then leaned against the wall. "*À propos*, today I received a message from the elder Lusignan asking for a maiden of high birth to marry his son. It seems the last choice has died." John laughed. "The man is unlucky in love." He nudged Isabelle. "I shall find a girl but shan't ask for a large fee, seeing as I robbed him of your company."

"Have you a maiden in mind?"

"None ill-formed enough."

"Perhaps . . ."

"One of the serving ladies. Not too highborn. Lusignan is Philip's man."

"I was thinking on that. His demesne is adjacent to our Angoulême. If you could bring him to your side, the two kingdoms

BEHOLD THE BIRD IN FLIGHT

joined would form a stronghold from which to win back Normandy."

John clapped his hands and rocked back on his heels. "Always my little plotter. You understand well." His laugh bounced off the stones. "So you . . ." He sobered and hooded his eyes. "Whom do you suggest?"

Isabelle dropped her chin and took a casual tone. "Johanna." Did his posture change? Stiffen? No, he was lounging against the wall, staring at her. She breathed into her words. "She is young. A long betrothal will give you time to win both father and son to your purpose."

"You would send her to Lusignan?"

Isabelle tilted her head and shrugged. Little cracks were opening along her sides, but she wouldn't mourn. This must be done. She lifted her chin.

John took her shoulders and moved her into the light. "You are sure?" He squinted into her face, his shoulders hunched, almost touching her.

Willing smoothness to her voice, she said, "Yes. I know Madame Lusignan. She will see that Johanna is properly raised both for her son and in honor of our trust."

John started to laugh. "What joy. He shall have not the mother, only the daughter." He let go of Isabelle's shoulders and strode down the hall. "The offspring of my loins." He flung his arm in the air. "I shall send for the Lusignans, père and fils, at once. Let them come and see how royalty lives."

Isabelle leaned out the window. Her sorrow at losing Johanna was overwhelmed by her pounding heart: Hugh was to come to England. She laughed into the dazzling day, but when she turned back to the shadowy room, she could scarcely see. Putting an arm over her face, she calmed. Hugh would come and she'd stand

255

beside her husband. She closed her eyes against the sun spots, the dancing light, the unacknowledged happiness. It shall remain as it should. She rested until her sight returned, smoothed her silk dress, gathered her mantle closer. She had sworn to be queen and would uphold that oath.

THE WEEK BEFORE the Lusignans arrived, Johanna ran everywhere, excited about her new overdress embroidered with daisies, and about the cart taking her to her new home. "Will there be a special flag?"

"Perhaps." Isabelle remembered her own wish for Angoulême pennants. If she had money of her own, even the rents from Niort, she could order as many banners as her daughter wished, but she had none and must ask John. He would certainly acquiesce when she said she was with child, a fact he hadn't yet noticed, being seldom of late in her bed. Praying briefly for a boy, she snared Johanna, who was running around the hall among the scatter of gossiping ladies, and beckoned the nursemaid. "Take her away. Let her run in the orchard. No," she called after them, "the stable. There's a new foal." The quiet seemed blessed until she realized soon it would always be so. She paced a little, nodded at the women, thanked God that she felt well, and turned her attention to details.

Using her mother's lessons, Isabelle ordered new feather beds for the guests, and because John had commanded a banquet in addition to hunting, new cloths for the tables. Now the silver salt cellars and plate must be polished, fresh reeds and marigolds brought and scattered, provisions acquired: mustard and capers for sauce, cheese for tarts, almonds for pudding, wine and eggs and mackerel. Three weeks earlier, suffering with morning sickness, she had avoided all thought of food, but now she talked equitably to the cook. Also with the bailiff, confirming there was hay and oats for extra horses. Nothing must be forgotten.

John had decreed the court would welcome the French guests at Corfe Castle. He'd spent a large sum fortifying it and lately added chambers where he and the ladies could live in comfort among seats, hangings, tables, shelves, and white window glass against the drafts; the men remained in the old keep. The newest addition, where the betrothal ceremony would be held, was a pavilion, richly built. Isabelle regretted the embroidered hanging with John's lion rampant lording it over the Lusignan emblem, but John would have the Lusignans in awe. She herself wanted to be seen as generous and kind.

During the day she could vanquish soft thoughts of Hugh through haste and industry, but at night she pondered how to receive not a letter but his living body. To face his curls while standing in the full pomp of court, John at her side. She decided she must release Hugh from his vow, a final break. As she envisioned the coming confrontation, a sharp fingernail ran between *the queen* and her inner self, the lining shredded but not falling away because even when John died, she would be a former queen, like John's mother, the old spider. She could use that power to direct lives, travel, enjoy her estates, even return to France. To go to Hugh's side would be unseemly. He must marry Johanna and be content.

IN MID-SEPTEMBER 1213, eighteen armored knights led by Lusignan Père and his son glittered their way across the misted valley from the sea to Corfe Castle. Isabelle stood on the castle walk holding the hand of the little fiancée-to-be. Below, the

Lusignan banner snapped; overhead terns circled, their cries not joyous but panicked. Like her breath. Her decision was firm—Hugh no longer held her in thrall—but when she considered the next three days, her bowels lurched. She swallowed over and over.

Because they'd watched the troupe's arrival, Isabelle came with Johanna late into the hall as the king bid the guests welcome. Never had the elder Lusignan bowed so deeply. Hugh, helmet in hand, paid quick homage, then scanned the room, eager to see his betrothed. Or so Isabelle hoped. She sent Johanna running to John but stayed in the shadow, studying both Hugh and her heart. Was this the man she'd longed for? The planes of his face seemed sharper, his cheeks wan, and there was a weariness in his stance, the same weariness that lived inside her. Would that the visit were over.

John pushed Johanna to the nursemaid. "Where is my queen?"

The newly glazed windows sent bands of sunlight shimmering onto the floor like rivers; Isabelle crossed, took John's hand, and the men bowed to her. Père's bald head caused an inner frisson of laughter, but Hugh's curls, matted with sweat, meant nothing, and she acknowledged him in safety.

John led the guests to a table set with refreshments; Isabelle noted with satisfaction the carefully laid cloth and the well-polished pitcher. Waving his hand casually to the stone seats set before the glazed windows, John said, "For comfort of the women." He turned, smiling, expansive, swept a flaunting arm at the elegant hangings, the cluster of carved chairs, and the massive fireplace, not necessary on the warm day.

Père smiled. "We have also made changes for the better at Lusignan. Rooms for the women, a space for my large inventory of bows, including those winch-driven, a true novelty."

BEHOLD THE BIRD IN FLIGHT

John nodded dismissively and led the guests through to the pavilion, which jutted toward the garden. There Père was silenced by the high ceiling cut by arches, finely painted walls, a herring-bone-patterned stone, carved trim, and in the window at the end of the hall: colored glass in the form of the Royal Lion. The nearby forest and hills crowded into the room through the many side windows. The group strolled and gathered in twos and threes to take in the view, John lording it over Père, William Marshal with Isabelle's sons, and at the furthest window the Bishop des Roches, brought from Winchester to say Mass. Isabelle was left next to Hugh. Neither spoke.

In a burst of laughter, princes Henry and Richard abandoned dignity and ran in a circle, mock sword-fighting.

"Your sons are well-formed," said Hugh.

She recognized longing; he had once looked at her as he now looked at her boys. Beyond the castle walls, the trees' green aged toward autumn rust. "John delights in them."

"I understand." Hugh stepped closer. "Once I too had; I only wish . . ."

The children's noise pounded away her sense, and suddenly the longing self she held inside emerged to Hugh's closeness. His faint smell of lemon. She forced herself to focus on his words. *I too had.* Delight in her? No, he was speaking of Henry and Richard. Perhaps he had—she stepped back slightly—sired a bastard with a harlot. Like a cork, the word stopped the genie of her other self; melting ceased, and she straightened, embodying the queen. "Sons are gifts from God, but must be reined in." William had broken up the mock fight, and the boys were walking meekly at his side.

"Fathers of sons are blessed." Now he turned his yearning to her. "I would also be so blessed."

259

His eyes. His hair. Her body inched toward his touch, but John clapped his hands and laughed at something Père said. Her queenship settled over her like a perfectly fitting dress, soothing in its richness, in its weight, and she was able to say calmly, "Johanna will bear you sons. She is of John's seed, sturdy and able."

Servants came into the pavilion, offering basins of water before supper, and Hugh walked away with a slight gesture of his shoulder. She followed the beauty of his back, his legs, his . . . No. A servant knelt before her, and she washed her hands. Her center had only wavered, as was to be expected in the first moments, but she had remained poised, broken nothing.

During the meal, Isabelle held serene, but underneath she imagined Hugh with another woman, fathering a child with a concubine. *I had, I wish.* Perhaps the woman had died. Or the child. The words were little knives sharpening her resolve to be distant.

At the betrothal ceremony, John affixed his royal seal to the charter giving Johanna to Hugh. Gifts were exchanged. Isabelle received hers without touching Hugh's hand. Afterward she walked among the knights, stroking here a sleeve, offering there a smile. At the mock tournament, she gave one smitten lad a scarf to carry as a token. She asked John to come to her bed. But Hugh was everywhere, smiling, capable, well-liked.

THE NEXT DAY, the marriage contract that confirmed John as Père's overlord was signed and he commanded both Lusignans to inventory the extent of his new holdings: manor houses, improvements, livestock. Henry and Richard were called to the table to learn about the new lands, theirs through their sister's marriage. Richard, the youngest, fidgeted, but Henry, almost six, asked about the cows and John's mustache lifted. A brilliant child, fit to rule. Plus the figures were vast; his dealings with the louts had brought him only increase.

Hugh rose, stretched, and asked permission to stroll in the garden with Isabelle. "'Twould be shameful to waste this beautiful day."

Reflexively John growled, but then took into account the wrinkles in Hugh's hosen, how his hair stood awry, and his lack of jewels. A powerless churl whose father treated him like a lackey, and who rode like a farmer, the first to be unseated in the tournament. John replayed the scene with delight, noting that Isabelle had neither gasped nor fluttered. Bah. Their connection was years ago. Nothing to fear. Thinking of his own nights with Isabelle, John loosened. "Of course, a walk in the garden. Have her show you the new bench. Cleverly carved. Dragons. Goats."

As Hugh and Isabelle were leaving, John remembered Chinon. Best send an obstacle. "Isabelle," John called after her, "take your youngest son. He needs air."

The bench John had recommended was in plain sight from the new windows. In a few minutes, he would call for wine, stroll across the room, and look down on them.

FOR TWO DAYS while riding, dancing, or walking, Isabelle had been Hugh's lodestar. Little pulleys urged him toward her, but he avoided entering her halo of beauty, afraid that his hand or his desire would rise of its own accord and show forth to all. During the festivities, he'd been invited to dance with various court ladies but never the queen, and he coveted the smiles and pleasantries she gave to others. She'd been merely courteous to him, as if she'd forgotten their afternoons under the trees, the flickering light, his hands on the arch of her waist, her body fitting to his.

Surely John's presence forced her silence. The first night, as John and his father drank, boasted, and played chess, Hugh stood at the stairs leading to Isabelle's chamber, prepared to risk all to remind her of their vows, but he hesitated. He would dare the consequences, but how could he force them on her? The next day, he saw a chance. Forcing ease over his ardor, he requested a walk in the garden. Delight at John's acquiescence soured slightly when they were joined by little Richard, but would a child notice a furtive touch, a murmured vow?

The garden had been specially prepared for guests: roses forced, orange lilies set against banks of lavender. The scent of potted gardenias—heavy, sweet, overpowering—exactly mimicked Hugh's longing. He glanced back; the pavilion overlooked the garden, but the king and Père sat at the far end, away from the windows. He touched Isabelle's hand. "I have wanted to speak to you."

"And I to you." She withdrew her hand. "Richard, your maman desires a sprig of lavender."

When the boy left, Hugh stepped close and noticed how her dress vibrated over her heart. She was frightened. He backed away slightly. "Shall we sit?"

"Let us wait for Richard." Her touch burned through his silk sleeve.

She looked again at the child, plundering the distant flowers, then said, "I must." She caught her breath and looked directly into his eyes. "I release you from your vow."

His body flamed in protest, but her eyes were unflinching.

"I have long been married to John, and although troubadours sing true love cannot exist between husband and wife, I am content." Her voice trembled only slightly.

BEHOLD THE BIRD IN FLIGHT

He tugged his hair into disarray, aghast. What could she mean? All the letters, desire, absence, for nothing?

Very softly, she said, "You shall have sons with Johanna."

Sorrow weakened his elbows, but anger wintered his voice. "Only God can know who shall have sons. He gives and takes." He clutched a rose, pricking his thumb to blood. "He is like a false lover." Hugh beheaded the flower. "He has given to me once and perhaps shall again."

"You had a son. So I understood." The wimple shaded her face. "Who was your harlot?"

Harlot? Fury, worse than love's suffering, lanced him; he threw down the rose, grinding it with his foot. "I had none." Red on the path.

"But."

He clapped his arm across his chest. "I swear to you." The dangerous red.

"We need not speak of it." Isabelle bent to Richard, returning with a small twig of lavender. "That is fine." She took the flower. "We need two yellow flowers to make a posy."

Why was she talking about flowers? Hugh paced the path, trying to master himself, goaded by her beautiful son, his glistening blond hair. "Where are they, Maman?" The lilting voice.

"Over there, see?" She pointed to a far corner of the garden.

Hugh backed into the rose bed to allow the child to pass, hose catching, leg torn. Softly, dangerously, he said, "I had no concubine. But yes, a son." He snatched and flung another rose. "He too was comely." His voice quivered and he pricked his hand deliberately as the past roared into his mind. The tiny face. Marielle's cries fading to silence. His helplessness.

"Does he bear the Lusignan name?"

She had drawn close her cloak; the wimple denied even a

view of the veins in her neck. "No." He plowed further into the bush, pulling the flowers, shredding them. "He died." His loss swirled around him as Isabelle looked out over the lavender. He wanted to grab her arm, to hurt her, but the long-ago French afternoon rose, new-leafed trees, fragile newborn skin. Terns carving the sky. The arrow shot and blood running from the birthing room. He shook his head. "You were there." In his confusion—which loss caused this pain?—he put his hand on her cheek, shifted her face to his, murmuring, "You were there. You saw him." Then he kissed her.

ISABELLE SCARCELY HEARD his words. Inside the kiss, her body cast off the queen, remembering dappled light. Hugh in the sunshine. Hugh, always Hugh. She dropped into passion, his fierce kiss, then when he began to hurt her with his strength, she pushed him away, crying, "Did you love her?"

Hugh clapped his hands to his head and roared to the sky, "You held my son when he died." He flung away, trampling a bed of lavender, running back toward the castle.

Scent rose around her; air lifted her curls, touched her cheek, then Richard called, "Maman, see what I picked for you." She smiled automatically while Hugh's words unspooled inside her head. *You held him. He died.* Suddenly, she knew. Marielle. Hugh had fathered her friend's child. She grabbed her son's small hand, flowers and all. "They are beautiful. Come, let's sit." She dragged him through the arch of heliotrope onto the new bench. She must control her feelings. She glanced up to the window of the pavilion.

John's distorted face hung behind the glass.

The force of his eyes shook her to her feet. Richard fell,

BEHOLD THE BIRD IN FLIGHT

crying out, high and thin. Fear sluiced her; John disappeared.

Grabbing her son—"Maman, let me down!"—she tried to run, wobbling against his kicks, hissing, "Quiet!" in his ear. When she burst into the bailey, Hugh lay on the ground and John was unbuckling his sword.

Isabelle threw Richard to his feet. "Bring Sir William. Run!" She gave him a rough push and ran toward her husband. "John, no!"

John threw down his sword, roaring. "Aaaagghhhh!" In a howling fury, he kicked Hugh again and again. "You besotted, crapulent churl!" Hugh covered his head; his tunic bloomed crimson under John's boot.

"Stop! He means nothing." She grabbed her husband's arm, but he hurled her away. She staggered, remained on her feet, picked up the sword, dragged it, sparking, across the stones. The metallic screech mimicked her anguish. John grabbed her wrist, fingers hardened into a vise. *Slam!* He threw her against the stone wall. Her hip splashed into pain. Face inches from hers, he grabbed her hair. She saw not John but an animal, wordless. Raging eyes.

She clenched her teeth. "Your child!" Her voice rose and scraped. "Don't hurt the child I carry!"

He focused, eyes slits. "Mine?"

His fingers bruised her arm, ripped at her scalp; stone ground into her bones. "Yours alone."

Across the bailey, Père leaned over his son. In a moment, he would stand and draw his sword, king or no king.

"How can I believe you?" His voice raw. The stink of ale and garlic.

"'Tis your son." She gasped and found the queen she needed. "Touch my belly. Yours, John, only yours."

Behind them, William shouted. As guards thundered down the wooden steps, she spoke into the vortex swirling around them. "Four months, maybe more."

He wrenched away the sword she still held. "I am going to kill him."

A melee of shouting and clashing swords. Isabelle cowered, spent and breathless until the guards hauled the two men apart and Hugh staggered to his feet, alive but bleeding. William stepped in front of John.

"Sire. Refrain." His clear voice sliced through the chaos.

John tensed, poised to strike, then suddenly dropped the sword. He took three swift steps, yanked Isabelle away from the wall, and threw her at Hugh. "Take her. And her daughter. I never want to see either of them again."

For the tiniest of moments, Isabelle was safe. Hugh's arms supporting her, his scent and warmth. Then a drop of blood fell on her dress and the child quickened for the first time. Perhaps a son, royal. As she was royal. She pushed herself away, not braving Hugh's eyes. "William, see that he is cared for." Hiccupping with sobs, she ran after John.

PART SEVEN

The Path of War
1214–1216

21

A Tempest Stealeth
Him Away

John shrieked in the pavilion. "Slut! Jezebel!" When Isabelle rushed in, he bellowed, "I'm going to kill you. And Lusignan." His crown, thrown, clattered into the corner, and Isabelle fled in a blur of silk. An eagle gnawed at his chest. He raced to the window—was his rival alive? Below, his younger children sobbed as his heir tried to comfort them. "Henry!" John yelled against the glass. "No softness. Kings must be hard. Iron fist." John swung his own arm, envisioning a baron on his knees, pleading. Mowbray and Fitzwalter! He'd bring them all to heel. But first—*first*—Isabelle. He ripped away his bloody cloak, the better to strangle her, and charged the door.

William blocked it, sword drawn. "Sire, hold."

John panted, purple-faced. "How dare . . ."

"Give thanks to God the boy lives. I have sent for the apothecary." A servant entered, carrying a tray. The scent of spiced wine mitigated the smell of blood.

John crashed around the room. His throat hurt. His chest. His gut.

"Sire, you must calm yourself. Rage blocks your thoughts."

"How could she?" John shoved his face against William's. "Did you know?" William, as always, impassive, the hooded eyes that saw everything but gave nothing away. Loyal. He must trust him. So few trustworthy left. He drained a cup of wine. Paced, growled, had another, slowed.

"The queen is with child." William's endless courtesy.

"Christ. Not mine." John tossed away the cup. "Lock her away, let her starve to death. I have done it before."

"Truly." William retrieved and refilled the cup.

Slowly, John let himself be convinced that a child born within the next months must be his, but he vowed if it was not, she would die like Arthur, alone, forgotten. A stone fell into his gut, her beauty wasted. His treasure.

William bowed slightly. "We must offer a falcon to Lusignan to ensure the betrothal."

"Give him my daughter?" John's mind grappled through the wine. "Never, never."

"Sire, when you win back your continental empire, the alliance will serve England."

"Am I to bear this insult? My wife, embraced. My queen! Death to him, to his father. To Philip Augustus. I shall annihilate them all." John threw back his head, ejecting words like hot stones. "Why have I a false harlot for wife?" He grabbed William by the throat. "Is she truly with child?"

His children ran past on the stairs, crying for their maman, and he allowed William to duck away.

"Her doctor swears it."

John took the offered drink. A bird's shadow floated across the window.

"Perhaps a boy. More sons, better for England."

270

BEHOLD THE BIRD IN FLIGHT

"A third son." Wine unclenched his fists. "Never a king."

"You are a third son." A horse neighed below.

"Fourth: Henry, Geoffrey, Richard, me." The soothing claret.

"Ah, I forget young Henry." William took wine himself. "Many sons are better. Safer. The queen has given you two. Why not four?" He suggested Isabelle be sent to St Briavels, one of John's hunting castles with recently rebuilt private living chambers. A small stronghold on the edge of the Forest of Dean near the Welsh border, where, at the moment, calm prevailed. Should danger arise, Chepstow Castle, one of William's own holdings, was a mere hour's ride. "In winter, St Briavels tends to drafts and smoke, but a surrounding moat and the deep forest assure the queen cannot leave, or more to the point, be reached by a lover."

John nodded, but the stone remained. "Send her by cart. The harlot might think to ride to freedom." He picked up his cloak. "I shall attend our guests. And William, tell her she lives by my grace alone. I shall be watching."

So John's daughter was sent to Lusignan with a small chest—let her new family provide—and Isabelle was vanquished. Still queen and so allowed her bed, jewels, trunks of clothes, and cutlery, but forced into a hated cart, accompanied by mercenary guards. Also a maid whom John trusted.

AFTER SIX LONG days, when Isabelle climbed from the cart, bruised and exhausted, she could smell the river. The forest master, thin and heavy-footed—"Good morrow, my lady"—offered no refreshments, only a meager bow. He didn't remove his hat. The walls clamped around her as he led the way to a stone room with no window where her bed had been assembled. At the foot, a pallet for the maid.

Less than twenty souls gathered behind St Briavel's massive walls, including the forest master who patrolled for poachers and meted out punishments, his family, and a few servants. For Isabelle, the silence after years of traveling with John and the full court was immense. Stillness pressed her thoughts into panic, so she walked the castle, trailed by the sour-faced maid. Water dripped on stone; occasionally a blackcap warbled on the curtain wall. No gossip, messengers, servants, or squires. Her body swayed under a heavy cloak as she read from her breviary and sought to understand the life God had given her. She prayed for John to become a kinder king, for Hugh to love Johanna, and when the unearthly quiet threatened her wits, she took to murmuring, "For everything there is a season." This was her time to be mute. She had danced, laughed, and wept enough for several lives.

From John, she heard nothing.

Cold, short days and constant rain. No messenger. Perhaps John's silence meant she was to be killed in secret like Arthur. As long as she carried his child, she would live, but afterward? John, drunk, was capable anything. The baby kicked savagely against her ribs; she bowed her head and accepted the pain.

On Christmas Day, faint trumpet calls rode the wind from Chepstow, meaning William was in residence; surely he would visit and bring John's forgiveness, a Christian beginning to the new year. He did not. The castle stone glistened, wet, and she walked incessantly, ignoring the dour maid. In the midst of the silence, a flock of geese arrived to settle along the river, and her ears awoke to the birds, calling, splashing.

One night she dreamed of Angoulême, the orchard bobbing with apples as she ran in and out of the trees, laughing, "I am a countess, I am a queen." When she tired, a light push on the ground swept her over the ethereal forest and the silver curve of river.

In February, because of her sins, she bore another girl. The sword over her head sharpened. She slept fitfully, alert to the baby's cries; she had no wet nurse. In early March, she woke to a young woman leaning over the cradle. Was she to steal the baby for John? She called out for the maid. No answer. Isabelle staggered from bed, still weak from the birth. "Who are you?" She snatched up her child. "Get out."

The woman curtsied. "I am sent from John to wait on you."

"What proof have you?" Rudely wakened, the baby was crying.

The woman pulled a small packet and a parchment with the king's seal from her pouch. With shaking hands, Isabelle read. "I command you to name the child Isabella." Her heart rose. She was forgiven. She unwrapped the gift: embroidered shoes, not the usual jewel. She was not.

"Allow me to serve you. I've brought a wet nurse. You need your rest."

Isabelle sat on the bed and let the woman take the baby. "What is your name and lineage?"

Cecily was the daughter of an important baron and looked much like Marielle, long dark hair and full hips. Isabelle liked her immediately. In the following days she found, now that her body was her own, her inner queen returned; she banished the sour maid to servants' quarters, wept through the baptism in the local church, and resumed her vigilance.

One night when the moon sent a sword of light through the arrow slit, Isabelle was wakened by Cecily weeping softly and steadily on the pallet. Perhaps she was one of John's conquests, used and discarded, unable to find a husband at court, sent into exile. Isabelle curdled with anger—why were kings allowed lovers but not queens? Why were women powerless? In any case, it was not yet time for the girl to mourn. When she married, she would, but first she must learn to be strong.

She nudged Cecily. "Put on your cloak." On the castle walk, she pointed at three stars hovering in the immense sparkle of sky. "The middle star is yours. I give it to you." She put her arm around the shivering girl. "My papa gave me a star years ago. If I felt sad or unsafe, I was to talk to it. The star sent my thoughts and words straight to God." Thinking Cecily would want to pray alone, she added, "I'll leave you now."

"Please stay." The girl leaned close, so Isabelle remained, brooding. Above, unseen angels lived in perfection with God, of that she was sure. Below, men and women—she, John, William, Cecily—could only pray. Strive to accept fate. She pondered the heavens until the girl sighed. Afterward, they both fell quietly asleep.

WILLIAM CAME AT last to St Briavels, bringing two young men to serve the queen.

"I have no need." Unknown men carried John's threat.

"The king is particularly concerned for your safety while he is in France."

Had he spoken in kindness or while drunk? "When did John sail?"

"On Candlemas."

Wind whistled through the hall, but her heart lifted. Candlemas, before Isabella's birth. The sword she feared lowered; he'd not stayed away because of anger. "He will win back the Angevin lands?"

"God willing." William crossed himself.

"Why are you not at his side?" William hobbled, but he still rode, and pain had never kept him from John's need.

"I have pledged to two liege lords, Philip Augustus for my lands across the water and your husband. The knight's code does not allow me to fight with one against the other." William leaned toward the fire. "We will prevail. He attacks from the south to draw Philip. Emperor Otto will hit from the north. Our plans were long in the making and in finding adequate coin."

John, ever at war. The death, the burning, all for power. "And Johanna?" A memory of flowers crushed in a small fist battered her.

"She is sent to Lusignan to ensure their neutrality, if not support."

Her beautiful child, safe. Also Hugh. Her heart remembered his scent, his kisses, but no, he was forever lost. Why had God arranged it so? Maman said Isabelle must trust Him, but it was so difficult. She swallowed. "William, how am I to feed these new men? We are not the king; we cannot press the local lords for our needs. The cook asks for eggs and spices; we require oats to feed the young men's horses."

William blinked several times and turned away. "They have no horses."

No horses? How could that be? Even second and third barons' sons were given a horse and basic armor before being sent into the world. Before she could ask, William said, "I will see to your needs," and crossed to the fire. His shadow flickered across the floor and she dared but one request. "Take away the maid. You may tell John, one less mouth to feed." William nodded, then called the forest master and the cook into council.

At supper—William gone without a meal—she realized the new men were no more than boys, old enough to squire but not

275

to be knights. Why had John sent them? To spy? To steal her child? She slammed down her knife, startling the forest master who sat to her left. Lips tight, rage contained, she smiled at him and beckoned a young man to her table. "Who is your father?"

"Fitzwalter." A beard lay thin on his face.

"You have brothers?"

"Two sisters only, Madame."

She nodded dismissal. A first son, inheritor of title and estate. Why was he here? The sword rose, clanking.

Later, as Cecily brushed her hair before sleep, Isabelle said, "Sir William brought well-formed young men. Pleasant company. We should arrange some dancing." She stretched her legs for Cecily to remove her hosen. "Odd their coming. We have guards enough. Perhaps they are simply for your pleasure." A tear dropped onto her foot.

It seemed they were hostages, sons of barons who objected to John's wars and taxes and meddling with their estates, barons who refused to march to John's war. Cecily's grandfather and an uncle had been buried in unhallowed ground because of the pope's interdiction. "When the king asked for more scutage to fight on the Continent, Father lost his temper and struck the messenger."

The girl's father was a courageous fool and lucky to live. Isabelle crossed herself against memories of John shrieking against God, jerking his horse's head, shattering an ancient statue at Winchester.

Cecily crossed herself in turn. "What, Madame, will become of my grandfather's soul?"

Isabelle brushed a tear from the girl's cheek; she had no answer. They knelt together to pray, but for Isabelle, the holy words were buried by a question. What of her own soul? As

BEHOLD THE BIRD IN FLIGHT

John's wife, was she culpable? She was powerless to stop him. She also could not confess to the priest without revealing the depths of his distrust, anger, and savagery, sins that were his alone to expiate. With a tremor, she said a *Salve Me* and slid into bed. "Please leave the candle burning." Tonight she would not sleep in the dark.

Deep in the night, realization startled her awake: The young people had been seized and sent as a test of her loyalty. She would hold them hostage, ensuring their fathers didn't rebel while John was in France. She was their jailer. The candle guttered; the black room shuddered.

DAILY DOWNPOURS LEFT tree trunks glistening and the air smelled of rising plants, not ice. Despite the coming spring, the cook said no eggs were to be found. No honey, no dried peas, no salt. Only dried apples, rye pottage, cabbage, carrots. No word came from William about supplies.

Trees pricked into harsh spring green; bluebells flaunted. Isabelle kept Cecily ever by her side and gave the young men tasks, drawing water from the well, clearing old rushes and spreading new. None were allowed outside the castle grounds and none complained.

Still no delivery. Suppers dwindled to bread, pottage, watered wine, dried fish. When Lady Braose and her children had starved, John said they'd been lost among the tremendous detail of administering a kingdom and Isabelle forced herself to believe him. But now she saw how easy it was to disappear. Her one comfort: William wouldn't forget a promise.

Another week, no word. Spring clouds spread like curdled milk, Fitzwalter shrank inside his tunic, the wet nurse thinned,

Baby Isi screamed with hunger, Cecily's elbows sharpened, and Isabelle fell into bones as when she'd longed for Hugh. Hunger and loss and cold was what it meant to be queen, which she as a foolish child had chosen. She could have married Hugh, been satisfied with esteem, but she had to have love. Now Hugh was gone and yearning glazed her days.

In April, Isabelle called the head cook. "Give whatever milk is available and any dried cod to the wet nurse." Rain sheeted past a tiny window. "Have we wheat for bread? Other supplies?"

"Pottage and bread can be had for belike a month. The boy goes out every morning, but no fish stir. We lack rye, honey, fennel, oats."

When death crept past Isabelle in the hall, she sent for the forest master. "No doubt you suffer as do we. Supplies are needed. My daughter's nurse requires meat."

"What would Madame propose?" His beard straggled over a slight smile.

"Go into the forest for a doe, rabbits, a brace of birds."

"Forest game is the king's property. He alone may hunt there."

"I am his queen. He will be ill pleased if his new daughter dies."

"'Tis only a girl." Muttered.

Her arm swung like a club against his head, knocking him against a stool. "Get away from me," she barked. Her beautiful baby, the dark eyes, the tiny smile. "You will take your meals below with the other servants." He staggered to his feet and limped away. She rubbed her stinging hand. 'Twas time to act, to reclaim her power. Not as the queen, but as Isabelle d'Angoulême, who had dared visit Hugh under John's very nose, dared to kiss him, who had saved his life. John had put her here, but she wouldn't let him win.

BEHOLD THE BIRD IN FLIGHT

She thought long, spoke to the wet nurse, then gathered her young hostages. "We are short of supplies. While the king tends to more pressing matters, we must save ourselves." The boys stood, eager. "Cecily shall go to St Briavels and beg for eggs. Wear your oldest cloak." Cecily bobbed a curtsy. "Fitzwalter, can you manage a longbow?"

"Yes, Madame." His pride shimmered.

"And you have such?"

He nodded.

"Go into the forest. We must have meat."

"But the king's edict forbids it."

Isabelle took off the ring that bore her oval seal. "Show this to any who question you." Escape leapt into Fitzwalter's eyes. She understood his need but sought to curb his desire. "If you do not return, the king's men will find you and you'll be hanged for treason." She put a hand on his shoulder. "We simply want to live, do we not?" She brushed his neck with her fingertip; the rising flush told her he would return.

"And me, Madame?" Young Reginald stepped forward, a mere stick of a boy, narrow-shouldered and famished.

"You shall accompany me to Chepstow. Bring your hunting knife. Sir William may not be in residence, but stores will be set aside. You must lead my horse and act as protector." She might take a horse from the stable, but no woman rode alone. "I doubt we can return by evening, but the two of you must be here for supper."

"What if there are questions?" Cecily, alert to danger.

All her life, danger everywhere, some of it from God—illness, accidents—but most of it from men. She must ready these children. "You are to say I am ill."

"Reginald will also be missing."

"Say the young lord drank too much and is taking fresh air. God will understand our lies. He wants us to live." At the last moment, she remembered a guard sometimes stepped into her room. "Cecily, you shall sleep in my bed. Pile your pallet with clothing. Speak of this to no one, especially not the forest master. Freedom will not be won from him."

WILLIAM WAS NOT in residence at Chepstow, and the guard refused to admit her. She urged her horse closer to the massive wooden gate. "I am the queen."

The man looked her up and down, lifted off his helmet, rubbed his hair awry. "What proof have you?"

Isabelle's mud-spattered gown belied her words and Fitzwalter held her seal. She should have worn a jewel. Reginald began to speak, but Isabelle silenced him with a nudge of her toe. "Sir William is well-known to me, as is his coat of arms. Gold and vert with a gules lion rampant."

"Known to many." A great stone tower loomed overhead.

"Not his aching hip, the shuffle when he walks."

"You need only to have seen him."

Isabelle glanced at her young companion. If she failed to get supplies, he would run for his freedom and his life would be lost. She dismounted and stepped close to the guard. "What have you heard of the queen?"

"Beautiful. Hair like gold. Seductive." He sneezed. "More Jezebel than Isabelle."

Ignoring *Jezebel*, often whispered at court, she pulled off her hood and cap. "Is not my hair golden?" Even under the dark clouds, it shone out. "I am Isabelle and my party at St Briavels is in need of food."

"If you are indeed the queen, look to the king." The man snorted. "Mayhap he treats you like he treats his subjects. We have little enough here."

When he turned away, she touched his sleeve. "Sir William does not supply you?"

The man shuffled slightly. "He obeys the law of God." He crossed himself. "Unlike the wicked king, defying the pope, ransacking abbeys, driving out holy men. And as you cleave to him, so are you defiled."

Isabelle had prayed on this and now her soul blackened at the edges, but crossing herself, she fought back. "As the weaker vessel, I must honor my husband." Reverting to girlhood, she shook her hair, smiled, touched his arm. Abashment scrambled in his face.

In the end she was allowed to stay, aching through the night on a scatter of straw, Reginald on watch. In the morning, they were sent away with a measure of barley, a knob of garlic, dried apples, peas, and a precious pot of honey. The guard bid them farewell. "Naught do I believe you be queen. But our Lord said *do unto one another.* Today I earn a remission in purgatory."

As they approached St Briavels, damp through and exhausted, one of the wintering geese in the moat rose slowly from the water, frantic wings, feet churning the surface until it found the air and circled away. The thrill of that moment lifted Isabelle. "We shall bring our bounty directly to the kitchen." She hadn't been in a kitchen since Chinon.

From inside came laughter and the smell of roasting meat. Fitzwalter had been successful! Her mouth watered; it had been more than a month since meat was to be had. Reginald opened the door and she stepped inside, holding up the honey and garlic with a laugh. "Here's spice for our dinner."

Faces snapped in her direction. "Madame." The cook stood, knocking over a stool. Laughter fizzled. The forest master stuttered, "Madame. You—You have, we were . . ." The company bowed deeply, eyes on the floor. Children gathered behind a skirt.

Why the terror? She brought food. She smiled. Before her a pheasant turned on the spit, a row of pasties lay on the table with a jug of ale and—Cecily's success—a great egg custard. A true feast.

The smallest child whined and the hearth hissed as a bit of food jumped from the pot of porridge. Porridge? Was the child sick?

A rapids of confusion tore her thoughts. "Where did that bird come from?"

The forest master was trying to edge her from the room. She planted her feet. "Did Fitzwalter bring it?" Royalty shot through her voice.

He flinched, barely whispered. "No, Madame."

Now she noticed bags of wheat, oats, onions; a small spice chest; dried eel and bottles of wine. Fitzwalter had not achieved this bounty. "Who?"

The forest master's wife spoke. "My husband may hunt to supply our needs."

"And not ours?" Silence. The fire crackled and the porridge boiled as Isabelle inventoried pots of confit, honey, and oil arrayed on a shelf. *William.* They were not forgotten, but his shipments had been kept secret. She turned to Reginald. "Arm yourself, but hold unless I say." He unsheathed his knife.

"You will attend me." She beckoned to the forest master's wife who came slowly, years of poverty grinding in her walk. Stifling empathy, Isabelle said, "You have not starved." She pointed at Reginald. "He has. So, too, has all of my party. Why would you deny us?"

BEHOLD THE BIRD IN FLIGHT

The forest master's servility fell away. "A pox on William Marshal, the king, the whole lot of you. My son accused of thievery, warn't he? A terrible amercement levied. Forty pounds the bailiff demanded, more'n a lifetime's wages. How should we live?"

"A trial found him guilty?"

"Trial? They are no more, only the judgment of the king's man."

Judged herself by the court, by John, by God, Isabelle had a stroke of pity. "What was stolen?"

"A mere flagon of wine." The man flung out his arms. "He was foolish, with bad companions, but they took him away. His mother weeps and the unfair amercement remains." He shook his fist at Isabelle and his wife grabbed his arm. "Ancient law requires the king leave us enough to live. Should my other children starve?"

Now her anger flashed like a fish. "And my companions?" Isabelle stepped forward, radiating power, no need for weapons.

"Christ's blood!" The forest master shook off his wife's hand. "The country suffers. The king wastes us with wars."

"Wars for lands that are ours. Yours." A vision of Angoulême flickered, its apple trees white with bloom, its lavender.

The man righted the overturned stool and sat heavily. "What use to me are those distant fields I shall never see?"

Chinon's shining river. The sea-haunted cliffs. The bird of longing awakened, but she jerked away from the images. "You are no longer master here. Tomorrow you and your family will leave." Spangled with anger, she commanded Reginald to lock him in a room.

"I cannot leave you alone, Madame. I fear . . ."

"Go." When the forest master and his family were gone, she

commanded the remaining men. "Bend knee to me." Slowly, they did.

The meat burst into flame and the cook rushed to turn the spit, her hand shaking.

"You," Isabelle pointed, "will serve tonight." The woman curtsied to the floor. "Bring this meal to the royal apartments." Tomorrow Isabelle would find another cook. And she vowed if they were ever released, she would take her daughter and go to France.

Afterward, she could scarcely climb the stairs, weighted by her queenship, but at the top, just beyond light flaring from the arrow loop, stood Cecily, Fitzwalter, Reginald, and the wet nurse holding baby Isi. She had saved them all. For now.

22

Curse Not the King

In La Rochelle, John paced the beach, waiting for news. His attempts to force the lords of Poitou and Aquitaine to his side had failed, and the last hope for the restoration of his Angevin Empire lay with Emperor Otto battling King Philip in the north. If Otto lost, the ancient lands of his parents—Chinon, Angoulême, Poitiers—would be forfeit. He strode through fog, growling, slashing his sword. God owed him this; he had submitted to the pope. Was that not enough?

Down the strand, his men gathered, reliving lost battles. Men paid with coin he'd taxed, fined, and forced from his barons, the louts who refused their sworn duty to fight, leaving England to teeter on the brink of rebellion. Traitors like Mowbray and Fitzwalter exhorting others against his kingship. For their treachery, he had seized their sons. If the mendacious plotting cowards continued to defy him, their sons would die. He plunged his sword into the sand.

The messenger arrived at last, bowing low, afraid to deliver the news that left John shrieking. "Useless shite!" Flames lit his throat and chest. Damn Otto! His own nephew fleeing the battle-field like a helpless girl. Christ's blood! He flailed his sword at the world's unfairness, roaring damnation against Philip, kicking at the sand.

A voice rose from within the gathered men. "With my knife, I slashed at the enemy and brought them to their knees." Brazen liar. John charged into the group and placed the tip of his sword on the man's chest. "What say you? We were soundly beaten." The words filled him with shame.

"Sire, I held fast long as I was able and barely escaped with my soul." The man carefully ducked away from the sword. "My horse was not so lucky." John lowered his weapon and the man bowed. "Terric the Teuton, at your service."

The other men hooted. "Seeking favor? Best kneel." "Germanic bastard."

John slashed his arm for silence. "Your horse, lost?"

"Slaughtered in the melee." Terric's bow deepened. "I remain your loyal servant, Sire. Sadly, now a foot soldier."

Again hooting. "Scurvy foreigner." "Go home. You've naught to do here."

Terric whirled. "We all serve a master. I serve this one." Wind lifted his torn and bloody tunic. "By the grace of God, you and I escaped. Countless others were slaughtered."

Terric spoke the truth: many had died. John sheathed his sword, beaten. Against the barons, these few warriors remained. But a slight glimmer: here, a boon. A loyal fighter. "You shall have a horse when we land." He paused. Best be cautious. "But cross me and you shall hang."

Terric repeated his bow and the murmuring men slid into the fog.

John trudged the beach, brooding against the stink of rotting seaweed and screaming birds. God had put him on the earth to rule. Why then abandon him? Under knife strokes of dark cloud, the sea puckered like black silk, and when he turned, his boot prints had washed away. He shuddered. To be king meant little. Pain and struggle and rage. A stone effigy in a cold church. A name in the chronicles, wars and deeds. Nothing would remain of his soul, his striving. He sorrowed and seethed until a misty sun raised his head. No choice but to go on. He had now only his crown, his will, his divine right. And Isabelle. Her name fluttered deep within his chest. Isabelle, who faithfully guarded his enemies' sons. He would send William for her. His treasure.

IN SEPTEMBER 1214, John signed a peace treaty with Philip Augustus in Chinon and returned to England and William's greeting. "You are greatly welcome, Sire. And much needed. The country boils like a black eel in a great iron pot." John pushed him aside, took brief shelter in Isabelle's body, then, as trees exploded into autumn red, rode with his mercenaries from castle to citadel, demanding fealty. He returned when possible to Isabelle who remained under guard in Winchester for her safety, galloping into the yard, taking her to bed. Afterward, he'd pace the room roaring of great lords cajoled and threatened, of bribes and drawn swords. His kingship on him like a mass of crows.

ISABELLE STILL HELD the hostages, helpless to release them lest John turn on her. Nights when he was away, she'd command the wet nurse to bring the baby. She rocked Isi, tickled her cheek into a smile, then, grasping a tiny foot, slept.

Days in court, she noticed that although the women still

formed buzzing knots into which she wasn't welcome, the men who'd often paused to talk with her before striding to their horse or mistress now assembled in thrumming groups. In hallways and stairs, wind-sharp whispers flurried around her skirts, hatred piled in the corners, treason sluiced stone. *Ira et malevolentia—* anger and ill will.

A savage wind was stripping trees bare of dying leaves when she could take no more and went to William. She found him in his room, drinking hot cider before a great fire. Anxious and frightened, she ignored required pleasantries. "Why do the barons rebel against my husband? He works vigorously in his kingship."

"Madame." William rose and offered cider.

"Please sit." She crouched on his carpet, shaking her head. "I must know, William. You see me as merely his queen, a jewel at his side. But I feel danger." A shard of panic scraped her chest.

"I think you are not . . ." Flames flickered.

"William." She leaned close. "Did I not help you with Langton and the pope?"

He set his tankard carefully on a table, considering. She waited, face smooth, hands calm, until he nodded. "Your husband is a ruler unlike Richard or even his father. Old ways have been set aside. He spends prodigiously and his meddling often impinges on old honors or estates. He seizes sons for leverage, as you yourself know. He imagines kindness lessens his power."

Again offered cider, she accepted, thinking of Fitzwalter, Reginald, and Cecily. Of the forest master's son, the guard at Chepstow. Even her own life: harried, followed, spied upon, clutched, abandoned. There was no kindness in John.

William sighed. "Better the king hunted or went on Crusade." He warmed his fingers on the tankard. "But it seems he cannot."

A flare licked the blackened mantel. "When the barons refuse to pay, when they side with the pope or speak slander, he deems it treason. His ire leads him into danger. He harms rather than corrects. The French take every opportunity to probe his weakness. To attack. But Madame, the barons are angry only with the king. You are not their concern."

When she left his room, Isabelle fully understood what William did not: she was invisible and thus vulnerable. If John fell, the barons would choose their own overlord, possibly a Frenchman, who would murder her and her sons. There would be no outcry. William Marshal would think of her, but he was old. From Hugh, betrothed and settled, she could expect nothing. A moment's comfort—Johanna safe—then threads of fear stitched her gut. She was no one. She had no money, nowhere to sell her jewels, nothing but a title. She needed allies, men for protection, men who would accept her son Henry as their king. She must rise above wife and enter John's realm, if only on the edges.

She devised a secret plan.

In every castle where the court established itself, be it Winchester, Cirencester, or Reading, she wore her richest mantle, left bits of hair to curl from her wimple. Only twenty-six, beauty unmarred, she accosted men on a stair or after a dance, snagging here a stray baron, there an earl's son, to chat about weather, touch a sleeve, take a hand. If the man didn't flee, and few did, she'd praise her son. "Have you seen Henry? So strong. Body of a great warrior. Good with the lance. Generous. Doesn't speak a word of my language. An Englishman through and through."

Sometimes eyes left her body long enough to hear her words. To nod. To think of a king other than John.

JOHN DRANK LATE into the nights, wrapping his fist around plans, sending to manor houses and countering plots, then woke to ride until his back ached and age crept up his spine. He'd never give in, but today he needed the relief of Isabelle. He ordered a length of silk and traveled to where he'd installed her and his daughter. Exhausted, beset on all sides, he intended to eat, decline the evening's dancing, and retire—he would bed his wife in the morning when fresh—but at the evening's high table, glances from men in the hall brushed Isabelle and his gut wrenched. He'd been too focused on the barons, too little on his wife.

"John, you are growling."

He turned to her. "Pardon, my lady." He offered her salt, then drank through the evening's dancing, watching her as she swayed and turned, flirting her sleeves, accepting the hand of whatever churl stood before her in the rondelet, glittering her teeth in smile after smile. He had forgotten her long neck and dainty feet. Against her youth, he felt his age. Under the table, his thighs shot with pain. His hands cramped from gripping the reins of his horse. Of his kingdom. And here, Isabelle, free and smiling. He twisted in anguish. Women demanded everything. Jewels, attention, flattery. Constant guidance. She would live on after him and then she could . . . He upset his wine and rose. Music stopped; heads turned.

"I am tired. As is my queen. We shall retire." She bowed and walked to him, charm quenched, Chinon again where she'd fooled him and gone to that base cur. He would send her away . . . No, he hadn't time. In the hall, he captured her arm, noting its slight quiver. In bed, he was rough.

The following day, he appointed Terric the Teuton as her guardian, growling, "For your safety, Madame."

BEHOLD THE BIRD IN FLIGHT

ISABELLE EXPECTED TERRIC to be another shackle in her life. She'd seen him bragging, laughing, always the loudest in the room, dropping his helmet with a clang, heaping salt when he could, challenging other knights. But he eased into her household, telling stories that made Cecily smile; Reginald and Fitzwalter valued his advice when driving their lances at the quintain.

Then once she came upon him tiptoeing after the baby. "Here, kitty, kitty." Isi crawled away from him, giggling. He wiggled his fingers and meowed; Isi crawled faster, until he caught her up with a guffaw and popped her into the air. She began to trust him completely, until one spring afternoon.

Habitually she stopped to gaze out through an arrow loop on the staircase leading to her royal apartments. Today the furrows prepared for planting stretched under a sky rippled with thin clouds, and she was pondering why men claimed the land even though it so obviously belonged to God when a fight broke her thoughts.

Terric and Reginald were shouting. At a scream, Isabelle flew up to find the men thumping each other, fists to torsos, and Cecily struggling to separate them.

Isabelle roared, "*Quelle est la problème?*" Faces snapped toward her. Reginald ran, but Cecily grabbed Terric's arm and pulled him in a walk around the room, leaning to him, whispering.

Had they formed an attachment? Impossible. She was noble; he, although a skilled knight, lowborn. She must sort this out. "Terric, you may leave us. Cecily, come here."

The girl's brow was pinched, her lip between her teeth. Isabelle spoke softly. "Is all well?"

She nodded slightly and hooded her eyes against light flickering from the window.

"Then why this altercation?"

Cecily shook her head. Shrugged. "An argument about how best to kill a man if you hadn't a sword."

"And practicing on each other?" Cecily's face bloomed red, but she laughed. The girl's relief was real; the explanation not. Isabelle would wait and watch.

THE CHRISTMAS SEASON arrived in Marlborough. Joyful celebrations, the church draped with holly, mulled ale with apples, villeins dancing and singing carols on paths of frozen mud, free from work for a fortnight and expecting gifts from their lords. None of it brought Isabelle cheer. John, ever dark, foul-mouthed and shouting, continued to fight the pope, King Philip, the barons. To her relief, he planned to remain in Winchester with William and des Roches for Yuletide. Striving for gaiety, she brought Cecily to the high table to preside over a jolly crowd of villeins and servants. Drink passed freely down the tables, and soon enough ale-sloshed men began throwing trenchers at the guards and one another, shouting for gifts of cloaks and coin. Isabelle stood to order a halt, but in the melee the Yule log rolled from the fireplace, setting a serving maid's long kirtle aflame.

In a swoop, Terric rushed her away. "'Tis danger, Madame." He escorted her out the door, his hand urgent on her elbow, up to her quarters. The haste, the faces; Isabelle hadn't lived years at court for nothing. She pushed past Cecily to the window and caught two men galloping across the snow-spattered field. Reginald and Fitzwalter. A thrill for their escape was followed by a faintness that almost dropped her to the floor. This time John would do more than throw her against a wall. She forced herself upright.

Terric blocked the doorway. "The moon is bright tonight." Eyes narrowed, he lowered his chin.

"Some are rejoicing under it." She crossed her arms and closed her eyes to a vision of John's contorted face. Then opened them to Terric, his own life in peril. Hoping their plan was sound, she acquiesced. "I rejoice as well." She knew he could see her heart pounding. Even hear it. Moonlight sliced the still room.

"Madame, I think it prudent that you take to bed. Cecily shall attend you. I regret you will miss the celebrations . . ."

The horses had disappeared into the forest, and Isabelle understood his offer. "I have not felt well for several days."

Terric bowed. "Perhaps you will be ill until Epiphany."

The weakness returned. Time enough for one of John's men to kill her and quietly dispose of the body. Terric would be powerless against the king. She clenched her bowels and nodded.

Terric's soft words, barely audible. "I vow your safety, Madame."

Now, a daily theater outside her door: Terric shouting accusations about escaped men, Cecily refusing him entrance. "Go away. Madame is ill. Your noise disturbs her." Truly, Isabelle was ill. Her breath cut off by a ball of fear as she awaited retribution.

Late one night, Terric entered. Isabelle pulled the coverlet and furs tightly over herself. "John has come." She crossed herself.

"I expected him, but he has not. I believe him sorely pressed by the northern barons. Blood will be spilled."

"Mine?"

"No, Madame. I remain by your side."

News came of John in Marlborough, Cirencester, Gloucester. Isabelle waited to die, spent time with her daughter. When John joined her, he spoke not a word about the escape. Was he playing with her as he caressed her in bed? She struggled to remain pliant against the ever-present terror. But then she learned there was to be another baby and breathed easier. Still, if John came for her, she would need coin to escape. Her jewels would be useless; only land had real value. She required the dower she'd never received.

February in Berkhamsted, she danced for John, then revealed the coming child. As he kissed her hands, she said, "When I give birth, I should like to receive the rents from Niort as promised when we wed." John's head snapped up. She didn't quail. "You gave it to me as dower."

He squeezed her fingers. "You are cold. Only ask and I shall provide." He smiled at her, eyetooth gleaming through his beard. "You must remain warm and give me another son. I shall order fur-lined gloves and a matching mantle. Do I not take care of my treasure?"

"John, I *am* asking. The income from Niort." He crushed her fingers against her rings. She bore the pain. "You are not always with me. I may need something when you are not. Remember St Briavels."

He tensed and she thought he was going to roar, but he gathered himself and stroked her neck. "See, is my hand not soft?"

The fire of his anger flickered at her feet, but she did not give way. "Niort?"

He dropped his hand and rose. "If it is a boy." His voice, a winter wind.

The next day, he sent fur-lined gloves and mantle with a message: *Bear me a son. Then we shall speak about Niort.*

He was gone again, flailing around the country, traveling from baron to baron, from duty to duty. Isabelle prayed for a lingering winter; when the earth was frozen and the trees bare, war was impossible, but eventually ice inched back from the rivers and safety became tenuous. John sent her to await the birth at Winchester, where Bishop des Roches watched over her sons. They had much changed since Isabelle had been forced to give them up: Henry, at eight, grown taller and cool; six-year-old Richard still gamboled. No matter. They would become men like all men: grasping for more, never mind the cost.

Winchester stank of wet wool and black earth as if from open graves. Terric brought rumors of northern armies, Wales in uproar, blacksmiths laboring late on horseshoes, axes, picks, bolts for bows. Horses galloped into the bailey day and night, men shouting, leaping from their saddles, slipping on wet stone, running up stairs, dropping rolls of parchment. John, tight-lipped and ever angry, forbade Isabelle to leave the castle grounds—for her safety. She remembered Angoulême, St Bri-avels. All punishments were cages.

To pass the time, she watched her boys play draughts, paced, prayed, and cradled her belly. She expected a daughter who she'd name Eleanor, hoping to gift her with her grandmother's strength.

Bubbles of leaf appeared, miniature yellow flowers; peonies and iris bloomed. May second was hot. Isabelle sat with her sons as Isi toddled around the room trailed by Cecily. The boys were talking of the May Day festivities—the dancing on the green, the puppet show—when John slammed in, shouting. "A plague of barons." He threw down his helmet. Little Isi jumped into Cecily's arms; Isabelle's unborn child smashed into her rib.

"The traitors will take my kingdom."

Ungainly, Isabelle stood. "John, what has happened?"

"They hold London. They will force me to bow to their de-mands." He kicked the helmet into the wall. "This is war."

The declaration was a form of relief. After months of strug-gle, something definite. Isabelle sent Cecily away with Isi and tried to contain her sons who'd begun a mock battle. She must calm her husband, help him think, but before he could shout again, William limped in. "Sire, we must . . ."

Isabelle held up her hand and hissed at the boys for quiet. "John, you are king. What demands?"

"Things I cannot give. They would make me a slave. They deny legitimate fees. Take amercements into their own hands. Christ, shall I be impoverished?" John flailed the length of the room. "And the French threaten to overrun London. Philip will take the country with the barons' approval. I shall hang them all. No trial. Their treason obvious."

Isabelle crossed herself, remembering the forest master's plight.

William leaned, favoring his hip. "They only request you uphold the ancient laws."

John halted, threw back his head, and roared. "I make the laws."

William straightened. "But your father and brother . . ."

"Do not talk to me of them," John screamed. "I am not Richard. I am not Henry." He slapped the wall. "I am John, King of England, Count of Angoulême."

William's glance required Isabelle's help. She grabbed her eldest son roughly by the arm—how small he was—and dragged him to John. "And king you must remain. Do you not want Henry to reign?"

"They will leave him nothing."

"Only if you refuse their requests."

"Demands." John whirled away.

"Think like a king, John." Her words pulled him. "You are not an injured villein. Not a helpless animal."

He arched away from her eyes, but his fire wavered.

"God made you king."

BEHOLD THE BIRD IN FLIGHT

"God? He is treacherous as a baron."

William crossed himself. "He will be your rock."

"He gives me only sorrow."

"He gave you me." Isabelle yanked Henry before him. "And sons. I see no sorrow there." In the pause, the rage in John's eyes waned; the man she had married, the man in the garden at Angoulême, flickered briefly. So long ago. "Go with William. Plan their defeat. You are king and so you shall remain."

"Sire." William bowed. "Come, let us talk this through."

That night Isabelle dreamed her papa walked in Angoulême's orchard. Pale blossoms blew like a blizzard, obscuring his face, but it was he. Hugh appeared, his curls blessed with white petals. Isabelle smiled at him. Her father crossed himself, and the two men walked to the end of the row, receding until Papa seemed to melt into the earth. Isabelle ran toward Hugh, her love even now, but suddenly, there was John, his face black, his mouth shooting fire. The orchard began to burn, the apples to bake. Isabelle could smell them, could hear the crinkle of the skins. She held her hands toward John and cried at him to stop.

"Madame." Cecily shook her shoulder. "Madame, waken."

Isabelle came slowly into the real world. A scent of mossy stone and a candle flickering mild fingers across the floor. "'Twas only a dream." But John was Count of Angoulême; her marriage and her father's death had brought him to her home. After Cecily lay down, Isabelle shuddered long under her coverlet.

WHEN JOHN COULD no longer defy his barons, he went to Runnymede and signed the Magna Carta, guaranteeing to uphold the ancient laws, affirming the right to trial, to widows' dower, to reasonable taxes. But for Isabelle, sent to Gloucester for the birth

297

of her fifth child, the Great Charter changed nothing. And shortly, John reneged. The barons raged; the pope was brought into the fray. War would come.

The baby, born in September, was baptized Eleanor. There was no gift, no visit, no mention of Niort. Isabelle understood John was fighting for his life, for his very kingdom, but she was tired. She prayed daily that her plan would work, then lay in bed with the baby, singing and cooing, feeling for the first time like a real mother. This tiny girl, with her dark curls and perfect mouth, she would keep. John would not have her.

Throughout the summer and into the fall, letters from John arrived, beginning with the required protestations of love—*The king to his beloved wife, Queen of England, greetings and affection.* Perhaps he did love her, or had at one time, but now he was all grievance. *With the connivance of our barons, Louis endeavors to take our kingdom.* Louis's entrance into the war alarmed her. He was Philip's son and heir to the crown of France. Was England to fall completely?

Terric came to her quarters, standing wide-legged to convey news. "Armies are gathering, Madame. The northern barons have broken every promise and are fortifying their castles."

She had been walking up and down with Eleanor, trying to lull her to sleep, but now she stopped. She must know everything. Her children's lives depended on it.

"Loyalists have been mistreated and they killed a sheriff in Northumberland in retribution." Terric put fists on his belt. "Would that I could fight. I would slaughter the traitorous curs." He bowed quickly. "But I have vowed that Madame and her children will remain safe."

Always he spoke of safety. Isabelle had learned as a child: such did not exist.

For weeks, she refused to play queen, remaining in her room, asking Cecily for court gossip, watching little Isi struggle through her first steps, rocking Eleanor in her cradle, singing to them both. The boys, immersed in studies and training, slipped out of her heart. They were royal, an honor bestowed on men and offered only reluctantly to wives.

She was teaching Isi a clapping game while Eleanor slept when John crashed through the door in armor. Isi hid behind her mother. "Don't be frightened, *ma petite.*" Isabelle forced her body into softness. "That is your father."

John took off his helmet and set it on the floor for the child to examine. "I am sending you to Bristol." Eleanor wakened and Isabelle picked her up. "You'll be safe there. 'Tis well fortified. I spent enough, God knows." John reached for the baby. "A fine daughter." He kissed her fuzzy hair. "We shall marry her to a baron if we live."

Isabelle wanted to grab her baby and flee. Instead, she clasped her hands behind and while Isi, ever the imp, kissed her finger, pled for a different place of safety. "John, we should go to Angoulême. My mother . . ."

"France?" John crashed his hand against his chest. "Never." Eleanor began to cry. Isabelle reached out, but John, his fatherly duty over, called for the wet nurse. "Terric will accompany you. I shall also send my sons."

She was to have all her children. But Bristol? Her sons a magnet for revenge. "Perhaps in Angoulême . . ."

"Do not speak to me of France." Now both girls were crying. "I won't be questioned."

After he had gone, Isabelle went to the chapel and prayed for the lives of her children.

John judged correctly: in June 1216, England fell to Louis

who marched into London to the acclaim of the treacherous barons who swore allegiance and did all but crown him. England was at an end.

MORNINGS IN BRISTOL, when the river fog slithered up the valley and isolated the castle, Isabelle rose early. Were she still a child, the gauze of mist stretching out below her feet would have seemed like heaven, but now she awaited French swords to slash from the white.

Through the days she held her little girls. If she were to die, she would have them to the end. The boys she'd already relinquished. She asked Terric to train them, a small gesture against the coming attack, and he organized mock tournaments and galloped madly with them to strengthen their horsemanship. At nine, Henry rode well; seven-year-old Richard whined, longing for the pony he'd been forced to leave behind in Winchester.

Nights she lay awake in horror: if they were captured, Louis would kill her sons like John had killed Arthur. The ball of fear took over her entire chest. She sent a letter to her mother. *Alert my daughter's betrothed.* The words caused unexpected tremor, but her love for Hugh must remain ash. *Because of our past, I trust him. We require a ship to take us safely to France.* Not daring to say where they were staying, she hoped the messenger would name Bristol. Now she could but wait. Pray.

In August, John joined them for three days, gray and gaunt, the rage of war eating him from the inside. He ranted and swore, ordered a heavier sword, drank late into the night over maps and plans, and came to her bed too wine-sodden to make love. She combed his hair and told him stories of his children. How Richard beat Henry at draughts, how they'd hidden from their

BEHOLD THE BIRD IN FLIGHT

tutor in a barrel. How little Isi begged to go to the kitchen and stir the big pots. When at last he fell asleep, she rose and stood by the window to watch for lights coming up the river, remembering John in the garden at Lusignan, his courtesy and warm hand.

The morning he left, he looked long into her eyes. "My choice for wife has been well paid." He took a gold-and-ruby ring from his finger and gave it to her. "I regret Niort."

The ring was but a bauble, meaningless; distance blew between them. She remembered his love of fine clothes, of jewels. Their trip to the fair. When the portcullis thudded into place behind his leaving, she ran up to the castle walk, tore off her wimple, loosened her hair, and willed him to look back, to remember her strong and bright. His strength, his treasure.

JUMBLED IMAGES SPLASHED behind John's eyelids: a bubble of red wax around his seal, riding through a blur of branches, peaches piled on a silver plate. One image swung past over and over like the priest's censor: sunset over The Wash, the red ball sinking into an iron sea, horses foundering. Every time it appeared, he shouted at the men. *Save them.*

"Sire?"

Someone leaned close. The bishop?

"Sire, 'tis William. Can you hear me?"

The crackle of parchment unrolling. The dull thud of a sword on a man's neck. The cries of drowning horses, the whips, shouts. Under it went, all of it. Crowns. Crossbows, iron-studded chests, tents, food, jewels. The tide . . .

"Sire, can you drink this?"

Yesterday, peaches. Today, wine with grits in it. His gut

clenched in pain and he pushed the cup away, spilling it on his face. A spasm of dread. The stink of feces. He mumbled, "Send for the priest." Then, miraculously, a light in the distance. His golden Isabelle. He opened his eyes to darkness.

ISABELLE DROPPED THE message. "Terric! Come!" She rushed from window to window. Outside, a clear October day; inside, her plan unfurling. She must succeed. When Terric arrived, she stopped so suddenly her long skirt swirled around her feet. "The king is dead." She pointed to the messenger. "At Newark Castle."

The messenger bowed. "The gates of hell opened for him."

"Get out." She turned to Terric. "You now take orders from me."

"Madame, I am not . . ."

"In charge." She stepped closer, cutting off his flow of words. "I am your queen." *Your former queen*, but no need to say that. "I trust you. Trust me." Quickly, over his confusion, she added, "Have you a man who rides well and is loyal?"

He nodded.

"He shall take Richard to Ireland. Quietly. If Henry is crowned or killed, Richard shall be safe. There is a packed trunk in my room. See that they leave today." Isabelle wished to retire to bed with her baby, but she called up her reserves. "Prepare the other men. Require polished armor, horses bedecked with the finest bridles. The horse master has clean pennants. We ride tomorrow."

"And your daughters?"

She turned away to catch her breath. Not hers. They belonged to England, to their brother. To be his as pawns, as they'd been John's. She had always known they must stay but never allowed herself to think of it. A brief memory of Maman combing her hair before sending her to Lusignan. "I shall leave them with Cecily." Quaking at the loss—the little mouth, the stirred pot—she looked into great hall's arches until she gained control. "No one will bother with them."

Little Richard waved and waved as he rode away to Ireland with his guard. She watched until he disappeared, then called Henry. "We are to ride to Gloucester. Wear your new green silk with the red velvet cape."

"Where is my brother?" When he heard Richard was gone, Henry cried until she slapped him. "You are king now. You must be strong and live."

She gave the ruby-and-gold ring to Cecily. "Take care of my babies . . ." Breathing was hard, but this must be done. Without her dower, she could offer them nothing. They were princesses; they would learn to live with that. "William will send for them and then you may return to your father."

The young king-to-be traveled in a shining cavalcade, the earth trembling under hooves, swords flashing. In every village, Terric, as Isabelle had ordered, galloped to the green, reined in suddenly, reared his horse and shouted, "The king is dead! Long live King Henry." Men gathered; women and children peeked through doors. When Henry appeared on his own horse, his blond hair pulled villagers around him like a maypole. Master after castle master bent knee, swearing loyalty. A new king, an English king. Hope taking root, the French not required.

At night, lying in the tent with him as oil lamps carried by the guards floated past, Isabelle tried to rid herself of the queen, but it clung to her. She wiggled her shoulders, arched her back until Henry said, "Maman, we cannot sleep." That word—the royal *we*, Henry assuming his kingship—released her. She became simply his mother. "I will be still now, Sire." Henry giggled and slept. She thought again of Maman sending her away. How had she borne it? She hadn't asked before, but now there would be time.

In Gloucester, William greeted them with a deep bow. "My king."

This time there were no giggles. Henry said the words Isabelle had coached into him, "We have sent our brother to Ireland for safekeeping." He was helped from his horse. "We should like to be crowned immediately for the good of England and its peoples."

There was nothing royal about the ceremony; the cathedral pillars loomed over the small boy-king surrounded by advisors and guards as he would be from now on. No one had given thought to a crown and there was shouting and fumbling until Isabelle unfastened her own circlet, the one given her by Hugh, and handed it to the bishop. Her neck ached, empty.

Just before the crown was on his head, Henry whispered to Isabelle, "Where are the trumpets?" Then it was done. Isabelle marveled at his pride and his pliancy. Was this the child who'd toddled across a great hall, chuckling? In Winchester? Marlborough? Now that he wore the little circlet, the men bent to him with respect. A king. She left the cathedral, followed by William.

In the courtyard she said, "I give him over to you. Guide him well."

"Stay." He touched her sleeve. "See him to his full kingship."

"No, that is for you." She hoped Henry would be a kinder king than John.

"Madame, I am old."

Ah, William. She'd been eleven when she first encountered him in Lusignan as she clicked her new shoes. "The barons will accept you, not me."

"I will die before he comes of age."

She nodded. He was tired and in pain, but she knew his will. "You must stay alive."

He bowed. "Madame."

She was done. Her children gone, burdened with royalty. Her own queen shattered, pieces shimmering on the ground; she had no desire to pick them up. She wanted Angoulême. "I ask only that I should receive my dower as it was given to me by John. Niort and the others."

There was shouting outside the courtyard. "They know they have a new king."

Men carried Henry away, a prize to be used. Isabelle touched William's sleeve. "Will he live?"

"The barons will recognize an English king before Louis."

"Then I am free to go." She conjured sails and whitecaps, the first glimpse of land, the sand, the trees. "One more thing. I shall need escort."

"Who would you prefer?"

"Terric. He will keep me safe."

"Godspeed, Isabelle de Angoulême."

SEA SPILLED INTO the sky, water tinged with green, clouds with blue. Far out a flock of birds bobbed, along the sand a bristle of weeds. Isabelle stood on the broad beach near Gosport and dreamed, her mind soft, fluid, stretching in all directions. Behind her lay Gloucester, St Briavels, St. Bartholomew's Fair. Those strands of herself she let drop, tangling over the forests and castles, thin as spiderwebs, barely touching England's earth. In front of her, water; beyond, Angoulême, Lusignan, Niort. Had she a map, she would mark them with gold. And Chinon? Mark it with a ruby for blood and suffering, for herself and for Hugh. His name opened gardens in her heart. Soon, she could . . .

A single bird lifted off the sea, headed toward France, in full flight.

23

AFTERWORD

William Marshal died on May 14, 1219, after issuing new versions of the Magna Carta and gaining support for the young king, Henry III.

Isabelle returned to her beloved Angoulême, retained her title as queen, and became an ongoing pain to her son with demands and threats as she struggled to be ceded Niort and the other gifts bestowed on her by John. Eventually, she prevailed.

She also shocked the medieval world by marrying Hugh, usurping her daughter's betrothal. Proving she'd learned something about politics under John, she sent a clever letter to her son claiming his land in France was in danger so *"we took said H[ugh], count of La Marche, as our lord; and God knows that we did this more for your advantage than for ours."*

Possibly her marriage was more a strategic move than a love match; when John died, her rights to Angoulême fell into danger. As Hugh's wife, her rights were reconfirmed.

On the other hand, the fact that she and Hugh had nine children in fifteen years argues for love.

Author's Statement

This novel started with two sentences outlining a bit of British history unfamiliar to me. In 1200, King John of England abducted Isabelle of Angoulême from her fiancé, Hugh de Lusignan, and married her. As queen she gave John heirs, but when he died she returned to France, married Hugh, and had nine children. I was immediately intrigued.

My BA in history, with an emphasis on medieval Europe, had taught me that, with few exceptions, women in that era were bargaining chips for power or wealth; their main duty was to bear sons. But what role had Isabelle played in the abduction? Women had to consent to marriage. And why had her fiancé waited? There was a great story there.

I gave each main character a point of view so as to write about the events from all angles. Isabelle came first, almost twelve, the age when she'd be considered marriageable. I invented the trauma that sent her to Lusignan to be fostered, a common medieval practice, then followed her into womanhood, the abduction, and her years in England, admiring (creating) her capability to maneuver in constrained, often dire, circumstances. Historically, Hugh seemed weak; John captured him in battle. But he also must have loved deeply—after all, he didn't marry in the sixteen years of Isabelle's absence. To complicate things, I envisioned a lost love for him. Finally, I wanted to give John some humanity after the drubbing he usually takes in history; he may have been a narcissist, mad, impetuous, insanely jealous, but he was a good administrator of the country—some would say too good, too invasive—and I wanted to find or invent reasons for his decisions. Also, a lot of speculation swirls around the abduction, a leading factor in John's loss of British territory in France. I decided that Isabelle had the personality to attract him, and that over time she used this personality to gain some control in her life. Not a modern woman, but recognizable in her strength.

Research at the Library of Congress, in history books, and online supplied information about the seventeen years covered in the novel. I read about the Magna Carta, of course, but also researched celebrations, falconry, childbirth, superstitions, religion, mores, and popular *lais* (songs) in order to recreate the tenor of everyday medieval life. Using a timeline of John and Isabelle's travels and biographies of the king's trusted knights, I built the story.

I will confess to a historical problem caused by my first reading: the original book, one designed for tourists and sold at Windsor Castle, claimed that Isabelle returned to her original fiancé. Sources I later found stated her original fiancé was Hugh's father. There are many Lusignan Hughs—they were an important family in both the Crusades and France—and documents are rife with contradictions. Luckily, I'm writing fiction, so I have chosen to make the original fiancé the younger Hugh. It made a better story.

ACKNOWLEDGMENTS

I couldn't have written this story without feedback from writing friends. In particular, Ann Gronowski, the best critique partner anyone could have, supportive, full of ideas, keeping me honest. Other writing friends may not have read or commented on this novel, but you all have sustained and encouraged me for years.

From a group that began over ten years ago at The Writer's Center in Bethesda and morphed from there: Cat Lazaroff, Sue Corby, Holliann Kim, Ayesha Ahmad, Mel Barber, Susan Corby, Suzie Eckl, Yuko Frost, Cassandra Israel, Nancy Jarmin, and in memoriam, Jeri Eaton. Our retreats were so special. From Kseniya Melnick's workshop at George Washington University: Carrie Callaghan, Felix Amerasinghe, Kate Wichmann, Richard Agemo, and Mark Travassos. From Rebecca Makkai's advanced workshop at the Lighthouse in Denver during the pandemic: Jacalyn Eis, Lexi Pandell, Kim Henderson, Monica Villa-Vicencio, and Stacy Allen. And from John Cotter's excellent class: Cindy Savage, Jessica Glynn, Jennifer Peters, and Jeff Golden. Not to forget Carly Heath, one of my first readers.

Thanks to the Sewanee Writers' Conference and Lighthouse Writers in Denver for accepting me into the fold. To She Writes Press, Lauren Wise, Sheila Trask, Julie Metz for the beautiful cover, and especially Brooke Warner, a wonderful advocate for authors. And finally, Barbara Beste Esstman, the first teacher who told me I had the wherewithal to write a publishable novel.

Although I wrote a novel, I have tried to remain true to the spirit if not the exact dates and places of the historical events. Huge thanks to Sharon Bennett Connolly, a Fellow of the Royal Historical Society, who patiently answered all my questions, and to Eleanor Leeson, a perceptive developmental editor based in England. Any mistakes are mine alone.

CREDITS

In April 2021, two sections of this novel and the author's statement were printed in a slightly different form in *Embark: A Literary Journal for Novelists*, Ursula DeYoung, editor. Thank you, Ursula, for your belief in this story.

https://embarkliteraryjournal.com/issues/issue-14-april-2021/behold-the-bird-in-flight-terri-lewis/

Further Reading

There are many online sites. Of course, you can look up the individuals. Other ideas:

—To envision the Lusignan castle, albeit some years after Isabelle's sojourn, search for *Tres Riches Heures, March*, and click on Images.

—To get a feel for John's itinerant court, https:// neolography.com/timelines/JohnItinerary.html shows where he was almost every day of his seventeen years as king.

—I am leery of Wikipedia in general, but this site has a decent overview of John's life: https://en.wikipedia.org/wiki/ John,_King_of_England .

—If you want an in-depth look at the Magna Carta, try the Magna Carta Project at https://magnacartaresearch.org/. It contains translated excerpts from John's itinerary and diary, organized week by week. And sadly was not available during the first drafting of the novel.

—For a brief history of Isabelle after John died: https:// erenow.org/biographies/queens-consort-englands-medieval- queens/9.php

—And finally, for fun, a site about who ran the castles, the medieval counterpart to Downton Abbey: https:// www.worldhistory.org/article/1234/the-household-staff-in-an- english-medieval-castle/

Over the years I have collected several shelves of books about the medieval period. Those listed here most deeply informed this novel. Not all of them are easily available, but they are worth the trouble to find:

An easy-to-read biography of William Marshal and his many exploits:

—Duby, Georges. *William Marshal: The Flower of Chivalry*. Translated by Richard Howard. New York: Pantheon Books, 1984.

A fresh look at John's kinghood:

—Church, S. D., ed. *King John: New Interpretations*. Woodbridge, UK: Boydell Press, 1999.

Pictures of medieval women at work:

—Fox, Sally, ed. *The Medieval Woman: An Illuminated Book of Days*. Boston: Little, Brown and Company, 1985.

To discover other women who claimed some power:

—Connolly, Sharon Bennett. *Ladies of Magna Carta: Women of Influence in Thirteenth Century England*. Barnsley, UK: Pen and Sword History, 2020.

To read actual medieval voices in ballads, letters, and other documents:

—Cantor, Norman F. *The Medieval Reader*. New York: HarperCollins, 1984.

Digging deeper into the daily lives:

—Duby, Georges, ed. *A History of Private Life: Revelations of the Medieval World*. Translated by Arthur Goldhammer. Cambridge, MA: Harvard University Press, 1988.

QUESTIONS FOR DISCUSSION

1. As a child, Isabelle's mother taught her to care for a castle and set rules for behavior. John even comments on her good manners. Given that Isabelle lived over eight hundred years ago, was this a surprise to you?

2. In Isabelle's era, as many as one in twenty women died in childbirth. Nineteen percent of children died before the age of two, fifty percent by five. Does this in any way explain or mitigate the legal age of marriage being twelve for girls?

3. What do you think gave Isabelle the strength to survive her marriage to John?

4. Compare the way Isabelle and Marielle talk about men, sex, romance, and marriage with modern teenagers.

5. The medieval period seems remote. Did any of their ways of living—food, travel, managing property, entertainment, manners—surprise you?

6. What role did William Marshal play for Isabelle? For John?

7. Was Hugh worthy of Isabelle's passion?

8. Medieval history as taught in school focuses on power and men, but in the novel, Isabelle uses her own power to affect events, persuading John to accept the pope's bishop and to consider the Magna Carta. Do you know other women who maneuvered behind men of power to make a difference in history?

9. John, as king, held all the power. Did you see any similarities between Isabelle's position and that of the barons?

10. If this book were adapted into a movie, who would you cast in the roles of John, Isabelle, Hugh, Marielle, and William?

11. How does the title relate to the story?

12. Imagine you can time travel. Which character would you most like to meet, and what question would you ask of them?

About the Author

Before she became a writer, Terri Lewis had a career as a ballet dancer in German opera houses, got a BA in history and an MA in theater, toured with a circus, and ran a dance company in Arkansas. Eventually, she settled down to write, her childhood dream.

Her love of medieval history started in college. Not the dates or wars, but the mysterious daily lives of the people. Building on this love, she read widely and traveled, marveling at Europe's preserved towns and castles. Finally, two sentences in a book bought at Windsor Castle led her to write *Behold the Bird in Flight*.

She has taken master workshops with Jill McCorkle, Laura van den Berg, John Cotter, and Rebecca Makkai and published short stories in literary magazines. She was accepted to the Sewanee Writers' Conference and advanced workshops at the Lighthouse Writers Center in Denver. Her reviews for the Washington Independent Review of Books have been excerpted in BookMarks. In 2025, she won the Miami University Novella Prize.

She lives with her husband and two lively dogs in Denver, Colorado.

For more information or to contact her go to her author website at https://terrilewis1.com/. Or sign up for her Substack blog at https://terrilewis1.substack.com.

Looking for your next great read?

We can help!

Visit www.shewritespress.com/next-read
or scan the QR code below for a list
of our recommended titles.

She Writes Press is an award-winning
independent publishing company founded to
serve women writers everywhere.